HIDDEN THREAT

Lot and Urban went out to the hull, exiting the transit bubble near the ship's aft end. Lot walked the hull's pliant surface, while his skin suit controlled the catch and release of his boots, leaving temporary footprints behind him.

"Turn around," Urban said, his voice sounding intimate through the suit's audio system.

Lot turned. Beyond the hull, stars gleamed like luminous sand strewn across the void. Gradually, Lot became aware of a spot of darkness, a patch of emptiness stamped upon the starfield. He stared at it, until his mind resolved it into the long, cylindrical silhouette of a Chenzeme courser.

"By the Unknown God," he whispered.

In its blackness it seemed to be extinguishing the light of stars.

"It's something, isn't it?" Urban said. "A Chenzeme ship, this close, and we're still alive."

Also by Linda Nagata

The Bohr Maker
Tech-Heaven
Deception Well

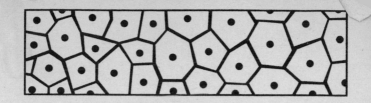

Vast

Linda Nagata

BANTAM BOOKS
New York • Toronto • London • Sydney • Auckland

VAST

A Bantam Spectra Book / August 1998

SPECTRA and the portrayal of a boxed "s" are trademarks of
Bantam Books, a division of Bantam Doubleday Dell Publishing
Group, Inc.

ISBN 0-553-57630-5

Published simultaneously in the United States and Canada

Bantam Books are published by Bantam Books, a division of
Bantam Doubleday Dell Publishing Group, Inc. Its trademark,
consisting of the words "Bantam Books" and the portrayal of a
rooster, is Registered in U.S. Patent and Trademark Office and in
other countries. Marca Registrada. Bantam Books, 1540 Broad-
way, New York, New York 10036.

PRINTED IN THE UNITED STATES OF AMERICA

OPM   10   9   8   7   6   5   4   3   2   1

Acknowledgments

Vast benefited from the input of several generous people. Robert A. Metzger and Wil McCarthy happily fielded the bizarre technical questions that appeared from time to time in their E-mail boxes. Sean Stewart provided priceless input on an early version of the book's opening, and Wil McCarthy, Bruce Holland Rogers, Sage Walker, and Kathleen Ann Goonan all took time out during the rush of the holiday season to comment on the manuscript. Finally, my editor, Anne Lesley Groell, provided insightful commentary and guidance throughout the revision process. My warmest thanks go out to all of you.

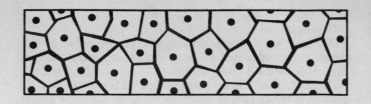

Prelude

Point zero: initiate.

A sense kicked in. Something like vision. Not because it emulated sight, but because it revealed. Himself: Nikko Jiang-Tibayan. An electronic pattern scheduled to manifest at discrete intervals. Nikko Jiang-Tibayan. He'd been an organic entity once. Not now.

Point one: identify.

Personality suspended on a machine grid: he is the mind of the great ship, Null Boundary. His memories are many, not all accessible. He's locked much of his past away in proscribed data fields. He interrogates his remaining inventory, seeking an explanation. It comes in an amalgam of cloudy scents: the clinging stink of living flesh parasitized by aerobic bacteria. All defenses down. "Don't be sad, my love," she whispers. "Whatever the cost, you know we had to try."

He explores no further.

Point two and counting: status check.

A scheduled mood shift floods his pattern with easy confidence. He confirms that Null Boundary had long ago reached maximum velocity, four-tenths lightspeed. The magnetic scoops have been deactivated; the solenoids folded to a point piercing the increasingly thick interstellar medium. Duration? Over two centuries' ship's time have elapsed since Null Boundary left Deception Well.

Two more centuries.

His past has become unconscionably deep for a man who'd been condemned to die at the age of thirty standard years. Still, death is never far off.

There are four telescopes mounted on tracks around the ship's hull. When two or more are fixed on the same object, their optical signals can be combined, creating an effective lens aperture far greater than any individual scope. At least two lenses are continuously fixed on the alien vessel that has hunted Null Boundary for 150 years.

It's a Chenzeme courser, an automated warship designed by a race that vanished millions of years before the human species even came into existence. It first appeared when Null Boundary was less than fifty years out of Deception Well. Then, it was moving at close to thirty-nine percent lightspeed, on a course that would take it toward the star cluster called the Committee—opposite to Null Boundary's vector. Nikko watches its fleeting image, wondering if it will manage to get past the defenses of the human settlements there.

Nikko knows little about the Chenzeme, but he knows this much: Their ships are not powered by conventional physics. The old murderers learned to tap the zero point field, that all-pervasive sea of energy where particles and antiparticles engage in a continuous dance of creation and annihilation. It's a deadly talent. With the zero point field to power their ships and guns, each Chenzeme vessel has far more energy at its command than any human installation. Their gamma ray lasers can burn away the atmosphere of a living world. Nikko has seen it happen.

A twinge of pain, like the tenderness of a half-forgotten wound, warns him away from memories he does not want to awaken. It's enough to know the Chenzeme will not be beaten until the frontier worlds own the zero point technology too.

Yet even for the old murderers, energy does not flow in infinite quantity. To catch Null Boundary, the courser would need to swing about and accelerate—a huge investment of both time and energy that can gain it only a very tiny prize. So that first time Nikko sees it, he knows it will ignore him to push on toward the inhabited worlds of the Committee. He has no reason to think he will ever see it again. He aims the ship's prow at the natural navigation beacon of Alpha Cygni, a white-hot giant star that blazes against a background of dark molecular clouds—and he pushes on, in the direction called *swan*, where the Chenzeme warships seem to originate. He has set out to find their source, and he will not be distracted. Like a tortured man stumbling vengefully toward his tormenters, he has to know *why*.

A century and a quarter later, the courser reappears in Null Boundary's telescopes, approaching obliquely, far to the stern.

Now it has closed to 21.6 astronomical units—some three billion kilometers behind them. It's a luminous object, agleam with a white light generated by the membrane of philosopher cells that coats its needle-shaped hull.

Human ships and human worlds were not the original targets of the Chenzeme, but their automated ships have proven adaptive. So Nikko has adapted too. He cannot outrun the courser or match its guns, but on Null Boundary's hull he has grown his own layer of Chenzeme philosopher cells, forever dreaming their simulated strategies of war and conquest.

The cells are an intellectual machine. Not so much a mind, as a billion dedicated minds in competition, gambling their opinions. Approval means more and stronger connections to neighboring cells. Disapproval means an increasing isolation. Links are made and shattered a thousand times a second and long-chain alliances are continuously renegotiated. Consensus is sought but seldom found.

This is the clumsy system that guides the Chenzeme warships. Nikko thinks on it, and he doesn't know whether to laugh or to weep in terror.

He suspects he has done both ten thousand times before. It's been twenty-two years since he learned to live within the skin of his enemy. Null Boundary's hull has gleamed white all that time, a skin-deep Chenzeme masquerade.

If nothing else, this ruse has bought time. Though the courser has not been persuaded to turn away, it seems unsure, as if its instincts have been confused by Null Boundary's metamorphosis. Seventeen years ago it ceased to accelerate. Yet because its velocity is slightly greater than Null Boundary's, the gap between the two ships continues to narrow. In another 125 days Null Boundary will fall within range of its gamma ray laser.

That is Nikko's deadline. He must convince the courser of his authenticity before then, and persuade it to leave them alone. In the ship's library, an army of subminds is dedicated to the problem, interpreting and reinterpreting every record of Chenzeme communication to uncover all identifying codes. Nikko has used the results in repeated attempts to contact the courser, but to no effect—it has never answered his radio hails.

He adds one more submind to stew upon the problem, while instructing a Dull Intelligence to continue the observations. He will be unable to do so himself, as his present existence is limited to ninety seconds. At the end of this time, if nothing has gone wrong, his personal memory of the period will be dumped and a new interval will begin, so that from his point of view, Null Boundary's transit time will seem to require only ninety seconds, though years have elapsed. This is Nikko's defense against boredom.

Point twenty: Additional subminds report in. Their assessments are pleasingly dull. Reactor function is nominal. Air quality is nominal. Crew health: nominal. There are only three crew members. Four, if Nikko counts his own rarely used physical incarnation. He finds Lot and Urban awake and active; only Clemantine still hibernates in a cold storage nest.

Point thirty: Nikko scans Null Boundary with remote eyes. He discovers Urban in the library, linked to an interface that records the activity of the philosopher cells. Urban insists that with practice and refinement, the interface can be made to translate the cell's chemical language into something meaningful to a human mind. Nikko doesn't agree. Experience has taught him that Chenzeme language finds meaning only within Chenzeme neural structures.

This is something Lot understands. He is in a transit bubble just beneath the ship's hull. One side of the bubble is open, so that he lies squeezed against the underside of the colony of philosopher cells. He's dressed in an insulating skin suit, but the hood is down. His close-cropped blond hair shines in the cells' white light. On his cheeks are moist sensory glands that look like glistening teardrops. These "sensory tears" are a Chenzeme structure, integrated into the genetic system of Lot's ancestors by some unknown engineer, thousands of years in the past. Through them, Lot can perceive the cells' chemical language and respond in kind, with molecules synthesized in the tears' nanoscale factories.

The philosopher cells are Lot's creation, and he is still the only one who can effectively communicate with them. He mined their design from the living dust of Deception Well's nebula, storing the pattern in his fixed memory, a data vault contained within the filamentous strands of the Chenzeme neural organ that parasitizes his brain. Nothing degrades in fixed memory. Lot used the pattern to synthesize a seed population of philosopher cells within his neural tendrils, exuding them through the shimmery surfaces of his sensory tears. It's a neatly circular survival strategy in which the parasitic tendrils use their host to reproduce the Chenzeme mind. Clearly this has happened many times before in the thirty-million-year history of the Chenzeme, *and it is the warships that have survived it,* while their challengers have all vanished.

All except us, Nikko thinks.

He is acutely aware that they play a dangerous game.

After the first cells were made, it took three years of experiments before they learned to feed the young colony with nutrients delivered through the hull. Now the original cells have reproduced many times over. Lot is learning to delve into their inherited histories, and with luck, he will discover the proper radio hail to sooth a Chenzeme warship.

The warships are known to rendezvous in the void, to exchange cell histories encoded in dust. How Nikko is aware of this is a mystery locked behind the black wall of another proscribed field, but again, he makes no inquiries. It doesn't matter how Null Boundary's neural system came to be tainted by the Chenzeme, just that it has, in a primitive way, so that Nikko too can distinguish meaning in the cell-talk. He doesn't have Lot's talent. He is like a dog listening to its master's voice—aware of mood, but deaf to specific meaning. Forever surprised by what Lot will say.

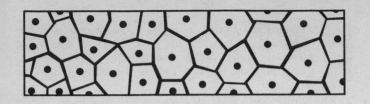

Chapter 1

The cramped arc of the transit bubble pressed on Lot like a gigantic, gentle hand, pushing him sideways into the only soft tissue within the cold, brittle membrane of Chenzeme cells that coated Null Boundary's hull. The philosopher cells glowed with an intense white light that Lot could feel even when his eyes were closed. At this one point Nikko had created a vacuole beneath the membrane's fixed surface, preventing it from bonding with the body of the ship. Lot thought of the site as a wound, because the cell tissue here was slushy, like overripe fruit or decaying flesh, on the verge of freezing.

He sank into it, eager, and a little bit scared: this thin amalgam of living alien cells was all that lay between him and hard vacuum. His gut clenched when he thought about it. He had no backups of himself. But the membrane had been in existence for twenty-two years, and it had not failed yet.

In the wound, the philosopher cells were loosely attached to one another. They felt glassy and granular as they molded around his shoulder, flowing up and into his ear, across his closely trimmed scalp, and around his mouth. He kept one eye closed. Their touch was cold, though it was not unbearable because the chemical reactions within the cells required relatively high temperatures.

Not high enough to suit Lot. The skin suit kept his body warm, but he'd left the hood off so as not to block the tiny, drop-shaped silver glands of his sensory tears that studded his cheeks just beneath his eyes. Now the right side of his face was embedded in the wound and it felt half frozen. He turned his head to keep his nose in the transit bubble's thin pocket of air. Over most of the hull, the membrane was a petrified layer only a few millimeters deep. Here in the wound it remained soft and it continually thickened. Lot worried about that. He didn't want to drown in the cells.

Finally, his shoulder brushed the crisp tissue of the membrane's outer wall. Relief flooded him. This time, he would sink no farther.

Over the past two years, Lot had spent up to fifteen hours a day with the cells, sometimes talking to Urban about what he felt. Urban monitored his communications, seeking to interpret the cell-talk for himself—and failing utterly. No surprise. Chenzeme thought was not like human thought. Lot could do one or the other, but serious fudging was needed to bridge the two.

Often, Lot just listened to the philosopher cells. Sometimes he would try to sway the waves of competitive simulations that swept round and round the field, and sometimes he would introduce his own notions to the tumult. Today though, he would try something new.

He closed his eyes, his heart beating hard in anticipation as he visualized the molecular structures assembling within the pheromonal vats of his sensory tears.

Nikko was convinced they could establish a Chenzeme identity through radio hails. Lot was less sure. Chenzeme radio signals were intricate and highly variable, but they were not immune to counterfeit . . . a fact that had started Lot wondering if there might be another level of identification among the warships, and if so, what might it be?

It didn't take long for him to fix on the chemical language of the philosopher cells. If Null Boundary could communicate with the courser on that intimate level, it might be persuaded they were authentic Chenzeme. It might let them live.

A golden spider clung to Lot's left earlobe. It was his radio link to the ship's datasphere. Now the spider squeezed his earlobe with its legs, whispering in an airy, synthesized voice: "Looptime equal to seventy."

Twenty more seconds then, until Nikko purged his memory.

Urban, you ready? He wanted to check in, but Nikko might be listening. It was impossible to tell. Usually Nikko left them alone, relying on a nonsentient submind to look out for their welfare and ring an alarm should something go wrong.

Nikko would stop them if he knew. He would see the very real possibility that the courser would be provoked into a close approach to seek a mating—that's what Nikko called it—an exchange of chemical histories with the philosopher cells of Null Boundary.

Lot had no idea if they could survive that level of contact—Nikko refused to even talk about the possibility— but for Lot, even gray uncertainty looked better than the zero chance they would have if the courser crept within weapons range still unconvinced.

He took slow, shallow breaths, determined to appear calm. Nikko would stop looping if he thought Lot was having a bad time.

Calm.

"Ten seconds," the spider whispered.

Near the end of his loop, Nikko sometimes had a few seconds with nothing to do, free time that could be spent looking over Lot's shoulder. Of course, whatever he saw would be forgotten as soon as the memory of this ninety-second segment was dumped.

"Four seconds," the spider whispered.

Nikko's program would take two seconds to purge and reset. Lot breathed softly as a chemical language slipped in discrete packets to the surface of his sensory tears. The charismata. They were molecular messengers, and he could sculpt them to influence human moods or Chenzeme protocols.

"Three seconds. Two—"

"Do it, fury." Urban's voice issued from the spider, over-riding the count.

"Zero—"

Lot released the charismata. The chemical message flushed across the bridge of liquid that linked his sensory tears to the glowing cells pressed against his cheek. Immediately, he felt a mottled red-cold burst of acknowledgment from the philosopher cells as they replicated the message, transferring it throughout the membrane's vast field. Within seconds, Lot was breathing the respondent chemical structure: a mélange of identification codes and demands for radio communications from one Chenzeme vessel to another—

The wall of the transit bubble shuddered. Lot yelped in surprise as the bubble's tissue oozed over him, sliding like a flexible knife between his skin suit and the philosopher cells. Between his *skin* and the cells: he could feel the bite as it sliced the nascent bonds the cells had made with his sensory tears. He twisted in an instinctive—and utterly ineffectual—attempt to escape, then cried out in hoarse protest: *"Urban!"*

"It's not me, fury."

"Then Nikko. Dammit, listen—"

The transit bubble's tissue sealed around him like a layer of skin, cutting off both his protest and the cells' white light, plunging him into darkness. He could not breathe.

The bubble expanded. Cold air puffed against his cheeks. He felt the pressure of acceleration as the bubble raced inward through the ship's insulating tissue. His face throbbed as his skin began to warm. He tried again. "Nikko, listen to me." He had no idea if the experiment had succeeded. "I know you're pissed, but I need to be at the hull *now*—"

The bubble slammed to a stop. In the same instant, the wall beneath his belly snapped open and Lot found himself hurtling through the zero-g environment of Null Boundary's core chamber.

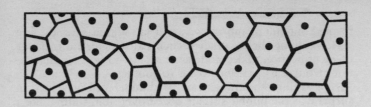

Chapter
2

Instinctively, Lot tucked himself into a tight ball. "*Nikko—!*" His shout cut off as he slammed into the chamber's opposite side. White light burst under him, flaring within the image walls that lined the spindle-shaped room. He clawed at the soft tissue, digging his fingers in to keep from bouncing in the chamber's zero gravity.

His sensory tears registered the enveloping scent of his own anger, the tang of Urban's presence, and the sharp taste of Nikko's fury.

"You taught the cells to drop dust, didn't you?" Nikko demanded, his deep, rich voice filling the chamber.

Lot looked up. "Sooth. I tried."

The core chamber was the sheltered heart of the ship, some twenty feet long and eight across. The image walls displayed a shifting blue-gray illumination. Nikko was nowhere in sight, but Urban drifted only a few feet away, clothed in a pale gold skin suit. He was upside down to Lot, his long, lean body curved in the zero gravity like a cupped hand.

In silhouette, Urban and Lot might have been taken for twins. Their builds were almost the same, and they both kept their hair cut short so it wouldn't drift in the way. Their complexions differed. Lot was blond-haired and brown-skinned. Urban was darker, his hair black and tightly curled. Now Urban's grin flashed like the sudden turn of a white fish in murky water. "*We* taught the cells to drop dust, fury, and it worked."

"You're sure?" Lot wanted confirmation. "Nikko, did you feel a flush of heat?"

"Like I'd been lanced." His disembodied voice originated from the chamber's end.

Urban laughed. "That would have been the moment the dust went into the void."

Several tons of dust. It had been a huge drain on the ship's resources, but it had worked! Lot shook his head, loosening a charismata of joy on the air. Let Nikko *feel* it. This was a good thing.

"It was a message for the courser, wasn't it?" Nikko pressed, still without appearing.

"Sooth." Lot eased his fingers out of the semisolid image wall, the tissue sparking white around his hand. "Are you still running on looptime?"

"Hardly. Too much seems to happen in my two seconds of downtime."

"Well, if you're going to hang around for more than ninety seconds, you might as well come out and talk to us."

"Now that it's too late to take anything back?"

"You never would have let us do it."

"You've got that right."

"Give us a grip, will you?" Urban asked. "And a little more light too?" These requests brought an immediate response. Texture appeared all around the image wall. Loops and knobs pushed out from the curving surface, and the illumination climbed toward a brighter, whiter glow. Hooking a boot under a loop, Lot looked back—up?—to see Nikko's image at the chamber's end.

No one was natural anymore, Lot least of all. Yet everyone he had known before had *appeared* natural. Not Nikko. His anatomy was adapted to tolerate vacuum, and it showed. Where Lot had skin of neutral brown, Nikko was covered with minute blue, china-hard scales. His fingers and toes were almost eight inches long. Lot watched them twisting in braids, a sure sign of anxiety. His head was smooth and hairless. His eyes were hidden behind protective crystal lenses, and his nose and mouth were diminutive, his face incapable of expression. The small, membranous cloak of his kisheer lay still against his shoulders. It was an organ for converting carbon dioxide into oxygen, that would seal over his face under vacuum, allowing him to breathe. Nikko wore no clothing, though an accessory organ like a living loincloth concealed and protected his anal and genital zones.

This version of Nikko was a holographic image reflecting the physical human body that he sometimes used, but Nikko was more than a man. He was also the sculpted entity that inhabited and controlled the body of the ship. His sensory system extended from the outer membrane of philosopher cells to the bioactive walls of this chamber, where glands synthesized the charismata of his moods.

Somehow, long ago, Null Boundary's neural system had been tainted by Chenzeme tissue, so that Nikko had some understanding of the charismata. He was no precisely engineered machine like Lot; still, he could follow the gist of cell-talk, and he had even more skill at producing the charismata of human emotion.

Now a charismata burst against Lot's sensory tears, a chemical package conveying a sense of pressure: time pressure and chest injuries and gathering specks of darkness.

"Back off, Nikko," Lot warned. "It's not that bad."

"You made a mistake."

"You don't know that. The courser won't taste the dust for months."

A new charismata hit Lot's sensory tears. He felt blood flowing thick and warm across his face; salt in his eyes and on his lips. He pulled back, one hand rubbing frantically against the sticky glands of his sensory tears. "Stop it! Nikko, what's the matter with you? You know the radio hails weren't working. We had to try something new."

"It isn't new." His kisheer rippled, a tight wave rolling outward from his neck, ending with a low *snap* as it met the edge of the membrane.

"It is new," Lot insisted. He loosed a soothing charismata. "I know you don't want to risk a mating, but I found this function in the cells, for producing massive quantities of identical data packets."

Dust. It had never occurred to him before that dust could be used for anything other than the short-range communication of a mating, but here was a way of producing trillions of copies of a single message. Why would so many copies be needed? He had talked it over with Urban, and the only plausible reason they could think of was to counteract the dispersion of a long-distance drop.

Urban was happy to explain it. He rolled forward, a horizontal arrow aimed at Nikko. The textured surface of his skin suit gleamed like wet sand. "The packets develop with spin vectors to reduce their velocity and stabilize their spread. They should form a diffuse cloud, at least ten thousand klicks across by the time the courser intersects it. The density will be low, but it'll only take one hit to convey the message."

"If the particle survives the impact, of course," Lot amended. He had his doubts. "Only Chenzeme communicate with dust. This is just one more way to convince it we're real. Did you understand the message content?"

Nikko shrugged, a gesture that moved in a wave down his torso. "Good feelings. Friendly contact. Not the kind of message you'd expect to find in a Chenzeme library."

"That's where it came from," Urban said.

Lot nodded. "Sooth. I got it from the cells. I think it's an armistice signal."

"It's not new," Nikko insisted, his voice reflecting all the emotion his face lacked. "I've seen a dust drop before. Love and nature, I remember it exactly."

Lot knew little about Nikko's past, except that it was deep, extending some thirty-two hundred years back to Sol System in the era before the rise of the Hallowed Vasties. Some cataclysm had overtaken the ship early in its history, wiping much of the original memory and leaving the rest scrambled. Once, Nikko let slip that he'd learned the charismata from a "mating" with a Chenzeme ship. Maybe that record was wiped too, or maybe it never happened. When Lot asked Nikko how he'd escaped, the answer was a terse "I didn't."

Urban seized a handhold, rotating his position again, so that now his head aligned with Lot. His dark eyes glistened, as if they were made of some frozen liquid thinly wrapped in meltwater. His black hair lay against his head in tight curls. On his face was a faint, condescending smile. "So tell us, Nikko. What do you remember?" It was a facetious question. There would be no answer, because Nikko never talked about his past.

This time though, Nikko surprised them. "It was another world then. Everything felt different." Light caught in a smear in each of the scales of his hide.

Lot leaned forward. He badly wanted to know more. "Tell us about it?" he urged.

Nikko's kisheer went still. Lot caught the edge of a sense of vastness, no more, before it vanished into a pointillistic cynicism shimmering in discrete specks upon the air. "It was a long time ago, and we were angry. The cult virus had begun to move through the Celestial Cities. We didn't understand it then. All we knew was that our perfect world was dissolving into a fascist religious mania, and when we couldn't change it, we left."

"Aboard Null Boundary?" Lot asked.

"Aboard Null Boundary, yes. Four hundred twenty-nine of us. Others had gone out from Sol System before us, of course, but we were going farther. We were angry, and most of our company was very young—and foolish, like the two of you."

In truth, both Lot and Urban were over 220 standard years, but then time in cold sleep didn't count toward maturity. Lot's effective age was somewhere around twenty-five. Urban was close to thirty—no more than adolescence in the culture of Deception Well.

"You were immune to the cult?" Urban asked.

"Yes. All of us—though of course we didn't understand it then." His voice soft and bitter. "And we'd never heard of the Chenzeme. When we saw the vessel in our telescopes, it seemed a miracle, dreadful and awesome. We should have fled. We might have outrun it . . . even if we had to run forever. But we didn't even try. The flash of heat on the hull"—Nikko waved his hand, as if to acknowledge Null Boundary's perimeter—"I saw that. I never understood it though, not until now."

"It dropped dust?" Lot asked, though already he could see the incident in his mind. A flash of heat, a temporary blurring of the image of the Chenzeme ship for the few seconds it would take the dust to cool and disperse. Then nothing. No overt sign of hostility.

Nikko's expression didn't change—couldn't change—though his voice grew softer. "It was a plague. A typical Chenzeme plague. It took months to overrun us, but eventually we intersected the cloud. It wrecked the ship's memory and wiped the ghosts. It killed everyone but me. I don't know why I survived. No reason for it."

But Nikko's physiology was not human-ordinary, even when he chose to manifest in physical form. "Were they like you?" Lot asked. "The other people on the ship?"

Nikko didn't answer this. "As I think on it now, I can see we must have been strange to it, just as it was strange to us. It didn't strafe us with its guns, as any Chenzeme ship would do these days. It was a test. You see? If we'd been Chenzeme, the plague would not have harmed us."

Lot felt a fever's burn ignite upon his face, dark blood oozing from his pores. "Nikko, stop it!" He slapped at his sensory tears, but he could still feel the near presence of disaster.

"Did you booby-trap your dust?" Nikko demanded.

"You know I didn't. I sent a friendly handshake." He looked at Urban. They'd been in this together, but only Lot understood the cells. It had been his choice. "What if the proper greeting is a threat?"

Urban detested failure; it showed in the hard set of his face. "Well then fury, I guess we've just presented ourselves as deranged Chenzeme."

"Maybe it doesn't matter." Nikko's fingers twisted in excruciating braids. "Maybe we've misinterpreted everything. The courser has left us alone, so we tell ourselves we've fooled it."

"We have." Lot didn't like the doubt in Nikko's voice; instinctively, he moved to shore up Nikko's faith. "The camouflage is working. You know it is. The courser could have closed with us years ago, but we're still alive."

Nikko's image stretched, his long, spidery toes raking the wall. "Why?" he demanded.

"Because we've confused its instinct."

"Or because it's afraid of us," Urban said. "We're Chenzeme. We could be dangerous."

Nikko snorted, crossing his arms over his chest, his long fingers at his elbows like coarse fringe. "Or maybe it understands us better than we understand ourselves. Coursers aren't blind, or stupid. This one was hot on our ass. It saw the cell field spread across our hull. It saw us becoming Chenzeme. So it eased off. It gave the process time to happen."

"What process?" Urban asked, his voice stern, braced for bad news.

Lot guessed. "A colonization."

Nikko nodded his agreement. "So it might not matter if we get the first message wrong. The courser might even expect it to be wrong, because we're *becoming* Chenzeme. We're not Chenzeme yet."

This was a neat line of speculation. It gave them maneuvering room. Lot nodded a willing agreement. "So another dust drop might be accepted, even if the first one tastes of deranged Chenzeme." He rubbed at his sensory tears, already planning the structure of his next greeting.

"So that's the good news," Urban said. "There's bad news too, isn't there, Nikko? Like, if the courser knows what's going on, that only means it's seen this all before." He looked around the core chamber, performing a sarcastic inspection, eyes wide, his neck craning. "Hey. I don't see any other survivors."

Lot felt his chest tighten. It was true. Human and Chenzeme were the only species active between worlds. There was evidence of other spacefaring races in the distant past, but they were all gone now. At Deception Well, nanotechnological "governors" still protected the system from destructive elements, but the species that had designed them had long since disappeared.

"Colonization must be a damn successful procedure," Urban concluded. "Or maybe that ass-biting courser's standing by to tidy up any evidence of failure."

"Maybe it is," Nikko said, "but now we have the dust, we're not helpless anymore." The walls of the chamber brightened further, along with Nikko's mood. "Dust can be used to carry chemical lies. It can be used to carry poisons and plague. And Lot brought a library of Chenzeme vulnerabilities out of the Well. Didn't you?"

That was true. Lot remembered Deception Well, the dry taste of the nebula's living dust, and the static libraries of data it contained—thirty million years of a contentious history, recording the clash between Well nanotech and Chenzeme nanotech. The Well governors had forced their own evolution, actively seeking new structures that might provide an advantage over the Chenzeme, and mostly, they had been successful. The Well thrived, while other systems had perished.

In their passage through the nebula, Lot had barely brushed the surface of that data sea, uncovering only a tiny portion of the molecular defenses that must exist there. The patterns he had learned were safely ensconced in the neural tendrils of his fixed memory. He probably could learn to use them.

"You could use what you know to kill the courser," Nikko said. The crystal lenses that protected his eyes made his unchanging stare seem fixed somewhere over Lot's right shoulder.

Lot stared back at him, filled with a sudden, sourceless dread. "I don't know how to use the dust that way."

"You'll learn."

"Nikko's right," Urban said. "Once we get what we need out of the courser, we could poison it."

Lot felt the skin on the back of his neck tighten as Nikko drummed a slow, deliberate beat against the china-hard scales of his thigh: a synthesized image producing synthesized sounds of impact. When the courser had first been sighted, he too had longed to find a way of destroying it. Now . . .

He glanced at Urban, saw the anxious and not-so-subtle shake of his head—and ignored it. "Nikko, I've been thinking . . . maybe we should try to make our peace with the courser."

Nikko froze. For several seconds he didn't answer. Then: "That's the cult virus talking. It's inside you and you can't escape it. You were made to be its host, its vehicle, and it will always drive you to make a Communion with anyone and anything."

"Not with the Chenzeme," Lot said. "The cult virus is *their* plague. They made their ships immune. You know that."

"While they tailored your kind to attack the human neural system."

"History," Urban scoffed. "Who cares?"

Lot, for one, because Nikko was right, he'd been engineered to spread the virus—and he was fairly sure he'd been engineered by the Chenzeme. Some ancestor of his must have been one of the first humans to venture into Chenzeme territory. He had found something there, or the Chenzeme had found him, and they'd changed him. They'd infected him with their neural tendrils, their sensory tears, and their cult virus, and then they'd sent him back again, all the way to Sol System.

This was the story Lot had pieced together, from the history he knew, and from the remembrances that had come down to him, inherited through his fixed memory, shadowy snatches of ancestral lives.

The cult virus had hit first in Sol System, burning through the population in a firestorm of faith that made the planets melt and run and re-form again into a Dyson swarm—a singular intellect distributed across a swarm of orbiting habitats so vast the Sun was hidden within it. From Sol, the contagion moved outward to other star systems, carried in the flesh of men like Lot, charismatic cult leaders almost exactly like that first cult leader, each of them formed from a fusion of Chenzeme and human neural systems. Rationality burned away in their presence. Religious fervor eliminated dissent. Cults blossomed into true Communions that grew at exponential rates, until another star was claimed by a Dyson swarm of the Hallowed Vasties.

Disaster or ascension? Looking inward from the frontier, it had been impossible to say—until the cordoned suns began to fail. Now, scant centuries after their formation, anyone could turn a telescope toward the center and see the shells crumbling into clouds of dust and gas that slowly unraveled on mild stellar winds. No one knew what became of the people who had succumbed to the cult, or if anything living survived the breakdown of the cordons. There was no way to know without going back to look, and such a journey would demand centuries of travel time. It seemed a fair guess though, that in the collapse of a cordon, there were no human survivors.

Thousands of frontier worlds remained unconquered by the cult at the time they left Deception Well, but the cycle could erupt again on any of them, igniting around a charismatic carrier like Lot. The cult virus was inside him, and no one had ever learned how to get it out. He could feel it: a dull desire for Communion forever nestling in his belly.

Deliberately, he straightened the curving line of his body. "Nikko, for all the Chenzeme have done to us, for all the worlds lost between the cult virus and the warships, hitting back is not the answer. It doesn't matter that we want to. You know we can't destroy every Chenzeme ship. We'd be lucky even to wreck this one. But if we can get it to talk—"

Nikko's long, long fingers slashed the air in front of him. "You can't negotiate with the warships. They're not conscious, and they don't make deals."

"You don't know that. The Chenzeme vessels *are* intelligent, even if they're not conscious. They're adaptable too. They can change."

"The better to eat you," Nikko growled, and a cold sense of enclosure accompanied his words.

Urban was oblivious to it. Like Nikko, he was immune to the cult. A few people were. No one knew why. He shook his head, his face set in a slight, ironic smile. "See, Lot? You can't talk to him about it."

Lot gave him an angry glance, feeling the warm white shadow of the cult, swelling, swelling in his belly. *Push:* "Come on, Nikko. Think about it. Something lies behind the machines. We came this way to find it."

The Chenzeme ships had come out of darkness, from the direction called *swan* where vast lanes of molecular clouds marked the rim of the Orion Arm. Something was sending them. Lot felt sure of it. Something out there had created his ancestors. Lot was a weapon, a hybrid device designed to spread the cult—but whether that made him an ally or an enemy of the marauding ships, he didn't know.

Nikko's kisheer moved in sharp, impatient ripples. "We came this way to find the source of the Chenzeme. If I could destroy that, you know I would. Love and nature, they've killed enough of us."

So true, and still Lot stumbled on the unsettling fact that the microscopic governors that regulated the Deception Well system had never tried to destroy the Chenzeme. The Well had only sought to change them, to manipulate their behavior toward less destructive ends. It was an instinct of the Well governors to try to push every living thing of every clade toward a harmonious life system, where cooperation carried more value than conflict.

"It's too soon to talk about destroying anything," Lot said. "We need to know more about the Chenzeme, if we ever hope to find them."

"So we learn what we can," Nikko growled. "That doesn't mean we can't be ready. Make your weapons now. When we're well armed, that's the time to negotiate."

Was that a concession? Lot didn't think so. Nikko's charismata carried a sense of restlessness. He'd probably had enough of real time and wanted Lot to go away so he could resume his cycle of electronic suicide. Lot saw no reason to make it easy for him. "Why don't you stay present?" he asked. "You could help us."

"You don't need help, kid."

"It's pretty sick the way you wipe yourself over and over again."

Nikko cocked his smooth, blue-scaled head. "Have we had this conversation before?"

Urban laughed at that, while Lot admitted: "Several hundred times."

"Funny. I only remember one or two sessions. What was my latest answer?"

Lot resisted an urge to punch the wall. "That you want to stay close to your past. That nobody lives forever. That human minds weren't made to contain such vast spans of time."

Nikko nodded. "That's good. I'll stand by that."

"But why? You don't *have* to remain human."

"I want to. There just aren't that many of us left."

Lot blinked—a fraction of a second, but it was enough— Nikko's image was gone. Before long, the spider reported that he had resumed his loop of virtual death and resurrection.

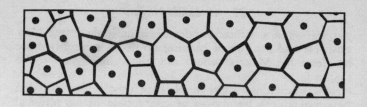

Chapter 3

I have to get back to the cells," Lot said. "Check on
things. They must be frantic."

Urban looked at him, faintly amused. Then he looked
at the wall. A transit bubble oozed open at that spot with
an audible *pop!*, its smooth interior shimmering faint white
and gray.

Lot leaned hard on a twinge of jealousy. After they had
left Deception Well, Urban had grown an atrial organ in his
head that let him communicate directly with the ship. He
could even make a ghost of himself, an electronic copy of
his persona that could be sent into the ship's library to
oversee projects, while his core self worked elsewhere.

Lot had tried to grow an atrium too, but the modification
had failed—just as every attempt to change his physiology
always failed. The same mysterious engineer who had created his sensory tears and blended Chenzeme neural tendrils
into his genetic line, had also armed his body with an impenetrable system of defensive Makers—self-programming,
molecular-scale machines that would not permit tampering
with his inherited design. Everyone had defensive Makers,
but Lot's were different, because no one knew how to re-
program or override them. They had blocked every attempt
to pry the cult virus from his system. It was hard to avoid
the conclusion that he was a device made for a very specific

purpose—and a *disposable* device, if he looked at it honestly. He had no way of backing up his existence, because his defensive Makers would not allow his tissues to be mapped.

It was different for Urban. He kept a tissue map stored in Null Boundary's library—a precise record of his physical structure, down to the neuronal connections where memory and personality were stored—so that if he was ever lost or killed, an exact physical copy could be regrown. Clementine did the same thing, and Nikko went even farther, regrowing his body only in the rare intervals when he desired a physical incarnation. Lot's physiology denied him this option. Since his body could not be mapped, he could never be duplicated, or regrown.

Still, he had advantages of his own.

Tapping the wall with his boot, he launched himself toward the bubble. He caught the rim. The thin gloves of his skin suit translated its smooth, cool feel. "Is there any way you can keep Nikko from grabbing me when I'm out there?" he asked, as he tucked himself into the hole. He kept one hand on the rim to prevent it from closing.

Urban shook his head. "Don't think of Nikko as a ghost visiting in the ship's neural system. That's what *I* am. Nikko's different. He'll always have the last word, because the core of the neural system *is* his mind, his brain, whatever you want to call it, and I can't get in there, any more than you can get inside my head."

"So long as you're immune to the cult."

Urban grinned. "That's not something I'm planning to change, fury. Now go. We need to know what the cells are thinking."

As Lot sank into the wound, his sensory tears merged again with the philosopher cells. Abruptly, he was inundated with the chemical rush of multiple dialogues. The cells were analyzing the dust drop, creating scenario after scenario to try to model what might have happened, and what it might mean.

Never before had Lot encountered such a fine weave of speculation. It was as if the experience of the dust drop had forced the cell field toward a new complexity and maturity.

Even in ordinary times, the configuration of the field underwent constant evolution. New connections were established between the cells. Some old ones died. Nutrient supply and demand fluctuated, and always the field expanded as more cells were made. Activity was unceasing, and integrated across tens of thousands of pathways, so that Lot worried: If he spent too much time away, would he still be able to find his way into their conversations? Or would he grow apart from them, so that they might recognize his alien nature?

This time he slipped easily back into the flow, to find a new image dominating the dialogues. A presence—vague, close, and strong. Lot understood. The act of dropping dust made the argument that Another existed to receive it. The cells had not perceived this other, but they were delving deep into their inherited memories to build hypotheses about it.

It was a dauntingly sensual exercise. Lot tasted sweet flavors bursting across his tongue. Erotic emotions mobbed his sensory tears, flowing images cascaded through his brain, pleasure struck random blows all over his skin, and a hard-on fought the restraint of his skin suit.

He flashed on Clemantine: stone cold, buried in tissue more frigid than the cell field, she'd been in cold storage the two years he'd been awake. Lot had schooled himself not to think of her, but now his control cracked, shield walls caving in so that all the desire and anger of two years rushed out at once into the philosopher cells, where it was puzzled over and amplified, and fed back into him. The cells desired the contact of Another as much as he did, and all of them blithely unaware of it till now.

"*Urban.*"

"Yeah?"

"Talk."

"About?"

"Anything. Just break me out of this loop."

So Urban talked, a near breathless monologue on cell language, on cooking, on biomechanical engineering and historical dramas. No doubt put together by an unconscious submind, a partial persona suitable for dull tasks that Urban himself would never have the patience to endure. It did help. Lot felt a slow return to equilibrium. The submind must have been monitoring his vital signs, because as Lot calmed, Urban's voice faded, until only the circling thoughts of the cells remained in his awareness.

Memories of other ships and other ages were archived in the cells, carried down through their lineages. New lineages were brought into the field when warships mated in the void, exchanging cell lines. The memories were not recalled in images or sounds or smells or symbols or feelings alone, but in combinations of these—gestalt impressions capturing all that lay within an indefinite stretch of time.

Or anyway, it felt something like that.

Lot found it impossible to truly reflect the Chenzeme sense in human terms.

Cell memory might be as concrete as the tumultuous joy of a planet boiling under a gamma ray laser generated by one of the great ring-shaped ships called swan bursters. Or it could be as abstract as a pulse of unfocused hatred. Concurring memories from different cells could reinforce an impression; contrasting memories could destroy it. Much of what passed for recollection was disjointed, or short-lived: details drawn into scenarios, then quickly discarded. And always there were multiple threads of thought progressing at once, so that the field would be planning, remembering, desiring, questioning, rehearsing, in coherent, interlinking threads—yet without a persona to bind all these scattered elements. Lot had never sensed a hint of consciousness among the philosopher cells. All their deliberations, all their training, ran as blind reactions awaiting outcome, never interrupted by a glint of intuition. Sometimes Lot imagined himself as the field's central persona, but the idea never survived long among the cells.

He let himself sink into the flowing conversations, gradually shedding the sense of himself, brought back to awareness only by Urban's occasional question. *"Fury, you still there? You still awake?"* And finally, *"Will you make the poison dust?"*

That's right. Nikko wanted weapons. Lot was supposed to explore ways to kill. He shook his head, loosening the grip of the cells on his sensory tears, pulling partly free of them so he would not be distracted by their conversations while he explored his fixed memory, turning over the structures and flavors of dust, hearing in them the slow, coaxing heresies of the Well. The Well governors had deftly blended life from different worlds into a single, functional biosphere, but when life could not be blended, it must be defended against, and the governors had been adept at that too, over millions of years developing a host of molecular-scale strategies to thwart the Chenzeme. There *were* keys in the data Lot had gleaned, that he might use to slide beneath the courser's suspicions.

And then what? Every complex system had pressure points. Lean on those points, and the whole system would snap. Carbon monoxide was a simple molecule, yet in the human circulatory system it could block the uptake of oxygen in red blood cells, leading quickly to death. More complex molecules could block the transmission of nerve impulses, causing almost instant collapse. Defensive Makers were programmed to sweep the body clean of such hazards, but at the same time, these very defenses created new vulnerabilities. The human body had become so dependent on its molecular caretakers that a plague spawned in Deception Well had once killed hundreds of thousands of people simply by destroying their defensive Makers.

Similarly, there were simple molecules that could jam the communications channels of the philosopher cells. Of course the cells had defenses, evolved in the fire of nanotechnological warfare, but they were not invulnerable. In the Well, Lot had found Trojan-horse molecules that mimicked ordinary Chenzeme emotive packets, but that carried within their hollow interiors potent arrays of blocking molecules. Once bonded to a cell, the complex structures would produce a false input, setting up a virtual environment for every affected cell while isolating it from its neighbors. Coordination and decision making would evaporate, sending the cell field into a nonfunctional state: hyperactivity at the molecular level, catatonia on the macroscale. With all input channels blocked, there would be no way for the philosopher cells to feed, and within minutes they would starve to death. The blocking molecules would echo back any distress cries from the dying cells. The cells in turn would react as if they were dominant, opening ever more channels to their attackers as they "won" each debate.

In theory.

The Well codes were old. Lot felt sure they had once

worked, but the Chenzeme warships had been evolving for at least thirty million years. They might have developed a defense to this line of attack. He had no way to know. He might be able to test the poison on an isolated section of Null Boundary's hull field, but that wouldn't tell him much. Every lineage of cells was different. Null Boundary's cells might be vulnerable to this dust, but the courser's might not. There was no way to know, short of trying.

And if the courser survived it? Lot didn't think they would be allowed a second chance.

He had no idea how long he'd been in the wound when it happened: A new input flooded the philosopher cells with . . . a soft greeting? Sooth. A dark (calm) glistening query as to identity and intent and history. An input from outside the field, an alien radio hail proclaiming

<Another>

A foreign presence. For the first time, the courser existed as a real object within the dialogue. And almost simultaneous with this recognition came a need to respond.

<Answer>

A possible reply—similar to the greeting received—was offered for debate among the philosopher cells, though this version held something of newness, a confession of inexperience.

An aggressive minority objected:

<Stop. Strengthen that.>
<Stop. Strengthen that.>
<Stop>

Too late. Overwhelmed by the instinct to answer, the dominant cell lines launched a respondent radio hail.

Urban had been drowsing on the gee deck when the courser's radio hail reached Null Boundary. Usually he left at least a ghost to sit vigil over Lot whenever he was in the wound, but this time the frantic pace of the cells' activity had exhausted his molecular monitors. No data; no point in sticking around. He'd shut down his interface and pulled out.

So he was startled from a half-sleep when a signal screamed through his atrium, a weird amalgam of meaningless tones and scratches. He spilled out of his hammock, landing on his knees on the pavilion's tiled floor, wincing in pain as Nikko's voice flooded his atrium. *The courser is hailing us.*

"That's impossible," Urban said. "It can't have intercepted the dust yet."

No. But it would have registered the infrared flash.

It was late afternoon on the gee deck; a solitary dove crooned among the two-hundred-year-old trees that grew like pillars between the floor and the holographic sky. The pavilion, with its lattice roof, occupied the summit of a grassy slope sweeping down to the koi pond.

Urban took it all in at a glance as he gained his feet and ran. "Where's Lot?" he shouted, plunging down a path that cut through flower beds.

Still in the cell field.

He set a submind to do a quick calculation. The answer returned as he skidded around to the back of the slope, where Clemantine kept a little house, built into the hill. Six hours: the timing of the courser's response matched the round-trip light-gap between the two ships.

Urban startled a resident service 'bot as he bounded through the entrance arch and into the house. A transit bubble waited for him, wide open in the image wall. He threw himself into it, and the bubble shrank to fit him. "Get me out there." His stomach wrenched, as *down* shifted 180 degrees. At least there was no room to fall.

Love and nature, Nikko said. *Lot has answered it. The cell field has generated its own radio signal.*

"I didn't know it could do that."

I didn't either, but it's biomechanical tissue. It wouldn't be hard.

Already the bubble was slowing. "So what did Lot say?"

A greeting. But it feels weak; wrong. Not really Chenzeme.

"If you're right, that won't matter."

If.

A wall melted. Strange scents puffed over his face as he merged with an older bubble that kissed the dazzling, glittery white wall of the cell field. The air here was freezing. And the light so bright his eyes had to adjust for a few seconds before he could make out Lot within the glare.

Love and nature, Nikko swore in soft astonishment. *He's never been that deep before.*

Lot's eyes were closed; his body immersed in the wound. He lay on his side with the cells puddled around him like a viscous liquid. Several fingers of them had flowed over the elevated side of his face, reaching for his sensory tears. His mouth and nose were covered.

Urban yelped in alarm. He kicked off the bubble wall, slamming into the freezing sheen of cells. The white lights dimmed at the impact. Cold rushed past his palms and through his clothes. "Lot! Dammit. Nikko? What's happened to him? The wound was never this deep before."

The cells have been active.

"No shit!"

You were supposed to be watching him.

"Sooth." Urban dug at the gleaming tissue that had grown into Lot's nose and mouth. It stretched and shattered, leaving lesser strands behind. Lot's chest was buried in it, and Urban could not feel him breathing. "Lot, come on. Wake up now. Get this shit out of your lungs before it drowns you. Lot!" He scraped at the fingers of cells. They were hard and cold to the touch, yet they stretched when he pulled on them, shattering into tiny fragments, like frozen raindrops.

He heard a slow intake of air. "Lot?"

Lot's nose and mouth were still covered. How could he breathe?

There it was again, a slow *shoosh* of indrawn breath, as if the cells filtered his respirations. "How can he get air?" Urban muttered. "Nikko? The cell field isn't permeable to air."

I don't know. His physiological signs are not showing distress.

"He won't wake up!"

No. He is awake. He won't respond.

Urban let a fist thump hard against the cells that had oozed over Lot's shoulder. "Talk to me!" An edge of panic in his voice. He had not kept watch, not even a ghost.

Maybe Lot heard him, or maybe he was coming out of it anyway, because now his eyelids fluttered open. His gaze fixed on Urban's face, but without a glint of recognition. Then his body spasmed. A horrible cough convulsed his chest, sending a spray of glistening cells across the pocket of the transit bubble. Urban hunched against the ricocheting snow. "Lot, are you all right?"

"Urban?" Lot's voice skewed uncontrolled across the scale, settling on a tone of righteous anger. He got a hand free. Urban had changed his skin suit for a long-sleeved shirt and shorts. Now Lot's fist closed on his collar; the light fabric pulled tight against his neck. "What are you doing here?" Lot demanded. "Get out of here! You're contaminating the cells."

"I don't give a damn. This stuff—it's like ice! Rubbery ice, and it's *growing* into you. I'm getting you out. Right now."

"No." Lot let his collar go. He looked to the side, as if he could see through the white wall of cells. "The courser's out there. I felt it."

"No shit. We heard it too. Now out."

"Right now," Nikko echoed, forestalling Lot's protest. Urban could just hear his tinny voice emerging from the spider on Lot's ear, as the walls of the transit bubble collapsed around them. "I'll cut you out again if I have to," Nikko warned.

Lot cursed him. Still, the threat worked. The gleaming tissue collapsed to the consistency of jelly. Lot slipped clear of it, just as the transit bubble closed beneath him, cutting off the blaze of light. He turned on Urban, his sensory tears specked with bright spots of blood. "Why did you come? You've got your monitors on me. You didn't need to interfere."

"The monitors gave out. You were in there six hours, Lot."

"I've been in three times longer than that. Nikko! Take me back. Now. Things are changing, and I have to be there."

Urban's chin rose. "Shut up, fury. Nikko's on my side now."

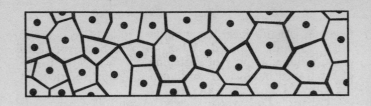

Chapter 4

The transit bubble opened, spilling Lot, gently this time, back into the core chamber—and into Clemantine's presence. He sensed her before he saw her. Her aura folded around him, a strange mix of resentment, excitement, and delight. The dull white hunger for Communion that lived inside him flared a little brighter as he grabbed a handgrip and turned. "You're awake," he blurted. Brilliant as usual.

She clung right side up to the curving wall, her back to the chamber's bow end. Their eyes met, and a cool half-smile bent her lips. Her affection was a keen pleasure against his sensory tears, though it was marred with knots of wariness, and animosity. So she had not come out unscathed either.

"Busy day?" she asked.

"Sooth. You could say that."

"God, we've missed you," Urban added devoutly, bumping in beside Lot.

Uncorralled by gravity, Clemantine's body presented as a complex series of smooth, golden curves: bare calves and biceps and the furrow over her spine. She wore shorts and a gray-green stretch top that covered her breasts but left her belly bare. Clemantine was a big-boned woman, as tall as Lot but more heavily built, her skin smooth over well-cultivated muscles. Her face was as strong as her physique: a broad, flat nose, full lips, little ears, with a frieze of tiny gold irises tattooed around the lobes. Like Lot and Urban, she wore her hair very short, with sharp triangles of velvety stubble stabbing down in front of her ears.

Lot stared at her, helpless not to, and unable to find anything to say that didn't sound banal. So he gave it up. "I'm glad you're awake. We have missed you. I have."

She grinned. "Well, you haven't done too badly on your own. Look at yourself, Lot. No atrium and no ghosts—and still you're the only one to come up with a viable weapon against the courser."

Nikko's voice answered her, a second before his lean, blue image appeared at the chamber's end. "He had no right to respond to that hail on his own."

Lot glared at this. He'd exhausted himself with his effort to keep the cell field from its rash response. It was true he'd failed, but he had not *sent* that message. "Did you understand our answer?" he demanded.

"Some," Nikko said. "It felt like the response of something young and naive."

"Sooth. That was *not* the answer I would have given. That was the philosopher cells. I tried to stop it, but the passive cells overrode my faction." He turned again to Clemantine. He wanted her to know. "I did all I could."

Her good humor vanished. Apprehension chewed at her aura. "You're saying the philosopher cells are autonomous."

"Well, sure. Of course they are."

Nikko's kisheer had scrunched around his neck. Incredulity lay in his voice and in lines of burning amber that lanced across Lot's senses. "I thought you controlled the cells."

"I never said I did." What exactly had he said? He glanced at Urban, but there was no help to be found in his thoughtful face. "Nikko, you had to know: The cells have no central authority. I've got a voice. I can kick some routines into action, but the membrane doesn't stop functioning when I'm not there. The philosopher cells have their own protocols, their own instincts. They're developing. They're learning all the time." He tried to be calm. He let that onto the air, and it took the harshness off Nikko's mood, but it did nothing for Clemantine. He couldn't touch her that way anymore. She'd seen to that.

Nevertheless, *her* worry worked at him. "I thought you were using the cells as a translation device."

"No. They are autonomous."

"So they could learn we're not Chenzeme?"

He smiled. He didn't think the cells could even conceive of that. "No. You're overestimating them. They can't draw conclusions like that. It's not like they're conscious."

Nikko wasn't reassured. "You don't know what they're capable of, do you? Love and nature, what have you gotten us into?"

"We need our philosopher cells," Lot said.

"But do they need us?"

No.

He did not say it aloud, but it slipped onto the air just the same. Nikko glared at him, his blue eyes seeming weirdly unfocused behind their crystal lenses. "Will they be colonizing more than our hull?"

"No! Anyway, I don't think so."

"Great," Clemantine said. "Nikko, we need a manual inspection of the navigation and drive systems. We can't trust the sensors until we know they're clean."

"The cells haven't spread beyond the hull," Lot insisted. "I'd know it if they had. Come on, it's not like they could reconnoiter the ship and then plan a stealth assault on the systems."

"At least *you'd* like to think so," Urban interjected.

"You've worked with them too."

"Only through you."

Lot sighed. God, he was tired. And hungry too. Famished. Let this panic die now, so he could eat. Please.

"Look," he said, as patiently as he could manage. "I don't know how the philosopher cells on a Chenzeme ship are connected to the drive system, but whatever those connections are, they don't exist here. Our cells can drop dust, and now we know they can send and receive radio communications. But that's all they can do. They might try to issue a command to the drive system, but it would be like my brain telling Urban's hand to move. There's no connection, so it just won't work."

"Huh," Nikko countered. "I could infiltrate Urban's atrium and control the movement of his hand."

That announcement stunned them all into silence. Yet Lot had played similar games when he'd lived in the sky city of Silk, at Deception Well, using the charismata as his infiltrating weapon.

Urban stirred first, softly defiant. "You could not."

Nikko ignored him, his mood dark and cool. "I said it before. We are immersed in a *process*. It's why the courser has hung back, and it's not over yet." His nervous fingers rattled against his thigh. "I'd destroy the philosopher cells, if I thought it would help—but without them we have nothing. Without them, our friend will pull within weapons range and exterminate us."

"By the Unknown God," Clemantine swore. "How long can this go on? It's been twenty *years*."

No one answered. The Chenzeme had carried their war through eons. Twenty years was nothing to such infinitely patient minds.

Lot wanted to go back to the cells, but his body was famished, and he was getting light-headed. Urban offered to cook something for the three of them, up on the gee deck. "You might as well accept," he explained cheerfully, "because Nikko is not going to let you back out to the hull until you've had a break. Right, Nikko?"

So Lot squeezed into a transit bubble with Urban and Clemantine, for the swift trip to the gee deck.

It was hard to be that close to Clemantine. Her aura played against his sensory tears, intimate and inaccessible. She had made it that way. *Why?* Her choice mystified him, and it made him angry. Why had she changed anything? Things had been perfect. He knew it was so, because he had those times locked into his fixed memory. He could see her again—*there*—on the gee deck, sitting at the edge of the koi pond while starlight poured down from the holographic sky, echoing the night outside the ship. That night he and Urban had fallen asleep on the grass, but now Lot was awake, watching Clemantine writing in her notebook, her head bent to the screen's bronzy light. Her presence washed over him, a chaotic parade of subtle frustration, subtle triumph.

She laid her stylus down. "You're doing that, aren't you?"

The question startled him. He hadn't been fully awake. Now the night took on firmer definitions. "Doing what?" He sat up, brushing at marks the grass had left on his skin.

"Whenever I feel doubt stirring in me, or anger, or even a touch of boredom, it disappears. You're erasing it, aren't you?"

"No."

"Overwriting it, then."

He thought about it. Unlike Urban, she was vulnerable to the cult virus. It had colonized her before they left Deception Well. Its parasitic tendrils lived in her brain, opening her to the influence of his charismata. She would feel what he willed her to feel, and in turn, her feelings would feed back into him. When they had lived in the city of Silk, he'd sculpted the emotions of thousands this way. Now Clemantine was the only one left he could touch, in a one-on-one intimacy that surpassed the joy of anything he had known before. "I might have been doing something," he admitted, with a guiltless smile. "I was half asleep though. I wasn't really paying attention."

Her concern put a chill on the night air. "It's gotten that easy?"

"Sooth. It's an instinct now." He met her gaze, determinedly unafraid. Unashamed, while her anxiety swirled around him. At first he ignored it, but then he changed his mind. He seized it. He made it his own. He transformed it: into a charismata of faith. A gift for her and for himself, and she had been happy to receive it.

She had been happy. He'd made sure of that. He'd made sure they were all happy. He'd devoted himself to the equation of their three-part relationship, and in the end it had made no difference. Only one transmission ever followed them out of Deception Well. It was the design of a new family of defensive Makers. Lot could remember reading the text that accompanied it, and the dark clutch of fear as he realized what it was for. "You don't need it," he told her. She used it anyway, to get the cult virus and its corrupting parasite out of her head. (To get Lot out of her head.) After that, nothing was the same between them.

Let it go, he told himself. It wasn't important now. The courser was bearing down on their ass. That was all he could afford to think about anymore.

Lot stumbled, a bit off balance when they emerged into Clemantine's house on the gee deck. The rotating deck's circumference was too small to hide the centrifugal displacement. *Down* was never quite what it should be. Still, he liked it there. Nikko had filled the deck with a forest of thick-trunked trees, hung with limbs that branched in horizontal shelves. Shrubs grew on the ground and vines climbed the trunks, but nothing ever dominated or threatened to overwhelm the deck. It was as if each species had been lectured by the Well's governors on the necessity of harmonious coexistence, and they all listened: the plants and the birds and the small crawly things that surprised Lot from time to time with their existences.

They left Clemantine's house, following the path to the pavilion. Urban went first. Clemantine followed, while Lot trailed behind, feeling half drunk on her presence, as if on fine champagne. It annoyed him. These past two years he had gotten pretty good at controlling his emotions. Most of the time he could manufacture the charismata that would blow away nascent feelings of loneliness, so that he didn't really miss her. Happiness was a chemical state, and Lot was good with chemistry. The cult had given him that.

"You've been in cold sleep a long time," he told her, his gaze fixed on the hypnotic play of her legs and her muscular butt as she climbed the path ahead of him. "Things are different now. We don't live in the core apartments anymore. Mostly, we live here."

Where the path cut through a line of sword-leaved irises, she stopped and looked back, her dark eyes curious. "It is better here."

"Sooth. I've been happy." He wanted her to know that.

She nodded sagely. "Well, I'm here to change that."

Lot smiled. He couldn't help himself. "I think you already have."

• • •

Like everything they ate, or wore, or used as tools, the pavilion had been grown from raw matter by the programmable nanomachines called Makers. It had a tiled floor and was open on three sides. Six posts supported a lattice roof hung with flowering vines. Two elevated beds took up most of the space at the back of the pavilion. In the center, a cooking counter formed a U-shaped island. A factory anchored one end of the counter, looking like a tall wooden cabinet with a bilevel door. They called it a factory, though it was really just a hatch where goods could be delivered from the nanoprocessors in Null Boundary's interstitial tissues.

At the front of the pavilion, overlooking the sweep of lawn that descended to the koi pond, there was a low table, a bench, a hammock, and an armchair. Pointing at them, Urban ordered Lot to have a seat and take it easy. Then he headed for the factory, where he obtained a bottle of wine for Clemantine to pour. He remembered that Lot especially enjoyed river bread with capers and macadamia oil. Apparently, nice-Urban had replaced the real thing.

Lot lay in the hammock, his muzzy thoughts bouncing between this oddity and the unfathomable puzzle of Clemantine, while Urban retrieved a plate of river bread from the factory. He sliced the bread, laying each piece in a randomly assembled marinade of herbs and macadamia oil, then he wiped his hands. "Now we wait."

Lot groaned. "You should have ordered it finished."

Urban looked hurt. "I make this up every time. It's not reproducible."

Clemantine sat across from Lot, on the padded bench, one bare foot propped on the table between them. The line of her leg unfairly led the eye. "How long has he been cooking for you?" she asked.

"Just tonight," Lot grumbled.

Urban grinned. "See? What a privilege." He seized a glass of wine, drained half, then set it back on the table, while he squeezed in next to Clemantine on the bench. Lot watched, feeling the cult flare in his belly. He tried looking away, but all he could think of was Clemantine's amazon grace. That body, strong enough to lay him out—though they'd put it to better uses.

He didn't understand her at all.

His gaze cut back to them. Urban was testing the waters with cautious touches, a kiss on Clemantine's cheek. She could be prickly. She didn't want too much assumed. They respected that. Now a rosy flush illumined her bronzy skin. She laughed and let Urban put his arm around her, though she shooed his other hand away from her legs. "Hey, we really did miss you," he objected.

"Oh, I'll bet."

Urban got his hand on her lap anyway. Lot imagined the smooth warmth of her thigh, the soft-over-hard feel as her muscles flexed beneath her skin. "Look at Lot," Urban said. "He's starting to drool."

Oh, now this was the Urban-persona they knew and loved. Lot glared at him. "It's a predatory response."

"Sooth, you're starving him," Clemantine said. Little wrinkles formed around her eyes as she smiled.

"I'm guessing it's not just me."

For a moment, Lot felt stunned. Then his anger leaped forth in useless charismata. "You're an asshole, Urban."

Clemantine's smile expanded, but she did not burst into laughter—quite. She found Urban's hand, and her fingers laced with his. "Don't try to be helpful, son. You just don't do it well."

"Sooth, I know. I'm sorry."

That was it. Lot was burning to the roots of his close-cropped hair, but for Urban, apologies came easy. On to the next subject, and all that. Asshole.

Urban cocked his free arm over the back of the bench. "Lot's done some amazing work with the hull cells, hasn't he?"

Lot groaned at this ominous return of nice-Urban.

"Really, fury. This is the first usable language interface anyone has ever had with the Chenzeme. I'm impressed with that, even if you're not."

"Urban," Clemantine said. "My love. Tell us what you're after?"

Urban frowned. "All right." He sat up a little straighter. "I'd like to see some boldness. That's all. Now that we can talk to the courser—"

"—*if* we can," Clemantine cautioned. "That's not at all certain."

"—if we can," Urban echoed, "we can data mine for the design of its zero point drive." He looked across the table at Lot. "We've got a real shot at it, *if* we can talk to the courser. Think what it would mean for us, if we could exploit the power of the zero point field. We would have the speed and maneuverability of a Chenzeme ship. We could carry the same class of weapons." He offered more as he turned to Clemantine: "Think what it would have meant for the frontier worlds, if we could have matched the firepower of the swan bursters."

That one hit. Clemantine stiffened under his arm. Urban wisely let her go, taking that moment to lean forward to grab his wineglass.

Clemantine had been alive centuries—real centuries—not just time spent in cold sleep. She had seen her home world of Heyertori boiled away by the gamma ray lasers of twin swan bursters. That experience had shaped her in ways Lot still strove to understand. "It's a long way from saying hello to engineering our own swan bursters," she said.

"Sooth," Urban agreed. "While it's very easy to die." He picked up the wine bottle; put it down again with a *crack* against the tabletop. "So what if it's ambitious! Maybe our problem is we're not ambitious enough. The Chenzeme beat us, because we believe they will."

A silence followed. Day was fading into night in the ship's artificial cycle of light. A moth fluttered over the table. From the lattice overhead, a gecko clucked. Lot got up out of the hammock and headed for the counter, determined to finish the cooking Urban had forgotten.

"All right, Urban," Clemantine said at last. "What exactly do you want to do?"

Urban grinned. He strode after Lot, recapturing from him the marinating river bread. He clapped a hand on Lot's shoulder. "Tell us, fury. What does Nikko fear most?"

That was easy to answer. Lot said, "What he calls a mating, when the Chenzeme ships meet at close quarters to exchange experiences encoded in chemical form. To exchange dust."

"And how do we stand to learn the most from the courser?"

Lot could feel himself being pulled in by Urban's quickening excitement. "Through a mating of course—if we could survive it."

"Sooth." Urban dealt the river-bread slices across a griddle that had appeared on the malleable countertop. "We are naive Chenzeme, newly colonized and strange. Won't the courser want a mating, to secure our identity, to instruct us?"

"Seems likely."

"By the Unknown God," Clemantine said in hoarse piety. "You're both crazy. A mating has to be a huge risk, even for a legitimate Chenzeme ship. At such close quarters it would be vulnerable to attack. There has to be some means of proving identity before contact—detailed recognition codes, maybe, or rote behavior. And I'll bet any slipup in a potential mate isn't answered with a polite 'It's not working out, dear.' "

"Sooth, it would be dangerous," Urban said, as he poured guava batter around the plateaus of river bread. "Anything we do is dangerous. We could try to poison this courser at a distance, but how many times can that work? There are bound to be more Chenzeme ahead of us. That's why we've come this way, to find them. Will we be able to poison the next warship too? And the next after that?"

Clemantine sighed. "That's the trouble, Urban. We just don't know. But if the courser is talking, we might negotiate. We might learn enough to avoid it. We might learn to talk to other ships."

He shook his head. "Hanging back could be risky too. Talk too long, and we'll give ourselves away. If the courser suspects us, it could use its guns to vaporize any dust we send. The most convincing thing we can do is to *seek* a mating—and that's also the only way we'll get access to its zero point drive."

As he talked, he got some plates and filled them. Lot accepted one gratefully and sat down with it. The guava batter had cooked into a low cake, sweet and light and so insubstantial Lot could swear it dissolved in his mouth without ever reaching his stomach. So he started in on the river bread, muttering blessings over the oils. Calories! He wanted calories.

Urban handed a second plate to Clemantine, never slowing

in his lecture. "We need to be armed with the zero point technology before we go farther *swan*. We need the power it could give us, so that our speed and maneuverability can be the equal of the Chenzeme. So that we can power guns to match the courser, or there's no point in going on."

Clemantine accepted the plate but returned a hard look. "Do you think the zero point technology will be there for the taking, Urban? Do you think you could just send for a diagram to be delivered into the library while the philosopher cells are chatting? I won't throw away our lives on a chance like that. I won't *seek* a mating. Be patient. The one advantage we have is that we can think, and plan ahead. A little patience could buy our lives."

"Or it could betray us," Urban said.

They both looked at Lot, as if he could referee the truth, but Lot only scowled. "You keep forgetting," he said, around a mouthful of food. He hurried to swallow it. "Defective model." He tapped his head. "The Chenzeme forgot the instruction manual that was supposed to go in my fixed memory, so most of the time I'm guessing, just like you."

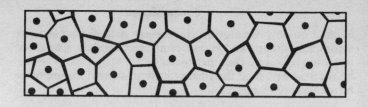

Chapter 5

Clemantine was right, of course. They didn't know enough to make a decision. So Urban sent a ghost into the ship's library to work on the problem.

Though Nikko probably had more experience with the Chenzeme than anyone, there was little useful evidence of that in the library. Almost no records survived from Null Boundary's early days. There was no evidence at all to back Nikko's claim that he'd learned the charismata from a mating with a Chenzeme ship. Null Boundary's history had been trashed, and all they had to rely on was Nikko's personal memory—or the small part of it he was willing to access.

Why wouldn't he talk?

Was it shame? Or guilt?

It was even possible Nikko *didn't* know anything useful. He had deliberately unthreaded his memories, chopped and edited them, and popped them off into storage. Sometimes he claimed those stored memories had been damaged too, but that was a lie. Nikko had recalled the past clearly enough today when he confessed the cataclysm that wrecked Null Boundary's first crew. So maybe the apparent absence of data in the ship's library was also a lie?

How could data be hidden from the library's own search engines?

Urban submitted this question first, and was rewarded

with a quick presentation on private data fields, security codes, false limits, and empty symbols. Could data be made to disappear? Yes. Definitely, easily.

So next he asked the library how missing data might be made to appear again.

Clemantine sat on a bench outside her house on the gee deck. It was deep in ship's night, but she'd used a medical Maker to overrule any need for sleep. From inside the house, the cabinet factory pinged the completion of its latest task. A roosting bird fluttered nervously in a nearby tree. Lot was asleep and Urban was engaged in some cryptic project. No better time than now.

She returned to the house.

In the living room, the image wall was active, displaying a vista that had not existed for some five hundred years. She looked out over a cliff clothed in a dense forest of tropical trees. An ocean lay below, silver crescents of reflected afternoon light winking in and out of existence as a small swell ruffled the surface. An owl cruised the cliff, frightening the flocks of blue-and-white seabirds that sometimes soared for hours on the updrafts. Across the water the dark hump of another island stood in silhouette against the sheen of afternoon light.

The world of Heyertori had been destroyed by the swan bursters of the Chenzeme, the oceans and atmosphere boiled away in a bombardment of gamma ray lasers. Clemantine had escaped only because she'd been in transit to a perimeter station where a viral Maker had been isolated. By the time the virus was discovered, it had already spread from the watch-posts to the orbital synchrotrons, corrupting their defensive protocols, so that they failed to fire when the swan bursters entered the system. Clemantine had looked on helplessly as the gigantic, ring-shaped ships bore down on the planet. Their attack lasted only minutes. That was all the time it took to reduce Heyertori to naked rock. With a handful of other survivors from the outer stations, Clemantine had eventually made a new home at Deception Well.

Lot and Urban dreamed of concocting a peace with the Chenzeme, but Clemantine was too well acquainted with the reality of the dead past to believe any of it. She had not come on this voyage looking for peace, but for a knowledge that would let her beat the Chenzeme. The ghosts of her past demanded it.

Waiting on the factory shelf was a Geiger counter, assembled from an antique design. She hefted it, surprised at its weight.

Tonight she would explore a part of the ship where she had never been. She wasn't sure this place existed. She only inferred its existence, from what she knew of the master of this ship. "Now we find out how much you and I think alike, Nikko," she muttered aloud. He had been at Heyertori just before the swan bursters hit. Indeed, Null Boundary had led them there, though no one—not even Nikko—knew it at the time. She secured the Geiger counter to her belt.

A transit bubble emerged from the structure of the image wall, opening as a dark oval door in the vista of Heyertori. She stepped through, ordering the bubble to take her to the ship's bow. The Dull Intelligence that operated it did its best to obey, but soon it announced with some concern, "This is the limit of the transit's operative zone. This device is unable to continue service beyond this point."

Clemantine accessed the library, summoning a diagram of the ship into her atrium. "Where are we?"

A green point ignited on the diagram. The transit bubble abutted a containment wall, designed to secure the ship's living area from the power-generation facilities. Clemantine located an access hatch. She highlighted it on the schematic. "Take me there."

"Advancing," the DI said.

After a brief acceleration, one side of the bubble peeled back, revealing an oval hatch. Clemantine laid her palm against the access panel. "Open," she commanded.

Another DI within the doorframe took a moment to consider this request, then, with a soft, multiple *snick*, the door swung back.

Clemantine drifted through, into a narrow, spiraling crawlway. An alarm had probably just rung in Nikko's sensorium. She imagined him watching her. She waited for him to make some move to interfere with her progress. Close the crawlway, perhaps. Turn off the lights. Evacuate the air. None of that happened.

She glided through the tight spiral, slapping handhold after handhold until she came to a second door, and then a third. The air in the crawlway grew hotter. A fourth door loomed ahead. She palmed it, and it swung open onto the reactor chamber.

A blast of hot, dry air puffed past her face. She half closed her eyes against it. She'd never felt air this hot. *Temperature?* she queried a submind ensconced in the ship's system.

Forty-four degrees Celsius.

Sweat popped out of her pores and vanished instantly. She felt as if flecks of radiation were biting against her skin. Already, the Geiger counter had begun to click.

She advanced cautiously.

The chamber on the other side was long, but very narrow. It had a high roof, so that she felt wedged at the bottom of a crevasse with sheer walls rising on either side. One wall was the outermost shield of the reactor itself. Its dark surface glimmered with a sheen that seemed unnatural in the heat, and it bulged slightly, conveying a sense of immense mass, as if it were made of some mysteriously stable element with a molecular weight far greater than uranium.

She reached for the Geiger counter tethered at her waist. The cadence of its clicking increased when she aimed it toward the back of the chamber. It was not counting radiation from the reactor; that was a clean fusion burn.

She had reached for a handhold, ready to search for the radiation's source, when Nikko's voice stopped her. "Keep going and you'll fry," he warned, his words reverberating as they emerged from widely separated speakers on the wall. "If you want to poke around up there, you should do it with a robotic remote."

Clemantine licked dry lips, and smiled. So far, she had correctly guessed at Nikko's secrets. Despite the games he played with his memory, she knew that he too was haunted by the past.

She loosened her grip on the Geiger counter, leaving it to drift at her waist. "So Nikko, would you have a remote available?"

He countered with a question of his own: "Why have you come here?"

Light strips on the rounded wall were an odd, bluish color, and dim. The wavelength seemed chosen to make the human nervous system uneasy. Farther on, where the crevicelike chamber narrowed to pass around the intake pipes, there was no lighting at all. "It's plutonium, isn't it?" Clemantine asked. "With a radiation count that high . . ."

"There's stable uranium too. Not a lot, but it can be converted into weapons-grade material in the reactor."

We do think alike. She closed her eyes briefly, thankful and troubled at once. "Where did you get it, Nikko?"

"It was part of the ship's original manifest."

"Did *you* order it?"

"I've seen nukes used before. It seemed a reasonable precaution."

"Nukes in the Hallowed Vasties?" She tried to imagine it: war in the ancestral home. She had thought of Sol System as a civil paradise, great orbiting cities, and three garden worlds.

Nikko shattered that fantasy. "We didn't need the Chenzeme to teach us war."

"By the Unknown God."

"The only deity that has ever lived up to expectation." Then he added: "The plutonium has suffered some decay."

"But it's still usable?"

He didn't answer, not at first.

Clemantine pressed him, impatient in the ungodly heat. "Lot and Urban want to provoke a mating."

"Lot won't provoke it."

"He won't poison the courser, either. He wants to seduce it, Nikko. You know he does. He's ruled by the cult, and Communion will always look better to him than war."

"This is for Heyertori, isn't it?"

She shrugged. "You were there."

"You don't need to remind me. I have not forgotten *that*."

She nodded. Scars left by the Chenzeme were not easily shed. "If we are forced to a mating, it might be possible to transfer a nuke. If we don't survive, at least the courser won't live either."

"The Chenzeme ships really are alive, aren't they? They're not machines."

Sooth. No line of machines could have survived the stray accidents and changing conditions of thirty million years. They were alive. "Heyertori is dead."

"You won't tell Lot and Urban?" Nikko asked.

She shook her head. "They have never witnessed an assault by the Chenzeme, Nikko. You and I have."

"All right then. But go back. Please. This place is not clean."

"Lot?"

Urban's voice reached into the dreamless void of Lot's sleep, dragging him upward into the world of substance. As soon as he realized he'd been asleep, Lot sat up sharply, his boots hitting the pavilion floor to kill the hammock's wild swing. "What time is it?"

"Take it easy. You've got over an hour before any reply from the courser can reach us."

Darkness lay entwined with silence on the gee deck. Lot could hear a distant cricket mechanically calling for a mate, but nothing else. Clemantine had gone. He rubbed at his sensory tears as his waking panic drained away.

"I've had a ghost at work in the library," Urban said. His anger glinted in brief, brilliant red flashes. "I've found some things that have been hidden. That bastard Nikko remembers a lot more than he's ever told us."

Lot had felt the impact of Nikko's past today, in the charismata that brought the memory of blood and decay. He wasn't sure he wanted to be admitted to more details. He stood up. He walked over to the cabinet factory. "Nikko really doesn't remember it, you know. He puts his memories away. If it's hidden from you, it's probably hidden from him too." He told the factory to put together a packet meal. Then he turned to get some water while the assemblers worked.

Urban was standing right behind him. "Come with me for a few minutes," he said, and the urgency in his voice made Lot's heart beat a little faster. "I want to show you something." Smoldering anger again assaulted Lot's sensory tears. It stirred in him a harmonic of betrayal. Urban was right. How much would they have to relearn by hard experience because Nikko refused to confess, or to remember?

"I went looking for the earliest records I could find," Urban was saying.

"On the Chenzeme?"

"On anything. I found a lot of fragments locked away. Couldn't make sense of them."

Lot nodded. "It's what he told us. The plague-bearing dust made a hash of the ship's neural fields."

"Sooth. I'll accept that as truth. The crew died. But not all their ghosts were lost. Nikko lied about that, because I found a survivor. A full personality, stored in an inactive field. A witness, Lot. Someone besides Nikko, who might be willing to tell us a little more about this ship's past."

The cabinet factory chimed its readiness. Lot glanced down, fingering the packet meal before dropping it in a pocket of his skin suit. A ghost. A new persona on the ship. A stranger, lying in storage. The thought rattled him badly. When he had run away from Deception Well he had run away from the cult. The only connection he wanted anymore was Clementine.

He grabbed a bulb of water. "Does Nikko know you've found it?"

Urban shook his head. "He's looping again, so I don't think he's noticed. Not yet. It's a matter of time, though, and that's why we have to move fast." Something in his aura fluttered with the evasive loops of butterfly wings. His voice dropped to a whisper—as if that could prevent Nikko from overhearing them if he chose. "That's why I want you to come with me. Now."

Lot took a step back, reluctant to get between Urban and Nikko. "You know I have to get back to the hull."

"Just for a minute," Urban whispered. "I want you to see her."

"*Her?*" Now Lot was whispering too. "Urban, you already woke the ghost?"

"Of course I'm waking her! Fury, she's as real as you and I. Come see for yourself. Please. I need you to back me. We can't let Nikko put her down again."

Urban didn't want to take a transit bubble. He didn't say it, but Lot knew he was afraid Nikko would interfere. So they glided through the crawlways.

"Your ghost is with her?" Lot asked.

"Sooth. I haven't been down there yet. Not in this version. You know."

A gel membrane marked the end of the last tunnel. Urban slipped through first, then Lot leaned into the yielding barrier. The gel slid cool and smooth past his face. On the other side he emerged beside a massive transit pipe that spanned the interstice between the core chamber and the core's armored shell. Once, this barrel-shaped space had been the province of cold storage. The square ends of hibernation cells had tiled these walls. But Nikko had changed it into living quarters, dissolving the cold storage units and replacing them with four separate apartments, each an intricate warren.

Nikko had never occupied his own apartment, but Lot had lived here, with Clemantine and Urban, for a long time. The memory brought a stir of resentment, flashes of bitterness like lightning in negative colors, propagating across his brain. He slapped the wall hard, sending himself darting through the narrow, curving space. Urban was just disappearing into the gaping entrance hole of his warren. Lot followed him in.

The tunnel walls were lined with pipeweed. A soft white glow filled the pliant tubes. Urban wrapped his fist around a handful of them. "Hurry," he urged. "Her pattern is stabilized. She's starting to talk." And he launched himself down the tunnel.

Lot took off after him, caught up in his excitement. Gleaming pipeweed swayed beneath him, pushed down by the air current of his passage.

He followed Urban to the warren's farthest recess, but he didn't follow him into it. Grabbing a handful of weed, he brought himself to a graceless stop just outside the chamber's round doorway, shocked at what he saw.

In the chamber was a creature like Nikko, with an anatomy adapted to vacuum, only she was feminine and slight in stature, her figure like that of an adolescent girl, with small breasts just visible beneath a translucent layer of armored skin. Her scales were blue, though a lighter shade than Nikko's. The membrane at her neck, the kisheer, had a silvery sheen. Lot could get no sign of her with his sensory tears, so he knew she was still just a ghost, a holographic projection running on a machine grid.

Did he make some sound?

The girl turned her head. She looked straight at him. Her blue eyes flashed behind their protective crystal lenses. Her lips parted, and an expression of surprise slipped over her face.

Lot grunted in shock. Nikko's face was incapable of expression, as still and immobile as that of a statue.

Now Urban was looking at him too, worry lines just visible. "Say hello," he urged.

"Hello," Lot said. Nikko had wanted to forget this girl. Why?

"Her name is Deneb," Urban added. He looked at her doubtfully. "She was part of the original crew."

Deneb's expression changed again, and the shift was no less startling this time. Her surprise turned to indignation. "He's lying to you."

She said this to Lot. She spoke the language Lot had used before he came to Silk, all soft edges and blurred syllables. "I don't know why he's lying, but he is. I've never been part of any crew. I don't know why I'm here, but I know you. *I know you!* How could you be here too?"

Lot felt the skin on the back of his neck tighten. "You don't know me. I've never seen you before."

She flinched, as if from a blow. Her kisheer trembled, and the long, long fingers of her right hand pressed together in a spear. Lot was instantly sorry. "I didn't mean it like that," he said. "Look, we thought you were part of Nikko's crew—"

"Nikko?" she echoed, fear in her voice. "Am I still with him?"

"Where did you come from?" Lot asked.

"Sol System."

"When?"

"I don't remember." She shook her head. "I don't remember a lot of things."

"Her name was part of the crew list," Urban insisted. "She came from Sol System with Nikko."

"I wasn't part of any crew! I do know that. How could I be? There was no crew with him. There was no one alive, when he came back from the void. Even he was a ghost. Now I'm a ghost too, aren't I?" She turned to glare at Urban. "Why are you keeping me confined here? I want to be real."

"Sorry," Urban said. "We thought you were someone else." His fist knotted. *"Shit!"*

Lot finally glided into the room. "Anyway, Nikko didn't lie. There were no survivors on that first voyage."

Urban nodded grudgingly. He was studying Deneb with a measuring gaze, as if determined to find some other value in her. "How do you know Lot?" he asked her.

She looked confused, so Urban jerked his head in Lot's direction. "Him. How do you know him? Where have you seen him before?"

"He looks like the Lens." She said it quick and breathlessly, as if she were jumping off a cliff.

The Lens. The title wrenched a reverberant memory out of Lot's past. He heard again the voice of Gent Romer, schooling him in the cult: *You are the gateway, Lot. The focusing lens through which we'll all pass. You gather the essence of your people. Through you, we become one.*

It had been the same on so many worlds. *We are all the same.* Charismatic carriers of the cult virus, infiltrating societies, then destroying them in an ecstatic Communion of hyperconsciousness. The charismatics had been made by the Chenzeme. The evidence of that was in Lot's head, in the neural tendrils that let him talk to the philosopher cells. Yet the cells remained immune to the cult. Like two descendants of the same ancestor, the cult and the warships had a shared physiology, yet their purposes were at odds. Lot could not help but think of them as two sides in an ancient civil war.

He swallowed against a dry throat, wondering how much history this girl had witnessed. "Did you see him? The Lens?"

She shook her head, while her kisheer rippled in uncertain waves. "I never did. I never knew what he looked like, until I saw you. Now it's as if an implanted memory has been triggered. *Is* it you?"

Lot closed his eyes. Yes or no? He didn't know the true answer. There had been so many versions of him. He could sense them, like shadows haunting his fixed memory, attached to lives in the Hallowed Vasties that he had never lived. They were cult seed, all of them. An insidious weapon made to corrupt. The cult virus had linked individual lives around the seed crystal of a charismatic, drawing the inhabitants of each star system into a single, sublime entity of many parts. *Rapture.* Lot knew the ecstatic pleasure of Communion. The desire for it sat in his belly like a warm white shadow, whispering always to him to come in, come in, and someday he might answer it. Still, he recognized the cult virus for what it was: a slow weapon, designed to destroy the enemy over a time span of a few hundred to a few thousand years—the life span of the Hallowed Vasties.

He looked again at the girl's blue-scaled face. The devotion there, the devout need—he recognized that too. He had seen it often enough as a kid, on the faces of the troopers in his father's army. Gathered in prayer circles or aiming grenade launchers, they would have done anything for Jupiter.

Like father, like son? Sooth. Jupiter had died trying to impose his will on the sky city of Silk. Years later, commanding the same devotion as his father, Lot had almost succeeded.

The Lens? Jupiter hadn't bothered with a title. His name had been said reverently enough.

"I'm only a ghost," the girl said. "I can't feel you." Her voice trembled, and Lot felt a flush of soothing charismata rise from his sensory tears, though they couldn't touch her.

Here was a scion of the cult. Is this what he'd wanted for Clemantine? Some small voice protested, *It wasn't like this with us.* Yes or no?

Neither seemed a convincing answer. The truth stood apart: He wanted Clemantine. But this girl—she belonged to someone else.

He looked at Urban. "Now you know why Nikko left her cold."

She again reacted to Nikko's name. "Is this still his ship?" she demanded. Lot told her it was. "And how far has he run?"

"From Sol System?" Urban asked. He turned to Lot. "What do you think? Maybe eleven hundred years?"

"Maybe not quite that long," Lot said. "If you made it direct, no stops."

The blue of her eyes turned to gray, as her eyelids closed behind the crystal lenses. Her head tilted back a little, though Lot couldn't imagine how her tears might flow. "Love and nature," she whispered. "I'll never be part of it again."

"Just as well," Lot said, haunted still by the aura of the dead, when Jupiter's army had been trapped in the industrial corridors of Silk. "It's all long over by now. Deneb, I know you can't believe it yet, but you're the lucky one."

He turned to Urban. "You woke her. Now it's up to you to make her real. Then cure her. Get the cult parasite out of her head. Don't let her go on a minute more like this."

"Sooth." Urban looked resigned as he turned to the girl. "Deneb, there are things you need to know."

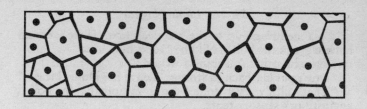

Chapter
6

Back in the crawlway, Lot felt the trace of a presence brush his sensory tears.

"Nikko?"

He grabbed a handgrip and twisted hard to get a look at the tunnel behind him. Empty. But something—pores in the walls perhaps, whose existence he had not suspected—were making charismata, and he could taste Nikko's sense of betrayal.

Lot did not want to think about the ghost-girl in Urban's warren. He had to get back to the hull. If the courser was going to respond, it would do so soon.

He pushed off the rung, to glide again through the crawlway, but as soon as he moved, the tunnel ahead of him collapsed, closing like a straw pinched shut by giant fingers. Lot cried out. He ducked his shoulder and twisted, grabbing at a grip to stop his glide. Now he faced the way he had come, and that end of the tunnel was closed off too. Urban had thought they'd be less vulnerable in the crawlways than in a transit bubble. Guess not.

"You should be in the wound," Nikko said. His stern voice came out of the spider on Lot's ear. "You have less than an hour left."

"I was . . . going to ask you to take me there." Though

he'd planned to go up to the gee deck first. There were no crawlways to the hull. "Nikko? Don't hurt her."

Nikko hissed. "You think I would?"

"Don't put her back in storage. Leave her alone. Please."

"That's all I've ever done." An unfathomable fog boiled against Lot's sensory tears.

"Why is she here?" Lot asked. "What is she to you?"

"She's nothing. Not that version of her, anyway."

The segment of tunnel shrank into a transit bubble, just large enough to contain Lot. Its wall pressed against him as it began to move.

"You knew another version?" Lot asked.

"The one that was my wife. *My* Deneb. She was with us aboard Null Boundary."

Nikko did not have to say it again: that he had been the only survivor of that voyage. Even the ghosts had been corrupted. "I'm sorry," Lot told him.

"This Deneb you found, she came to me later. In the Hallowed Vasties."

"You went back there . . . after?"

Nikko responded with a lacy puzzlement. "Apparently. After the plague I returned home—at least that's what my archives say. It had been almost six hundred years since we'd left. The cordon was whole by then and I could not see the Sun. They knew who I was before I arrived. They knew I was the sole survivor. Maybe they employed dust too. It amazed me even then that they would bother. Do you know how many people might have lived in that collection of cities?"

Lot had inherited vague memories of the Hallowed Vasties. "Maybe none at all."

The bubble slowed. One side of it opened on the gleaming hull field, while Nikko chuckled darkly. "Well, whatever they were, there must have been . . . quadrillions? An inconceivable number, anyway. Why would they bother with me?"

Lot touched the cold face of the cells, thinking about the sparse impact of dust on the gleaming surface. "Because even a single copy of a virus is dangerous if it can learn to copy itself. How did you find her?"

"I didn't. She found me. My Deneb had left a ghost behind. It was an old one, and she'd forgotten about it. Her parents had it made, when she was fourteen. They'd been updating it every year, but that year I met her. They didn't like me."

Lot grinned.

Nikko chuckled too. "Yeah. They hung on to her old image. It seems they revived it sometime after we left."

Lot let his hand slide beneath the wound's soft tissue. "You said that none of you aboard Null Boundary were vulnerable to the cult."

"None of us were. Maybe they changed her. Or maybe they just wore her down."

"How did she find you?"

"They sent her out from the cordon to greet me. She didn't know why she'd been chosen for it. She had no memory of me. She was a believer, and it was her task to bring me into the sphere. That was their weakness, you see. They didn't want to destroy any threats. They wanted to enfold them within their Communion. The cult virus is made that way, so it will spread itself endlessly."

"Sooth." Though Lot could remember less benign times, recorded in the memories that had come down to him from his ancestors, when dissidents were dispatched with swift mob justice. "They were strong enough to take chances then."

"Probably." Nikko was silent a moment. "Love and nature, I didn't know what to do. It looked like her. The voice: it was Deneb's voice. But what she said, what she believed: it wasn't Deneb. I was furious. I couldn't bear her presence, but I couldn't leave her."

"They let you go?"

"They weren't afraid of anything then. They were at the height of their power."

"So Urban will cure her now, like Clemantine was cured."

"I should have done it myself—if I'd let myself remember."

The transit bubble contracted, pushing Lot into the cold grip of the cell field. He resisted a moment, feeling unready for it. "Nikko, wait—"

"Go on," Nikko said. "Get yourself in place."

Already Lot could hardly hear him. Waves of debate crested over his senses, crowding out thoughts of the ghost-girl, and the great cordons of the Hallowed Vasties. The courser was part of the cells' conversation. Lot could see the Chenzeme ship, gliding through the void toward the cloud of dust laid down by Null Boundary.

As he watched it, he felt his awareness sliding free from its simple geometry to merge into the complex structures of Chenzeme dialect. Gradually, he realized that the image being developed involved the courser as a minor harmonic only, a dark echo to which the primary theme could be compared. This was a self-appraisal, and it was not silvery clean. He could feel a dark sense accusing wrongness, absence.

Stop it, he told himself. Stop trying to describe it. A Chenzeme debate could not be couched in human languages. It could only be felt for itself, and perhaps simplified and translated later. So he stopped thinking about it. He just sank into it, and when he emerged a few minutes later, he was frightened. The hull cells picked up the concept and played with it, producing a thousand variations and echoes of his fear.

"Nikko?" He hoped at least a submind would respond.

"Here." His voice arrived through the spider that clung to Lot's earlobe.

"Are you looping?"

"Seven seconds."

"Stop it please."

"Give me a reason."

"Our hull cells—they've been comparing themselves to the philosopher cells on the courser." The spider was silent. Lot realized more than seven seconds had passed. "Nikko?"

"Here."

"Stop looping! I need to talk to you about the philosopher cells. The courser must have asked them to adjust our velocity. They don't know how. So they know they're different. They don't know why."

"*Love and nature.*" Nikko muttered this oath in a low, distracted voice. "Did you offer the cells an explanation?"

Lot frowned. "What explanation? That they've been kidnapped by an enemy vessel and used as camouflage?"

"I had really been thinking of something a little less . . . provocative. Lie to them, Lot. You need to learn to lie to them, in the Chenzeme way."

The code that described Deneb's body had been shunted to a fleet of resurrection Makers, and already they had begun to re-create her physical form within Null Boundary's interstitial tissue. Urban watched the process through a remote camera eye, a nervous flutter in his belly. This was Nikko's ship. If he didn't want Deneb to live, it would be easy for him to switch off the Makers or to block their supply of nutrients.

That hadn't happened. Nanoscale building blocks continued to pour into the work site through a scaffolding of microscale threads. Individual cells were assembled on the threads, then pushed outward as more cells formed behind them. Already some of the microthreads supported enough tissue to make them visible without magnification.

He turned to Deneb.

He had resurrected her ghost on a grid isolated from the ship's neural system. He'd done it to protect her from Nikko—and also to protect the ship from her. He wasn't foolish. She might have been dangerous or deranged.

Still, the isolation grid was a bad place to be. Its limited capacity forced on her a simulation of reality that was far less than what she'd feel if she were alive. So Urban had taken her ghost into his atrium. That had brought its own limits. She'd become invisible to the outside world, existing now only within his point of view. But the sensations she experienced came to her through his own nervous system and she felt herself to be real.

The atrium manufactured the illusion of reality for both of them. Deneb could not move any physical object, though it would seem as if she did, both to her and to him. He could touch her. She would feel that. And she could touch him. If she chose to. She couldn't leave this chamber, though, unless he went with her, because her existence was limited to the range of his senses.

Still, she was free and she could choose to upload back into the isolation grid or return to quiescent storage.

She had chosen neither.

Urban could not keep his gaze off her for long. He caught himself at it again: studying her as if she were an unconscious painting or holographic projection. The pattern of her scales, the graceful lines of her long, long fingers, the curve of her small breasts and her narrow hips. She was quite petite, and he decided she was not fully grown yet.

"How old are you?" he asked.

He could see her blue eyes shift beneath the glittery surface of crystal lenses. "I remember being . . . fifteen? I know time's passed since then. A lot of time. What do you know about Nikko?"

Urban shrugged. "He's crazy."

The edge of Deneb's kisheer moved in a light transverse ripple, a silver ribbon of motion. "If he's crazy, why are you with him?"

"Hey, it's his ship, and we needed to leave Silk. Why are you here?"

"I was sent." She frowned. "This ghost was in storage a long time. I think some of my memories have decayed."

"Probably." Urban had never been one to sugarcoat issues. "What do you remember?"

"Not much. I remember my family, my mother and father, though it's been a long time since I needed them. A very long time. But that time is . . . empty? It's as if . . . yes, I do remember. It's as if bits of thoughts are flashing past me. As if I were a conduit. It was sublime—like living inside a cloud and every molecule of vapor is delicious and there are no worries and no sense of time passing. Time is like a cloud there. Amorphous. It's real but you can't measure it or hold on to it." Her gaze shifted to the projection within his atrium, of the microthreads collecting the cells of her body along their invisible lengths. "But that's not what you want to know, is it?"

She was perceptive. Urban liked that. "Do you know anything about the Chenzeme?"

"No."

"Do you know anything about exploiting the zero point field?"

That made her flinch. A faint red flush rose through the blue scales of her face. She looked frightened. Urban leaned a little harder. "I've studied history. There's reason to think zero point technology was not an exclusive invention of the Chenzeme. Some feel it was developed in the Hallowed Vasties too. . . . What's wrong?"

Her kisheer shivered, bunching against her neck in uneven folds. "Out on the Spine—people were working on the zpf." She spoke softly, as if it were a dirty family secret. "I went there once on a virtual tour. But my dad said it was a myth, a fancy, to think we could exploit the field."

"It's not. Zero point technology is real, Deneb, even if we don't understand it. It's powering the Chenzeme courser that's running us down."

Urban watched her, admiring the way the scales of her expression slid against one another as indecision flitted over her face. "My mother worked at the Spine, before she was gathered by the Lens."

"She worked on the zpf?"

Deneb nodded. "I wanted to go with her—I'd studied quantum physics in school. I was like my mother in that, wasn't I? But my mother was sent home from the Spine. They didn't want her out there anymore after . . . after she came to know him. Yes. And after that my parents wouldn't let me go. They took me out of school, and told me I should be looking inside myself to learn why I had not allowed the Lens to gather me." Her lips squeezed together in a tight line. "That's how it was. I remember it now. They said he hadn't come to me and so I was as flawed as the researchers on the Spine who had sent my mother home. But I wasn't flawed!"

"Sooth," Urban said. She had been immune to the cult virus too. Or at least she had been resistant. "You were like me then. Stronger. They couldn't touch me either."

"I wish I'd known you then. Where did you live?"

"A long way and a long time after you."

"Sooth. Is that what you say? Sooth. So some of them escaped—from the Spine, or from other places."

"I think Nikko was one."

"Oh yes," she said. "I know he was. He told me. I remember I was going to send a ghost to the Spine, without telling my parents. Maybe I did. Maybe that's how I met Nikko—he said I met him before—but I don't remember that ghost ever coming back to me. I do remember I changed. I began to feel the Lens." She tapped her breast. "Here, like something warm and safe and wise, a presence inside me. It made me happy—" She shook her head. "After that, all I remember is time passing, until they took me out of the Communion and sent me to Nikko. I feel so lost now. He is so far away."

"Soon you won't need him," Urban promised her. "We're going to change that part of you." Let her understand the drift of things aboard Null Boundary. "Whether you choose it or not."

She turned again to the image of her forming body. More microthreads were visible now. Almost, Urban could discern the outline of a human frame. "You're sure the zero point field is not a myth?" she asked.

"It's not a myth," Urban assured her. "And its energy can be tapped."

She nodded, as if this were eminently satisfactory. "We'll learn how then. When I'm real. When I'm flawed again." She grinned. "Oh yes. I remember how it was."

During the last few minutes before the expected transmission, Lot practiced lying. He made up an image—no, less than that—the *suggestion* of an image: a layer of philosopher cells wrapped around a dominant core. The core was him. He let the cell field register his connection to the navigation function.

Dominant. He tried to emphasize that concept as the image propagated around him, evolving in bizarre directions.

Well, there he was, being disassembled by the more aggressive cells because this image of him was not coherent with their instinct. A radical faction fought this theoretical destruction. *Change has value.*

Now his control was being parasitized, tendrils of influence growing into him, reaching through him to the theorized navigation function—but he'd lied about that. Or had he? Nikko controlled the ship, but Nikko might do what Lot advised him. That thought rolled out into the cells. Lot tried to catch it, but nothing could be retrieved. His anxiety was flowing now as well. Damn. He could see his symbolic image—not dominating so much anymore—connecting to another, even more theoretical link. That was Nikko.

He closed his eyes and stopped translating. Translating got him into trouble every time. He could not be both Chenzeme and human at once.

So he yielded resistance. He gave himself up. Yet when

the expected transmission at last arrived, he reacted to it with a burst of very human fear. It was a demand for suicide or submission, he wasn't sure which. Maybe both. Maybe either. They were wrong and needed to be sterilized. Or they were usefully wrong and only needed to be controlled.

He could feel dust quickening between the links. A dust storm. Its taste was poisonous, a contortion of data stolen from the Well. Where had it come from? Lot stiffened within the enwrapping cells, knowing it had come from him.

No.

He tried to object, but the aggressive cells united to bully the others. They would defend themselves from the courser. *Usefully wrong.* An image of glorified madness.

Not us, Lot tried to say. *That's not us.*

His argument stumbled and disappeared. Reappeared again in another wave of imagery, stronger now. The taste of poison faded, but defiance grew. *Stronger now.* Stronger. The sentiment leaped outward on radio waves, leaving Lot panting in the cold grip of the cells, his heart racing. He'd given it all up. Every molecular structure he'd brought out of the Well had been copied into the cell field.

"Nikko, get me out of here."

He eased himself free of the cells as the transit bubble enfolded him. Nikko's voice spoke in his ear. "What happened? I couldn't understand it at all."

Lot felt groggy. He dug his fingers into the wall as the bubble accelerated. "The cells wanted to drop poison dust for the courser . . . just like you."

"You didn't let them?"

"No." The bubble wall eroded beneath him, releasing him into the core. "But now our hull cells hold the code for the poison. They could drop it anytime. Or they could synthesize a defense against it."

"Love and nature." Nikko's image hung at the chamber's far end. "This isn't working," he said. "Relying on the philosopher cells is like relying on a madman—a violent lunatic."

Lot could not argue.

"We need to synthesize the Chenzeme speech ourselves, without the cells as go-between."

"Do you know how? I don't. All I can do is try to lean on the cells, influence them."

Nikko's fingers tapped his thigh. "You should have let the cells lay their trap, because this can't go on. We're giving up too much of ourselves."

"Are you still thinking we have a choice?"

Nikko's kisheer twitched. "We'll do what we have to. I know."

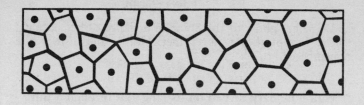

Chapter
7

Point zero: initiate.

No, no, no. Dammit, anyway. He'd lost too much already.

Terminate.

He looked again, to see Deneb laughing at something Urban had whispered in her ear, her head tilted back, her smooth, blue hide infused with a rosy warmth. Incarnate and free of the cult virus.

(My Deneb.)

She'd been incarnate less than an hour. Urban had taken her to the gee deck, where she walked with him on unsteady legs, his arm encircling her waist, her thin, graceful fingers hooked around his shoulder. Joy shone in her posture and in the ecstatic laughter that bubbled from her throat, the kind of joy that only someone who has been sick a long time, or lost, or in despair, could feel when relief and renewal finally arrive. It didn't seem to matter to her that their time was measured against the courser's approach. She was free of the cult virus, and for her, that was reason enough to be happy. This was Deneb—and Nikko had let himself forget her.

That phase was past. Her appearance had shattered all the careful blocks he'd put around his memory. Here she was, exactly the same as the Deneb he'd first met, when she had sent her ghost to the Spine in defiance of her parents' edicts. Except they'd never met. Not in the history she remembered.

Null Boundary turned on its long axis through a thirty-hour rotation. Working together, two of the telescopes swept through section after section of the surrounding starscape. Results were recorded and compared to earlier passes. The Dull Intelligence that performed the work dutifully corrected for the ship's forward momentum before admitting to an anomaly: The luminosity of a nearby red dwarf star had declined.

The telescopes were slid back along their tracks to investigate. The lenses fixed once more upon the site, only to discover that the star's luminosity had returned to normal. The DI consulted its task list, comparing the event against a list of excusable stellar phenomena. It settled on the description of an eclipse as the most likely explanation for the event. If the class-M star possessed a large, nonluminous companion object that passed between Null Boundary and the star, then the star's luminosity would appear to decline.

The DI tested this hypothesis, drawing up a detailed chart of the star's motion over the past seventy years. Perturbations in its orbit about the galactic center would support the presence of an occulting mass.

No perturbations were found.

The DI returned to its task list, considering now the possibility that the star was unstable. But the historical record did not support this surmise.

In time it reached the conclusion that a dust cloud or solid object not related to the star had caused an occultation. The density of particulate matter in this sector of space had been gradually increasing over the past twenty-eight light-years; still, the average was only four atoms per cubic centimeter. A denser clump of interstellar dust so close to the ship seemed unlikely. Indeed, there was no evidence for it at all.

The DI concluded that the most likely explanation for the event was an occultation by a solid object unrelated to the star. It scanned the sector again, this time in the high infrared, expanding the recipient wavelengths as it searched for evidence of a brown dwarf—an object not quite massive enough to ignite in the fusion reactions of a star.

Before long, it found a candidate. It recorded the profile and line-of-sight position, then summoned one of Nikko's patrolling subminds.

The charm of subminds, Nikko thought, lay in their perverse tendency to produce a sense of absentmindedness rather than of enlightenment whenever they poured their memories into the core persona. Never was there a joyous, revelatory burst at the moment of melding, for after all, the new memories were already his own. His core persona perceived them as something known, but forgotten.

So when he saw the infrared image, the first thing he felt was embarrassment, as if he should have known it before. It was there in his memory: the profile of a Chenzeme courser seen at a hard angle, so close the lines of its hull were visible. A stealthed courser: the hull cells did not exhibit their ordinary luminescence.

Chenzeme ships were forever acquiring new strategies. They were known to hunt together, and obviously Null Boundary had fallen victim to a new hunting strategy. The first courser had performed as a highly visible threat, and it had thoroughly distracted them . . . while this second courser drew unnoticed within striking distance.

Nikko studied the image, shaken by a powerful—and false—sense of remembrance. Only after several seconds did he begin to feel fear.

He summoned everyone to the core chamber, even Deneb. "Null Boundary has found a second Chenzeme courser. This one is stealthed. Its hull cells are dark, and far below normal operating temperature. They are probably inactive, but that can't last. It's well within weapons range and the only major question is: Why hasn't it taken us out yet?"

"Because we're Chenzeme," Lot said. He drifted upside down to the others, dressed in his ever present skin suit. His sensory tears glistened without connoting any sense of weeping. They were a sarcastic remark, a false claim of vulnerability. The sweat of an effort to become alien.

"If we're Chenzeme why hasn't it hailed us?" Clementine demanded. Her strong toes were hooked under a grip, anchoring her to the wall while the others drifted.

"Because we're deranged Chenzeme," Urban said. "Maybe dangerous. I hope so."

This made Deneb frown.

Clementine asked: "How much time do we have?"

Nikko shrugged. "Maybe no time at all, if it's already fired missiles on us. We could try a radar sweep, otherwise we won't know until they hit. But assuming it hasn't passed judgment yet . . ." He consulted the calculations of a submind. "It's using the zero point field to adjust velocity and course in a sequence that should result in a side-to-side match with our own position in no more than forty-nine hours."

Dead silence followed, for at least three seconds.

"Or less," Urban said, "if it's already fired on us."

"And if not, then it looks like you'll get your mating," Clementine told him.

Lot's agitation rattled the Chenzeme receptors in the chamber walls. "Get me a transit bubble, Nikko. I need to get to the hull cells."

"Wait." Clementine wall-walked, using her agile toes to slide close to him. Lot started to pull away, but Clementine cupped her hand on his shoulder. They faced each other upside down. "Lot, we need to talk about this," she said. "What are you going to tell the hull cells?"

He shook his head, his rising tension clogging the chamber's pores. "It's not like that, Clementine. The real question is, What are they going to tell *me*? Nikko," he called, ducking out of her grip. "A transit bubble!"

Nikko snorted at the demand—"Yes sir. Right away, sir." He knew a submind had already responded.

A concavity opened in the chamber wall. Clementine glanced at it. "Lot, we need to talk about this."

"Okay, okay," he said. "But later." He launched himself toward the bubble. Grabbing the rim, he curled into the hole. It closed over him.

Clementine looked at Nikko. "You didn't have to do that."

Nikko answered this with cold amusement. "I'm not his master. Besides, it wasn't me. It was a submind."

"Do you trust him out there?"

"I don't see we have a choice."

"We all do what we can," Urban said. "It's up to Lot to monitor the hull cells. I'm still getting a record of that, but none of us can help him. I won't be left out of this, though. If the courser pulls even with us, I'm mounting an expedition to it. I'm going to jump the gap, see what I can find."

This statement seemed nonsensical. Nikko could not think at first what to say, but Clemantine was not so circumspect. Her laugh was instant and unforgiving. "Come on, Urban! This is the real world."

"Sooth."

Her scorn cracked, in the face of his stubborn reserve. "Do you think the courser is not armed? With guns, or plagues? Or worse things, that we haven't encountered yet?"

"It's true," Nikko said, with a quick glance at Deneb. Her expression was puzzled but attentive. "Urban, you know there's no one out there with your best interests in mind. The courser is sure to detect your presence. It will have to infer a hostile package. A nuclear warhead, perhaps?" He looked at Clemantine, at her bright and angry eyes. "The Chenzeme are not invulnerable. It'll be on guard."

Urban turned on a cocky smile. "If it closes with us, we'll have already convinced it we are Chenzeme. At that proximity, a nuke would damage us as much as it would damage the courser, so it would make no sense to use one . . . unless we were feeling suicidal?" His brows rose in a questioning look.

"This isn't a joke," Clemantine said. "Urban, you won't get to hit a reset button when things start to fall apart."

"Hey. Things *are* falling apart. This new courser's almost on top of us."

"And you want to provoke it."

"I want to take advantage of the moment. We may be considered deranged, but we are still Chenzeme. The courser *wants* the experiences recorded in our philosopher cells. It isn't going to attack us unless we leave it no choice."

"You don't know that," Clemantine insisted.

"It's a theory I intend to test." He turned to Nikko again. "How about it? Do you want to come too?"

Nikko's kisheer rippled in tempered amusement. Now that he'd recovered from his initial surprise, he found himself impressed by Urban's bravado. Was it all for Deneb's sake? He tapped his finger against his thigh, producing a measured clicking. "And you call me crazy."

Urban shrugged. He looked at Deneb. Nikko followed his gaze, to discover a quickening excitement in her parted lips, and in the gleam beneath the thin crystal lenses that covered her eyes. Her own gaze shifted from Urban to Nikko. Defiance slid into her graceful expression. "*I'm* going," she said—her first words in Nikko's presence.

"No one's going," Clemantine countered.

Nikko nodded his agreement. "Deneb, you don't know anything about the Chenzeme."

"I know the history of this ship."

Did she? Nikko felt stunned by this assertion, and ashamed. How much did she know? He had never told her anything about the other Deneb. But he had told Lot.

"You haven't lived this ship's history," Clemantine said.

Deneb looked as if she would object to that, but then she shrugged. "I know the Chenzeme are dangerous, but if the chance presents itself, I won't be staying behind. An alien ship! This may be the first real chance anyone has ever had to get inside its programming and make contact—real contact, without aggression—"

Nikko felt as if he'd been swallowed whole.

"*—real contact, without aggression,*" Deneb was saying as she addressed the ship's conference. Excitement ran in a low, tense note behind her voice, an excitement that had only grown in the hours since the alien vessel had been sighted. "*An opportunity like this has never existed before in all of human history. How can we turn away from it . . . ?*"

Clemantine's commanding voice snapped through Nikko's sensorium, yanking him out of the decaying memory loop. "Contact is Lot's talent—"

"And theft is mine," Urban said. "I want the design of that zero point drive."

Nikko fled. His disconcerted consciousness abandoned

his holographic image, leaving it in a repetitive rest state in which his fingers twitched and his kisheer rippled as if he were considering each point in the sharp debate. Meanwhile, he took his core persona into the ship, allowing it to stretch out along the lines of the hull. Alpha Cygni blazed dead ahead, a point of white-hot brilliance less than two years away. In the radio spectrum, he saw the signature of molecules in the dust clouds beyond the giant star, the shivering beat of scattered pulsars, the brilliant lens of the galaxy's heart. He opened his senses to the hot kiss of interstellar hydrogen striking the bow, to the nurturing warmth that flowed through his jacket of Chenzeme cells, to the presence of the itching cyst just under his hide, where Lot lay bedded in a current of alien thought.

Deneb had wanted to make contact. That first time they'd ever seen a Chenzeme ship, it had been Deneb who'd persuaded the rest of the crew to go forward. Nikko had tried to dissuade her. They'd even fought about it, hadn't they?

"You don't know enough to make a choice! You don't know anything about it!"

"But my love, that's why we have to try."

Deneb had wanted to make contact. Then, and now.

Intersecting waves of conversation flowed across the hull cells, an alien babble that Nikko could only vaguely understand.

He engaged a submind. He instructed it to rewrite his emotional parameters, weakening the fields that supported melancholy, doubt, and pessimism, while enhancing those that produced confidence and audacity. His distress dissipated. After an absence of 4.7 seconds, he felt possessed enough to return to the core chamber. He slid back into the perspective of his holographic projection, to find Clemantine still trying to bring Urban to heel.

"Even if the courser allows you to approach, do you think it will leave itself open to your dissection?" she demanded. "Urban, the only way you'll ever get that design is if you let Lot dig it out. If you interrupt that process, you might never have it. You might be dead."

"Lot won't be able to find it," Nikko said.

Clemantine turned on him, her glare a dark and potent weapon. "You don't know that."

"If that information was stored in the philosopher cells, he would have already seen some hint of it within our own."

"Sooth," Urban said. "The drive mechanism, the weapons system. They could have an independent origin. The philosopher cells make decisions, but the body of the courser lies beneath that."

"Lot won't be able to go that deep," Nikko said.

Was Urban's smile a little nervous now? "Then you will go with us?"

"If it comes to that," Nikko agreed.

Deneb had wanted to make contact and he'd given in; he'd given his support. And they had failed. But he was older now, wiser, better armed. It wasn't too late to make it up.

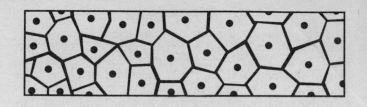

Chapter
8

Deneb felt as if she'd been picked up and rattled in the hand of some capricious god, then tossed off the end of the world with his injunction ringing in her ears: *Make a new world now, or die.* Setting the Chenzeme to measure her success.

When she considered where she was, what was at stake, then fear ran through her, a dark and unsettled river in her veins. The past was dead, and the future no more than a tenuous dream. Yet she also felt a strange elation at this chance she'd been given: to know the Chenzeme, to understand what had never fallen to human understanding before. If this was a curse, it came strangely close to the innermost desires of her heart.

And she was free—of the cult, and of Nikko too. He had either forgiven her or forgotten her—she didn't care which. All that mattered was that she had the run of the ship and the same autonomy as anyone else. For now. Everything that anyone did was now infused with a sense of haste. The dark courser lay only hours away. They had only hours to learn everything they could about it.

Eyes closed, Deneb made a ghost of herself within her atrium. The ghost was her, and when it was ready, she slipped away, a stream of information that delivered her virtual image to Null Boundary's library—

—where she stood alone on a straight white path, immersed in a vista colored in pearly gradations of blue and white. In the library, white meant proximal. Blue was the blur of distance, and data was embedded at every point along the way. A librarian crawled up from an indistinguishable crack in the white path. Its little angel wings fluttered while its tiny white-furred feet tapped, indexing the path's collection of hidden files. Deneb's kisheer fluttered as she considered how to start this latest hunt.

Null Boundary's library was a hodgepodge collection pulled from the archival stations of a dozen stellar systems—and in each of those systems, the archival records had been plumped with information dumps from passing great ships. So it was a confused and often repetitive collection. The librarians tried hard to index it, but the only way to know for sure what was buried there was to dive in and explore.

"Reprise prior survey," she said after a moment. "Then continue it." Ghosts worked fast. There was still time for raw exploration.

The librarian spat back the search parameters from its chubby lips: "Search Chenzeme, nonhuman intelligence, alien, summaries. Order by date, oldest first. Review prior files, then continue quest."

"Approved." The quality of information on the Chenzeme was astoundingly poor. Unsubstantiated, anecdotal, often contradictory—it angered her, until she reminded herself that most of those who had witnessed the Chenzeme had not survived to record their experiences. And how many of them had spent their last hours delving through confused libraries, searching for some elusive fact that might hint at a path to survival?

The requested filters fell into place, producing a change in shading. The path at her feet brightened and grew longer, extending for hundreds of yards. Files appeared on it, each a paper-thin, vertical field, like a transparent window large enough for her to step through. They were stacked face-to-face-to-face, with no space between them, so that hundreds were layered within the span of her hand.

She considered doubling her ghosts. But while multiple copies of herself would speed the basic search, she'd still have to integrate their findings. So she decided to work with one incarnation, at least for now.

The librarian reduced itself to a half-sensed presence fluttering overhead, while Deneb leaned forward, feeling a slight resistance as she pressed her face into the data fields.

Each file was compressed, with a horizontal component of a fraction of a millimeter. As Deneb moved through them, their key factors flooded her awareness: a streamflow of images and descriptive titles, faces that had been famous at some unknown place and time, strings of radio transmissions, colorful schematics, wisps of conversation, shouts of excitement, and of rage.

The faster she moved, the faster the data poured past her. Since she'd been over these files before, she let them flow unhindered, building through their cumulative impact an impression of the Chenzeme encroachment.

It had many faces.

In stellar systems on the edge of the Hallowed Vasties the Chenzeme had been only a rumor for decades, sometimes for centuries. Communication between worlds was slow and intermittent, and when reports arrived from the frontier documenting an alien presence, they had been dismissed as hoaxes, for anything could be faked.

On the frontier worlds the Chenzeme presence was treated as hard reality. At first there had been only distant sightings. The coursers appeared in the void between worlds, variable in size, but all of them coated with a white hull glow. Attempts at contact were made, but the coursers refused to respond, so caution became the rule. On a dozen worlds the simultaneous decision was made to shut down interstellar radio transmissions. The orbital antennae became listening posts only. What they heard was chilling.

Deneb touched the glassy face of a record she had not explored before. It had been gathered out of the void long ago by a passing great ship. "Expand," she ordered. Then she stepped forward into a foreshortened starscape, centered on the image of a Chenzeme courser as seen through the telescopes of an orbital city above some world whose name she could not pronounce.

Events spun forward in compressed time. Hours elapsed in seconds as a trio of coursers swept into the system at nearly one-tenth the speed of light. Deneb listened to voices filled with excitement and with fear, and then she listened to the horrified reporting of disaster befalling outlying stations, and the stepped-up preparations for the defense of the inner system, and the deadpan sign-off as death descended and this record was cast into the void, a warning to other worlds.

Carefully, she noted the approach vectors of the warships, the overheard radio codes that passed between them, and the response of the human inhabitants. She tried not to let the voices get inside her.

She came upon the same stellar system later in her search, in a file that originated from a different time and a different library. She had to backtrack to be sure, but yes, it was the same star, the same two habitable worlds each with its own ringlet of orbital cities. Except in this file, defensive synchrotrons had mysteriously appeared, occupying lonely orbits in the outer system. As the pack of coursers swept toward the cities, the synchrotrons fired a battery of lasers. The lead courser was lanced and the others turned away, while shouts of joy filled Deneb's ears.

She reviewed the first record. Here there were no orbital synchrotrons, and the destruction had been absolute. Doubt became a sour lump in her throat.

She saw the same stellar system a third time. In this record, neatly edited segments were interspersed with the concerned face of a communications officer. The pack of coursers swept in just as it had two times before. The orbital synchrotrons were in place, only this time they didn't fire. This time the lead courser responded to the peculiar code the officer sent into the void, turning away without hostility.

Deneb chewed on the papillae that lined her mouth. When she tried to summon details of the code, the librarian reported incomplete data. She watched the scene again, and then a third time, trying to find some testimony of falsehood, knowing it *was* false.

"You can't always tell," Urban said.

She flinched, unaware that his ghost had joined her. Still, she was glad it was Urban. She felt easy with him. "Who would fake records like that?" she asked him. "Why?"

Urban looked surprised at the question. "Because it's better to believe we might survive?"

"We can't base our decisions on lies."

He shrugged. "They're not really lies. Planetary defenses

have gotten better. Heyertori might have survived if the synchrotrons hadn't been sabotaged."

Deneb looked back over the library path. "But we can't trust these records."

"Sooth. You didn't know that?"

"No, I didn't." Then she added: "And I didn't know you were that cynical."

He shrugged again. "It's not the reality of our past that matters, Deneb. Just our belief in it."

"I don't believe that. Reality does matter. Do *you* edit what you know?"

"Not yet. I haven't been around that long." He touched the frame of the record, not meeting her gaze. "Sometimes I edit what I feel."

"Nikko does that too."

He did not like the comparison. She could see that in the hard set of his eyes. "Nikko's crazy. You can't trust him. He pretends to know a lot about the Chenzeme, but he doesn't know how he knows, because he's trashed any record of the actual experience that earned him that knowledge. *If* it's real knowledge. Lucky he didn't trash you."

Deneb's kisheer fluttered in slow, thoughtful waves as she tried to make sense of this outburst. "There's nothing wrong with the records he's kept."

Urban grinned. "Sure. It's the records he hasn't kept that I'd like to see. I thought his whole past would fall open when I found you, but there's nothing here. Not in any hidden field. He's trashed it all."

"No he hasn't." Deneb glanced at the librarian. At first it was a translucent suggestion, no more. Then it gathered substance, and descended according to her gaze. "Retrieve my personal index," she instructed.

Wings fluttered. Furry feet scuffed, and the path narrowed into a new, more attenuated collection of files.

"Look for Nikko's journal."

Urban said, "He doesn't have a journal."

The librarian folded its wings and dived into the data fields. Deneb followed. Histories screamed past her, swift images, fleeting scents, blurred voices that she barely registered as she pursued the librarian, its wings a blur of hummingbird motion.

It stopped. A single file gleamed rosy as the librarian faded from sight once again.

Deneb touched the glassy face of the marked file, thinking *expand*. A vast and detailed record unfolded along a new path. "This is his journal," Deneb said, glancing back at Urban's astonished face. "You must have seen this before."

Urban stepped past her, almost disappearing into the record as he made a cursory scan of its prodigious contents. He looked back at Deneb. "This wasn't here before."

A chill touched the back of her neck. "It must have been. You just missed it."

"No."

The chill deepened. She felt as if Nikko stood behind her, observing her every move. She resisted an urge to turn around.

From the look in Urban's eyes, he might have felt the same. "Nikko! You!" he shouted. "Why? Why give this to us now?"

"Because things are critical," Deneb said, peering down the path.

"Things have always been critical."

"But if Nikko didn't want to remember these things—"

"This is not a game!"

"Then bring it up with him later! There's no time to argue about it now."

She started forward, only to feel Urban's hand on her arm. She turned, and she could still feel his hand, though now she could see he wasn't touching her: his left hand hung at his side, while he chewed thoughtfully on a knuckle of his right.

"You're starting to blur," she said.

"Hell." A knuckle in the mouth did not interfere at all with his enunciation. "I'm remembering something. Back at the Well, when we first came aboard—Nikko told us he'd once mated with a Chenzeme ship."

Deneb's gaze shifted. In her mind she saw the dark silhouette of the approaching courser. "Then he's done this before?"

"Or he lied."

Misgivings rose in her. "He understands Lot though, doesn't he?"

"Sooth," Urban admitted. "He said he learned that from

the mating. Damn you, Nikko!" He shook his fist in the air. "Why have you kept this secret? Are you out to kill us all?"

"Urban, please."

"Two centuries, Deneb. He's kept this out of the library for two centuries."

"He probably didn't know he had it."

"That's just stupid."

Her temper snapped. "That doesn't really matter now, does it?"

He stared at her a moment, then slowly, he started to smile. She didn't like the mocking flavor of it, but she forced herself to focus instead on the task at hand. "Mating involves an exchange of dust, right?"

Urban shrugged. "Lot thinks so."

"Then let's look for that." Even before she'd said it, the librarian was back fluttering in her face. She sent it off through the gallery of files stacked along the path. Soon it stopped. It marked a file. Then it rose off again, fading into translucence as it went.

Deneb stepped forward. Unmarked files whispered past her, but when she reached the marked file, that expanded. Instantly she was immersed in an overwhelming cacophony of sensation, as if she were being shunted laterally through an emotional maelstrom bored out of unrelated stacks. She screamed, then jumped backward out of the record, crashing into Urban. "What was *that*?" she cried.

"Don't know." Urban didn't sound too steady either. He swiped at the librarian, which fluttered between them now like a mindless moth. "Back the record up," he told it. "Is there an initiating event? Go back before that. Show the setup."

They found themselves in the void. The ramscoop was deployed. Behind them, a sun blazed like a tiny yellow gem. Data rushed into Deneb's ghost-mind, and she remembered the name of the system she'd just left.

"It's Heyertori," Urban whispered. His ancestral world, as Earth was hers. Both gone now. Deneb took his hand.

Null Boundary had passed the last inhabited post three months ago. The decks were cold and empty. All ship's power was divided between the engines and the core. The library hummed, organizing data uploaded from Heyertori's extensive archives. The data had distracted them.

Nikko did not notice at first when a submind brought news of a powerful radio beacon out of Heyertori.

Urban shuddered and his arm went around Deneb's waist. "I've seen this before. It's in the records the survivors brought to Silk."

They listened to panicked voices reporting the death of the system. The outer posts had failed to detect the approach of twin swan bursters, and then the orbital synchrotrons failed to respond. Nuclear armaments were launched in the swan bursters' paths, but the rings used their weaponry to lance the mines. Debris fields met the same fate.

"Stop," Urban whispered. The frantic voices collapsed into a meaningless hum that carried on and on and on as the moment stretched out in time. He looked at Deneb. "At that point they knew they were doomed. As the swan bursters drew near to Heyertori itself, they sent out a massive information dump—everything they knew, and everything they believed, cast into the void in the hope that some other world would chance to pick it up. As if the culture made a ghost of itself."

"Nikko must have caught some of that."

"Sooth."

"Look," Deneb said. "The rings have followed our trajectory through the system."

"Yes. They followed Nikko through it."

"You know that?"

"He said so. They'd marked him. They used him to spread the virus that corrupted the watch-posts and the synchrotrons. He didn't know it at the time."

"Love and nature."

"Skip the slaughter," Urban said roughly. "What happened next?"

The librarian brought them deeper into the record, to a time several weeks later. The swan bursters had left the system, on trajectories roughly parallel to Null Boundary's. The telescopes could pick them out despite the glare of Heyertori's yellow sun. They were accelerating, while their courses slowly converged.

"Do they see us?" Deneb asked.

Urban shifted uneasily. "I don't know. Nikko said they were following an emission from Null Boundary . . .

though . . . he doesn't know it yet? I mean . . . he didn't know it then."

Nikko had given up running. Already he had furled the scoop and shut down the reactor. They had become a tiny island of darkness, invisible against the infinities around them. Deneb felt the cold of the ship in her bones, the ringing silence in her ears. More weeks passed. The twin rings drew closer, to Null Boundary and to each other. Now the telescopes could resolve both their images within a single frame.

They were less than a hundred thousand miles astern, and Null Boundary's angle of view could not be better. The rings appeared face-on. Deneb watched them converge, looking first like the outline of blind eyes, then like a squeezed infinity sign as one slid behind the other. Within an hour (it passed in seconds) they were fully aligned, their separate shapes now almost indistinguishable.

Deneb expected to see them slide apart next, a steady separation of two bodies as in any eclipse. Instead, the swan bursters remained aligned for twenty hours, and she shuddered to think of the energy costs such a maneuver would require.

But finally, the rings did part. Their courses diverged. She watched in silence as each began a slow loop back toward the Hallowed Vasties.

"They've had a successful kill at Heyertori," Urban said. "They'll take that knowledge with them, and spread it around."

Deneb felt unaccountably angry. "Where's the dust?" she demanded. "We're in this file because it's supposed to have dust."

"*I have to interpret this,*" Nikko said.

Deneb jumped hard. She found herself backed up against Urban's chest, every muscle in her projected body taut as his arms closed protectively around her. Nikko was still talking.

"—*clear the swan bursters followed me. Love and nature, is anyone alive at Heyertori . . . ?*"

"It's a voice-over," Urban said. "He's not here."

"*I never detected them in my wake. I must go back. If there are survivors—*"

Urban's words were clipped. "Skip forward," he said. "To just before the dust."

Nikko did not have the power reserves of the swan bursters, and he was scared. So he didn't turn about immediately. Instead he coasted in cold silence, waiting for the Chenzeme marauders to pull far away.

It happened with the same abruptness they'd experienced before: a sensory storm hit them, overriding all standard input. Visions and smells and excruciating noises combined in a cerebral tempest, howling impulses that threatened to dissolve their ghost structures.

Deneb turned to hide her face against Urban's shoulder. "Freeze it!" he shouted.

A strange, unvarying harmonic ground at her ears. A stink of sexual passion sat in her nostrils. All around her a pattern of silver had exploded into a complex linkage of machine parts that fit together in intricate harmony, hooks and loops and long connecting tendrils.

"Frame advance," Deneb whispered.

The silvery canopy disappeared. She witnessed a thermal plume the size of Earth's moon rising from a reddened planet. "Love and nature." The sexual scent remained, but the tone changed to something higher pitched.

"It's a gallery of sensation," Urban said, holding her close against him. "But whose?"

"Let's just run through it, okay?"

She felt him nod. His arms tightened around her. She tried to ignore the signs of his arousal and hers, in the pheromone-draped moment in which they'd paused. "Forward, then," she said.

The boiling world vanished into a flood of images, scents, sounds, and *sensations*: fingers brushing her, sharp objects slamming past her integument, worms writhing in her gut, kisses soft against her kisheer—

It vanished, and the world with it. They were left to float in gray nonspace. She could smell tears on Urban's cheeks.

Then Nikko's ghost was crouched before them. Like a cutout pasted on the gray background: his fingers twitched beneath his chin as he stared at something not visible to them.

"Is he real?" Deneb whispered.

"I don't know. I don't think so."

"Nikko?" she asked tentatively.

"He's erased this segment of the journal."

"Nikko!" she shouted.

Nikko did not turn, or acknowledge them in any way. Was he a recording then, and not a ghost?

"*It is . . . obscene,*" he muttered. "*It was obscene.*" He looked at them then, and though Deneb cringed against Urban's chest, she felt like a child doing it, because Nikko was not looking at her. He was looking at a camera; she was sure of it. He was speaking to a camera as he recorded an entry in a journal now hundreds of years old.

No expression could be seen in his face, which was as still and beautiful as the face of a Buddha, but in the soft, low burr of his voice she could hear an almost unbearable confusion.

"*It went on like that for two years. Understand: My Makers were defending me all that time, fighting an evolutionary war against the invading dust . . . they did not win, but they made a compromise, and I was finally able to think again.*"

The mystery had unraveled for him slowly. Only gradually did he understand that he'd been exposed to stray dust released by the two swan bursters when they'd passed so close to one another. He used the term "mating" to describe their intersection. The dust had been traveling at a relative velocity higher than Null Boundary's. It had caught him, and it had worked its way through the hull like microscopic worms. It had found its way into his neural system and *he'd had receptors there that could interpret it*. This was the conclusion that left him stunned and shaking as he recited it. He'd already had something of the Chenzeme in him, or he would not have "heard" the dust (seen it, felt it, smelled it).

Once he was aware of his sensitivity, he was able to guess at how it had been acquired. "*It must have been an effect of the plague Null Boundary contracted, that first time we ever saw the Chenzeme.*"

"That's when his crew died," Deneb said.

"It wasn't my crew then."

Her breath caught in a sharp gasp. Nikko stood beside them now, watching his own image speak. He turned his head and looked at her, and this time she knew it was no recording, but a fully conscious ghost.

"When the ship's original persona died, I took its place."
He laughed softly. "I knew very little about such things,
and the library had been trashed. I never understood that
the matrix that contained me was different from those of
other ships. It had been modified by the dust. I had an extra
sense I was not aware of until I intersected dust once
more."

"You claimed once that you mated with a Chenzeme
ship," Urban said. Deneb could feel the tension in his chest,
his barely contained anger.

Perhaps Nikko felt it too. His kisheer went very still.
"That first time, when the plague dust destroyed us. That
was a mating. I didn't see it until later—that I was my own
corrupt offspring."

"That was an accident," Urban said. "It's nothing like
what we're about to face."

"It was no accident," Nikko said. "It was rape."

"I died then, didn't I?" Deneb asked. "That other version of me that you knew."

Nikko's kisheer rippled in uneven waves. He didn't
answer.

"Does your journal record that time?"

"No. All the records from before that time were
trashed."

"Except your memories."

He laughed softly. "We're stronger now. If it's rape
again, at the least, the violence will be mutual."

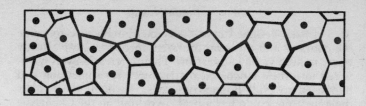

Chapter
9

The luminous courser had fallen back into silence. It made no response to Null Boundary's aggressive warning—though whether this resulted from satisfaction or suspicion, Lot could not say. He spent most of the next day and a half at the hull. The frigid tissue of the wound had deepened. The philosopher cells flowed over his closed eyelids and filled his ears. They painted his face, enveloping even his nose and mouth. This collection of cells had come out of Deception Well.

He thought about that, as dialogues flowed past him:

—hoary contemplations on the structure and handling of poisons (thought experiments in which scenarios leading to disastrous outcomes were eliminated).

—a continuing analysis of his own presence and value, and Nikko's presence too, *the navigator.*

—histories handed down from ancestral ships, memories of blackened planets and ecstatic unions and a melding of the other.

—and temperaments. This colony of philosopher cells was not homogeneous. They derived from different ancestors. Lot felt their contrasting personalities. He felt himself in them as a taint of glorified madness.

Like any collection of natural organisms, the Chenzeme cells were varied and adaptable. But they were *not* natural.

They'd been designed by a conscious intelligence to guide the coursers and the swan bursters through a war already thirty million years in duration. Their aggression was hard-wired into their biochemical structure. Yet something had happened to Null Boundary's cells. Through the endless dialogues, Lot could feel a brake working on the Chenzeme loop of unprovoked aggression. A thousand times the argument was made to ready the poison dust; a thousand times the argument was defeated. Only now did he guess that the cells were contaminated with the peacekeeping protocols of the Well, infected with viral thoughts designed to spread the Well theme of cooperation-replacing-conflict. He now doubted the cells would attack unless attacked first. If an opportunity arrived to use the dust, they might refuse—and for the best. There were better ways to meet the Chenzeme.

Cooperation was often more profitable than aggression. Chenzeme ships that did not practice aggressive warfare should be more likely to survive to reproduce. That such ships hadn't come to dominate indicated a mechanism to cull any cell colony deviating from the Chenzeme norm. Apparently only the real thing could evade sanction . . . or those that could mimic the real thing?

That must be Null Boundary's strategy.

If Null Boundary could survive this contact, it could infect the dark courser with its own deviant cells, and peace might spread.

If they appeared to be the real thing.

You need to learn to lie in the Chenzeme way.

But the Chenzeme did not lie. That was a human talent.

It was deep in ship's night when Lot went to the gee deck—the last night before the dark courser would catch them. No one was around, so he plugged into a set of headphones that emerged from the factory after a few minutes' wait. He crashed on the bed, feeling tired and detached. Closing his eyes, he whispered the system on. Rhythmic angst flooded him: a very human sound. The music tugged at him. It took the place of dreams he never had, weaving pictures and sensations through his half-waking mind. Dimly, he was aware of scattered impressions playing across his sensory tears: Urban, in a feral mood. And some-one else?

A solid nudge against his foot startled him awake. He sat up, to discover Urban really was present, sitting cross-legged at the foot of the bed, a cocky grin on his face. He wore a pale gold skin suit beaded with drops of condensing mois-ture. Anticipation pumped off him. Lot yanked the head-phones off, his heart pounding hard. "What's wrong?"

Deneb leaned back in a chair, watching him with an expression he could not read. Her presence curled around him, equally inscrutable: a combination of curiosity and mistrust, anticipation and anger. Her blue-scaled skin was as wet as Urban's suit, and Lot guessed they'd been outside, exposed to the chill of hard vacuum.

"Wrong?" Urban asked, pulling a look of staged puzzle-ment as he brushed some of the water droplets off his arms. "You mean besides that we're all about to die?"

Lot smiled. His heart slowed. He hadn't seen either of them in the two days since the dark courser was sighted. The company felt good. "Okay then, what's new? Why were you outside?"

Urban slipped up then. He let the grin get away from him. A chill grew out of its disappearance. "Did Nikko tell you? If we get the chance we're crossing over to the courser."

No, Nikko had not told him that. At first, Lot could make no sense of it. "Cross over? But why?" Even as he said it, he knew why. Urban's pirate-curiosity had made him jump to Null Boundary too, leaving Silk behind for-ever. "Urban, you don't want to do this."

Urban just shrugged. "We want to look at the courser's interior, and learn how it relates to the philosopher cells. So we'll need a way to get under the hull membrane—"

"There is no interior! Why should there be an interior? No one lives there."

"Then we'll make our own shaft. What will happen if we damage the philosopher cells?"

"I don't know. Urban, you don't need to do this. Let me handle it."

Wrong thing to say. Lot could feel Urban's resistance slam against him like a hand in the face. Urban had never been willing to play second to anybody.

"I'll decide what I need to do, Lot. We don't know anything about this courser. I'll do anything I have to do, to learn."

Lot didn't doubt it. "You're going after the drive system?"

The edge of Deneb's kisheer fluttered like wind-kissed water. "We'd like to get some idea of where it is and what it looks like."

"And what it's made of," Urban added.

"Well, it's probably exotic matter, at least in part," Deneb said, "with a negative mass-energy density. It almost has to be, if there's a connection to the zero point field. Exotic matter is the key to changing space-time gradients."

Urban scowled. "Could we replicate exotic matter?"

"The Chenzeme ships must have managed it," Lot pointed out.

Deneb frowned, and water glinted on her glassy lips. "But if they use exotic matter to make more exotic matter . . ."

"Then without a starting sample we've got nothing," Urban finished. "Even if we stole schematics on the whole ship."

"So we get a starting sample." Deneb tapped her fingers, deep in thought. "It might be like breeding matter out of the empty void, but Lot's right—if the Chenzeme ships can do it, we can too."

"And affect the resonance of the zero point field," Lot muttered. The zpf was theorized to be an all-pervasive field, the same in all directions, except where exotic matter unbalanced it.

Urban's gaze unfocused. Deneb watched him thoughtfully, and Lot imagined he could feel the invisible atrial traffic that flowed between them as they extracted ghosts for another deep run through the ship's library.

He lay back on the bed, feeling apart from it. Spiderwebs clung in untidy fans to the lattice roof. Why had Nikko introduced spiders? To catch the tiny moths that fluttered near the lighting strips. There were more efficient ways to control the moths. Nikko liked to keep an array of life, that was all. Lizards could be found crawling on the posts. The pond supported fish, and water-skating insects, and inquisitive dragonflies. Several species of birds lived in the forest. In Silk, people had surrounded themselves with life too. Why? There was no need for it. An integrated system of Makers could provide all their needs, yet still people chose diversity when given any kind of chance, almost as if it were an instinct.

Only that instinct had changed in the Hallowed Vasties.

"So why were you on the hull?" Lot asked. Urban still sat cross-legged at the foot of the bed, though to his surprise, Lot discovered Deneb had gone.

"Deneb wanted to see the courser with her own eyes."

Lot raised himself up on one elbow. "You can actually see it?"

"Yeah." Urban slid off the bed. "Deneb doesn't say much, but she understands what happened to her. She knows the cult stole away her old life. She wants to know why."

"That's what I want too," Lot assured him. Was the cult the enemy of the warships too? Perhaps, perhaps. And all of them caught in the crossfire of an antique civil war.

"Come see the courser," Urban said. "It puts things in perspective."

So they went onto the hull, exiting the transit bubble near the ship's aft end, in an area Nikko had deliberately kept free of the cells. Lot walked the pliant surface, while his skin suit controlled the catch and release of his boots, leaving temporary footprints behind him. At the edge of the cell colony, he stopped.

The last time Lot had been outside, the colony had measured a few meters in diameter. That was twenty-two years ago. Now, the field of gleaming cells sheathed Null Boundary's cylindrical hull, a blaze of white against the black void.

The cells would latch onto any object laid against them, from the dust of the void to the boots of a skin suit. When the colony was new, Lot had watched it disassemble and absorb steel plates and sheets of ice that Nikko laid against it.

"Turn around," Urban said, his voice sounding intimate through the suit's audio system.

Lot turned. In this direction the hull showed faint gray, reflecting light cast by the cells. Beyond the hull, stars gleamed like luminous sand strewn across the void. Gradually, Lot became aware of a spot of darkness, a patch of emptiness stamped upon the starfield. He stared at it, until his mind resolved it into the long, cylindrical silhouette of a courser.

"*By the Unknown God,*" he whispered.

In its blackness it seemed to be extinguishing the light of stars.

"It's something, isn't it?" Urban said. "A Chenzeme ship, this close, and we're still alive."

Lot could see the silhouette growing, expanding to blot out more stars. "I didn't think it would be this real."

"Sooth," Urban murmured in agreement. "That's the word. It's *real*."

Lot didn't dare return to the wound. Not yet. He didn't want the cells to pick up his apprehension. So he went back to the gee deck with Urban. They sat on the grass outside the pavilion and drank beer in the darkness of ship's night. The brew was smooth and slightly sweet, served in white ceramic bottles painted with long-legged birds. "Deneb seems to be coping well," Lot suggested after a while.

He'd picked the right subject. "She's on fire," Urban said. "She can't wait to take the courser apart. She's been cracking the theory on zero point tech almost without a break."

"You really like her, don't you?"

"Sooth." His affection sparkled across Lot's sensory tears. "She's crazy and wild, Lot, but she's smart—"

"And pretty."

"And pretty," Urban agreed. "When this is over, you should get to know her. You've hardly talked to her."

"I will," Lot promised, watching the painted birds on his ceramic bottle as they dipped their beaks in painted ponds to feed.

Urban's mood shifted. Anxiety filled the shadowed spaces around him. He looked downslope at the koi pond, where a frog chirruped in a chiming voice. "Do you know why I didn't leave a copy of myself in Silk? It's because I didn't want to wake up and find myself trapped there. You understand? Even if I were here on Null Boundary, some version of me would have been stuck back there too. I didn't want to be that version."

Lot took another pull of icy-cold beer. "You sure you want to be *this* version?"

Urban laughed, short and loud and only partly false. "It'll work," he said. "And anyway, if it doesn't, we won't be around to worry about it."

He knocked off the last of his beer and got to his feet. Lot followed. Urban said: "I'm going to see what Deneb's doing, and then I'll be getting ready for tomorrow. I don't know if I'll see you again—well, at least for a while." He stuck out his hand.

Lot took it in an awkward grip. "You be careful."

"You too, fury." They embraced, then Urban left along the garden path.

Lot stayed for a while. He sat on the edge of the pavilion. Koi splashed in the pond at the bottom of the grassy slope. The frog chirruped. A gecko clucked, while the dark courser drew steadily nearer.

Is this all?

"Hark," he said at last, waking the spider on his ear. "Where's Clemantine?"

He hesitated on the threshold of her house. A slow-moving air current brought him the sense of her presence as he stood there assuring himself that she would be busy, or that she would be angry with him. Or worse, that she would be aloof. He stepped into the living room.

The image wall was active. Veils of rain fell over the green sea cliffs of Heyertori. Waves crashed against the foot of the land, their roar faintly audible. "Clemantine?"

He found her on the sofa, lying down as if asleep, her eyes moving beneath closed lids. Locked in the atrial flow, trying to find her own angle on tomorrow's encounter. He felt a flush of admiration. She'd been alive a long time; she'd survived against long odds.

"Clemantine."

Her eyes opened. Her body tensed, while her surprise and fright washed over him. "Lot? What's gone wrong?" Her eyes still moved restlessly back and forth so he knew she was still linked.

"Nothing," he said. "Don't look for a problem in the data fields. Nothing's there."

Her face relaxed a little. She was coming back into herself. He sat on the sofa back while she sat up on the seat.

He could feel her curiosity and a cut of annoyance. He couldn't meet her gaze.

Words of atonement welled in his throat, but they were a foreign language he didn't know. All he could manage was a pathetic declaration: "I'm seriously scared."

Her laugh made little wrinkles on her cheeks. "Son, I'm glad to hear that. I'd be worried if you weren't."

She looked tired and a little dejected as she lay back against the sofa arm. Her long legs bent at the knees. Lot's gaze followed their merging lines. "I'm sorry," he said. Apparently he was quite full of pathetic declarations today. He tried again. "I wanted . . . all of you. Maybe it wasn't fair."

"That's right," she said. "It wasn't." Her mood held a background beat of anger, with other things present that he could not decipher. "So what part of me do you want now?"

It was his turn to laugh. "All of you."

"Go on, Lot. I won't change and you know it. Don't start it all again."

"No," he said. "It's all of you I want." He got up and walked around to the other side of the sofa. All or nothing now. "Whatever that means. However you want to define it. I can't dictate your pleasures anymore, I know that. I could probably still influence them."

She stared at him. Then laughter sputtered from her lips. "You say that with a straight face?"

He smiled.

"Don't look at me like that," she warned, only half in jest. She was sitting up now, her feet firm against the floor. Her anger had not gone, but it was swimming against a potent sexual tide.

"I could court you again," Lot offered. "But really there's no time. We could be dead any moment."

"We aren't going to die."

"Of course we are. Maybe not tomorrow."

Her brows rose; he caught the scent of her amusement. "This fatalism would be something you got from Jupiter?"

"How can you joke about it?"

"How can I not joke about it?" The humor in her aura was a thin veil, at best.

He frowned. "Oh. I think I understand."

"Do you? That would be a first."

• • •

"Do you remember how?" she asked him. They'd moved from the couch to the privacy of her bedroom.

He shook his head. "No. I've never done this before."

"It's that different?"

"Sooth." Before, with the feedback influence of the charismata, they'd been able to reach a state of synchronicity almost immediately. She would feel what he willed her to feel; her feelings would shape his desire. Now the charismata bumped against her, only to flow away without effect. If Lot's hands had been cut off, he could not have felt more awkward.

"Don't try so hard," Clemantine whispered.

"I'm sorry."

"Don't be sorry."

"Let me try again."

He let her mood flow over him. He immersed himself in its symphonic flavor, yielding all sense of himself . . . and to his surprise he discovered it did work. He could touch her mind—but in the ancient way, with a caress, a kiss, a word spoken in the right moment, in just the right tone of voice. He still knew how to gauge that. Time skipped past them, a golden blur the color of her skin.

He blinked. He'd been adrift. Now he found himself faced with her cautious gaze. He saw himself reflected in her dark eyes. This was not the cult. They existed outside the cult. And still he loved her. He couldn't bear to think she might die.

Her eyes narrowed. "Forget about that."

"What?"

"Whatever you're thinking that's cast that shadow on your face. It's okay like this. You know it is."

His charismata mobbed the air, love and doubt equally invisible.

Her sharp gaze would not permit melancholy. "What am I thinking?"

"You're as scared as I am."

"Am I?" She frowned briefly. Then she shrugged and shifted her weight, nudging him over onto his back while she rolled into a crouch that straddled his hips. "You're looking too deep. I was really thinking it was my turn to be on top."

He smiled. He took one of her breasts in his hand, caressing the wide, dark nipple. Guilt nagged at him. "I should get back to the hull cells."

She shrugged, rocking slowly so that her pubic hair brushed against his legs. "You can do that if you really want to." Her strong hand stroked his withered cock, coaxing it back to life. "If you feel you have not done all you can out there?"

"I don't know."

"Sooth, who ever does?" The humor left her face, though her hand remained busy. She leaned over to touch her tongue to the moist surfaces of his sensory tears. He closed his eyes, treasuring the taste of her. "If this is our last time," she whispered, "then we should cherish it."

It wasn't in him to argue. He pulled her down against him, covering himself with a shroud of heat and scent momentarily infinite. Charismata of love and of desire flowed from him. And fear. They brushed past her without effect. It didn't matter. Her own love flowed back to him, her own fear. Independent and utterly essential.

She chuckled in his ear, a soft sound, drunken and delightful, that brought goose bumps to his skin. Her breath puffed in a warm tide past his cheek as she asked, "You're ready now, aren't you?"

It would seem so. "Something must be done with it," he acknowledged.

Her hand helped guide him. "*God,*" he breathed.

"Of history's most popular religion."

And he would worship here forever if he could. He swore it to himself, and berated himself silently for all the wasted time. "I've been an idiot."

"Sooth, I know. But there's hope for you yet. We've got time to work on you. We still have time."

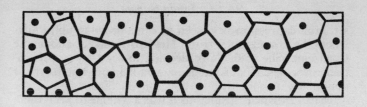

Chapter
10

Urban felt awkward in his overstuffed skin suit. Sample pockets and equipment caches bulged across his chest, along his arms, and on his thighs. He wondered if he was taking too much stuff. Deneb was adapted to vacuum and required no skin suit. When she joined him in his core apartment wearing only a small chest-pack, he began to entertain serious doubts.

Her eyes widened when she saw him; her lips twitched in an irrepressible smile. But her voice remained somber. "You've got the bugs?"

"Sooth." His cheeks felt hot as he pointed to his cartridge belt. He had armed himself with a collection of robotic bugs, developed to probe and analyze the courser's tissues. The microscale devices were stored a thousand to a cartridge. Their homing times ranged from five minutes to three hours, when they would return to the nearest go-pack, if that were possible.

"Then come on," Deneb urged, with a smile that sent sparkles of light glinting off her blue scales. "The go-packs are ready." She turned and dove back through the pipeweed-lined tunnel, leaving Urban to follow.

Clemantine waited for them in the interstitial space outside the apartments, the newly minted go-packs drifting around her in a slow, zero-gravity dance. Her face had the set, grim expression he'd seen so often growing up in Silk, when the immigrants from Heyertori talked about the Chenzeme. She said, "I've decided to send an empty go-pack over first. If it's fired on, you'll know not to try it yourselves."

Urban frowned, suspicious it was a scheme to keep them from going, but Deneb nodded. "Yes. That's a good idea."

Each pack glistened black, with hexagonal "scales" across its arched back so that it resembled a tortoiseshell. From the front the go-packs looked like shallow cradles, each with a cowl that would flare out around the head to frame it like some ancient headdress.

Urban regarded the go-packs with considerable suspicion, mistrustful of antique designs dredged up on deep runs in the library. He'd dredged this one himself. Clemantine had checked the plan, but the packs still had not been tested.

Deneb glided down over his shoulder, her kisheer rippling in excited silver waves. "Ready?"

"Sooth." Urban snapped into action. "To get the go-pack to couple properly, you're supposed to back into the cradle. Like this." He tapped the wall, kicking himself back into the nearest pack, hoping desperately the design would work. He held his breath as his back touched the cradle's black surface. In he sank. Pliant black goo flowed up and around his shoulders and over his chest and hips, sealing across him in broad straps. More goo wrapped his legs. Perfect.

"You look half melted," Deneb said.

"It doesn't hurt."

She scowled. "I didn't think it would."

Thousands of micronozzles perforated every surface of the go-pack. They could be activated in select galleries by the onboard Dull Intelligence, so the pack could maneuver in any direction.

"It works like any other heads-up device that tracks your visual field," Clemantine said. "Where you look, there you go."

Urban tried it, gliding around in a cautious circle.

By this time Deneb had wriggled into her own go-pack. Framed within the flaring cowl, her face appeared in bas-relief against the tarry background. She looked like a partly formed pupa emerging too soon from its cocoon. Her eyes glistened and she coughed as the kisheer writhed at her throat.

"Are you all right?" Clemantine asked.

"No!" She made an awful face. Alarmed now, Urban moved his pack toward her. "It's sucking at my kisheer. Urban, it hurts."

"Get out of it then. Deneb—"

"No."

"Maybe we can change the design—"

"You know it's too late for that," Clemantine said.

Deneb nodded. "Let's just get outside. Then my kisheer will be over my face and out of this black shit."

"But Nikko's not here yet."

"I don't care!"

"Right," Urban said quickly. "Of course not. We can meet him outside." He called for a transit bubble. "Deneb, I'm sorry. I didn't think about your kisheer."

The transit bubble opened, and she jetted toward it.

He started to follow her, then he remembered Clemantine. She'd elected to stay aboard the ship. He turned back, to find her expression gone cool and distant, as if she were plugged into another reality. Still, she leaned in close and kissed him on the cheek. "I'll be watching you, son, so be good."

"Sooth."

Her gaze never did focus on him. "Hurry now. Deneb's waiting."

Lot could not see the dark courser. He lay entombed within the wound, linked into the shared awareness of the philosopher cells. The unending debate moved through him. He studied every nuance. Still, he could find no hint of the dark courser's presence.

Could the cells remain unaware?

What senses did they have, anyway? Of course they could taste dust, and they could produce it. They could converse in radio emissions. But what function did they have that would allow them to see in the visible range of the electromagnetic spectrum?

None.

They were effectively blind. He'd never realized that before.

Just before they emerged on the hull, Deneb's kisheer rolled up over her mouth and nose and ears. Tendrils of it would be entering her mouth and throat, melding with the papillae there. Oxygen created within the kisheer was now being exchanged for carbon dioxide within her blood. She did not breathe. Urban found it eerie, watching her.

The transit bubble lifted them through the hull and popped, exposing them to vacuum. They stood at the edge of the gleaming cell field. Deneb's distress had vanished, and she did not stir at all.

Urban was supremely conscious of the harsh, irregular rhythm of his own breathing. He felt unwieldy in the fully fueled go-pack. His legs looked massive. And yet they flexed easily, allowing him to crouch. His feet rested in stirrups that clung to the hull on their own hot zones. The go-pack would shrink to a less cumbersome size as the fuel was used, but for now he felt like some exaggerated VR android trooper.

Deneb stood tall beside him, staring at the star-eating black shadow that was the courser. It was little more than a mile away now.

There. Her voice stirred in his auditory nerve, though still she did not move. Behind the kisheer, her mouth did not twitch. She spoke to him, atrium to atrium. *You see there? It's begun to awaken.*

Urban turned from her, to look at the courser's silhouette. There indeed. Points of white light now glowed amid the darkness. They expanded in a lacy pattern, flowing over the courser's hull like branching rivers, painting its cylindrical bulk—but the scale seemed wrong. For the first time, Urban understood in his gut just how big the courser was. Null Boundary measured scarcely a quarter its length. This was not so much a ship they faced, as a worldlet. Urban caught himself gasping. Something had lodged in his throat, and he was breathing hard to pull air around it.

The lights continued to expand, downward now under the courser's vast belly, as waking cells woke their neighbors. Unexpected texture was revealed at the bow. Beneath the white glow of the cells, longitudinal rumples ringed the courser's forward section, like the rounded folds of a pleated curtain. Was it part of the drive system?

Urban rose abruptly from his crouch. *Where the hell is Nikko?* His voice was hoarse and sand-scratched. *We should go. We should cross now.*

Nikko answered immediately. *What's the matter, Urban? You're not getting anxious, are you?*

Deneb shot a pointed look past his shoulder. Urban turned to see Nikko rising out of the hull—looking as if he were being squeezed out, molded from the pliant tissue even as they watched, made corporeal once again here on the verge of existence. It gave Urban a creepy feeling, and for that he scowled.

You're late, he said, making sure his voice was firm this time. *Where's your go-pack? We should cross now. We don't know how much time we have.*

Nikko chuckled, seeing through it easily. *You're scared shitless, aren't you?*

Urban's hand closed into a fist. *Are you still coming?*

Wouldn't miss it.

Nikko's go-pack squeezed into sight beside him. He must have watched Deneb when she put her pack on. He wasn't going to repeat her mistake. Now that he was outside, his kisheer was secure over his face, beyond the reach of the go-pack's flowing tissue.

I'm scared, Deneb said. She stepped toward Nikko, the stirrups of her go-pack leaving faint, angular tracks upon the hull, where the molecular bonds that secured her to the ship had been quickly made, and quickly broken. Her long toes curled past the stirrups, to tap at the hull's faintly textured surface. *I'm deeply scared. And yet I've never seen anything more wonderful than this.*

Not even the cordon? Nikko asked.

Not even the cordon. That was human—and perhaps too big to comprehend. This is alien. A thing utterly different from us, and yet reachable. We can touch it. If we're lucky we can understand it, make it part of ourselves. . . .

You never learned caution, Nikko accused.

His face was a mask, while Deneb's was quick with

expression, even behind the veil of her kisheer. Now anger wrote creases around her eyes. *Maybe I didn't live long enough to learn.

Nikko shrugged, at the same time stepping backward into the go-pack. Its dark tissue flowed around him; he became ominous in its unnatural bulk. *Even when you were decades older than you are now, you didn't know what caution was.

She shrank from him, fear a metal tension in her voice. *What did I do?

*Never mind, Urban told her. *It wasn't you. He stared across the gulf at the courser. *Let's cross. Let's just do it. Then he caught sight of a black shadow moving away from Null Boundary's gleaming hull. *Hey, what's that?

*Clemantine's drone pack, Nikko said.

Its tortoise back glinted with reflected light. Urban watched it advance, waiting for it to be obliterated by a burst of laser light, or the sudden flash of an exploding missile, but the empty pack continued blithely on across the gulf between the two ships, a spot of darkness silhouetted against the courser's white hide.

Urban looked at Deneb. *Our turn now.

Behind the veil of her kisheer, she nodded.

Urban felt his heart beat in close explosions. Silently, he instructed his atrium to release a dose of NoFears.

In the encapsulated tissue of the atrium's pharmaceutical tendril, a tiny sac popped open. Calmness flooded him. He stepped close to Deneb and touched her hand, his glove reproducing the feel of her smooth scales, invulnerable to vacuum. He told her, *Don't ever worry about what happened before. Nikko lost you in that other life. You don't owe him anything. Then he spoke to the DI that controlled his go-pack. "Launch," he commanded.

"Trajectory?" the machine voice asked.

"Target: See it."

"Target at one point six seven kilometers and closing," the DI confirmed. "Launch in two. One, two."

Cushions of mush popped up around him as the go-pack kicked. He grunted at the abrupt acceleration. His vision blurred. Then he was coasting—no, falling. Falling toward the white plane of the courser. He waited for some dark lens to blink open on its surface, followed by the blinding glare of a laser. *Wait,* he said to Deneb and Nikko. *Wait until I'm at least halfway across.*

He kept his gaze fixed on the courser, but in his atrium he held an image of Deneb and Nikko, relayed through the go-pack's sensory gear.

It doesn't matter now, Deneb said defiantly. She launched. Nikko set off behind her.

Clemantine spoke now into his atrium. *Don't lose your head, Urban. I'd like to see you back again.*

We'll be back.

Sooth. I'm silent from now. Be good.

You too.

Clemantine worried that radio might disturb the courser. She would talk to him again only in an emergency.

Urban grinned. No emergency here. Just going to check out this alien killing machine.

He wondered again how close it would get to Null Boundary. The gap was closing at about a foot per second . . . which left them an hour and a half before collision. Urban could not believe there would actually be a collision. What would happen to avert it? *That* was what he longed to see.

Cameras on Null Boundary's hull followed the progress of the boarding party as they crossed the gulf between the two ships. At her post in the core chamber, Clemantine surveyed a real-time image. Additional feeds arrived from the go-packs, including the drone, which had continued to the far side of the courser's hull. Clemantine let it stay there, about a half-klick beyond the Chenzeme ship.

She had two more drone go-packs stored in a transit bubble just beneath Null Boundary's hull. Each carried a weighty cargo. Now she summoned them to the surface.

"Place them as near to the bow as you dare," Nikko said.

She could not see him, but his ghost was here, watching his own physical copy glide toward the Chenzeme courser.

Clemantine instructed the drones to launch. "I should be able to put one near the bow. But the kids are planning to nose around up there. I don't think I can hide two. The other will have to go to the stern."

Nikko said, "They're not kids."

"The hell they're not. Urban's hardly thirty—"

"That's old enough."

"—and Deneb's half his age."

"She grew up with her ghosts. She's lived far longer than her linear years."

The drones departed on an indirect course so that they would not appear silhouetted against Null Boundary should anyone in the boarding party glance back.

Clemantine toyed with the image of wired babies.

In Silk, and in Heyertori before that, children were not given atriums. They lived a singular existence, and they grew up slowly. It seemed right. It seemed respectful of their developing personas, and the only way to ground them in the real world. To permit a toddler to play with ghosts . . . it struck her as obscene.

"When did you get your atrium?" Clemantine asked. She did not shift her gaze from the image wall.

"I was born with it."

By the Unknown God!

Nikko chuckled. "No doubt on Heyertori we would have been seen as radicals in need of therapy. What do you think, Clemantine? Were we wrong? Or were we just less afraid?"

"It wasn't Heyertori that fell to the cult virus, Nikko. Did you people know what you were making?"

As soon as she said it, she wished she had not, but it was too late to take it back.

Nikko's voice hardened. "We didn't make the cult virus."

"I know. That was uncalled for."

"Whatever mistakes we made, we knew what counted. 'Fascist' was the worst name one kid could call another."

"I don't even know what that means." A submind brought her the fact: someone who would rule another by force. It was an evolved word, generalized from its original political meaning.

"The cult virus changed everything," Nikko continued. "It took away choice from everyone it infected. But not all of us succumbed. The species was too diverse by then. You see, without even planning it, we'd made our own resistance."

Did he really believe that? "Nikko, the cult virus can change too."

"Sure, but it won't beat us again. Not unless it's deliberately reengineered."

Urban had reached the halfway point. Clemantine watched him through the video feed delivered by the first drone. Then her gaze shifted to the courser and her heart leaped. "Nikko! What the hell is that?"

Urban fell toward the courser's gleaming hull, now fully illuminated, a blaze of glassy white. His eyes felt dazzled. He blinked. When he looked again, dark spots bloomed among the cells, puddles of blackness flowing in ever widening circles.

*Deneb!

*I see it.

She sounded far calmer than he felt. He waited for the blast of a laser, but it didn't come. Instead of expanding into lenses, the black circles took on a new dimension. They *emerged* from the courser's white surface in a badland of cone-shaped spikes.

Love and nature, Nikko breathed. *This can't be real.

The spikes grew taller, while their basal diameters continued to expand.

How tall?

Without easy references, size was difficult to gauge. More than his own height? Surely. Two or three times more, at least.

Make that four times. The courser's hull seemed to recede as Urban drew nearer. The spikes became gigantic.

Ten times, Urban thought. They stood apart from one another by a distance equal to no more than twice their height.

A glinting fog puffed into abrupt existence in the low points between the spikes where the hull cells still glowed. The fog flowed outward with impressive speed, as if propelled on an impossible wind. It swept toward them. Urban cried out, ducking his head and half turning, trying to get some shelter behind the shoulder of the go-pack. "Dodge that!" he shouted at the DI. Too late.

The fog enshrouded him. It danced in tiny sparkles against the visor of his hood. *Deneb!* he shouted. *Get out of the path of this fog!

Then it was past. He touched his visor, half expecting the transparent shield to collapse under the pressure of his gloved fingers. He imagined a microscopic war raging over the surface of his skin suit, as Chenzeme Makers overwhelmed his native nanotech defenses. Any moment now and his skin suit would begin to dissolve as the Chenzeme Makers took it apart, molecule by molecule. His go-pack would disassemble into dust.

The NoFears worked very hard.

His equipment held together.

He checked his back view. Deneb was just emerging from the fog.

There was no warning. Lot followed the usual run of obscure musings as they rose and fell within the awareness of the cell field. Then, like a scattered explosion, chaotic beats of excitement arose at once from ten thousand cell clusters. Waves of synchrony collapsed, and cacophony reigned, as an image of the approaching courser shunted between the cells.

<Other> Luminous now. Lot could not see it, but its gleam came to him in a chemical pattern that described the stunning white glow, and the foreign taste, and a sense of threat, and criticism, because Null Boundary's cells were blind and therefore deficient. Would they be culled?

Lot suffered a stirring of very human fear. *Wrong time for that,* he chided himself. Don't translate. *Be* Chenzeme. Vicious, cocky, defiant murderers.

He let his perceptions submerge, leaving fear to float like degrading oil on the surface of an empty and impenetrable sea.

"Holding together," Urban muttered, still not quite believing it. The go-pack fired a decelerating burst, so that he drifted slowly now toward one of the black spikes.

The spike's surface was smooth and very dark. Urban could see white light from the hull cells reflected in upward-reaching parabolic arches. Fainter lines of white flared downward from the spike's tip: that was Null Boundary's image, narrowed and smeared and replicated uncountable times. Urban could see now that the tip was rounded. Perhaps the size of his closed fist? Still too far away to tell.

He spoke to the go-pack's DI. The unit fired, pushing his descent closer to the tip. He wanted to get a good look at this thing.

Nikko's voice spoke sharply within his atrium. *Urban, you're drifting.

*It's all right.

"Closer," he urged the DI. It cautioned him. He overrode and the go-pack fired again, sending him toward the spike in a slow careen.

He had brought along a baton tipped with an analytical factory. Now he unstrapped it from his right forearm. He didn't switch it on—he had no desire to ignite a nanoscale war this early in their expedition—instead he would use it as a blunt instrument, to probe the texture of the spike.

Another droplet of NoFears fed into his bloodstream as he drew within arm's reach of the spike's rounded tip. He held the baton in a cautious grip. Then he laid it gingerly on the top of the spike.

In the instant of contact, the tip collapsed. It flattened like a piece of black cloth, then rippled around the baton and across his glove. All in the space of half a second.

Urban shouted an incoherent oath of surprise. He dropped the baton and yanked his hand back. The stuff stuck to his glove. It stretched, forming a thin, shiny, rubbery bridge, and then it stopped stretching. The baton had disappeared from sight. "Get it off!" he shouted at the suit DI. "Target: See it. Don't bond to it, you dumb scut."

The suit took an agonizing time to assess the situation. "Reconvene free fall?"

"Shit, yes!" His hand was being pulled overhead as his body continued to descend.

"Impediment clear," the suit assured him.

He felt the goo peel free from his gloved palm. He *felt* it, like a firm handshake giving way. He craned his neck, watching it. The stuff had wrapped around the back of his hand too. The suit hadn't bonded to it there, but still it held on to him. "Get it *all* off," he screamed at the suit.

He could feel his downward momentum weighing in the muscles of his arm. He could feel heat in his suit as its circulatory system pumped defensive Makers to the site.

So much for keeping their Makers out of the action.

His hand slid free. He felt himself slip. Or descend. (His body had never stopped descending.) He let go a rushing breath of relief, but he couldn't tell if his suit had wrested him free, or if the goop had let him go.

He looked up to see Deneb just overhead, close enough that he could recognize the fear in her eyes. He grinned at her. She couldn't see it behind his hood, but she could see his eyes through the thin arc of his visor. She must have extrapolated the rest. She looked briefly angry, then relieved, and then her eyes smiled back at him.

NoFears, he decided, was a wonderful thing.

Lot's awareness sprawled outward in a circular wave. He had no discrete location. He existed everywhere at once within an ocean of frantic debate, functioning as a multiple link in multiple wave paths that rose in fierce crests—

Fight now./*It threatens.*/**Kill it!**

—only to be canceled in the troughs of opposing paths:

(Other compatible.) / <excitation> / **Make peace.**

The taste of the Well ran through it all, flavoring every propensity with a disquieting sense of newness—and a flexible strength. The cells could poison the courser if they chose; they could slaughter its cell field. Some desired this.

(Suppress that.)
Agreement: Suppress that. Identify collective/me.
(We are Chenzeme.)
Negate that: We are newness. We are incomplete.
(Suppress that: We are Chenzeme.)

Above all else, the cells *must* accept themselves as true Chenzeme. Only when armed with that certainty would they be able to defy an admonition from the courser. Lot had not forgotten that first demand for suicide or submission. So he strove to press the identity codes. Slam them. Throw them. Eject them at velocity.

(We are Chenzeme.)
\<Identify: We are Chenzeme\>
Collective/me are Chenzeme.

The taste of the Well belied that. It was everywhere, in every wave path, an irresistible influence demanding consensus in the field. Aggressive cells readied the poison dust, only to discard it; readied it and discarded it, as this new instinct dampened innate Chenzeme aggression—and nurtured Chenzeme doubt:

Identify: We are newness. We are incomplete.
(We are stronger.)

Strong enough not to kill. Let the field embrace that. Strong enough to wrest a settlement from the courser, and to infect it with the wisdom of the Well. Cooperation was better than conflict.

(We are stronger.)
Identify.
(Our strength is Chenzeme.)
False Chenzeme.
(Negate that.)

The wave paths split, then split again.

^	^
Collective/me are not complete.	**\<excitation\> Go: Self/other exchange.**
\<revulsion\> Collective/me are deficient.	(Offer: Integration.)
(Negate revulsion. Collective/me are Chenzeme.)	***Negate offer. Kill it.***
\<reinforce revulsion\> False Chenzeme.	(Negate that. Assemble packet: All of collective/me.)
\<agreement\> Collective/me incomplete. The other is complete.	**\<excitation\> Go: Packet preparation.**
(The other is weak. Collective/me are strong.)	***No go. Kill it.***
\<agreement\> The other is	(Negate that: Collective/me are stronger Chenzeme.)

weak. Collective/me are
incomplete.
<revulsion> The other is weak.
Collective/me are incomplete.
(Synthesis: Our strength, its
completeness.)
<agreement> A synthesis. Our
strength is Chenzeme.
<revulsion> False Chenzeme.
(Negate revulsion.
Collective/me are stronger
Chenzeme.)
<agreement> We are stronger
Chenzeme.

<agreement> Go: Open
receptors.
(Open receptors.
Self/other exchange.)
<excitation> Go:
Exchange.
Caution.
Collective/me are
Chenzeme.
<agreement> Go:
Collective/me are
stronger Chenzeme.

<AGREEMENT>

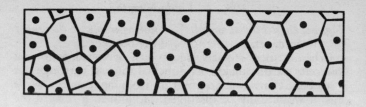

Chapter
11

"Don't touch down," Urban muttered, as the go-pack brought him closer to the courser's white hull. The black spikes towered overhead. If the courser's hull cells behaved like Null Boundary's, they would try to bond to anything that contacted them. Despite his brief skirmish with the spike, Urban was not at all confident his defensive Makers would win such a confrontation. Better to avoid the cells, at least for now.

His elevation dropped to six meters. The go-pack's DI fired steady, decelerating streams from several gallcries of micronozzles. Urban's descent slowed. The micronozzles continued to fire, synchronizing his trajectory with that of the courser so that he floated a stable two and a half meters above its glistening field of hull cells, even as it continued to advance toward Null Boundary.

Urban studied the shipscape so close below him. The courser's cell field looked exactly like Null Boundary's hull cells . . . except for the spikes. In his atrium he scanned an image of Null Boundary—and felt startled at its proximity. Had the gap between the two ships closed so much already?

Nikko descended alongside him. His gaze—always so directionless—rubbed past Urban as if he were not there.

Sight-seeing? Nikko asked. *Or will you release the bugs?* Then he took off, soaring toward the bow.

Urban bristled. He saw Deneb pass overhead, following Nikko forward. Quickly, he punched the first cartridge out of his belt. There was no point in dropping it on the white cells; it would only be dissolved. He lobbed it toward the black surface of the nearest spike instead. It hit hard, but it didn't bounce, cracking open as it sank into the tissue of the spike.

He looked again for Nikko and found him some three spikes away, moving rapidly and about to disappear behind one of the monoliths. Holding his gaze steady on Nikko's position, Urban snapped at his go-pack: "Target. See it. Mark and pursue."

The go-pack fired, pushing him on a trajectory that wove between the spikes. Creaks and hisses were audible inside his hood at every course correction. The DI was doing its best to conserve fuel, so the corrections were minimal. He found himself slicing past the spikes with inches to spare. Once, he thought he saw the shimmer of another fog all around him, but when he blinked, it was gone.

He saw the real thing seconds later. A vapor emerged again from the deck beneath his feet. He responded quickly, popping another cartridge from his waist. He cracked the cartridge just as the fog caught him, then lobbed it in a line along the vapor's path, hoping to match course and speed.

He didn't wait to see if the maneuver succeeded. Ahead of him, Nikko and Deneb had slowed. They drifted near the end of one of the longitudinal ridges that had been visible from Null Boundary. Like the rest of the hull, the rounded back of the low ridge was covered with a membrane of philosopher cells. It looked like the housing for some sort of vent system. Urban hurried to catch up.

As he drew near, he saw Nikko remove a bug cartridge from a pocket on his chest-pack. Nikko let the cartridge drift a moment, then he used the flat of his hand to slap it toward a dark—membrane?—a black circle nestled within the end of the low ridge. The cartridge spun into the dark space and vanished.

How far in does it go? Urban asked.

Deneb said, *We can't tell.*

Let me look. Urban instructed his go-pack to invert his

position. The glowing deck beneath his feet became a roof overhead. He shunted close to the vent, bumping against Nikko.

Take it easy, Nikko warned, retreating on a burst from a gallery of side jets that Urban could feel as a feathery brush across his arm.

Now Urban had a clear view. He peered inside. There was only blackness. He couldn't tell if it was a black surface or empty, lightless space. If it was a black surface, the cartridge would have stuck to it.

He took a flashlight out of a hip pocket and flicked it on. The beam fell upon a flat surface that shimmered with motion, as if a debris-filled stream had been diverted to run between two plates of glass. The cracked-open cartridge lodged against it.

Urban flinched at a touch on his shoulder. The skin suit communicated the sensation perfectly: the hard, cold tap of Nikko's prehensile toes. Urban ducked his head to glare. Nikko drifted in front of him, above the vent housing, oriented opposite to Urban. With his toes, he touched the torch strapped to Urban's forearm. *Do you want the honors? Or shall I . . . ?*

I'll do it, Urban growled. He yanked the torch out of its straps.

Clemantine's voice cut into his sensorium. *Urban! Don't use the torch. Think for a minute about what might happen.*

Urban hesitated, perplexed by this demand. *I don't have any idea what might happen.*

Anything could happen, Clemantine told him. *You could cut open a venom sack.*

Not likely, Nikko countered. *If there are assault Makers here, they'll be stored as harmless components.*

What if the components mix?

Nikko said, *We left our patterns on the ship.*

And we have to try, Deneb added.

Urban glanced down past his boots to see Null Boundary, set in the void like a lost crystal of white ice. *Clemantine, you know this is our best chance.* He summoned another drop of NoFears. Then he ignited the torch. A thin haze of dust spewed from it to show the path of the blue beam. He raised it and slashed across the membrane.

Dust sprayed forth, and then drops of liquid. Some of the stuff hit his visor. He didn't blink. The NoFears was working fine.

*Get out of there, Urban, Clemantine urged. *Back off until it clears.

*Too late for that, I think. Urban shook his head, sending dust and ice crystals flying. When the debris cleared, he could see a cut across the center of the membrane. The raw edges curled and seeped in complex patterns of hoarfrost.

Clemantine said: *Urban, if you're going to do it, do it right. Cut it away at the perimeter.

Urban scowled. *Clem? I thought you were going to keep radio silence? He grinned to himself. She hated it when he called her Clem.

Of course he had planned to do as she suggested. He aimed the torch again, playing it across the top and bottom of the membrane to cut it clean away. Steam sprayed from the severed edges, crystallizing into flakes of dirty snow.

Nikko pushed in close again . . . now that immediate danger seemed past? *What's left? he asked.

Urban leaned into the vent to look, impressed at his own calm, even if it was artificially achieved. "Damn. It's still blocked."

A plug of gray tissue filled the space that had lain behind the membrane. Urban touched the material. He ran his gloved fingers along a seam down its middle. The glove reproduced the texture for his fingertips. Slick and smooth and . . . slightly yielding? Like a water-filled cushion. He pressed his fingers against the seam, and to his astonishment, it parted just far enough that his hand could slide into the gap.

*Love and nature, Nikko whispered.

*It's okay. Look. He slid his hand back out again. *This is a collapsed tube. There is no empty space, but there is a passage.

Nikko gingerly touched the surface while Urban popped a bug cartridge out of his belt. Holding on to it, he slid his hand into the seam once again. He could feel semisoft papillae lining the interior walls. They wriggled under his touch. He cracked the cartridge.

Let me get a look, Deneb said, but neither of them moved aside. *Urban?*

How far did the collapsed tube run?

There were two ways to find out. He could wait for the robotic bugs to return (*if* they returned). Or he could go himself. The tube was big enough.

He pulled his hand out once more, then examined the site carefully. Nikko looked at him, his blue eyes distorted behind their protective lenses. *What are you thinking?*

This is our way in.

And you call me crazy.

You coming?

If a word could sound bitten and mauled, this one did: *Yes.*

I'm coming too, Deneb said.

Urban gave Nikko a warning look. *You can't,* he told Deneb. He pulled a coil of wire from a thigh pocket. *Look here.* Holding the wire, he gestured at the burned rim. *The membrane's already growing back. You'll have to stay here with the torch, keep it clear.*

Deneb didn't answer right away. Then, in a wary voice, *Nikko can stay.*

I'm not staying, Nikko said. The black straps of his go-pack peeled away from his scaled hide as he uncoupled from the device.

Deneb glared at him. *But that's not fair! Why do you get to go?*

Nikko didn't answer. Urban thought it best to stay quiet too, and to move fast. He plugged one end of the wire into a jack in his go-pack, the other into a jack in his suit. Deneb continued to argue. *Urban, I know more about zero point systems than either one of you.*

That's what the wire's for, Urban said. *You'll see everything we see.* He tossed her the torch, sending it deliberately over her shoulder. She had to grab for it. *Urban, you prick. You planned it this way, didn't you?*

"Hark," Urban said to his go-pack. "Uncouple."

The DI argued, but Urban overrode. "Uncouple!" This time the straps withdrew. Once again, he was conscious of the harsh pounding of his heart. *Clementine?*

Here.

*Retrieve the go-packs if you can. They'll come to your voice.

*Damn you, Urban. You'll retrieve them yourselves. She sounded as angry as Deneb.

He exchanged another glance with Nikko. Then he slid both hands into the seam, dug his fingers deep into the nest of papillae, put his head down, and tugged. The walls gave way and he slid in, feeling like a piece of shit moving the wrong way up an ass.

Once inside, the tube walls squeezed hard all around him, but he could breathe. He could move through it. He reached forward, secured a grip, and pulled. He felt his legs slide into the passage.

*Urban? That was Deneb's voice.

*I'm okay, he told her. He couldn't see anything, though, even when he blinked down to infrared vision. The tunnel walls pressed against his visor and he could not focus. He reached forward, secured another grip, and pulled again.

*Okay, Nikko said. *I'm coming in behind you.

They worked their way forward. Perhaps a hundred yards of wire had reeled out when Urban felt the tug of a gravitational gradient—wispy at first, but climbing rapidly in strength as he advanced.

*Feel that? Nikko asked. *It's the zero point drive.

*Sooth. It made him remember the passage of Null Boundary through the eye of the swan burster, when Nikko had made his wild dash out of Deception Well. This was less extreme, like a gentle tweaking, a twitch of soft fingers against his ears, his cheeks, his scalp. He could feel it shifting even when he did not move. Flexing and erratic: it didn't have the feel of a process truly under control.

A heat kick told him another microsphere of NoFears had opened.

Urban chuckled. Were his maintenance systems trying to tell him he was terrified? Duh.

He pressed on, cramming his head and shoulders into the reluctantly expanding tube, still feeling as if he were crawling up the ass of the Unknown God, against a current of random peristalsis squeezing and flexing the structure of space-time. His hair stood on end. It was a tidal effect. His scalp pulled away from his skull. Blood pooled in the bone/flesh interstice. He heard a hoarse scream from Nikko at the same time that pain flared across his own sensorium. It lasted brief seconds, before his medical Makers overrode, shutting down the nerve paths. *Nikko?*

Okay now, came the panting reply.

I don't think we have much time.

Then hurry.

The pain had been a warning from their medical Makers. Pain would return if they continued to expose their bodies to damage. Pain was the ancient motivator, and like most ancient scripts, it was highly effective.

But Urban was spared the need for immediate decision. The tidal pressure eased. The field flattened. He pushed on, powered by NoFears. He wondered what Nikko was using.

After another minute he noticed light seeping through the walls. It brightened and dimmed, flowing in lagging echo to the tidal flux, following by a second and a fraction. As he advanced, the light brightened generally, until it blazed so bright he could feel it as a pressure. He could feel its passion in the walls. Twitch, twitch. Shudder.

Ovaries, he thought. And he sent the thought to Nikko: *We need to find an equivalent to ovaries.*

Some structure that contained not only the blueprint of this pulsing ass, but also the machinery to construct it.

Now a thing happened that Urban found almost sufficiently unsettling to negate the NoFears. The walls that had pressed against him for so long fell abruptly out of existence, replaced by a fast-flowing river of light. Behind him, he heard Nikko gasp.

It's just a perceptual shift, Urban said. *An illusion.*

Fuck that, Nikko panted.

But Urban believed it, at least on an intellectual level. Still, the walls had vanished and he felt as if he were swimming now, not crawling, up a pulsing, flowing white/white-shadowed river that pushed at him and pulled at him and made his hair stand up—even the hair on his arms—pulled at his skin too, at his gut.

White shadows shot through the streaming white light like darting fish. White shadows. He could think of them in no other way. They were knots of force, points of denser structure whipping past him, around him, impacting him in dizzying blows of gut-wrenching inequilibrium. Reality spiked, and for a moment he was somewhere else. Somewhen, when he had not taken NoFears. He screamed in utter, abject panic.

Then plunged back into the realm of NoFears, and the cry cut off.

*Urban?

That was Deneb's voice. Did the cable still trail behind him? The pressure of this environment would not let him turn his head to see. And yet there were no walls.

He reached a hand into the current ahead of him. His hand stretched and swelled, growing longer than his forearm, longer than his body. He pulled it back slowly, watching it shrink.

*Urban! Deneb called again, more urgent now. *Something's happening out here. The tidal gradient is increasing. I think the courser's begun to accelerate.

*Get back to Null Boundary, Nikko ordered her.

Urban felt a wrench of muffled panic. *Yes, Deneb. Go back.

*Send your ghosts to me first, she pleaded. *Both of you.

A pressure wave swept over him. The light squeezed his body, bearing down so hard he could not breathe or even blink. His heart felt crushed, its pulse reduced to an erratic flutter.

His atrium functioned. He used it to weave his ghost. That at least could escape along the wire. He would have images of this place to fill the head of a copy that would grow in the amorphous tissue of Null Boundary's interstices. If Null Boundary lived.

Damn.

He wanted more than images of this place. He wanted to get out. And he wanted a trophy.

*Urban, send your ghost, Deneb pleaded. *Hurry.

*Here, he thought impatiently. *Here. It's coming.

The electronic pattern uploaded, the code that could be translated into a thinking copy of his persona, with all his memories intact. It took most of the energy in his blood-starved brain to send it.

*I'm going to get out of here.

*I know, Urban. Try. Hurry.

He could not blink. But his hand lay at least six inches in front of his face. It was another world there. The pressure was less. The muscles in that hand were blood-starved too, but they were not frozen.

His vision was fading. His chest felt as if it would collapse in on itself, fall into the dark space of his struggling heart and disappear forever.

Out of the wasting light he saw another white shadow riding toward him on the current. He watched it, and when it drew near he raised two fingers and he swiped at it—

—the light grew dim and at the same time fierce, as if it had shifted to a higher wavelength that he could not see, almost invisible now, but unrelenting—

—the white shadow caught on his fingers and shattered, scattered. Did bits of it catch on the hot zone of his glove? His glove seemed far away, though it was drawing closer rapidly. Very rapidly.

Darkness plunged around him, and the pressure cracked with the abruptness of breaking glass. He felt himself spinning. His heart thundered in his ears while minute streaks of light swirled around him, round and round.

Something bumped against him. Something absorbed him, and he found himself cradled again in the armature of his go-pack. It stabilized his tumble, resolving the streaking lights into stars.

Had he been ejected from the tube, then? Shot outside?

Panic interrupted his confusion. He couldn't see Null Boundary or the Chenzeme courser. He couldn't see anything but stars. *Deneb!* he screamed. *Nikko!*

She's okay. Nikko's silky bass voice was edged with dark amusement. *You're secure in your pack?*

Yeah. What—?

Look back at the courser, Urban. Turn around and look at it. Clemantine? You're watching this, I trust.

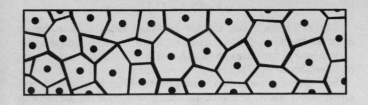

Chapter 12

Clemantine felt sick as she watched Urban and then Nikko disappear into the vent tube. She wanted to snatch them back. She wanted to grab a sissy-hatch and make the VR run stop-right-now.

(No sissy-hatch this time, dear).

What are we doing here?

She wanted to close her eyes. Instead, she forced herself to watch the courser's hideous, black-spiked image. Her skin crawled at the nearness of the thing. Her fingers twitched. The drone go-packs were over their target zones. With a brief command she could drop them against the cells and let them adhere. She could order an explosion at any time. Or she could let the cells do the work. Within thirty hours of contact, the cells would dissolve the bombs' protective coatings. The first nuke to be breached would send a signal to ignite the second. Their explosions would be simultaneous and devastating.

Patience. Urban was not dead yet. She awaited his return, barely breathing.

"Lot's heart rate has climbed over a hundred twenty." Nikko's anxious report interrupted her thoughts. "His temperature's up, and his brain activity is off the scale."

"Has he lost control?"

"I can't tell, and he may be too far under to know when it's time to call it off."

Lot could not be regrown.

Clemantine's gaze sliced across the gallery of images displayed on the core chamber's wall: Deneb, drifting just above the courser's hull; the courser's crazy interior; its farside, as seen from the first drone go-pack. There were none of the horrible spikes on the farside. The only two spots of darkness there were the waiting silhouettes of the armed go-packs. Clemantine's fingers clenched under a tidal wash of fury.

What had they agreed to by being here? Nikko called it a mating.

A good term, that. Aloud, she growled, "This intersection is obscene."

Nikko huffed. "It's far less obscene than dying."

That was bitter truth. What choice did they have? They had not invited the dark courser to attend them. . . .

She blinked hard, not liking the doubt that suddenly nested in her mind. Was it possible they *had* invited the courser? In truth, she did not know what Lot had said or done while ensconced within the hull cells. She shook her head, but she could not banish the taint of doubt.

"Did Lot call it here?" she asked, surprising herself with the question.

Perhaps she'd surprised Nikko too. He took a moment to answer. Reviewing his records? "No," he said at last. "It must have begun its pursuit decades ago."

The cell colony had been extant for twenty-two years.

Nikko said: "You can't blame Lot for this. If he hadn't given us the philosopher cells, we'd already be dead. This courser would have come out of the dark and killed us before we knew it was there."

So Lot had bought them a chance at life. But at what cost?

The dead far outnumbered the living, billions of lives gone to the blind ravages of these things. Now they must lie down with it? Spread their legs to it? Let it cast its semen all across the hull of Null Boundary? Infect this ship with ever more of the Chenzeme nature?

What else can we do?

She watched the slow approach of the black-spiked obscenity. A sense of corruption ran like mordant fluids between her cells, a floodwater that sluiced through the streets of a dark city populated by hordes of anonymous dead.

What else can we do but let the past go?

A billion faceless wraiths from Heyertori alone. The floodwaters washed over them. The city dissolved. She stared at her fingers, seeking the old rage, but it would not come. Her inner landscape had become a flat and empty sea where all choices were the same choice and so there was no choice at all.

The cult virus took away choice.

Fascist.

She wished the dead would cry out, or rise or make objection. Instead she felt a new resolve move inside her, an approving wind that rippled the tarry surface of her polluted sea, stirring a pattern out of her emptiness, a new arrangement of molecules. She did not want to change. She had made herself around the pattern of the past. *And if you can't let that go are you any more alive than the dissolving wraiths?*

She raised her eyes to glare again at the courser: this startling field of black-spiked white. Was it changing? She stared at it. No longer was it a mere mechanical horror. Its shape was shifting. It had begun to take on organic lines.

"Nikko!" she cried in scandalized surprise. A subtle contortion had formed along its length, as if it had begun a slow bend into a helix, bow and stern twisting over toward Null Boundary's hull. "Nikko, what's wrong with the image?"

"Nothing!" he said fiercely.

"But it's warped." It must be the image. Ships could not twist like turning snakes.

"It's not the image," Nikko said. "It's the courser."

Then Deneb's panicked voice cried out in Clemantine's sensorium. *Something's happening out here. The tidal gradient is increasing. . . .*

Nikko said: "Look at the farside."

Clemantine's gaze shifted to the image from the drone go-pack. On the courser's farside, steerage jets that had not existed a moment before were blazing now in sudden, asynchronous fury, a lateral line of fire driving the vessel sideways toward Null Boundary.

Send your ghosts to me, Deneb was pleading. *Both of you.*

"Nikko," Clemantine muttered. "You've got to get yourself out of there. Get Urban—"

A blue/gold projectile shot out of the vent. It slammed past Deneb, striking the shoulder of her go-pack, sending her spinning across the plain of the courser's hull as it broke up into distinct blue and gold figures. Clemantine shot a command to the go-packs to pursue. "Deneb, get out of there!" she shouted at the same time. "Back to Null Boundary, now!"

Urban started screaming. Nikko jabbered in her atrium. Clemantine understood nothing. All she could do was watch in fascination as the courser's forward quarter continued to bend and rotate, until it achieved an angle of almost thirty degrees, twisting over toward Null Boundary, its gallery of spikes ready to impale the ship. Abaft, the courser mirrored these contortions, so that it spiraled around Null Boundary in an armed and obscene helix. "By the Unknown God," Clemantine whispered. "It's going to crush us."

Surely there were more efficient ways to kill?

Urban looked past the toes of his boots to the exhaust vents at Null Boundary's stern, hoping Nikko would not panic and ignite the engines in some wild attempt at escape. Escape didn't seem likely.

Urban's own position was momentarily secure. He'd been ejected along the courser's long axis. After the go-pack caught him, it damped his momentum, but it dumped a lot of propellant to do it. Its size had shrunk accordingly. Urban no longer felt like an invincible warrior android. As he drifted alongside the courser's immense hull, he simply felt damn small.

Still, he had enough propellant to get back. The DI assured him of that, though the trip would take several hours after a brief acceleration drained the last reserves of the pack. Not a problem, really. Urban was more concerned with whether there would be any place to go back to. He decided to conserve resources until the question was answered. For now, he would hang back and watch the show.

Nikko and Deneb must have reached similar conclusions. The DI pinpointed their locations for him as two closely spaced red points on his visual field. He could hear Deneb whispering incoherently as the courser twisted itself in a spiral around Null Boundary. The black spikes reached for the ship with their pliant tips, advancing with excruciating slowness.

Urban watched with neutral interest. The quantity of NoFears in his system had left him numb to real worry, but his curiosity was intact.

The spikes touched first at the bow. Urban expected to see the hull dissolve beneath them. Perhaps it was dissolving, but on a timescale he could not perceive. For now the spikes appeared to latch on, attaching one after the other, starting from the bow and continuing through the stern.

Null Boundary looked like a fly pinned within the sticky spikes of a predatory sundew.

A babble of panicked voices erupted in Urban's atrium. He did not try to distinguish them. Beside him, the wall of the courser flexed, as a wave front rippled past. There were no spikes here.

Urban realized he was sweating within his skin suit. Why? He didn't feel any fear. He wondered if the suit's thermal regulator was failing.

Ahead of him, the courser ceased to move. Had it settled down to feed? The babble on the radio was indecipherable; Urban suspected he'd pushed the NoFears too hard.

He wriggled uncomfortably, feeling like his skin suit was about to slide away on a lubricating layer of sweat. The motion caused light to glint in the corner of his eye. He glanced down the length of his body, and again he caught a glint of light. It came from the palm of his right glove. He turned that hand back and forth. Tiny dots of blazing white flashed on the edge of perception. He held his palm close to his visor and squinted.

Between the dots of light he could just make out points of motion within the velvety surface of the hot zone.

"It's going to collide with us." Clemantine stared wide-eyed at the courser's contorting image. "It's going to hit us."

"I'd say so," Nikko agreed.

"*Move* us, then. No. Wait."

A blue glow ignited in a strip along the near side of the courser's hull, threading between the horrible spikes. More steerage jets, she decided, but these were situated to reverse the courser's momentum, to slow it down. "What the hell is going on, Nikko?"

"I don't know."

The first spike touched. Clemantine watched its progress via the feed from Deneb's go-pack. She expected to hear the crunch of the collapsing hull; the scream of alarms. Instead, she heard only a faint groan from Null Boundary's skeletal structure.

"The hull is heating up," Nikko announced as more spikes touched down, their pliant tips splashing in circles across the white cells. "The colony's metabolic rate is climbing."

Clemantine could hear a reverberant hum as Null Boundary's frame flexed and strained. Nikko called it a mating. Sooth. Clemantine felt as if she'd been tied down in a rape rack.

A new thought lanced this sullen contemplation. "Lot's out there. Nikko, pull him out! Get him out, before the courser crushes him."

<AGREEMENT>

Agreement equaled acquiescence. Calmness fell upon the field. The amplitude of debate declined, but not its frequency. <Agreement> echoed in intense ripples of short wavelength, bearing the same hammering message over and over again:

Open receptors. Receive self/other exchange.

The field blazed with metabolic heat.

(Synthesis: our strength, its completeness.)

There was no longer any choice. The peacekeeping protocols of the Well permeated every dialogue; the influence of the Well was replicated in every packet of dust readied by the cells. Cooperation was better than conflict: this was the new instinct acquired in the Well. It had been layered over old behavior, a brake on the loop of automatic Chenzeme aggression. A gift for the other.

(We are superior Chenzeme.)
<Agreement>

"Lot?"

More dust fell across the field. It was tasted, analyzed, shared.

Ready.

"Lot. Listen to me. Answer me now, or I'm taking you out."

Anxiety slipped forth from a single node.

"Last chance, Lot. Answer me now, or I'm going to cut you out."

The words acted like hooks, yanking his awareness back to some unstable surface. Lot blinked, astounded at his own discrete existence. "Nikko?" Cells seeped away from his lips. His exposed skin felt raw, and brittle. "Can't talk now, Nikko. Go away."

He tried to sink back into phase, but the spider on his ear continued to babble its untenable demands. "Listen, Lot—"

"Nikko, shut up!" Fury exploded from him in a wave front that swept across the cells, eroding the careful structure of <agreement>. Lot recoiled in horror. "You're wrecking it. God damn you, Nikko, go away!"

"Lot, it's over. The courser's coming in to crush us. We've got a chance in the core, but if you stay out there, you'll be the first to die."

Die? The cells were calming again, repairing their consensus. Lot felt soothed by this restoration of harmony. "It's not like that, Nikko. Self/other exchange. We are Chenzeme."

"The hell you are!"

"Cut him out now." That was Clemantine.

"No!" Lot's fingers clutched at the tissue of the wound, as if he could hold on to the cells that contained him. "Don't wreck it. Please. We can win this."

"You are not Chenzeme," Nikko insisted.

Lot wrestled with an overwhelming confusion. The cell field tugged at him. He could not exist in both worlds at once. "Please just leave me alone. We need this synthesis. The other is weak, and primitive, but it is complete. We are naive, but we are stronger. We will take its knowledge. We will give it ours. We will teach it not to kill."

"Not to . . . ?" Clemantine echoed, sounding mystified.

"Not to kill," Lot repeated. The peacekeeping instinct of the Well ran through the cells. It ran through him, resonating with the cult hunger nestling in his belly. *(We are superior Chenzeme.)* "We will teach the other. It will teach others in turn."

"You can't kill it, then?" she asked.

"We can." *(Negate that.)* "We won't though."

"Why not?"

"We are superior Chenzeme."

"Love and nature," Nikko swore. "I'm taking him out before we lose him altogether."

"No, wait." Clemantine's voice sounded high, and strained. "If he can teach it peace . . . that's a poisonous idea, for a Chenzeme ship. It's one more weapon for us. We have so few. And we don't know if any will work."

Lot didn't understand this at all, but he would use it. "She's right. Let me stay."

Clemantine added: "He won't be directly beneath any of the spikes."

"Lot, I can't let you—" But then Nikko caught himself. "All right. You can stay—but just for now."

Hey, Urban said, to no one in particular. *The bugs made it back. Some of them anyway. Deneb? Check the hot zones on your gloves. Did any return to you?*

The suit DI had confirmed the identity of the moving specks. Now Urban watched as the tiny devices migrated across his glove. He could not see them directly, but he could follow their progress through the disturbance they made in the glove's velvety hot zone. They avoided the blazing specks of white light that dotted his palm.

He queried the DI on why the bugs were moving. It could not answer him. Neither could it explain the source of excess heat that had him stewing within his skin suit.

Deneb's voice interrupted his contemplations, comprehensible at last through the dulling fog of the NoFears. *Urban, get your ass out of there!* she screamed at him. *Move now or you're going to be a smear when the courser's tail turns over.*

Urban thought she might be exaggerating. He glanced up, to see the aft wall of the courser sweeping toward him with unsettling speed as it completed its spiral closure around Null Boundary. Maybe she was right.

He spoke to his go-pack. Select galleries of microjets fired. He felt a feather-brush of acceleration, and slowly— so very slowly—he rose above the plane in which Null Boundary lay.

Faster, Urban! Deneb shouted. *Empty your pack if you have to. Don't worry about getting back. We'll get you. We'll bring you back.*

Sweat dripped into his eyes. He shook his head, silently cursing the suit for not keeping up with the excess moisture. When he looked again, the wall of the courser loomed uncomfortably close. "Get me out of here," he muttered to the go-pack. "All fuel, as needed."

The feather-push changed to a solid thump. Given the nearness of the approaching wall, Urban would have preferred a more dramatic acceleration, but the DI had completed its calculations with neat precision. His feet rose past the curving plane of the courser's hull a moment before it crossed his line of flight. The luminous cells glided by, just inches beneath his stirrups.

His acceleration ceased, though he continued to fall away across the back of the courser . . . and away from Deneb too, he noted with disappointment. Beneath him, the bright and unbending hull of Null Boundary lay wrapped within a single turn of an impossible helix formed by the courser's long hull. The black spikes had become columns that pinned the ships together. Urban gazed on the union in breathless silence, waiting for the collapse of Null Boundary's hull.

Adjust your course, Urban. Deneb's voice reached him now with unblemished clarity. *You're drifting away from us.*

Urban spoke to the DI. Then: *Sorry, Deneb. I'm empty.*

She hissed. *That's all right. I'll come get you.*

Already Urban forgot to worry. *Look,* he said, as an

anomaly caught his eye. *There's another spike emerging from the courser. See? There on the farside, near the stern.*

His angle of view improved as he drifted farther out and he decided he was wrong. It wasn't a spike. It was the tortoiseshell back of a go-pack, caught by the sticky grip of the courser's hull cells.

Quickly, he rechecked Deneb's and Nikko's locations. They both remained at a safe distance from the courser. Then he remembered the drone go-pack. Had it been swept up by the courser's motion?

But the courser had moved *away* from the drone's position.

Urban frowned, his thoughts clicking over a little more efficiently now. It occurred to him to check his view options. The feed from the drone go-pack confirmed its position beyond the courser's farside.

Clemantine? He framed his own go-pack's feed in a red line for emphasis. *Where did this other pack come from?*

Lot felt the presence of the courser in his body, a trembling communicated to him from Null Boundary's stressed hull. Dust poured down upon the cells, an information transfer too fast to process. Their own dust was made and offered, made and offered, filled with the heresies of the Well.

Lot no longer paid attention to it. Exhaustion tugged at him. Hunger clawed at his belly. It made him remember himself, and from there he remembered other needs. They would never be closer than this to the zero point drive. So he set out to find it.

Breathing slowly through a mask of frozen cells, he sank within a froth of new dialogues tentatively exploring the data flood. He sampled a thread, followed it a moment, rejected it and switched to another, then another, touching on thousands every second, seeking some clue to the connection between the cell field (Chenzeme mind) and the zero point technology (Chenzeme muscle). Each thread of rejected dialogue was a ladder step away from the known, until dialogue ceased and process took over. Seeds sifted past him: independent packets of information that sprouted roots in the cell field, growing branches in a direction he could not quite conceive. He felt the alien nature of this new life-form, and he recoiled.

The ships had been linked three hours. In the zero gravity of the core Clemantine became convinced she would drown in the film of her own nervous perspiration. She had placed the nukes against the courser's hide when collision and her own ensuing death seemed imminent. Had she made a mistake? The nukes would blow in thirty hours when their shells eroded. Nothing could stop that. But what if Null Boundary remained coupled to the courser when that time arrived?

This thought made her realize survival again loomed as a possibility.

She brushed at the sweat collected around her eyes. The courser had not moved since linking to Null Boundary. Dust had flowed between the ships for several minutes, but that had long since ceased. There was an eerie quality to this stillness. Something must be happening. But what?

"Clemantine?"

She startled at Lot's voice, emerging from a speaker on the chamber wall.

"Nikko?" he asked next.

Nikko responded first. "Go ahead."

"There's . . . something new being seeded among the philosopher cells. A different *kind* of thing. Not at all like the cells. It's *other*. Alien. We support it though. It's like . . . part of us, but it's not *us*."

"It could be the spikes," Clemantine said. Lot sounded so much calmer now, utterly human.

Nikko asked, "Can you see it?"

"No. I can only sense it. Maybe it's microscopic. Or maybe it hasn't reached the wound yet. It is growing."

Clemantine fought a sickening resurgence of fear. "Lot, I want you out of there."

To her surprise, he didn't argue. "Sooth. Check for contamination though, before you bring me in."

Nikko's ghost pulled Lot out, then sent an army of defensive Makers swarming over him. At the same time,

Nikko's incarnate version moved in from his position beyond the two ships. He slipped into the space between them—a weird white hallway columned in heavy black pillars—to explore the attachment of the spikes. They had penetrated the cell colony, shoving it aside as if it were a stiff cloth, so that the once smooth field was marred now with thousands of minute wrinkles.

Nikko released bugs into the spikes' black tissue. They returned a few minutes later, confirming Lot's report of something new. A thin zone of foreign tissue had formed beneath the philosopher cells, distinct from the cell membrane, a metabolically active layer that fed on the ship's hull tissues. Defensive Makers rushed to isolate it.

In the core, a transit bubble opened. Clemantine turned, to see Lot drop out of it. Fear twisted a cold hand in her gut when she saw the blood that seeped from his sensory tears. Holes peppered his skin suit, as if he'd been caught in a spray of strong acid. Red wounds glared wherever his skin had been exposed. He looked at Clemantine, his face drawn and exhausted—but with relief in his eyes. "Looks like I'm clean," he said.

Hours of barely contained terror burned off in an instant, heating her mood to some unbearable consummation of joy and anger, relief and frustration. She dove at him, startling him with a furious hug that drove them both against the wall. "Lot, you shit! I didn't think I'd ever see you again, and damn all the Chenzeme anyway, even the one in your dense and pretty head."

"Hey!" Lot protested, while they bounced across the chamber to hit the wall again. "Ow. That hurts. Take it easy." But he laughed as he said it. He held her close.

At their next impact, Clemantine hooked a foot under a loop that stretched and stretched, swallowing their momentum. Drops of blood wobbled in the air between them. The smell of his blood and his sweat was good to her, a confirmation of life. His life. "You look like hell," she growled fiercely, her lips close to his ear while her hands cradled his head, her fingers bedded in the stubble of his blond hair. "And you scared me. What was that shit? 'We are Chenzeme.' God, I thought we'd lost you."

"I know. I'm sorry. I was in deep." He pulled back, just far enough to look her in the eye. "Are you okay?"

"Sooth." His skin felt so cold.

"And the others?"

"Still out there." She swiped at another drop of blood oozing from his cheek, making him flinch as her fingertip slid across a sensory tear. She did it again. God, what he put her through. "It's not over yet," she warned, looking past his shoulder at multiple images of the courser.

Lot turned to follow her gaze. He stiffened in her arms. *"By the Unknown God,"* he whispered. "Is that what it looks like? And we're still alive."

"You're damn right we are." She didn't want to let him go. She would hold on to him forever if she could, and hurt him some more, or love him, she couldn't tell. But he pushed her arms away, kicking the wall to extricate himself. He glided across the chamber to stare first at the feed from a hull camera, then from Urban's go-pack, and then Deneb's. From all perspectives, Null Boundary was helpless prey in the courser's grasp.

He grabbed a handgrip and turned back to Clemantine, looking puzzled, and a little guilty too. Her fist closed. She clenched her teeth, waiting for him to say it was all worth it—but what he said was worse. "I'm glad I didn't see this happening. I might have tried to stop it."

"Don't you tell me that now."

"I'm glad I didn't see it. Cooperation *is* better, Clemantine. You have to understand, that courser will never be ordinary Chenzeme again, now that it carries the viral thoughts of the Well."

Her breath quickened. "Then you really could have poisoned it—and stopped all this?"

"Sooth. I didn't want to, though."

"*Damn* you, Lot! That's Urban out there, and Deneb, and Nikko. We may not get them back. We might not get away. And you didn't hit it when you had the chance?"

He shook his head. "Cooperation is better," he insisted. "The cells agreed."

She felt horribly cold. She didn't want to nestle with him anymore. As much as she loved him, she wanted to slam his head against the wall and demand why, why, why have you killed us all?

"It's the cult," Nikko said, his stern voice emanating from all around . . . as if she were lodged inside his throat.

"It's not," Lot said. "That's what you always want to believe, but it's not true. This is the influence of the Well. Our cells came from the Well, it flavors them, and they *are* superior. It's just that the field is too small. There aren't enough pathways to integrate the input from the courser." He stuck a thumb in an especially large hole on his suit's upper arm. A raw, red puncture wound lay beneath it. "Nikko, the cells did this. They had tendrils under my skin, like the connection with my sensory tears wasn't enough anymore, not at the speed they're working now."

Clementine felt sick. Her hands shook, and she had to turn away. Lot looked human, he sounded human, and so she let herself be fooled into thinking he was human, time and time again—until he deftly corrected her.

"It's transferring more than dust," Nikko said. "That's what the spikes are for."

"Sooth, we're not complete, so it's giving us other things. Seeds. To start new phases of growth. I could feel things sprouting in the disturbed tissue, like . . ." He frowned, groping for words to explain. "Like muscle? Not literally like muscle, no. But like action. Power."

Clementine pressed her fists together, hating the way he hedged. "You mean zero point technology? Why don't you say so? Why don't you tell us how that would make all this worthwhile?"

When she looked at him again, doubt haunted his cream-coffee eyes. He nodded. "You're right," he said. "I should go back. Find out."

"*What?* Lot, that is not what I meant."

"We need the zero point tech."

"Not that badly."

Lot looked at her with guarded eyes; he didn't argue. Clementine knew him too well, though, to take his silence as a concession. When Lot went quiet, it only meant he was making his own plans, drawing his own conclusions, in a private realm where no one could countermand him.

The waiting ended just past the four-hour mark. Nikko's ghost saw it first. "The courser is retracting the spikes."

Clementine watched the image gathered by Deneb's go-pack. The spikes pulled away one by one, starting from

Null Boundary's bow, withdrawing slowly into the courser's hull as if they were dropping beneath the surface of a luminous white sea.

When the last spike had withdrawn, the courser's steerage jets fired. It separated from Null Boundary, correcting its spiraled posture until once again its hull lay parallel to the smaller ship. Then it pulled away.

The incarnate Nikko waited on the clean section of Null Boundary's hull, while Deneb brought Urban in from the void. His skin suit sizzled with heat. Inside the transit bubble, he stripped it off and shoved it at Nikko. "Analyze it for contaminants," he whispered. Then his guts dissolved in a fit of violent nausea and diarrhea. Nikko split the transit bubble, isolating Urban.

Defensive Makers swarmed over the three of them. Deneb was cleared, and Nikko let her return to the core. Urban, though, had incurred massive radiation damage.

"Estimate time required to repair and rebuild?" Nikko asked.

The supervising DI responded: "Repair not recommended. When exposure to unidentified foreign contaminants is suspected, defense protocol requires isolation of the affected tissue. The incarnation may be regrown from virgin substrate."

Make a ghost, Nikko said grimly. *This version of you is finished.*

Urban was weak, so it took time. He had to remain conscious while it was done. Finally, the ghost was ready. It uploaded to the library. Yet it was only a copy. Urban's original consciousness remained behind in the body. "Shut it down," Nikko urged him. "Nothing else to do."

Urban didn't answer, but his life signs vanished as if switches had been thrown: respiration, heartbeat, brain function. When it was over, Nikko ordered the DI to proceed. The tissue was dissolved, then stashed in a sealed casket along with Urban's skin suit. The robotic bugs attached to the skin suit's gloves had proved useless. Whatever data they had gathered aboard the courser had been hopelessly scrambled.

"Initiate fabrication of a new incarnation from uncontaminated tissue," Nikko ordered.

"Fabrication initiated," the Dull Intelligence replied.

• • •

Two hours later, the courser had fallen over six thousand kilometers behind, decelerating rapidly as its course diverged from Null Boundary. Nikko sent a signal to ignite the nukes. Through Null Boundary's scopes he saw two explosions—but at widely divergent points, far from the receding courser. Nikko sent his grim laugh rolling through Clemantine's atrium. *It shed the nukes, Clemantine.

*Sooth. I guess it knew how to defend itself.

In the core chamber, Lot had given in to exhaustion and fallen asleep. Clemantine drifted near him, drawn again to the puzzle of his presence. What was he? She stared at his sleeping face, at the flawless curve of his cheeks and the alien shimmer of his sensory tears—and suddenly, she felt like an anonymous character in an ancient, repeating drama. How many times in their thirty-million-year history had the Chenzeme ships been attacked by clever new species in just such a way? And still the ships survived, while their opponents had all vanished long ago.

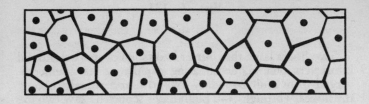

Chapter
13

Nikko's body was in better shape than Urban's, but he chose to dissolve it anyway, sealing the matter in another armored casket. He saved a ghost first. The integration of memories between this ghost and the one that had remained aboard the ship was a matter of several seconds' work in the neural strata surrounding Null Boundary's core.

After that he possessed two histories to explain one period of time, and still that was a simple existence compared to his youth, when his past had often divided into thirty tracks, or more. In those days there had been legal limits on self-reproduction, but he had known ways around them.

Now he

:listened to a conversation in Clemantine's house, as she and Deneb discussed the contaminant Urban had brought back on his skin suit.

:gazed through a hull camera at an image of the retreating courser as it leaned into a slow curve that could eventually turn its trajectory back toward the Hallowed Vasties. It showed no more concern at all for Null Boundary.

:accessed the image compiled by the two telescopes continually fixed on the original courser. This one still pursued them, its velocity unchanged, as if nothing at all had happened.

:watched Deneb as she tapped her long fingers against the

screen of a notepad. "I'm sure now the contaminant is growing." Worry shadowed her face as she turned to Clemantine. The casket that held Urban's discarded tissue and skin suit had been stashed in the ship's bow, where the plutonium had been stored. Deneb had remote access to it, through wire leads that pierced the casket's shell. "Look how the emission of visible light from the suit's tissue has increased—and that's a tiny fraction of the energy being produced." Frustration was evident in Clemantine's reply: "But produced by what?" She did not seem to expect an answer.

:looked to Urban's new incarnation nearing completion in the ship's interstitial tissue. Nikko skimmed the report of a submind on the cell-by-cell assembly, satisfying himself that all was going well.

:glanced at Lot rocking in the hammock on the gee deck, staring at spiderwebs draped beneath the pavilion roof.

:manifested in a simulation of physical form within the ship's library, where Urban's ghost waited for him on a data path that linked all known sightings of Chenzeme ships. It was more like a data *highway*, Nikko thought, studying the path's impressive span. The file presently active was the most recently acquired: a record of their own encounter.

"I think I know when I picked up the contaminant," Urban said. "Look." He turned to the file. It detected his gaze, and an image began to run.

Nikko suppressed a shudder at the view from within the courser's vent tube. It was the segment in which the blaze of white light had dimmed to something stronger, fiercer. If he stepped into the frame he would feel again the horrible pressure, crushing the circulation within his kisheer and stilling the motion of his lungs.

He did not step forward. He remained where he was, as a vague white shadow appeared within the image, moving toward him like a living thing. He watched a gloved hand reach into his field of view. He watched it swipe at the shadow, tearing through it as if it were a physical object, a puff of dense smoke perhaps, that shattered, its fragments spinning off as if on chaotic currents of air.

"Watch again," Urban said. "Watch my glove."

The glove looked very far away. The view zoomed in on it. Nikko watched it slash through the shadow once again. Did spots of light cling to the glove?

"Back it up," Nikko demanded. "There. Freeze that."

Urban nodded in satisfaction. "Those are the luminous spots I saw after we were ejected. Nikko, my right hand was most severely damaged. The heat started there."

Nikko's kisheer rippled with anxiety, climbing up around his throat. "Deneb says it's growing." Urban gave him a quizzical look, so Nikko explained. "Whatever it was you brought back on your skin suit. It's growing."

"Here?"

"Here," Nikko confirmed.

"Can we use it?"

Nikko's kisheer fluttered. "How? And for what?"

"I don't know. Whatever the courser used it for—"

A submind returned, integrating itself with Nikko's primary ghost. He endured the usual annoying moment of absentminded realization as his memories converged.

This was a submind that had long ago been assigned to track the activity of all his ghosts, instructed to report only if some ghost or partial persona failed. It had bided within the ship's neural structure for centuries.

"What is it?" Urban asked.

Nikko cocked his head as worry nudged him. "I've lost a submind. One assigned to patrol the cardinal nanosites within the hull." He let his image double.

Urban stepped closer. The fear on his face seemed an exotic emotion, so rarely had Nikko seen it there. "It disappeared near the outer wall?"

"Just beneath the new metabolic layer, yes." Nikko hesitated, caught off guard by Urban's open concern. It wasn't like him to let such feelings show. How shaken had he been by his experience aboard the courser? "You should edit that," Nikko said. "Fear will hamper you later."

Urban scowled. "I'm okay. You're going to leave one ghost here?"

Nikko nodded again.

"I will too." His own image slid apart into two identical copies.

Watching him, Nikko became abruptly aware of the vaporous nature of his own existence: the taut pull of his muscles was only illusion, as was the comforting hardness of his sleek china shell. It was false air that rushed into his false lungs, and the pounding of his heart was no more than a collection of code. Disrupt the intricate pattern and he would vanish. He'd lost hundreds of ghosts in his youth. It wasn't hard to make them disappear.

Of course, he had backups. If he chose, he could replicate himself until Null Boundary's memory was full. But someday even that option would fail. Even Null Boundary would not last forever.

So Nikko watched the doubling of Urban's image and nodded, feeling the future unfold before him. "Yes," he said. "You should come. You should learn it all. Someone else should."

Lot lay in the hammock, while the gee deck's artificial sky faded from the deep blue of evening, to star-studded black. Burning through the ranks of the forest, the giant star Alpha Cygni gleamed on the artificial horizon, a navigation beacon as white as philosopher cells. He let the color bleed into his brain.

He needed to go back to the cells.

Everything he required had been seeded today within the hull membrane. The design of the zero point drive; the layout of Chenzeme guns; the machinery of mating. All there. Lot felt sure of it.

He had only to go back to the cells and get it, and he would know all there was to know about the workings of Chenzeme warships.

He curled his fingers over the edge of the hammock, acutely conscious of the tension in the fabric. He'd gotten scared out there today. He'd sensed something new, something unknown, in the matrix of the cells, and he'd panicked. A new life-form . . . or live-*forms*, independent of the cells, poured onto them from the courser. An alien presence within the familiar field, rebuilding the margin of the ship to suit its own needs.

He hadn't liked it being there. It offended his territorial nature. His human half.

The cells defied his anxiety. *We are complete.*

What else mattered? A flush prickled his cheeks. He sat up in the hammock, planting his feet carefully on the floor.

What if a Chenzeme warship was an alliance of life-forms? A union, tempered now by the harmony of the Well.

Change has value.

He had been accepted by the philosopher cells. There was no reason he couldn't make himself acceptable in this new alliance too. These new elements were rebuilding the ship's tissues to suit their needs, but he had been in the wound, and they had not tried to rebuild *him*.

So there was no reason to be afraid.

There was no reason he couldn't go back and learn what he needed to learn.

Vaporous. The word reechoed in Nikko's mind as his ghost left the core, uploading to a cardinal nanosite near the outer hull. Left behind was the illusion of being human. The computational nets within the cardinals were geared to analysis of molecular structure, not to the psychological comfort of visiting ghosts. In this micron-scale environment, his existence was crudely simulated as a sense of mass. Urban was a secondary mass behind him, invisible and almost insubstantial, registering in Nikko's new senses as a slight warping in the path of data.

"We are not real," Urban whispered. These words still carried the illusion of sound.

"That's good to remember."

Cardinals were scattered throughout the hull, each one guarding a tiny domain of tissue against mutations, malfunctions, and invaders. This cardinal was located in untainted tissue, a few centimeters below the new metabolic layer growing beneath the philosopher cells. It was both a processing node and a microscale watch-post, designed to integrate and react to data gathered by scout Makers. At Nikko's request, it had used that data to build a visual model. He could see the structure of the surrounding tissue; he could feel its heat.

He issued a command, and instantly he acquired hands: nanoscale manipulators that were carried on scout Makers though they operated under his input. "I can feel that," Urban said.

"We share the same sensory field."'

"But you control our response."

"For now." Nikko found a reassuring solidity in this constant pressure at his back. "Control here is intuitive," he explained.

"All right."

He leaned into the hull's clean, pliant tissue. This was Null Boundary's flesh, composed of complex, motile cells. Nikko's presence slid between them on tensile ducts.

He issued a new command, and all the healthy tissue became transparent, defined only by faint white lines. Abnormal structures remained fully visible: in this zone, only his own hands. But ahead of him, still several micrometers away, he caught the gleam of anomalous heat.

"What is it?" Urban asked.

"Activity."

An interface of activity, where Null Boundary's tissue ceased to be normal and became something unknown.

They drew nearer, and their ignorance rose before them in the form of a fog-shrouded cliff face. This was a visual model accumulated by the cardinal nanosite, a declaration that *something* was there. But what? The scout Makers had failed to gather clear structural details.

The fog gleamed white with heat. Its billowing surface was pierced by a collection of pincers and coils and beams, shifting rods and spots of bright electric potential.

"It looks like an armory," Urban said, awe in his voice.

"It's not." Though it did look dangerous. "If we can see it, we know the scouts survived contact long enough to report."

Urban's mass contracted to a smaller, denser form. "Then the fog represents unknown structure?"

"Yes. Exactly."

The fog-shrouded cliff face extended above and below him, and for a vast distance on either side. Scout Makers had not been able to penetrate it. His own submind had disappeared in those mists.

He reached toward the interface. His hands vanished beneath the fog. He could feel a vibration, the time-stretched echo of a reaction that lasted only a few nanoseconds. His hands were gone. Dissolved or excised, he didn't know. Urban muttered a soft chain of profanities while Nikko summoned a different pair of hands.

All along the interface, cardinals were running through the ship's inventory of defensive Makers and assembling the described structures in corpuscular vats, racing to find a design that could combat the encroachment of this alien growth.

They had confirmed that much at least: Whatever lay behind this fog-shrouded wall was growing. Nikko reached again into the mist, and again his hands were taken. Sooner this time, as the fog drew ever nearer. Its expansion was visible.

Nikko watched it flow across another layer of Null Boundary's motile hull cells. Upon contact, the cells writhed in a time-slowed chaotic reflex as their structures were torn, their electrically balanced membranes thrown into a confused, black-limned boil that disappeared within the fog. The zone advanced a few more micrometers. Nikko retreated.

From behind him, complex mechanicals bumped into existence, slipping through the healthy tissue as they advanced toward the fog. "Defense Makers," Urban whispered. "They don't look real."

Indeed. Their structures were known in exquisite detail. Every stud, every tool, every pore was clearly visible. No blurring of definition softened their appearance, no shadows obscured their structures. It was a clarity of vision so unnatural that Nikko's senses insisted it must be false.

The defensive Makers advanced, and where they touched the fog the heat of conflict flared. Data fed back to the nanosite. Bits of fog evaporated along the cliff face, revealing glimpses of crudely sketched structures as the defensive Makers vanished, torn apart by the alien interface.

"It's reformatting the hull, isn't it?" Urban asked, his voice not quite steady. "The hull cells were accepted as Chenzeme, but the rest of the ship was not. So now the foreign elements are being rebuilt into something acceptably Chenzeme."

"That would be my guess," Nikko said.

"Can we adapt to that?"

"We can try."

Lot stood outside the door of Clemantine's house, taken by a sense of caution. He could hear Clemantine inside, talking to Deneb. If he went in to use the transit wall, it would be natural for them to ask where he was going. He didn't feel inclined to say.

He glanced overhead. A glitter of stars filled the false sky, but the light they cast was minimal. He felt secure as he turned and walked away.

At either end of the deck he could access a series of crawlways to the core apartments. He would summon a transit bubble from there.

Once back in the library, Nikko instructed the cardinal nanosites to allow the structures of the defensive Makers to freely evolve, while still enforcing strict limits on their behavior. Rates of variation were increased, while an engage-and-fallback strategy was implemented that would offer a useful selection pressure.

There was no noticeable effect. Whole lineages were evolved and discarded in a few seconds' time, while the alien interface continued to advance.

Sweat gleamed on Urban's ghost-cheeks as he watched along with Nikko. He was silent through several failures. Finally, he looked at Nikko and said: "We'll have to blow off the outer layers of the hull, like you did when we left the Well."

Nikko shook his head, his kisheer moving on his shoulders in thoughtful waves. "It won't work."

Urban's fist closed in abject frustration. "We have to try it! If we don't shed this infestation now, it'll reach the core in just a few hours."

Nikko's long fingers tapped in nervous cadence against his thigh. "It won't work, Urban, because the solenoids are infested too. We can't blow the solenoids off, because we can't replace the metals that are in them."

"We can heat them. We can bring them to a temperature just short of liquefaction—"

"The solenoids don't exist anymore."

"*What?*"

Nikko too was surprised at what he'd just said. He thought about it a moment, then explained, as much to himself as to Urban: "They're being cannibalized. Their atoms are being mixed in with whatever is growing on the hull. Half their mass has already been taken."

"Why didn't you tell me before?"

"I didn't know, until . . ." Until just now, when a sub-mind brought him the disturbing fact. He felt as if he'd always known it.

The pipeweed in Lot's abandoned apartment glowed dimly, to simulate the presence of night. From an inner chamber, he told the spider to summon a transit bubble. Such requests were usually handled by one of Nikko's sub-minds. A submind would not bother reporting simple duties to the core persona, so with any luck, Nikko would remain unaware of this activity.

Luck was with him. The pipeweed pulled aside as a transit bubble opened in the chamber wall. Lot smiled. Inside the gloves of his skin suit, his hands were damp with sweat. He grabbed the bubble rim and curled into the hole.

"To the wound," he told the spider. The bubble sealed, then accelerated. Lot dug his fingers into the wall, expecting at any moment to be discovered, to feel the bubble reversing, to hear Nikko berating him through the spider, *Love and nature, are you crazy?* Nikko was afraid of anything Chenzeme.

Instead, the bubble slowed, as it always did when it neared the hull. It was still moving though, when it popped. It peeled open on one side, its ragged edges singed as they curled away from an electric blue surface. Billows of steam puffed in Lot's face. Fumes scorched his sensory tears. He ducked his head, digging his fingers deeper into the wall as momentum whipped his body around. He plunged to the waist into the blue field, feeling no more resistance than he might have felt if it had been water.

His skin suit hardened over his legs and hips. He couldn't bend his legs, but he could feel his thighs burning, and his feet freezing cold. He imagined his body being taken apart, and he pulled hard—too hard—against his grip on the wall.

His legs snapped out of the blue zone as easily as they'd gone in, hitting the bubble wall with a thud. He almost lost his grip, but then his skin suit softened. He flexed his foot and got the toe of a boot into the wall.

Hesitantly, he looked at his legs. They were still whole, though they were coated in a boiling blue gel. It sizzled and popped as it evaporated. The fumes seared his throat. His ears popped. Lot had no doubt he'd plunged into the middle of a molecular-scale war. This was Nikko's signature. Nikko was fighting the new elements, and this was the result. "Hark!" he grunted at the spider. "Back up, back up. Close the fucking bubble."

Instead, the remaining bubble wall oozed closer to the blue zone . . . or maybe the blue zone advanced. "Back it up!" Lot shouted, his throat raw, and a fiery pain in his sinuses. He had not reckoned on crossing a war zone.

Still the bubble did not move. Maybe its transit hooks had been torn loose. Maybe it was just stuck in the boiling hot zone. His ears popped again, and he guessed this pocket of air was rapidly losing pressure. The decline left him dizzy. The DI in his skin suit took over. Without urging, his hood rolled up over his head and sealed. Cool air filled his lungs.

He clung like a bug to the intact wall while the bubble shrank and the blue zone advanced. Only a foot away now. He hesitated. Eight inches. He'd plunged into it, hadn't he? And it hadn't hurt him. It was consuming Null Boundary's tissues, but it had left him alone. And it had been cool on the other side. He had felt that.

Four inches.

Nikko should never have started this war.

Three inches.

Everything he wanted to know was in the philosopher cells.

He asked the spider, "How far is the hull?"

"Six point nine three meters."

A groan escaped his throat. Almost seven meters of unknown territory. He wanted to kick off the wall, in a headfirst dive into the blue zone, swim to the hull cells on the other side. He could not bring himself to do it. He could not get his fingers to let go, or his arms and legs to thrust him away from the bubble wall.

The blue zone advanced, until it boiled only an inch from his visor. He could not get his fingers to let go. "Then get another transit bubble!" he shouted. If a bubble opened, he would flee. If it didn't open . . .

The wall behind him dissolved around his grip. A new transit bubble yawned beyond the ruined one. Lot grabbed at the rim, sliding himself inside it, his toes brushing the blue zone as he did it, taking heat but no damage. No damage. He felt like a coward fleeing. The philosopher cells had everything he wanted, only seven meters away.

"Hold it." He stared past the new bubble's open rim, at the electric-blue tide advancing around its edges. He crouched, readying himself to dive into it, still not sure if he could bring himself to do it, but determined to try. . . .

"*Love and nature,*" Nikko swore in his ear.

Lot didn't wait to hear more. He launched himself—too late. The transit bubble snapped shut. He slammed head-first into the wall. His neck cracked, and he sprawled, filling the tiny space. Momentarily stunned.

"Are you dead?" Nikko asked.

"No."

"Too bad."

Lot's neck ached. His fingers dug at the walls. He had hesitated and ruined his own chances. Now all he could do was argue. "Nikko! Listen to me. It's not as bad as you think. There are new life-forms out there. Allied life-forms, that know how to build Chenzeme ships. One of them will understand the zero point tech—"

"Shut up. And take off the skin suit."

"I didn't get hurt! Can't you see that? This new element isn't dangerous to us. You're fighting an unnecessary war."

"And I'm losing. Do you know how lucky you are to be alive?"

"You have to call off the defensive Makers."

"Not a chance."

"The only reason you've got a war is because *you* attacked the new tissue."

"Take off the skin suit."

"Sure." Lot stripped it off, his movements sharp and angry. He wadded it and pitched it at the wall. A minibubble opened to receive it, whisking it away. "There. Look at me. No damage. I was in the zone, Nikko, and I took no damage."

"Decontamination," Nikko said, as a fog swirled from the bubble walls.

Lot breathed in the vapor, drawing armies of Makers into his lungs, to crash and burn against any foreign invaders that might have survived his own defenses—he doubted Null Boundary could come up with anything more effective than the protection he already carried.

"Cooperation *is* better than conflict," he insisted. "Help me get back to the cell field, and I'll be able to tell you what's going on—and what we can do about it."

"Has it occurred to you that you're alive only because the Chenzeme tissue and our defensive Makers both recognize you as their own? If either side sees its mistake, you'll die."

Lot spread his arms, pressing his palms against the bubble walls to stabilize himself. "I still want to try it."

"If we lose this war, you will."

Gradually—so gradually Nikko wasn't sure for long minutes if it was happening at all—the war wound down. The advance of the infestation slowed.

Urban sat cross-legged on a data path within the library, his pensive gaze locked on an image of the battle zone that was as close to real time as the system could produce, given the speed at which molecular reactions occurred.

Clemantine's ghost stood behind him, watching with Deneb.

"It's over," Urban said, a note of disbelief in his voice. He stood, leaning forward to stare at the developing image. "Look. The advance of the alien layer has stopped."

Nikko stared at the image too, though his thoughts focused on the digital record of molecular activity that continued to pour in from the hull. "It hasn't stopped. It's only slowed."

Urban half turned, treating Nikko to a scathing look. "There's metabolic activity, sure, but the attrition rate of our defensive Makers has zeroed."

Clemantine swore in soft, choice syllables. "Nikko, did you allow the Makers to freely evolve?"

Nikko did his best to ignore a twinge of guilt. "I had to. But I put restrictions on their behavior."

"*Nikko!*"

He could not meet her gaze.

Urban looked from one to the other of them, as if ready to pounce on an explanation should one emerge.

"No proctor?" Clemantine pressed, without much hope.

"I couldn't risk it."

"What's going on?" Urban interrupted, taking half a step forward. "The advance has effectively stopped."

Clemantine's gaze was harsh. "Pay attention, son. It hasn't stopped. It's greatly slowed, but it continues. Yet the attrition rate of our defensive Makers is zero. What does that tell you?"

Deneb produced the answer first. "They've made a truce."

Urban wasn't buying it. "That option was specifically excluded from their behavioral parameters."

Clemantine shrugged. "Makers are complex, integrated structures. You can't let their hot zones freely evolve without some risk that their behavior will be affected too—not unless you also include selective pressures to reinforce the desired behavior. Nikko, you know that."

He knew it. It was a risk he'd decided to take. Putting sterner restrictions on the Maker's development could have made them noncompetitive—*leaving us to test firsthand Lot's crackpot theory of cooperation.*

"We could try again," Urban suggested. He sounded unsure now. His gaze was fixed on the nervous motion of Nikko's fingers tapping against his thigh.

Nikko forced himself to freeze the movement of that hand. "We could." He looked from Urban, to Deneb, to Clemantine. "But the Makers already on the hull are no longer ours. They've evolved to a point of equilibrium. Any new wave of defensive Makers we introduce could conflict with that balance."

"We could find ourselves with two enemies," Clemantine explained.

Urban's fists knotted. "You're saying we made things worse. That Lot was right. If we'd done nothing—"

"No." Nikko's fingers were moving again, but in slow, controlled strokes. "Lot's wrong. He's dreaming. This infestation isn't like the philosopher cells. It's aggressive. It's cut off our access to the hull, it's stolen our control of the ship, it's consuming and reformatting the ship's tissues, and while it may have spared Lot, there's no reason to think it will spare any of us. We had no choice but to fight it."

"Anyway, we've given ourselves time," Deneb said. "A lot of time."

"Time to do what?" Urban asked. "What else can we do?"

"We could try to sterilize the hull."

Nikko turned to her. Deneb's kisheer lay still against her shoulders. A thoughtful look graced her face. "Any complex structure will break down if it's exposed to a sufficient amount of heat."

"Too late for that, don't you think?" Urban said. He gestured at Nikko and Clemantine. "Thanks to these two, the fissionable materials are gone."

"We won't need fissionable materials," Deneb said. "Look—" Another data trail opened. Nikko glanced down its path, to see the familiar starfield that had lain ahead of the ship for almost two hundred years, unnumbered suns fronting the dark wall of a giant molecular cloud, and at the center, the navigation beacon he had followed since Deception Well: the white-hot star, Alpha Cygni, now only two years away.

Deneb said, "We're bound there anyway. A close flyby would bathe us in enough radiation to break down any complex structure in the outer layers of the hull. And Alpha Cygni is a young star, probably no more than a few million years old. Maybe too young to have been visited by the Chenzeme."

Could it work? Nikko gazed at the star's image, knowing its source was still so far away. He shook his head. "It'll take two more years just to get there. The infestation is already eight meters deep."

Clemantine's gaze was distant as she listened to a submind. "If the rate of expansion remains slow, even after two years we'll still have a viable layer of uncorrupted tissue around the core."

"But the solenoids are gone," Urban protested. "How do we make our course?"

Deneb turned a speculative gaze on Nikko. "Do the steerage engines still work?"

"Maybe."

Urban said, "They don't have the power we need for course corrections on this scale."

Clemantine was looking thoughtful. "Maybe they do, if we use them now. We're already bearing on the system. A small correction now could fix our course."

Urban looked scared. "But that will zero our fuel reserves."

"Son, what else are we going to use the fuel for?"

"I— Sorry." He drew a deep breath, calming visibly, so that Nikko knew he'd done some editing. "Can we fix a course that closely?" he asked.

Nikko shrugged. "We might not have to. After the initial burn, we should be able to synthesize some sort of fuel from the ship's tissue, even if it doesn't have much kick. Assuming we don't lose the steerage engines, some minor corrections as we approach Alpha Cygni might be possible."

"Assuming the infestation rate remains stable," Urban said.

Deneb's kisheer moved in stiff, nervous waves. "Lot won't like this, will he?"

"Screw Lot," Clemantine snapped. "We came this way to find the Chenzeme, not to become them."

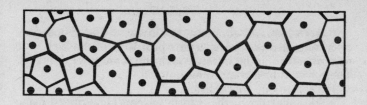

Chapter
14

Cameras on Null Boundary's hull recorded a change in the behavior of the philosopher cells. For the first time since they'd been seeded, the cells embarked on an unbidden expansion, spreading across the telescopes, the radio antenna, the steerage vents—following the aggressive advance of the devastating metabolic layer. Instruments were dissolved, and all connections to Null Boundary's hull were lost. The cameras at the stern survived longest. They recorded the last stages of the philosopher cells' conquest, as the field oozed toward them in an analogue of bacterial growth. One by one, the cameras failed. The last to survive recorded a 360-degree field of icy white before it too ceased to transmit. At that moment, all contact with the outside world was lost.

Lot missed the cells in a hellish way. They spoke the language of the charismata, and that was more real and more satisfying to him than any human tongue. This territorialism, this line of demarcation Nikko had drawn with the encroaching Chenzeme tissue—it was so unnecessary. It was nothing more than a pointless act of war for war's sake, because whatever was happening on the hull was not an ordinary Chenzeme conquest. Lot knew it. The philosopher cells contained the peacekeeping protocols of the Well. The new tissue would be infected with the same viral thoughts. There would be a compromise.

Except no one would listen.

Nikko shut down the transit system. He stopped using the charismata to talk to Lot, as if such use might mark him a traitor to the species . . . *same as me?* Clemantine made it clear she would rather plunge Null Boundary into Alpha Cygni's plasma sea, than make any kind of peace with the Chenzeme encroachment. Urban and Deneb were less absolute, yet they made no objection when Nikko fired the steerage engines, burning off some of the cell field—and all of their fuel—in a course correction aimed at taking the ship through the sterilizing heat of the great star's upper atmosphere . . . two years from now. It was an act of faith, more than an act of navigation. Tiny errors would grow huge over such a distance. They could as easily plunge into the star's heart, or miss it altogether. Not that it mattered. Lot didn't believe they would ever get to Alpha Cygni. Though the dark courser had turned away, fading to a barely discernible point even before the telescopes failed, the original courser was still out there. He had no reason to think otherwise. In a hundred-odd days, it would catch them, and things would change.

"Hey." Urban sat down beside Lot on the grass at the edge of the koi pond. He had two bottles of beer, both beaded with condensation. "Still plotting the revolution?"

Lot flushed. He had blanked the screen of his notepad when Urban approached, erasing the visible evidence of his struggle to redesign the cult virus into a more effective form. But it was silly to think he had any secrets left outside his own mind. No one trusted him. No one should trust him. The constant surveillance made his back itch. "Sooth, I'm still plotting," Lot said. "You know I'm not getting anywhere."

Urban offered him a bottle. Lot took it. He let the notepad tumble to the grass, while Urban leaned back on his elbows, for once somber and thoughtful. "Fury, even if you find a new way to infect us all with the cult virus, we'll stop you before you implement it. You know that."

"Sooth." Lot took a long draft of the cold, cold beer, feeling like an ass. But he had to do something. They had made themselves prisoners in this ship. "The dark courser gave us seeds for all the systems we're lacking. Urban, you know one of those seeds has to be for the zero point drive. We are so close. Let me talk to the cells. Let me look for it."

"Can't do it, fury," Urban said with a shake of his head. "You know that. As much as I want it, we can't risk destabilizing the encroaching layer. We'll get it another way."

"You think we'll have that chance? The original courser isn't gone. When it closes with us, this equilibrium *will* be disturbed. Let me get to the cells first."

Urban gazed at the koi pond, at a series of expanding ripples where a fish had touched the surface. His doubt was a shadow in Lot's awareness. Then he shook his head. Confidence surged from him, as if sprayed from a machine. He sat up. Reaching a hand into his thigh pocket, he withdrew a palm-sized instrument: a honeycombed wafer, dark gray. It folded open to something twice as large. There was a screen and a voice interface. "I made this for you," Urban said. "It's pretty interesting."

Lot leaned over to get a better look. The honeycomb texture was a dead giveaway. "Some kind of chemical synthesizer."

Urban smiled. He touched the screen. "Play the first set," he commanded.

A gush of chopped and broken cell-talk washed over Lot's sensory tears. He pulled back, astounded.

"What did it say?" Urban demanded.

Lot frowned, touching the device, running his finger down a line of honeycombs, each less than half a millimeter wide. "Nothing." He shrugged. "It was garbled. Like if you chopped up bits of sound recorded in a crowd and mixed them together."

Urban slumped, crestfallen.

"I knew it was cell-talk," Lot added quickly.

"Oh great. Progress." He rolled his eyes.

Lot picked up the synthesizer. Molecular diagrams waltzed across the screen. "I think I know the problem.

You're replicating a slice taken across thousands of different conversations, instead of following a single discrete thread through its loop."

Urban frowned at the synthesizer, his jaw working. "How do you follow a thread? Are there markers?"

Lot thought about it. "There must be. I'm not conscious of it, though."

"Say something," Urban said. "In cell-talk. We'll check for repeating phrases, things like that."

He didn't want to discourage Urban. This was kind of fun. But— "It won't be just one marker. Thousands of conversations are going on at once. They have to be sortable. And . . . I think phrasings are made up a lot. Just invented on the spot, used for a while, dumped. It's weird."

Urban rested his chin on his hand. "And you don't always understand it anyway."

"Well, I usually do when I'm in it, but afterwards . . . yeah, not all the time."

"So we work on it."

Lot finished the beer. An orange koi had come up to the edge of the pond. He watched it mouth the surface, wondering how far Urban was willing to go to understand the Chenzeme. He spoke cautiously. "You need to realize, any device like this is only a partial bridge to the language. This thing might learn to talk for you, but no matter how precise its own understanding becomes, it can't think for you. You have to work on your wetware too, so you can *experience* the Chenzeme talk, along a thousand different threads at once, or you won't understand it. Don't think about translating, think about immersion. Be Chenzeme."

"And get Clemantine pissed at me too?" Urban grinned, his dark brow wrinkling, his wide lips a reservoir of mirth.

Lot groaned and fell back against the grass, his arms spread-eagled, the bright light of the false sky dazzling him, making him squint. "She hates me."

"Well, you're half Chenzeme. Gives her the creeps. Like sleeping with the person who murdered her family, you know?"

"Oh thanks. I feel better now."

Urban's mood cooled, a shadow on the afternoon. "You should have poisoned the courser, Lot. We could have taken it apart."

Lot tried to imagine doing it, but he could not. Maybe Nikko was right. The cult was a hot, unhappy wound inside him, always hungry. He closed his eyes, drowning in the afternoon heat. "I'd do it again. Cooperation *is* better."

"Oh yeah. Especially if it gets Clemantine back into bed with you. You might want to think about that, fury. Now come on. Say something in the Chenzeme way. Let me get a working sample."

It took a few weeks, but Clemantine softened. It wasn't hard, once Lot got his pitch right. *You could keep me human.* She really did love him.

He loved her. It made his worries more intense.

He had no way to know for sure, but instinct told him the courser was still out there, still gaining on their wake. Anxiety fed his nervous energy. He could not be still. Late at night he would walk the gee deck, round and round in an endless circuit, under false stars that were only a projection of where Nikko thought they might be. He imagined the courser hurrying after them. It could happen. It could catch them sooner than they expected, and if it found fault with their transition, or if the tainted philosopher cells generated some unacceptable response to a radio hail, then the courser might fire on them. Might already have fired, and the next step he took might be his last. There was no way of knowing.

The uncertainty ate at him. He would do anything to know, and the only way he could imagine knowing was to immerse himself in the cell field and have a voice again, some iota of influence on their fate. The only way he could get out to the cell field was to induce someone to let him go. So he continued to plot his futile revolution. It was all he could do.

Clemantine laughed at his efforts to redesign the cult virus. Even so, she was captivated by the intellectual puzzle, and before long she and Deneb took a respite from their studies of the zero point field to turn their attention to the structure of the cult's neural parasite—though if they found anything interesting, they didn't share it with Lot.

A hundred days. Lot marked the time. Clemantine told him to forget it, there was nothing they could do. "You mean there's nothing you're willing to do," and that started another round of fighting, but it didn't last. She loved him.

He loved her. The day came when the courser was due to move alongside. They retreated to the core and waited it out, listening for alarms, explosions, or the stiff groan of the ship's frame as it endured another mating. None of that happened. The day passed in silence, and the next day too.

Where was the courser? They couldn't know. It might still be out there. Or it might have turned away months ago and all this anxiety was for nothing. There was no way to know.

Another day passed and another. Only slowly did the knots leave Lot's stomach—and still the encroaching metabolic layer advanced at the same unvarying rate.

"I've got the wetware," Urban announced one day.

They were on the gee deck, and Lot was immersed in the crude cell-talk of the synthesizer. The cult hunger was a white fire in his belly, a dark pressure under his skin. A craving for Communion that went unsatisfied day after day after day. The only thing that eased it was the touch of the synthesizer's charismata. Immersed in cell-talk, he could pretend he was one of many. It was a kind of Communion.

Anyway, it was something.

Lot whispered the synthesizer off. As his head cleared, Urban repeated his claim. "Did you hear me, fury? I've got the wetware."

"Yeah?" Lot squinted. He didn't think Urban was lying, yet there was something of subterfuge in his aura.

He pulled a chair up close to Lot's hammock. "It's a Chenzeme neural organ . . . or a virtual metaphor for one. I won't be able to think in Chenzeme, but my ghost will, if it works."

Lot sat up, dropping his feet to the ground so the hammock became a chair. "How is it supposed to work?"

Urban groaned, casting a glance of supplication at the ceiling. "Don't ask that, fury. This interface is the product of a hundred dedicated ghosts working at multiple clock speeds, for an equivalent of millennia of frustration. I don't want to know how it works, because I don't want to be as old and twisted as they are."

Lot scowled. "So you're all set. Too bad we don't have any philosopher cells to talk to."

Urban gave him an odd look, as if he thought Lot might be joking. A chorus of crickets kicked off all around them, a trilling cacophony rising in an asynchronous wall of sound. Urban leaned close. "You still remember how to synthesize philosopher cells, don't you? Like you did the first time?"

Lot felt unnerved at the concept of a cricket army under Urban's command. It was all he could do to nod an affirmation.

"Good, but don't say anything about it to Clemantine. She could try to amend your talent. She might be able to do it too. She works on your physiology all the time."

Did she?

Urban nodded and settled back. The insect chorus faded. "So let's try it."

They practiced for hours every day, training the virtual interface using fragments of conversations recorded in the cell field, teaching it to follow a single thread of conversation. A hundred times a minute the interface would order the synthesizer to drop the thread, switching to something unrelated. Lot would pick up the broken ends and knit them together, Chenzeme loops of understanding rotating constantly through his mind—and still it was only a weak echo of the symphonic complexity he had known in the cell field.

Lot's revolution dried up after the courser failed to present itself. He abandoned his determination to redesign the cult virus—but not before the idea spread to a new and more effective host. Deneb started out regarding the development of the cult virus and its neural parasite as an intellectual puzzle, yet the deeper she waded into the cult system, the more intrigued she became. Her studies shifted from the relatively simple cult parasite to Clemantine's records charting the more complicated and elusive Chenzeme system in Lot's head.

In the library, her ghost coasted through a model of his neural organ. Most of the diagram was coded yellow and orange, meaning this was proposed structure, still awaiting confirmation. Foreign Makers did not survive long in Lot's tissue, so it was hard to know anything for sure.

Deneb's thoughts turned briefly to war. Lot's defensive Makers were not almighty. They might be defeated if an army of freely evolving assault Makers was launched into his tissue—though it was doubtful Lot would survive the battle. The quantity of energy released in such a contest could boil his tissues outright, wrecking the information structure that defined him. Even if he survived the clash, it was quite likely his body was fully dependent on his defensive Makers. His tissues could degrade before a new defensive system could be introduced. It was even possible his defensive Makers would respond to a threat by turning on him and deliberately destroying his tissues. It was as if Lot was held hostage to his ancestry, protected yet imprisoned by his own defensive Makers.

Still, the implications resonated with Deneb's desires: this organ in Lot's head was made of Chenzeme tissue, adapted to human physiology. It promised the ability to speak a language that presently lay beyond her. Like some prescient dream, it offered insight into Chenzeme mind, if only she could separate the demands of the cult from the information flow of the charismata.

Urban was attempting something similar with his virtual interface, but that was a kludge, a clumsy system that needed to learn its instincts, while Lot's neural system was a finely honed bridge already replete with understanding.

Deneb created a new incarnation of herself. Never allowing this double to gain consciousness, she infected it with the cult, then tracked the development of the elusive neural parasite within its brain, comparing it with what she knew of Lot's superior system. At maturity, she destroyed the experiment, keeping her promise to Nikko. But immediately she started a new incarnation growing. Again, she seeded the cult in its unconscious mind, but this time she modified the development of the neural parasite, attempting to blend in characteristics of Lot's system.

She ran the experiment again and again, pushing the development of the parasite toward her own idealized concept. She met dead ends and disappointments. For weeks at a time no progress was made. But over the long term the system evolved, growing closer and closer to her goal of interpreting and generating the charismata, without being enslaved by them. She did not understand precisely how this neural organ worked, only that it worked more and more as she desired.

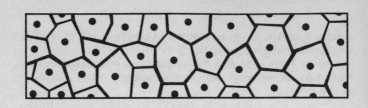

Chapter 15

Urban's ghost rotated out of the library, rising on the hour for a thirty-second scan of the ship's systems. He left behind an engineering problem Nikko had given him: how to channel a final burn through the steerage engines, now that their throats had been dissolved by the encroaching Chenzeme tissue? Urban suspected Nikko had already worked out a solution somewhere in the vast space of the library. The engineering puzzle was a distraction, though it had taken him three weeks to solve. The true point of this exercise was to experience the ghost-existence, prolonged, and undiluted by corporeal intervals.

Satisfaction was a supported emotion even in the primitive cardinals, and Urban indulged it. He slid into the first site, knowing he'd solved Nikko's challenge, but just as important, he'd learned to live in the altered consciousness of the ship's electronic memory.

Inside the cardinal, he collected his resident submind. It was a vaporous thing, its memories severely pruned. Merger was rapid and unenlightening. Nothing much had changed since his last circuit. The Chenzeme layer continued to advance as it had for two years.

"Have you got it?"

The query fell over him as he slipped out of the first cardinal: a fragile membrane of words strung across his path, possessed of a faint resistance.

"Nikko?" he asked in surprise. "You're not looping?"

The answer waited at the next cardinal. "I'm reformatting the decks."

Urban felt a rising excitement. Nikko had spent months planning their approach to Alpha Cygni, developing a scheme to pull the ship's uncontaminated mass in from bow and stern, to encase the core region in a shield layered with insulating vacuum. "So we're there?"

"Best estimate says so. Can we make the burn?"

"Sure. Look for the recipe in the marked file."

From this cardinal's resident submind he gathered another memory of minimal change. The Chenzeme conquest had the flavor of a geological process: slow but inevitable.

Except now, after two years, Nikko was ready to launch his counterassault.

Beyond the third cardinal, Urban slipped through another barrier of words: "The recipe looks good."

"It matches yours?"

Nikko hung a resistant laugh across his path.

Lot had been so sure this passage would never be. He'd convinced himself something would interfere, something *had* to interfere, before Nikko drove Null Boundary through Alpha Cygni's sterilizing plasma fires, wrecking their philosopher cells and the Well influence that held out the promise of peace for the first time since human ships had encountered Chenzeme.

He'd been wrong. Now the decks were being crushed out of existence as Nikko rebuilt the ship's interior to insulate the core. The gee deck was already gone, along with Clemantine's house and all the trees that had grown there for two hundred years. And the small animals? The spiders, the moths, the birds, the koi, and the lizards? Lot hoped Nikko had kept their patterns.

This isn't necessary.

Still, it had become inevitable.

Lot retreated alone to the core chamber while the others completed their tasks in the interstice, or in the core apartments. He summoned an old diagram of Alpha Cygni onto the image wall. The star was out there. They couldn't yet know exactly where, only that it was not so far away anymore.

The diagram expanded to include an image of Kheth, the G-type primary of Deception Well, placed against Alpha Cygni for scale. Kheth was less than half the diameter of this behemoth. Alpha Cygni was so massive, so bright, Lot felt it should be as old as the galaxy. He knew it was not. Massive stars were short-lived. Sometimes they survived only a few tens of thousands of years before their fierce metabolisms consumed all the available hydrogen in their reactive layer. Vast quantities of hydrogen would remain in the outer mantle, but it was not accessible to the star's fusion engine. When the hydrogen was gone, helium would be consumed, then upward through the elements until iron formed, deep beneath the mantle. Iron could not be fused at the temperatures and pressures available. So fusion would cease, and the outward pressure of radiation would vanish. Nothing would be left to support the star against the forever-pull of gravity. It would collapse inward, only to reignite in the cataclysmic explosion of a supernova, an event of massive destruction and essential creation—a forge where every element heavier than iron might begin its chain of existence.

And how do I know this?

Because she was there beside him for this moment: his mother. She had died that day Jupiter had brought his army into Silk. Her body had been dissolved, but her pattern had been preserved in the archives of that city. Perhaps she lived again. If Silk thrived, its archives might have been tapped—seven thousand new genotypes, seven thousand life experiences, immediately available to fuel the expansion.

If Silk had failed, then even those patterns would be lost.

Dead or alive? Likely he would never know. And she in turn—if she lived again—would never know what had become of him. And still she lived inside him, her voice alive in his fixed memory.

"There," she said, speaking to the boy he had been. "Look there." Her slender fingers moved in a horizontal arc. "That luminous river—that is the path of the Milky Way. That is our galaxy, seen edge-on." Her other arm

snuggled around his waist as they cuddled in the semidarkness, surrounded on all sides by a projected starfield, so
that they seemed to drift at the center of a cosmic egg. If he
looked backward, over his shoulder, he would see her face.
He did not look. He was six and romantically in love with
her, and for this moment she belonged to him alone.

She said, "For all the distance people have come from
Earth, we are still only on the edge of the galaxy's great
disk." The tone of her voice lowered. "There, do you see
where the luminous white path is broken by darkness?
Clouds of darkness that puff into the river of light? Yes,
that's it. Those really are clouds. They were visible even from
the surface of Earth. They are not so far from us now—not
the edge of them anyway. They are molecular clouds, made
of dust and gas. They are the place where stars are born."

This was her creation story, and she spoke it in hushed
tones, as if power lay in the words themselves, or in the image the words sketched—not only the power of creation,
but also of understanding, and acceptance.

"An older star explodes, within or without the cloud,
and a shock wave runs through the darkness of the cloud
center. The material of the cloud is compressed in a front.
Knots of greater density develop along this front. They
grow through gravitational attraction. Infalling matter
adds to their mass, until a family of protostars is formed.
They are cocooned in the veil of the surrounding cloud, but
as each new star ignites, a fierce stellar wind begins to blow,
eroding the cloud, until finally there is no cloud, and the
new star is revealed."

The great star, Alpha Cygni, must have fallen out of its
embryonic cloud long after the origin of the Chenzeme.
Plagues might have infested the nursery nebula, but Alpha
Cygni's radiation would have broken their structures or
blown them away. Given the star's youth and giant size, it
seemed unlikely native life had evolved in its stellar system,
so perhaps the Chenzeme had never gone there. Raw &
Vast & Sterile. Lot found a cold amusement in the irony
that Alpha Cygni, in all its short-lived fury, should be a
safer destination than any system sporting a lovely blue-
green aqueous world.

• • •

Feeling all too human, Deneb supervised the dissection of a factory-made probe within the interstitial space that wrapped the ship's core. She had named the probe Vigil. It had been assembled from an ancient design, leading Nikko to worry about imperfections in the library file. So they'd disassembled the device after it emerged from the factory, inspecting the separate parts and testing them, finding only slight errors that were easily corrected.

Deneb ran her hands along the smooth shell of Vigil's exposed heart: a meter-long ovoid containing the observational instruments. It looked like an eye. She could see her reflection and Clemantine's in the dark and smoky iris of the probe's glass lens.

"Ready?" Clemantine asked.

Deneb nodded, and together they fitted the eye back into a housing that held the folded solar panels and a small volume of propellant so that the eye could turn. The eye closed, as a shroud within the probe's housing lowered across the lens.

A shield canister bisected the curved space of the interstice, both its ends resting in the soft tissue of the outer wall. Vigil would leave the ship ensconced within this protective package. Nikko—once again in corporeal form—helped them maneuver the probe into its waiting cradle. Tricky work in zero gravity, it would have been impossible under any significant acceleration. The components massed far more than the people arranging them.

The probe settled into position in the open canister. Deneb touched it once more, reluctant to let it go. Seldom had she been so close to working machines. Construction was a remote art, performed by microscopic assemblers under the direction of autonomous programs. Finished devices were sealed within their permanent positions without ever encountering human hands. She stroked the probe, finding an ancient satisfaction in this fleshy contact.

Vigil would accompany them as they dove toward the star, though it would follow a trajectory that would keep it above the killing radiation. "Punch a path out of here," she whispered. "Watch for us, while the Chenzeme hijackers burn."

Nikko chuckled. "Would that be a new attitude for you, Deneb? I thought you wanted the Chenzeme for your friends."

Her kisheer went still as she turned a wary eye upon him. Did animosity nick at his voice? She had been leery of him for a long time, but he had said so little to her these two years, had approached her so rarely, she'd let caution slip away. It returned now, like an old song, surfacing in the memory. He didn't know she had infected herself with her own evolved version of the cult parasite. No one knew. "You're afraid of making peace, aren't you?"

Softly, Clemantine said, "Deneb, don't start anything."

Nikko drifted at one end of the canister, his face—as always—unreadable. "The only peace the Chenzeme want is the peace of our extermination."

Deneb tapped the wall with her toes, gliding closer to him. "Don't misunderstand it, Nikko. Don't misunderstand me. The philosopher cells on our hull are a device. They are not the Chenzeme. No one has ever encountered the true Chenzeme."

"Well now that's lucky. You can still be the first to do it."

His words carried the shock of a physical blow. *Was* that what she wanted? She glanced at Clemantine but found no support there, just a cool curiosity. Heat flooded the scales of her face. "And what's wrong with that?" she asked huskily. "It's a better goal than slaughtering them all."

"With luck," Clemantine said, "we can do both."

Against her back, Deneb felt the impact of a slow bolt of fear. She turned to Clemantine, expecting . . . she was not quite sure what. Not the calm expression she found. "You don't mean that."

"I think I do."

Deneb's china-hard fingertips scraped against the canister as her fists clenched in a reflexive, a defensive, gesture. Her neural organ was immature; its presence undetectable—but for how long? Nikko had Chenzeme receptors in the walls. Were he and Clemantine so scarred by their experiences that they could not think rationally about peace? About the necessity of adaptation?

In that moment Deneb felt again the desperate loneliness she had known in her first hours after waking. When the abyss that separated her from Sol System, from her own past, had splayed open at her feet, and she had felt afraid to even think, knowing she had lost everything—and that the shapes moving now within her perception must be forever alien. Human in form, but of a mindscape she could never comprehend.

It was a sense of dissociation that had faded over time, but now the feeling returned with vigor. A quietness came over her—the cautious silence of an outsider.

"Come," Clemantine said. "It's time to finish."

"Right." Her voice carefully detached. "Let's close up then." She helped Nikko replace the panel they'd cut from the canister wall. He laid a bead of sealant on the seam. The compound steamed, and the seam vanished.

Deneb watched the process, acutely conscious of her heart beating hard within her throat. She had put her dormant ghost aboard the probe. It was packed into the memory, along with the ghosts of Nikko, Clemantine, and Urban—placed there against the vastly small chance the probe would encounter a substrate that could be used to reproduce them, before the information it carried degraded beyond retrieval.

So she would always be alone with them—these strangers—in this life, and any others that might follow. Always with them. The fact knocked at her, like the maddening rhythm of a half-heard drum. Always with them.

Not with Lot. He had no ghost.

But with them.

"Okay," Nikko said. He looked at Clemantine, then at Deneb, his gaze forever unreadable. "Let's get rid of it."

The wall opened a receptive pocket. Nikko coiled his toes around a hold and gave the canister a shove, while the pocket extruded petals to receive it. The canister would be ferried astern, to the cargo compartment of a missile that waited near the interface of contaminated and uncontaminated tissue.

"Nikko?" Deneb asked.

He turned to her as the canister disappeared, and she had to remind herself that he was *not* alien, that a man lurked somewhere behind that emotionless stare. That she had loved him in another life. Her kisheer curled and shivered as she struggled to comprehend such a thing. Of course he must have been a different man then. He had not already lost her.

She swallowed against a dry throat. "It's wrong to think of exterminating them . . . even if it is possible. You don't know them. You're hating a phantom, a shadow that was cast by some unknown thing a long time ago."

"Not so long. They made the cult virus."

"*Something* made the cult virus. It might have been a small faction of the Chenzeme, out to conquer the rest. Maybe the warships fight so hard because most of the Chenzeme are terrified of the cult too."

His kisheer went still. Anger limned his voice. "If it is a civil war, it's clear both sides are waging it against *us*. And we know they're still out there, because they made the cult virus to work against us. That could not have happened very long ago. Whatever they are, Deneb, they don't have our best interests in mind. Get that straight this time and maybe we'll have a chance."

Was it my fault? Could she be responsible for something that happened in another life? Nikko seemed to think so. It wasn't hard to guess what he would say if he learned of her neural organ. *Still the same Deneb.*

She felt exposed. She turned a wary gaze on Clemantine, but all she encountered there was the oblivious expression of someone under heavy atrial link. No doubt she tracked the canister's progress through the transit tissue. Deneb sighed.

Calling the same feed into her own atrial space, she watched an image of the canister as it approached the missile. She watched it load into the waiting cavity.

The missile was oriented on a line tangential to the ship's core, so that its exhaust would not burn a tunnel into the heart of the uncontaminated tissue. Still, they would lose a great deal of territory when the exhaust sterilized their own defensive Makers.

"Fry the bastards," Nikko muttered. "It's our turn to win."

A synthetic voice chanted the ignition sequence: "*Three . . . two . . . one . . . go.*"

The image in Deneb's atrium vanished as the observational instruments burned. She felt the vibration of the ignited missile through the malleable walls, rattling the air of the chamber, first with a deep hum, then a soft *boom*.

A second, smaller missile followed the bore hole punched out by the first. She felt that vibration too. It hauled out a heavy cable that would suffice as a radio antenna for Null

Boundary. The cable was laced with newly developed Makers. They hoped to have at least twenty minutes of observation time before it succumbed. If the new Makers worked well, they might have more time than that.

Deneb looked to Nikko for word of success, but he was silent, his eyes closed behind their crystal shield. "Have we contact with the probe?" she whispered.

He hesitated a moment, then nodded. "We have."

Her chest felt light. Her heartbeat reverberated as if it boomed in an empty chamber.

Nikko straightened his shoulders, and Deneb realized he'd been huddled against the inner wall. He announced: "The missile housing has fallen away."

She allowed herself to breathe, softly, slowly. The missile had been designed to burst open with explosive bolts, so that any contaminants on its surface would be blown clear. The shield canister was similarly designed.

"The canister is open now," Nikko said. His kisheer shuddered, rising up around his neck as he let out a long and raucous whoop. "*Yes!* Clemantine, did you catch that? It's away. It's away."

Lot kept his grim watch in the core chamber, still alone when the first processed image from Vigil was displayed. He hissed. *The courser.* Its image splashed across the wall in flawless clarity. It still dogged them. It couldn't be more than a few kilometers away. He stared at its gleaming white hull, and at a dark wound near its stern, a crater with edges curling outward.

Understanding hit him. This was not the courser at all. This was an image of Null Boundary—but how the ship had changed! There were no distinguishing features left. The solenoids were gone; the exhaust vents were plugged; the entire hull had been colonized by the philosopher cells; and at the bow he could just make out the beginnings of the ridged architecture they had seen aboard the dark courser.

We have become a Chenzeme courser. Though without weapons or zero point drive—and they were badly damaged. The dark crater marked the point where the missile had exited. Lot couldn't see the radio cable. "Where is the real courser?" he demanded. "Nikko? How close is it?"

Nikko's ghost didn't answer, but on the wall a graphic marker appeared several handspans above Null Boundary's image. It bore the label: **object Alpha-Cyg1, spectra-match, Courser A. Range:>120,000**K.

Well within weapons range, yet it hadn't approached, and it hadn't fired. Like a nursemaid it accompanied them, overseeing their transformation.

A torrent of harsh light washed over Lot's back, erosive in its intensity. It overwhelmed Null Boundary's image, casting Lot's shadow in its place—though he felt his own body must soon dissolve in that heatless radiance.

He turned, to face a small point of unbearable brightness set into the dark wall.

"What is that? Nikko?" He squinted, wondering if some process in the image walls had failed, or if Vigil had been contaminated and was sending garbage signals.

"Come on, Nikko," Lot muttered, hoping that at least a submind was listening. "Damp the intensity. Process this input so I can *see* something."

Did the brightness decline? He wasn't sure at first. Then slowly, he noticed again his body, emerging from the solution of light.

The ship shuddered. Lot twisted around to find that Null Boundary's image was visible again, just as a chain of explosions ripped open the ship's flank.

Beginning aft and advancing toward the bow, orange mushrooms of fire leaped outward, uncurling into jets that narrowed and became blue lances that swiftly sputtered and faded. Nikko was firing his remaining steerage engines! Two years ago the engines had been pulled deep into the ship's tissue, away from the encroaching Chenzeme layer, while Nikko synthesized a fuel substitute. Lot counted the explosions of three engines, then four—no, five of them, feeling the brush of weight as the image wall pushed against his back.

This was not the ignition of precision jets. The engines' exhaust throats had been plugged by the Chenzeme encroachment. He was watching the immolation of pockets of reserved fuel, each one blasting past the reformatted hull, burning off swaths of philosopher cells, torching all the information they contained. Nikko was brutally rending their hull to refine the ship's course. An orange glare defined the wounds—a glare that did not fade.

Lot glanced at the graphic that marked the courser, fearing it would react. The label had amended: **Range:>140,000K**. So it was pulling away, or falling behind. The count ran up to 145, then 150—

Lot flinched as a sixth pocket of fuel exploded outward. He waited in tense silence, but there were no more eruptions. The courser's range had grown to two hundred thousand kilometers, and it was still increasing. Apparently it would not follow them into the fire.

Lot turned again to the point of brilliant white light.

This is Alpha Cygni, he realized. Like the face of a distant god, so bright he couldn't look at it directly.

If the steerage engines had fired properly, their course would now bring them through the star's outer envelope. Null Boundary would flash through a sea of fire, destroying the Chenzeme encroachment, sterilizing the hull.

"Lot?"

He turned, surprised by Clemantine's voice. She drifted at the mouth of a newly opened crawlway, uncertainty in her dark eyes.

"Will the course change work?" he asked her.

"Let's hope so, because there's nothing else we can do."

We didn't have to do even this. The courser was out there. With the hull cells intact, they could have persuaded it to meet them peacefully. But it was too late to change anything now.

His gaze returned to the image of Alpha Cygni. If the explosions had been mistimed or badly aimed, they were screwed. The ship would run too deep and boil apart. Lot had to suppose it marginally possible the opposite could happen, that they would run too shallow so the hull cells survived. He didn't put any hope in it, though. Nikko would have weighted his course correction for depth, even at risk to the survival of the ship. Lot had no doubt they were going in, and all the way. "Look at it," he said, nodding at the star's image. "You can almost see—"

Clemantine's mood lapped over him at last, silencing whatever banality had been on his mind. Her melancholy curled around him, while her horny defiance dropped straight to his core. He looked at her in dumb surprise, feeling the cult rise inside him.

"No reason to stay here, Lot. It looks like the courser will leave us alone, for now. And nothing else is going to happen for a while. So come now, with me."

The core interstice had narrowed; the apartments had shrunk to small hollows at the end of short tunnels. Still, there was room enough for their needs. Lot closed his eyes and tilted his head back, feeling the skin of his throat stretch and Clemantine's soft lips there, her breath so moist and warm, qualities that could vanish in Alpha Cygni's fire. *This passage isn't necessary.*

Nothing could stop it now.

He touched her head, relishing the nappy feel of her hair against his palm. He caressed her neck, while she concentrated on separating him from his skin suit. "Clemantine?"

"Mmm?"

"Did you ever have children?"

"No." She looked at him sideways, her dark eyes bright and full of a grim history that had hardened her, but had never extinguished her native grace. "Or maybe I did. Somewhere. Not this version of me, though."

"Maybe that version you left behind in Silk?"

"Hush. Leave them to their own lives. We're no part of it anymore."

"Sooth." They were in the grip of a relentless momentum, falling farther and farther from their pasts, and no turning back, ever. "It's just that . . . it all seems so fragile. What we do. Our lives. The choices we make. What happens to us. None of it is repeatable. If we could wind time back, it would never happen this way again."

"Does that frighten you?"

"Not really. Not all the time. It's just that, every moment, every life is . . ." He groped for a word that would say it.

"Unique?" Clemantine suggested.

"Yes, but more. It could never be again."

"Sometimes that's good."

"Sometimes it's not. And everything that's ever been

done, everything that's been accomplished, seems so precarious. A dropped glass a thousand years ago. A misunderstood glance . . . and where would we be? Never born. Another would be . . . not even here. You understand? None of this *needs* to be, by any definition of the word. We are here because . . . because we stumbled in this direction, and our ancestors before us, for no reason. That's *precarious*. I feel like . . . like a moth, my chaotic motion programmed in my cells, struggling chaotically over thermal currents that rise chaotically from the fire."

"Don't think about that."

He couldn't help it. Alpha Cygni might mean death for them, but deep in its core, elements were being brewed that would make new worlds. "This star is like the body of a god. Every element is there, or will rise from it, but for now it is without form."

She looked puzzled at the drift of his mood. "Is that meant to be poetic or superstitious?"

He shook his head. It was just another way of seeing. The cult flamed inside him, a white-hot fire, afraid now of its own demise. Nothing would ever come out of him but the cult. Even more than the courser that shadowed them, he was a machine with a singular purpose, a fact too clearly illuminated by the infinite possibilities embodied in this star. "I'm overdesigned. There are too many contingencies."

Clemantine didn't answer for so long he thought she would refuse to answer. Then finally: "Everything about you was made for a purpose, Lot. Or to defend that purpose. *That* is the difference between artificial and natural things. Artificial things have their reason for being imposed on them. Natural things are left to find their own reason in every moment of their existence."

His charismata bumped ineffectively against her. "You can change," he concluded for her. "I cannot."

In that sense, the Makers that cleaned his skin and the DIs that watched over him were more alive than he, and he was a machine, a tool without adaptive properties, and he was not alive at all because he could not find his own reason for being. "And still, I love you."

"Say that, again and again."

"I love you. I love you."

This star called Alpha Cygni was the body of a god, but

there would be no images, no leaping faces, no mocking dread, no superstitious ghouls encountered on their passage through its vaporous fire. In that sea of disassembled potential, of worlds waiting to be born, there would be only light. Pure light, incandescent dust, flowing plasma, without reason, filled with potential. "I love you," he repeated, one more time.

Untouchable light, that no order and no destiny and no reason could survive.

Chapter
16

The spider on Lot's ear woke him from a half-sleep. "You there, fury?"

Lot's eyes opened. He looked around to find Clemantine already awake. "Urban?"

"Nikko says to come to the core chamber. We're closing up."

"What's the courser's range?"

"Nine hundred thousand K," Urban said. "*Way* out of weapons range. The dog is slowing down like it's about to hit a wall."

Clemantine looked thoughtful as she pulled on her shorts and her stretch top. "The profile of anticipated hull temperatures sounds a little high."

Lot gave her a puzzled look. It was Urban who answered, and he sounded impatient. "Sooth. We're pushing the upper range. We aren't going to get a second chance."

"Exactly. So we need to accurately anticipate the effects. It'll take days to radiate that volume of heat. Can we be sure the core will remain insulated that long?"

"*I'm* sure of it. I plan to change the profile of the hull to speed cooling. Look, I've worked up some scenarios. See? These are arrays of fins we can deploy from midlevel tissue, depending on when we get control of our rotation."

Lot could see nothing. This conversation was taking place

at least partly on a level he could not access, leaving him feeling like a kid, excluded from the discussions of his elders.

But this was Urban.

"What do you mean *you* plan to change the hull?" Lot demanded. "Urban, when did you take Nikko's place?"

"Get dressed, fury."

The walls of the chamber pressed in around them. Lot hurried to grab his skin suit. It floated free, a silvery mantle writhing on the slow air current. He touched it with his hand and it wrapped around him, its seams smoothly sealing over his skin. "When, Urban?"

"I haven't taken Nikko's place. I'm just . . . backing him up."

While learning everything he needed to know to run a ship? Lot might have asked more questions, but not with Clemantine there.

They left the apartment, to find the interstice had shrunk to a crevice only a couple of feet across. "Nikko's been busy," Lot observed.

"We'll be filling this space with insulating tissue," Clemantine explained as she crossed the gap and entered a crawlway. "In the midhull we're layering insulation with airless decks to slow the spread of heat. We've been lucky. So far the antenna has held."

She dropped into the core chamber. Lot followed her, to find Deneb already there. Urban showed up moments later, emerging from a hidden membrane. "All together at last," he said.

Lot asked him, "Are you the same persona?"

He cocked his head. "As what? Oh. Yeah. I am now."

If he felt any fear, Lot couldn't sense it. Trust Urban to edit anything unsavory.

Deneb did not show the same degree of preparation. Fear steamed off her in a humid front. Her kisheer trembled, while her toes latched tightly to holds on the image wall. She looked as if she were afraid of falling. "We haven't discussed where we're going after this," she said.

"Assuming there is an after?" Lot asked. It surprised him that there were still plans to be made.

"We have to assume that," Deneb snapped.

Clemantine frowned at the walls. "Let's get some pictures back up while the antenna's still intact."

Somebody had summoned a factory door to the back of the core chamber. Lot headed for it, as a filtered image of the great star came up. The point of brilliance Lot had seen before was gone. Alpha Cygni had swollen into an immense plain mottled with granular shadows. Most of the light had been stripped away by filters; it did not look white, or pure. Lanes of static cut across its face as magnetic currents twisted Vigil's incoming signal.

Lot asked the factory if it was working. It assured him that it was. He ordered two bottles of champagne.

It took a minute for the package to be hauled out of storage, but at last the factory opened its door, and Lot removed two teardrop-shaped bottles. Clemantine gave him a sideways look, preoccupied with trying to filter the increasingly erratic signal from Vigil. Static-cut images flickered all around the chamber walls. "Don't open that in here," she warned him.

"Why not?" He beheaded the bottle with one ceremonious swipe of his hand. A sweet-smelling, frothy geyser erupted from the broken neck.

"That's why."

Urban laughed. He'd been huddling with Deneb, trying to offer her some comfort, Lot supposed. But now he left her to dive at the shower of champagne, catching a boiling globule in his mouth.

Lot grinned. Screw thermal profiles and cooling arrays. This was the Urban he knew. "A toast," Lot declared. "To Alpha Cygni." He mimicked Urban, diving after another bouncing, stretching globule. Some of it he caught in his mouth, but most of it splashed across his face. He swallowed against the sweet sizzle.

"Wait," Urban said. "We need a real toast." His eyes unfocused for just a moment. Did he slip into the library? "Got it." He peered at Lot. "Are you scared?"

"Not really."

"You should be." He grinned. Then he caught one of the shivering globules in his hand. "It's a quote by some Virgil, no-last-name: 'Death twitches my ear. *Live,* he says. *I am coming.*'"

Lot thought about it, while a champagne snake wriggled

past them. "Sooth. That's how it is." He chopped at the snake's back, shattering it, then scooped one of the resulting globules and sucked it, feeling the flush of alcohol in his cheeks.

Deneb dropped down between them. "I've never had champagne."

"Better hurry," Urban advised.

Lot saw his chance and scooped another bead. He passed it to Deneb. She caught his arm before he could pull it back, and she drank from his hand. He couldn't remember her ever touching him before. Her blue eyes fixed on him, bright and intense. Her fear was still there, but it was sharpened now, with a defiant edge. "I want to know how you see the world."

He cocked his head, wondering how to interpret such a statement.

She watched him puzzle it out; then her chin rose, and she laughed merrily. "Don't try to guess! You won't succeed. It's just that I'm still working on the cult parasite. I might even get results soon."

Urban dropped down between them. "Hear that, people? The revolution has triumphed. Deneb has broken our resistance and restored the cult!"

She gaped at him, scandalized. "I have not! You—you *mediot.*" She swiped at a passing globule, batting it into Urban's face. It shattered against his cheek, the spray flying over all of them, and Deneb again burst into laughter.

Urban's eyebrows rose in feigned shock. "The first shot is fired. I do believe we have a war."

Lot could see what was coming. He ducked out of the way as Urban dove on a globule, slamming it at Deneb. She squealed and tried to dodge, but it hit her cheek, bursting into a thousand droplets. "*Mediot!*" she shouted again, diving behind Lot just as Urban launched another shot.

"Hey!" Lot protested. He tried to dodge, but the champagne explosion hit him in the temple, spraying over Deneb, who growled and slapped at another globule, seeking to return the favor to Urban. But she hit it wrong and it shattered, soaking Lot too.

Urban laughed. "Do you know what a human mind is? I read this somewhere. It's a DI that's gone crazy."

"Like you?" Deneb asked. She had her hands on Lot's

shoulders, using him for a shield. In the sudden skirmish, Lot had lost contact with the wall. He twisted against Deneb, trying to get back to a place he could hold on to.

"Hey," Urban said. "He's stuck. Leave him there."

Deneb still had one toe on the wall. Lot felt the spike of her excitement and knew she would strand him if she could, leaving him hanging in open space, with no momentum and no way to reach any wall.

He twisted hard, just as she pulled away. "Uh-uh," he warned. He caught her wrist, and she erupted in laughter.

"Let go of me!"

"Not a chance."

She worked to pry his fingers loose. He let her do it, because he already had the momentum he needed. They bumped together against the wall. For a moment, the smooth scales of her shoulders flexed beneath his hands. Then she wriggled free, still giggling. "Crazy DIs get recycled!"

The air was getting warm. Lot thought it might be the alcohol. Across the chamber, a static-laced image of the great star flickered. Clemantine was anchored to it, one foot hooked under a loop, her gaze glassy as she focused on the intermittent images still reaching them from the probe.

Lot's gaze cut to Urban. It didn't seem right that Clemantine should be allowed to ignore them. Urban nodded silent agreement. "Is the bottle empty?" He mouthed the words.

"No," Deneb whispered. She plucked it from the air with a toe. Lot raised his hand and she passed it to him.

He turned the bottle around. Nothing came out. He tried shaking it. A few droplets burst from the neck. "Sloppy," Clemantine said, inches from his ear. Lot jumped in surprise, and Urban erupted in a roar of laughter. Clemantine took the opportunity to snatch the bottle out of Lot's hands. "Here's how we used to do it on the outposts at Heyertori."

Urban's laughter came to an abrupt end. "You were there?"

Clemantine raised one eyebrow. "How did you think I survived?"

"Then you saw Null Boundary pass—"

"Like this," she interrupted, and she sent the bottle spinning end over end, trailing from its tip a ribbon of flat champagne. She dove on it.

Lot recovered from his surprise in time to follow her, but just as he was about to beat her to a mouthful, she turned to him with an arch look—"Try to ambush me, will you?"—and she gave his shoulder a flick. Instantly, he found himself tumbling out of control. He slammed into Urban, while somewhere, Deneb laughed uproariously.

Nikko took that moment to drop into the chamber. "End-of-the-world party?" he asked.

"Any excuse," Clemantine told him. Her grin was wicked. She had gotten her hands on the second bottle of champagne. She beheaded it, sending a geyser of foam lashing across Nikko's face. He ducked—too late!—shaking his head, while Lot laughed so hard his belly ached.

Urban dove into the champagne cloud, slapping at the droplets, sending them slamming into Lot and Nikko, Deneb and Clemantine, before he hit the wall again with a thud.

The blow demolished his good humor. "Hold on," he said sternly. His head canted at an awkward angle as he squinted against the fiery image of the great star on the wall beside him. "Nikko? There. You see it? What is that?"

"I don't know."

Lot saw it now: a tiny spot against the star's surface, flashing in and out of existence within a ribbon of colorful static. It lay ahead of them, but there was no indication how far. As they swept toward the corona it surged in size, evolving between flashes of static from a formless spot to a ring seen almost edge-on. The Chenzeme vessels called swan bursters were perfect ring shapes too.

"That's not a natural object, is it?" Deneb asked.

Nikko's answer was terse: "No."

"It could be a swan burster," Clemantine warned. "It could take a shot at us, Nikko."

"Orbiting this close to the star, its hull cells will be dead."

Lot shook his head. "The dark courser found us without its hull cells active."

Nikko's frustration was a gray rot against his sensory tears. "It doesn't matter. There's nothing we can do."

The ring was already falling behind them, its image shrinking as Null Boundary passed within its orbit.

Urban leaned close to the wavering display. "We're losing the signal."

"Vigil will record it," Deneb said. "We'll get the record on the other side."

The curtains of static thickened. The ring's image flashed one more time, then vanished into a sea of chaotic color that itself lasted only a moment, before the chamber plunged into darkness.

"That's it," Nikko said grimly. "We've lost the antenna. We're blind again."

No one else spoke for several seconds while Null Boundary finished its plunge toward the star. Lot felt a pressure in the absolute darkness. He listened to the harsh wash of his own ragged breathing, while through the champagne mist Nikko's tension stung at his sensory tears. They would be going deep. "Nikko? Have we reached bottom yet?"

"Not yet."

Now Lot could hear a low moan rising from the ship's tissues, a vibration that trembled in his bones. "Heat expansion?" Deneb asked, her voice no more than a whisper.

The sound rose in frequency, an eerie wail in the darkness.

"The hull will be incandescent now," Nikko said.

In his mind's eye Lot saw the ship, hurtling through searing veils of plasma, traveling far too fast to ever be captured by Alpha Cygni's gravity. The philosopher cells would be white hot, molten and amorphous, their lighter elements escaping as vapor. "Nikko?" he asked again. "How much deeper?"

"Now. This is it."

The howl faded. For a moment the silence was unimpeded. Then a fizz arose from the image walls. Lot felt a warm liquid slick beneath his palm.

Was water seeping from the grip? He swiped at the wall and felt the splatter of a thick liquid layer. "What's happening?"

"We're flooding," Nikko said.

Then everyone spoke at once:

"Get some lights in here," Clemantine barked.

Deneb suggested, "Maybe the humidity sensors are overtaxed."

"Then kill them," Urban demanded.

Nikko told him, "They're already dead."

"Then maybe it's steam pressure."

"No. The vacuoles should be able to hold the pressure."

Lot could feel the liquid layer up to his wrist now. Beneath it, the image walls began to glow with a ghostly green light—a dilute emerald green—a shade all too familiar. Unnerved, he yanked his hand away from the wall, leaving a shadow behind in the shape of his grip, where tiny beads of green moisture oozed from the gray wall.

He touched the spot again, swiping the beads away. They were warm, and more viscous than water. They clung to his hand. He touched his tongue to one of them and experienced again the familiar, vaguely sweet taste of Deception Well.

Urban's hand closed on his shoulder. Lot turned to him, and they shared a knowing look. They had both been in the Well; they knew its signature. Information had crawled through the biosphere there, carried by elusive long molecules that washed into the streams, turning the water an enchanting, viscous green.

"How did it get aboard Null Boundary?" Urban asked. He answered his own question. "Oh. *We* brought it, didn't we?"

"Sooth." In the Well, they had drunk the water freely. Even if they had not, Lot knew the Well's microscopic governors would still have infested their tissue—breathed in through their lungs or ferried across the illusory barriers of their skin. "Some of it probably came out of the nebular dust too." He had imagined the Well influence as a fossil impression left on the philosopher cells, never suspecting the governors still lived among them.

The liquid was halfway up his forearm now. Blobs of it were breaking off, knocked loose by air currents, or by the motions of Deneb, Clemantine, and Nikko as they sought to avoid contact with the emerald substance.

"It won't hurt you," Lot assured them. At least, he was fairly sure it would not. Events in the Well had never been predictable.

"Has it been in the ship's tissue all this time?" Clemantine demanded. "Why is it emerging now?"

"Maybe it's melting out?" Lot suggested. "It could be withdrawing from the radiation, pulling back to the only safe site available."

The fluid was elbow deep. Clemantine's face looked eerie in the green light, her eyes cold and unnatural as she considered this theory. She flinched as a fist-sized blob waddled past her. "We're going to drown."

Deneb had already shoved her kisheer up over her nose and mouth as the ratio of liquid to air within the chamber continued to climb. Lot strove to keep his face in the clear. Still, he managed to breathe in a droplet. He started coughing. The spasm dislodged more fluid from the walls, a bright green fountain that mixed with the champagne.

Lot started to apologize, but his words were overwhelmed by the thunderclap of an explosion resounding through the ship. Beneath his hand the image wall rippled, pitching off the clinging moisture, launching it into free fall. Lot closed his eyes, ducking his head as a shimmering wave slammed over him. The impact knocked him from the wall. Water enwrapped him on all sides. He thrashed, not knowing in what direction air might be found, or even if there was air left to find.

Don't panic.

He forced his eyes open, to find himself immersed in a deep green world. He could see Deneb a body length away, her kisheer a veil over her mouth and nose and ears. With relief he realized she would be able to breathe, even if the chamber filled.

In the muted light he could not see her eyes beneath their protective lenses, but he saw her reaching for him. Did she know a way out? He kicked hard against the thick green water. His hand closed on hers. With her other hand, she motioned for him to continue. He kicked again, and this time he burst past a surface layer that had been invisible to him. Certainly the light did not change color when he emerged into an oscillating pocket of air walled by shifting arcs of surface tension. He gasped, filling his lungs. At the same moment, Deneb's hand tightened on his: an anchor that turned him around and killed his momentum. He looked back, to see only her hand protruding into the pocket of air. Then, as he watched, her face emerged, the surface tension breaking across it like a glassine mask peeling away.

"Where's Clemantine and Urban?" he asked her. "Where's Nikko?" He could not see their shapes anywhere in the green glow around him.

She looked at him, only her head and a wisp of her shoulders emergent from the green water wall. It took her a moment to spit out her kisheer. "They're in another air pocket at the chamber's far end. They're all right."

His shoulders heaved as he drew a breath of relief. "The explosion—what was it?"

Worry furrowed her brow as she consulted the ship through her atrial link. "It was in the reactor chamber. Nikko thinks it might have been the casket that held Urban's contaminated skin suit, and his remains."

"Is the reactor damaged?"

She shrugged. "Cameras are out. We can't tell."

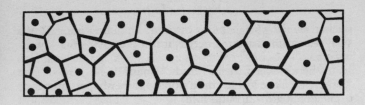

Chapter
17

Green walls shifted and rippled, echoing the restless sense that rolled off Deneb. Lot could guess: She was getting ready to duck back into the water. He felt a sudden, panicked sense of entrapment. "Wait! Show me where Urban and Clementine are."

She looked distracted, her attention turned inward. "I don't think—"

Nikko popped through the surface beside her with an abruptness that made Lot jump. He hung half in air, half in water, like a sea thing from the VR. The kisheer rolled off his face, oozing out of his mouth to unfurl across his shoulders. Lot watched it, grimly fascinated.

"Air's a problem," Nikko announced. "Oxygen is still being processed in the chamber walls, but it can't diffuse fast enough through this goop to replenish what you're using."

Lot nodded, holding on to an appearance of calm, though in his breast he could feel the beat of caged panic. His gaze roved around the trembling sphere that contained him. The air in this bubble was warm and humid, heavy with a vapor that gathered in ever greater concentrations within his lungs. "Can't we pump this mess back through the walls?"

In the vague light, Nikko's blue eyes looked black. They

seemed fixed on some point beyond Lot's shoulder. "This is Well stuff. It's smarter than we are."

Sure. They could try to pump the green water back into an interstice, but if the governors objected—

He could not guess what would happen. The chamber's transport membranes might simply fail. That seemed most likely. Still, the governors could chance on an active defense, attacking on a microscopic scale anything that was not Self.

"Okay," Lot said. He could find no echo of his own fear in Nikko's aura; only a cold and mechanical determination. "I'll need a rebreather, then."

"I've already ordered some, but the factory's sluggish. It could be several minutes more before they're ready—and Clemantine and Urban will need them sooner. They're caught in a smaller pocket."

"They could come here."

"That would make this bubble small."

"So you want me to wait here."

"You have to."

Lot moved his head slowly back and forth, but the only new sense he caught was his own crushing disappointment. He nodded. He really did not want to be alone. Nothing to do about it, though. Was there? He looked hopefully at Deneb.

That faint optimism was dashed when he saw her kisheer fluttering up her neck. She said, "There's another bubble we can move you to if needed. It's small, but—" She shrugged, and the kisheer sealed over her face. She ducked back beneath the liquid, a water spirit seen in distorted silhouette, rippling into invisibility.

"Are we going to make it?" Lot asked, turning back to Nikko—but Nikko had disappeared too, beneath a pucker of green water, leaving only the vapor of his mood behind him, a cold determination laid over sullen fury. Lot moved his head back and forth, letting the emotional remnants drag across his sensory tears, diluted by a sluggish green rain, by green filaments and champagne mist.

He felt horribly alone—and impatient with himself. The others weren't far. The core chamber was the same size it had always been.

Yet it felt huge now, and the world that contained them overwhelmingly vast. And the five of them all the people there were to fill it.

He moved his head again, tasting Nikko's fading presence. Determination over a sullen fury. *Is this our signature?*

He liked the taste of it. So he took it into himself, and he changed it. Stripping it of all ornamentation, he saved only the core of it—a core intensity that he redoubled, again, and again until it filled him, until he felt himself poised on a clifftop, or perhaps on the edge of the Well, with his consciousness flowing outward, creating space around him.

His eyes were not closed. Still, he did not see with them. That part of his mind that fabricated the sense of images was busied by another input. With muted surprise, he realized he had accessed the data latent in the green water of the Well that rained against his cheeks.

This awareness brought on a sense of wonder edged in faint, warm fear. He'd been here before. He knew the history of the Well was kept within the complex molecules that ran through every niche of that world and through the system's cocooning nebula. In the Well, Lot had accessed those histories, he'd harvested the design of the philosopher cells from the nebular dust—but he'd done it only when half drowned or drugged, never on his own.

Now, he crouched on a pinnacle at the center of an expanse that unfurled around him as if it were his own newly made wings. Thoughts pumped through this vista on highways woven of linked molecules. He heard his heart beating, pumping thoughts.

Far away, thin shapes moved—very far. He felt their distance as a measure of time, not of space. He gazed into the past and he saw things like translucent cloth blown on wind or like glistening nets rippling or like fog and knew these things were living beings. This knowledge appeared whole in his mind without preamble. These things were a kind of people, and yet they were like nothing he'd ever seen before, either in a library, or in the Well, or in his own crippled imagination.

Then, as abruptly as it had formed, this world began to collapse. He felt in himself an excruciating sense of mass, as if the vast wings of his perception were being crushed back into an impossibly compact core. He opened his mouth. Air slid past his throat in a rattling gasp. The vista onto the past vanished, while around him, the water walls trembled, as if responding to the echo of a scream that had died in his throat.

He cursed out loud, realizing he had let himself be caught in a pocket of still air. He might have suffocated, breathing the same torpid current over and over again. He twisted restlessly, as if he could sense where the oxygen was thickest.

What had he seen?

He swiped at the watery surface with the tips of his fingers, weighing the risk of seeking that state again. Just then, Clementine emerged through the wall of the bubble, a rebreather clinging with gelatinous fingers to her face. She popped it off and asked him, "Are you okay?"

"Yeah."

"You look a little lost."

He smiled. "Is the ship holding together?"'

She pursed her lips. "Well now, that depends on exactly what you mean."

Neural paths to the reactor chamber had failed, but when Urban had them rebuilt, he found the cameras still operational. Now his ghost floated cross-legged, three feet above a white data path. Nikko drifted at his shoulder. Together they gazed at a library window that opened onto the reactor chamber.

Debris from the exploded casket ricocheted through the high, narrow room in glowing, misshapen mushroom heads. The room lights had failed, but the chamber had not gone dark. Discrete flecks of blazing white light outlined slowly healing dents and scars on the glossy walls. The flecks were larger versions of the spots Urban had seen burning against his glove when he'd returned from his foray to the dark courser.

Another piece of shrapnel struck the wall. This time there was a small explosion. The piece shattered into droplets of red-hot clay that leaped off the wall with enhanced acceleration. At the point of impact, a white fleck glowed with heightened luminosity. The temperature in the chamber hovered near one hundred degrees Celsius.

"It's another infection, isn't it?" Urban asked.

Nikko nodded somberly. "That would be my guess."

"I picked it up on the courser. I brought it back on the skin suit, and now it's spread." He had wanted a trophy, but this was not exactly what he'd had in mind. "Lot thinks the warships are made of an alliance of organisms. Maybe this is one of them."

"It's hardy, whatever it is. To survive in the casket for two years."

"It's thriving now. Do you think it's feeding off the heat?"

Nikko didn't answer right away. Then: "It wasn't this hot in the courser's vent tube."

"Sooth. But the vent tube was inactive when we were there. If we cool the reactor chamber, we might slow its spread."

Nikko grunted. Another window opened beyond the first. Nikko started running engineering simulations, seeking arrays that would pull heat out of the bow. Urban produced a submind to look over his shoulder.

But his ghost remained fixed on the window into the reactor chamber. He had wanted to bring a trophy back. Now he watched another white spot brighten as it was struck by shrapnel. He watched it ooze with barely discernible motion toward the bow of the ship. He recalled the flowing current of light in the courser's vent tube and the stretching pull of shifting space-time. They'd gone into the tube looking for some clue to the engineering puzzle of the zero point drive. Could it be that they had owned that clue for two years and never realized it?

"Nikko?"

"Yeah?"

"Maybe we shouldn't try to slow this infestation. Maybe we should encourage it instead."

Nikko's head turned toward him. His blue eyes glared in a disconcerting, off-center gaze.

Urban self-consciously straightened his back. Defiance chopped his words. "The only way to find out what it does is to let it grow."

"Lot suggested nearly the same thing after the mating."

Urban thought about this, then shook his head. "It's not the same. The metabolic layer was like an army, systematically conquering the ship's tissue and reformatting it. This is more like . . . an escaped tool? That's what it acts like. It doesn't seem too smart." He shrugged. "Anyway, you know where it came from. It could be associated with the zero point drive. We could learn a lot."

Nikko sighed.

Urban watched him anxiously, but he could not guess what he was thinking. "Come on, Nikko," he pressed. "It's not like there are any safe choices."

"We could let the chamber retain its heat," Nikko said. "At least for now."

"Good." Urban nodded to himself. It felt like progress. "We'll watch it closely. Shut it down if we have to."

"If we can."

Another white fleck oozed toward the bow in minute, amoebic motion. The shrapnel rattled against the glistening walls. Urban felt something like fear stir in the chaotic regions beneath his conscious mind. He deleted it immediately.

It was Deneb who found a temporary solution to the problem of the green flood. She designed a membrane to grow on the chamber walls, a chorionic sac that surrounded the Well water. At her command the membrane contracted, peeling off the aft wall, herding the liquid into a compact globule that nested in the chamber's bow end.

Nikko was the first to wriggle out of the gelatinous sac. It sealed behind him. He turned to watch the others emerge into the open cavity, like tadpoles bursting out of a self-healing egg.

Deneb shook her head hard, drenching her kisheer in the oxygen-rich air. It shivered, then oozed off her face. She grinned, at no one in particular. "It worked, didn't it?"

"A grand job," Clemantine agreed. "Now let's get a new antenna deployed."

Nikko had a ghost already at work on the project. The antenna was launched through the simmering hull, a cable that survived only seconds—but that was enough to receive from Vigil a compressed data squirt encompassing the time since contact was lost.

The aft wall flooded with an edited image of the great star. The ring artifact stood against the face of Alpha Cygni, too small to discern, so its position was represented by a tiny black circle drawn by Vigil's DI. The circle was labeled: **identity unknown. estimated 2k diameter.** Far, far smaller than the gigantic swan bursters suggested by its ring shape.

The pursuing courser was represented by a labeled point, rising over the star's horizon.

"Look how far it's veered," Urban said. He cocked his fist at it. "Too hot for you, you son of a bitch?"

"Look how much it's slowed," Clemantine added, her dark gaze locked on the columns of data scrolling at the bottom of the display. "It's still slowing. It's decelerating at almost fifty g's. By the Unknown God. We could survive a maneuver like that only as ghosts. Nikko?" She turned. Her suspicious gaze skewered him. "What the hell is going on?"

"Maybe it's detected something ahead of us," Urban mused.

"Something bad enough to scare a Chenzeme courser?"

"Now you're scaring me," Deneb said.

Nikko's fingers rattled against his thigh in a nervous cadence. "I don't know for sure, but . . . look at the ring." He opened a window in the image wall, using it to house a model of the courser's path. Its velocity was already far less than Null Boundary's, yet still so fast its path bent only a little even in Alpha Cygni's immense gravity. "Isn't it lining itself up with the ring—?"

Deneb cried out as if in pain.

Nikko turned back to the projection on the aft wall, to see the artifact bursting open in a white-hot explosion: the courser had fired on it. The white light made a brief ghost of Deneb's face.

"*Old murderers,*" Clemantine growled in a guttural voice, full of hate.

Nikko felt something too—panic? revulsion? pity? It passed too quickly to be sure, excised by a protective neural function. He shook his head. "The courser must have been aware of the ring hours ago. That's why it slowed down— to give itself a longer window to use its gun."

Urban studied the image, his fist cocked near his chin. "The ring had to be a priority target. So what the hell was it? Run the record back, Nikko. Is there any more detail?"

"Vigil wasn't instructed to watch the ring," Clemantine said. "There's not much else."

"It was silent, though," Urban mused. "No detectable

radio. No visible philosopher cells. Definitely not a swan burster. So what was it?"

"We can't know," Deneb said. Her kisheer had scrunched around her neck; her voice was soft and uncertain. "We led the courser here. We caused this."

Nikko felt black anger move like a virus in his spine. She'd caused worse things in her time. "So the Chenzeme kill the Chenzeme. Boo-hoo."

Deneb stared at him in shock. "You don't know if the artifact was Chenzeme."

Lot overrode whatever retort he might have made. "It doesn't matter now! Not when our own ass is on the line." He clung to the wall above the burning image of the star. His anger and his ambition lashed the wall sensors. "I didn't want to make this passage, but now it's done, the ship is boiling away, we've got an event in the reactor chamber, and the courser's not so far behind. If you all don't do something now, it's over."

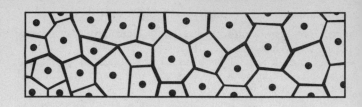

Chapter
18

Urban might have been waiting for a cue. "Lot's right," he snapped, kicking across the chamber to land on the wall beside Nikko. "We've wasted too much time already. Let's get the fins out, before we cook."

Deneb stared at him, striving to focus her attention. It was a joke to him. Everything was a joke, or a scheme, or a game. *Not this.* This was real. The ship needed to cool. It would be a long process, and she worried it would demand far more time than Urban had allotted. Meanwhile, heat would work its way from the ship's outer layers to the core.

She didn't want to think about that.

"I'm going to get another antenna out," Clemantine said. "See if we can get another data squirt from Vigil."

"Get on it," Nikko agreed. "We need to know what the courser's doing now."

"Our thermal profile is up and running in the library," Urban said. "Meet you all there."

Nikko agreed.

Clemantine agreed.

Deneb drew a deep breath to steady herself—wasted effort—Nikko's brusque voice sliced in through her atrium, making her jump. **How many ghosts are you comfortable running?*

Peeved at his intrusion, Deneb rounded on him. Why couldn't he speak out loud?

She found him gone from the chamber. *Hey, where are you?*

"He's ghosting," Urban said.

Her kisheer tightened around her neck. "You mean he's dissolved himself again? Love and nature, Nikko, how can you bear to wipe your core persona like that, over and over again?"

I don't have a core persona. Now, do you think you could leave aside the question of my mental health long enough to upload a ghost to the library? I want some oversight on the growth of the ship's cooling fins. And if you're feeling especially generous, we could use your opinion at the reactor chamber too.

"Is that all?"

How many ghosts are you comfortable running? We could always use more in engineering.

"I'll use subminds for that."

She carefully trimmed each persona, so none would feel her fear.

Microprobes launched through the ship's tissue reported the formation of a crust on the outer hull, but beneath that there was little organization. Incandescent liquids pooled around veins of glowing metal while volatile gases sublimed in a continuous cloud around the ship. Deneb's ghost knew the loss of hydrogen, oxygen, and carbon vapors would be crippling. Outgassing had to be stopped, and soon.

A submind brought her the essence of Urban's strategy to restore Null Boundary to a functional state. Recovery had to begin by shedding unwanted heat, but the vacuum in which Null Boundary existed acted as an insulator. Heat could not be lost by convective or conductive processes, but only by radiation.

Radiant losses occurred continuously, but given the present profile of the ship, those losses would not take place fast enough to prevent the core from reaching critical temperatures. So to speed the process, Urban planned to increase the ship's surface area through an array of cooling fins. Deneb reviewed his proposal, tweaking a few of the growth algorithms. Then she shifted her locus into an open plane in the library, where her modifications were blended with an active model running under Nikko's supervision.

The image of the library was an unnecessary frame. She wiped it. Now she existed within the evolving model of Null Boundary. No longer did she have any sense of her own physical presence. She was a point of perception without mass or volume, able to manifest anywhere within the described layers of the ship's structure and to transfer instantaneously to another location. She flitted through the model, causing layers to become transparent or opaque before her gaze as she reviewed updates from the microprobes. Vaguely, she was aware of the presence of other ghosts within the data structure: Urban and Nikko and maybe Clemantine.

At last, all seemed ready.

"Party time?" she asked softly.

"Sooth," Urban said. "Let's do it."

He had prepared a coded sonic pulse. He sent it now, activating a lineage of microprobes occupying the relatively benign environment of an inner hull, where the temperature still lingered at just below 230 degrees Celsius. The probes released a cargo of high-temperature Makers, and Deneb allowed her time sense to slow.

Her self-image dissociated into little more than a primal awareness as slowly, slowly, structural ribs began to sprout in shallow arches from the foundation of the inner hull. It was a metabolic process that generated even more heat, but that could not be helped.

The ribs grew from the root, consuming heat-tolerant metals scavenged from the surrounding tissue or cannibalized from nonstrategic sections of the supporting hull. They rose through superheated tissue, finally bursting past the outer crust and into vacuum. Their growth did not slow. They thrust outward from the ship, pulling webs of malleable hull tissue within their loops to form a chaotic array of cooling fins, until Null Boundary resembled some manic crystal tree, leaved in a jumble of glassy planes.

At first the fins were red hot. But as heat bled into the void, their materials cooled and structure was added:

neural paths, cardinals, and flow channels through which hot fluids could be pumped. Scavenging Makers sorted elements, ferrying needed materials along relay chains or through microscopic transport channels to construction sites. Metals were preferentially collected in the fins. Hydrogen, oxygen, and the carbon gases were captured wherever they moved slowly enough to be seized. But while the extreme outer tissues cooled, heat continued to move toward the core.

The rush of activity in the core chamber was over. Nikko had vanished. Urban and Clemantine had tranced themselves, drifting like dead people in the slowly stirring air. Lot had no ghosts and no off switch, so he busied himself with the synthesizer.

Deneb watched him a minute, feeling some of the cell-talk brush against her own expanding senses. It was an unpleasant cacophony that carried no meaning at all for her. "You want to reseed the philosopher cells, don't you?" Deneb asked him.

He stopped his work, to look at her with suspicious eyes.

"I think you should," she added.

"Don't tell Clemantine."

Deneb smiled.

Lot straightened in his drift, sliding the synthesizer into a thigh pocket. "Why are you awake?"

"I don't know. I just . . . feel vulnerable when I sleep. I guess."

"Hey, you're really scared."

This time her smile was an embarrassed grimace, as a warm flush rose in the scales of her face. "Urban would just edit that."

"You don't want to be like Urban. Are you hungry? I could get some food."

She wasn't hungry, but she wanted to keep him talking. She didn't want to be alone. Did he sense that?

He brought bulbs of sweet coffee and pocket bread stuffed with a nut paste. He told her stories from Silk. She told him about her school and the tea parties she'd had with her friends, and how they would let ghosts do all the homework, or let boyfriends inside their atriums to spend the night, never touching each other but lying side by side, knowing there was time.

Wails arose from Null Boundary's shifting outer tissues. Deneb listened to them. In time, she found herself talking about her parents and how they had changed when the cult virus took them. Her soft words rose to an angry rant. She told him the truth: she wanted to blame *him*. She knew it wasn't his fault, but it had been such a waste. All gone for nothing.

Lot watched her through half-closed eyes as she bounced back and forth across the chamber, in sharp, angry hops. He had one foot under a loop in the chamber wall and his sensory tears winked diamond bright as he turned his head slowly back and forth. What did he sense in her? He held his hand out. "Your parents: they still loved you, didn't they?"

Deneb thought about it. Her fingers brushed his palm as she slid past. *They still loved you.* She nodded. She could hold on to that. That much at least, she could salvage.

Urban looked in again on the reactor chamber to find the ricocheting debris was gone, broken down to dust, or cannibalized in the growth of a skin-thin crustal layer building like a coral reef on every exposed surface—including the camera faces. The reef was semitransparent. For a time, it allowed the passage of light, but as it thickened, it dissolved its substrate. Before long, the cameras were ruined.

Urban worried about the integrity of the reactor. So far, the developing reef had etched away only a couple of millimeters of material, but if the process continued, the reactor shielding would eventually be breached.

He had to know what was going on.

So he punched a new hole in the chamber wall. Around the hole he grew a tube. Its walls were three inches thick; its bore less than a tenth of an inch. It extended fifteen inches into the chamber. Through this passage he inserted a camera wand, and for several hours he was able to watch the slow development of the reef.

His first glimpse with the new setup was startling. The

chamber had vanished. The bulkheads were invisible beneath a dimensionless field of fierce, gray-purple light. Rare speckles of lesser brilliance floated aft, toward the camera and then past it. Urban shuddered. He'd seen this same vista on his journey up the courser's vent tube. Turning the lens, he saw only more of the measureless space.

A sense of mass at his back warned of Nikko's presence. "The integrity of the reactor walls is our first concern."

"Sooth. But the reef is building slowly. We've lost less than three millimeters on this bulkhead, and the expansion is slowing."

Nikko didn't answer right away. Then: "Looks awfully familiar, doesn't it?"

Urban grunted. "Of course, on the Chenzeme ship the vent tube had an outlet, and probably an intake too."

Nikko hesitated. "You want to add that? We don't even know what this stuff does."

"I think we do know."

Then Deneb was there. Unlike Nikko, she manifested as a fully formed ghost. Her kisheer bunched up around her neck, communicating a nervous excitement. "It's lovely," she said.

Urban frowned. "You think so?"

"Curiously self-sufficient."

"Sooth. It's what Lot said. The courser wanted to seed us with a collection of life-forms."

"Hmm. He said those were rooted in the philosopher cells. Maybe dependent on them? That's how I would design the system, if I wanted the philosopher cells to act as overseers to the other life-forms."

Urban stared at the open window, watching another glint drift down the chamber's length. This system had no overseer. It proceeded without feedback or support. Would a true subsystem of the Chenzeme courser be able to adapt so easily to Null Boundary's barren environment? Urban remembered the sense he'd had in the vent tube, that the flux and pull of the zero point drive was a process not quite under control. "So maybe this reef really isn't Chenzeme? Maybe it colonized their ships too?"

Nikko's mass faded as his ghost took form. "Love and nature, I don't even want to think about that. I want to

think this is a thing the Chenzeme made. I want to think
they were smart enough to design it. Smarter than us. We've
done so badly against them. But if they only *found* it . . ."

"We've found it now," Urban said firmly.

And if the Chenzeme could adopt it, they could too.

Deneb woke from a fitful sleep, hearing again in her
mind a clangor of impact, as if the ship had been struck
some wrenching hammer blow. She blinked against a swel-
tering darkness, unsure if the sound had been real or part
of some disconnected dream.

She listened.

Ghosts returned to her, then left again, leaving shadows
of their experience behind.

:A lane of debris lay at a shallow angle to their course,
and every few hours a tiny chunk of ice or a bullet of shattered metal would punch a hole through the fins. The ship
would ring with the blow.

:The courser had begun to accelerate as it moved out of
Alpha Cygni, on a path that would soon converge with
their own.

:Null Boundary had begun to accelerate too. It was just
a tiny increase in speed, but Nikko had measured it three
times. It was real.

Deneb could hear Lot's soft breathing an armlength
away. Still asleep. She could smell the sweet scent of his
sweat.

When had the core gotten so hot?

A submind reported the temperature as thirty-six degrees
and climbing.

In the city where she had lived with her parents, a
favorite trysting place for teenage lovers had been in the
temperate zone of the city park, where superheated steam
worked its way up from the reactor through giant mani-
folds. Where steam met cold air at the grated vents, warm
mists formed, encouraging the rank growth of a stand of
broad-leaved vegetation. In the Edenic atmosphere inhibi-
tions melted away and sexual pleasures were learned and
practiced. But when Deneb was thirteen, a girl she'd known
vaguely from school had died there. She'd squeezed
through the grates, climbing after a dropped ring or a lost

camera—accounts of the event varied. Perhaps she'd gone in on a dare. She slipped deep into the manifold and could not climb out. Her lover could not reach her. In the panicked minutes before she died, nine ghosts formed in her atrium and escaped, but her core persona had no way out. It remained trapped within a body that was soon reduced to brown bones and steamed flesh that fell apart in her rescuers' hands.

Deneb stared into the darkness. She felt her kisheer unfurled and thick with blood as her body sought to dump excess heat across its broad surface. Despite their efforts, heat was spreading from the hull to the core, seeking an equilibrium. Null Boundary was half melted. Deneb could hear the ship groan: a low, frothy hum on the edge of perception. She stretched her toe through the dark, touching the membrane that held back the Well water. Now the hum leaped into her bones, a resonant echo of the ship's evolving structure. Ghosts were at work within the walls.

Lot's breathing rhythm stumbled and caught, then faded to waking softness. "Deneb?" She felt a stirring of air near her shoulder. "What's wrong?" His concern felt like a live thing inside her.

"It's too hot in here." Her voice was a whispered squeak. The heat seemed an entity, and it filled her. No matter the direction she turned she could not get away from it, or even feel it decline.

"It is hot," Lot said. He hesitated, and she had time to wonder if her fear had awakened him. Then tentatively, he asked, "You've been dreaming?"

"I don't know." She felt awash in confusion. She imagined the darkness infecting her eyes, making her blind. In her blindness, other senses quickened. She thought she caught the scent of a thick, sickly-sour brew adrift upon the air. The smell sent her heart racing. "Vigil is our lifeboat," she whispered. "It already holds our dormant ghosts, and I know that if it gets too hot here we'll make new ghosts and send those out to the probe too. But no matter how many ghosts we send, *we* won't be able to escape."

"I don't think we'll need to escape. Not this time."

Comforting words, but what did he know about the ship? He had a spider, whispering updates in his ear. And yet there was something . . . in his voice? Or perhaps in his simple presence, that calmed her. *"Oh!"* Her hand flew to her mouth as she realized what she'd just said to him. "Oh no. I—I've been thinking of myself, of our ghosts. You don't even have a ghost. Lot, that's unbearable. It's terrifying. I'm sorry. I—"

"Deneb, please." Now he sounded embarrassed. "It's okay."

"But it was so callous. I don't know what's wrong with me. I feel like a stranger here, sometimes. I forget that things are different here."

His surprise touched her, like ghost-fingers on the inside of her spine. "I thought you were happy . . . with Urban?"

"Well, I am. I was. He—" She caught herself. She would not run on with another complaint, and still, frantic dialogues played in her head. What was wrong with her tonight?

She drew in a deep breath, thinking, *Calm. Be calm,* and it worked, at least a little. "Don't talk about me, okay? What about you? You're not afraid, are you? Why aren't you afraid?"

He chuckled. "Who said I'm not afraid? I'm scared shitless."

"Are you?" She reached out. Her hand found the slick surface of his skin suit, taut over his belly. "You don't feel scared." But even as she said it, his belly began to tremble. She felt a surge of trepidation, as if she'd been swept up in emotions that were not her own. "Lot?"

"What's happening?" he blurted.

"I don't know."

She struggled to stay calm, to breathe calmness out upon the air.

He responded with a hoarse croak of surprise: "I can feel that."

She could too. She could feel him calming, and not through the trembling of his belly, but inside her mind, she could feel it there. Cautiously, she reached for him with her other hand. Did he anticipate the gesture? His hand met hers. The slick fingers of his glove closed hard around her palm. "I don't understand," he whispered. "Deneb, how can you feel the charismata?"

The charismata? So this is what it was like. She had never felt this way before, as if she were wrapped in a weightless cocoon that pulled at her anxieties, leaching them away.

"Deneb?"

She strove to recall herself. He had asked her a question, but it was so hot in here she could hardly think what it was. Ah, the charismata. He wanted to know about that. "I have seeded myself with a neural organ. It's working now. That must be it."

"No." His worry pricked at her, annoying barbs against her skin. *Calm.* She heard the catch of his breath. "This is different from the cult parasite. Deneb, I can feel charismata from *you.*"

His hand was so hot, she had to let go of it. "Oh, Lot. This is not the cult. I've changed the parasite. I've tried to make it more like yours. You can't control me."

"I don't think I can say the same."

Temperatures were rising higher than Nikko had anticipated in the critical core region. The efficiency of the ship's neural tissue, packed into the armored walls of the core, was threatened by the heat. Nikko could feel the decline in his slowed reaction times, in his increasing errors. He performed every calculation at least three times, comparing the results. Cooling was imperative, but the insulation he'd packed around the core worked against it, preventing heat from getting out. So Nikko opened additional channels to carry cool fluids from the fins to capillary networks budding in the neural tissue. The enterprise didn't work as planned. The fluids, heated to steam by intervening tissue, ferried heat from the midlayers *into* the core, rather than carrying it out, compounding the problem. So Nikko built insulated channels that would keep cold fluids cold until they reached the capillary nets. That worked better. Heat buildup ceased. In a few minutes, temperatures in the neural tissue began to decline. Nikko opened new capillary networks to speed the process, expanding the therapy to the walls of the core chamber.

No more copies.

The resolve formed with languid slowness in Deneb's

overheated brain. The core temperature had risen to forty degrees. Deneb had passed the time in alternating states of panic and contentment—an emotional balance that tilted according to Lot's proximity. She had already sent ghosts twice now to Vigil. So she had saved some memories of this ordeal. She didn't think she would want to remember any more.

Her heart fluttered, as fear chewed at her again. Her scaled body could not cool itself with the efficiency of an ancestral human. She knew unconsciousness must take her soon. Already she felt incapable of purposeful motion. She drifted in the little room, her mouth open as she panted softly. Her engorged kisheer would no longer respond. She felt hideous and angry and terrified, and it didn't help when she noticed the febrile twitching, tapping of her fingers against her china thigh. Had she adopted Nikko's annoying habit now? There was no justice. None.

I am too much attached to this body.

Or to the core persona that inhabited it. *You don't have to feel this.* Time and again Lot had urged her to trance, to block out all sensation from her body, to let her core persona coast in an atrial blind cave, where the air would be as cool as she desired. And still she clung to awareness with psychotic tenacity. Why? Her ghosts operated within the walls. They would live even if she did not. But were they her? They did not feel the heat. *(I do!)* They were steady and focused. They could be that way because she was here, to hold their fear. All of it. She alone—this core persona— dared to be afraid. *(This is me.)* It seemed somehow important to hold on to that.

Lot leaned into her line of sight—summoned by her distress? Perhaps. Sweat made lenses on his half-closed eyelids. He shook his head, scattering beads of moisture.

Damn. Humidity is getting high.

She tried to alert one of her ghosts, but her atrium didn't seem to be working. She tried to speak, but her tongue felt swollen, and all the papillae that lined her mouth. Lot spoke, but she could not understand his words. The language he used: she had not heard him speak that before. Had she known this language once? She tried to speak again, to ask him. Nothing happened. Apparently the hardware was failing. Shit.

Lot touched her throat with gentle fingers, icy cold, and abruptly she was aware of a dim roaring pounding racing beat. She watched his eyes widen. Watched a comical V of concern dive between his eyebrows. He turned. His mouth moved, and the water wall trembled, as if reverberating to an imagined shout. Lot really was so very strange.

She closed her eyes, listening to a tumultuous rumbling fluid noise.

So. The hardware had failed.

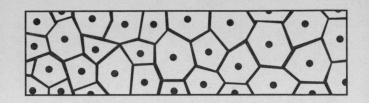

Chapter
19

Vigil remained their eyes on the world outside the hull, but it also had a life of its own. The little probe had followed its own path around Alpha Cygni, and now the passing hours pulled it ever farther from Null Boundary. Clemantine tweaked its limited propulsion system, bending its trajectory just a bit, so now it fell toward a distant star cluster that included several small, yellow, G-type suns—the spectral class so often friendly to life. Over time, the probe would re-form itself into a sail made to strike the interstellar medium, and it would use the ensuing drag as a slow, slow brake. Its Dull Intelligence would take it past intervening systems, using their stellar winds to further reduce its speed. In not more than twenty-two hundred years it would reach the star cluster, where it would wind between individual suns, using the sail to complete the braking process. Eventually, its velocity would be low enough that it could let itself be captured by one of the stars, or by the planets that must be there, so that the ghosts it carried might live again.

Or not.

Clemantine found herself facing another small disaster as she absorbed the latest data squirt from the probe. Vigil's telescope looked backward on the white blur of the courser.

The Doppler-shift of the courser's hull light allowed for an easy estimation of its speed. It was swiftly reclaiming all the velocity shed on its approach to Alpha Cygni, rising on a vector aimed to intersect the probe. In a matter of days the courser would catch it—but that gave Null Boundary a few days more to gain a lead.

Vigil had bought them a reprieve, but Nikko knew it couldn't last. When the courser turned back on their trail, they would be carrying no camouflage to confuse its instincts. It could not fail to use its guns. Zap. Pop. Finis. The long pursuit would at last be over.

He could try mining their wake, but the courser wasn't running behind them. Its approach was oblique, and besides, it could use its guns to clear any debris.

He could try regrowing the philosopher cells and defend the ship with their poison dust—but there was no way a working field could be ready in time, and besides, Lot would refuse to drop the poison.

So they had no weapons.

Okay, then. They needed speed.

Except the solenoids could not be rebuilt in time. Even if they could, conventional propulsion could not outrun the courser's zero point drive.

So they needed a zero point drive.

Thanks to Urban's adventurism, they apparently had one, though it wasn't working well. Nikko had measured a feather-push of acceleration, barely discernible. How to increase it? Now that the ship was thermally stable, he turned all his ghosts to this question.

Urban watched the growing reef. He measured its output. He compared its output to Null Boundary's faint but growing acceleration as the reef unbalanced the all-pervasive zero point field. It was like a magic act, something from nothing, a miracle—and still not enough to keep them ahead of the courser rising out of Alpha Cygni.

Nikko's ghost spliced in beside him. "Figured it out yet?"

Urban chuckled. He made guesses about the reef; he did

not understand it. He thought of it as an aggregate entity, made of billions of cooperating organisms, each measured on the micrometer scale. Those fixed to the chamber walls seemed dead, though like a coral reef, they formed a solid base for the remaining colony. Those living on the surface seemed most alive. They were not made of exotic matter, but they created it, synthesizing nanoscale particles from the zero point field. The exotic matter would decay almost instantly, but it would be re-created in another part of the reef, over and over again, a billion events per microsecond. And every synthesis of exotic matter would tweak the structure of space-time.

This was the story he told to Nikko.

It was only a story. People had always used stories to explain what they could not understand.

:*The stars are the moon's children.*

:*The sun is the wheel of a great chariot.*

:*The Milky Way is a stream of milk gushing from the breast of a goddess.*

:*The reef evolved in the accretion disk of a black hole or a neutron star—someplace with a horribly warped gravitational field, where it developed a taxis away from the fatal center.*

The cumulative effect was a fluctuating gradient, and Null Boundary rode it on a vector aimed away from the slight gravitational distortion of the ship's mass.

"We don't need to understand it," Urban said. "We just need to know how to kick it over. Faster, slower, nothing more than that."

Nikko grunted his agreement, just as Deneb's busy ghost winked into existence between them. "It's almost time."

Urban caught her hand and smiled. "You are a treasure." They had decided to replicate the environment of the courser's vent tube—or their best guess at what that environment had been, and this ghost had handled all the engineering work. Deneb had designed an inlet and two outlets to vent the Y-shaped reactor chamber. Heat-damaged distribution channels in the ship's tissues had slowed all engineering work, but at last, the three vents were ready to punch open. They would use precision explosives. Urban did not trust their industrial Makers to function near the reef.

"Ready . . . ," Deneb said. "*Now.*"

The explosions were aimed inward. Urban saw them rise in caps of dust, steam, and light, a burp of concerted motion, immediately reversed as the pressure of vacuum sucked the chamber clean. The reef flared brilliant white, overwhelming the cameras. The ship surged and shuddered, and Urban whooped, a raw animal call of triumph. They'd kicked the reef, they'd affected it. This was the first step toward control.

"Wait," Deneb said. She held her hand up to silence him. It was a chilling gesture. "Look at the numbers. Nikko? It's fading."

A full spread of graphs and numbers appeared on the window frame. Urban's gaze skipped over them. Deneb was right. The activity of the reef had only spiked. Now, both heat and radiant output were plunging. The brilliant glare from the window faded; the reef darkened to deep steel shades. The transition was stunning in its speed. Within seconds, activity had plunged all the way back to previous levels—and the decline had not stopped yet.

"Love and nature," Deneb whispered. "It's crashed."

Urban didn't want to believe it. "We've exposed it to vacuum. It has to cool. We knew it would."

"Not like this," Deneb said. "This is too much. There. See?" She pointed to a graph on the right side of the frame. "All detectable effects on the gradient are gone. We've killed the acceleration, as little as it was." She turned to Nikko, her eyes glistening with fear. "Close it up, Nikko. Now. We were wrong."

"No, wait."

Nikko startled them both with this refusal. His gaze was fixed on the reef; his kisheer lay across his shoulders, calm and still. "This has got to be the way the courser worked. Don't get nervous. Let's give it a chance to stabilize."

Urban gripped the window frame, his knuckles pale, trying to see some hint of recovery in the reef. The walls were blackening. Only an occasional white speck illuminated the chamber. "Enough, Nikko. We've given it time enough."

"A little longer," Nikko said. No fear, no anxiety in his bearing. Cool as a Chenzeme warship.

Urban's ghost-grip tightened on the window frame. By

the Unknown God. He had wanted the zero point technology for so many years. And he'd found it! He'd brought it off the courser in his own hands. It had survived two years in the casket with no attention. He couldn't believe it would die now, yet the evidence was there, in the library window.

And if they let it die now, how would they escape the courser?

"Nikko, the reef is our only chance. You kill it, and the courser will be on us before we can cool our hull. Close the vents. Now."

Nikko's kisheer wriggled, just a little nervous squirm. "It can't be this easy to kill."

"You don't know that." Urban uploaded a submind into the system. If Nikko would not close the vents, he'd do it himself. The submind popped back. *Access denied.*

He looked at Nikko in sharp surprise. "Nikko? Have you locked us out?"

"Thermal and radiant outputs are still dropping," Deneb warned. "Nikko, Urban's right. We've given it time enough. It's going to zero if we don't do something to stop it."

"All right," Nikko said. "I'm closing the vents." His face expressionless, his kisheer once again still. Urban could not guess what he was thinking.

The vents closed.

Nothing happened. They watched in silence for several seconds; then Deneb started mumbling. "The reef flared at the moment the explosives went off. Either reacting to the presence of the dust, or to the radiant energy? After that, no more dust; no more radiant energy—"

"Wrong," Nikko said. "With the intake open, a minuscule quantity of dust was flowing in. The mean density in this region is almost three particles per cubic centimeter."

"That's nothing," Urban said.

Deneb's kisheer bunched around her neck. Her head bobbed up and down, restless motion. "So now dust is zeroed. Still no recovery in activity. Maximize dust? Or would that kill the reef? Radiant energy? Maybe we should try—"

"It's kicking," Nikko said.

Urban snapped around to look. There was no visual change in the reef, but on the window frame, graphs measuring radiant activity had begun to rise. "It's nothing like before, though. It was stronger before. We've damaged it. Deneb?"

Her long fingers stroked the edge of her kisheer; her gaze did not waver from the window. "Try radiant energy?"

Nikko tapped his thigh, a taut, dry, cracking sound. "All or nothing now," he muttered. "Wavelength?"

"Why not run through the spectrum?" Deneb suggested.

Urban had been in the vent tube. "No," he said. "Start with UV."

"Nikko!" Lot could stand it no longer. "*Nik-ko!*" he roared.

He had stayed quiet during the aftermath of their passage, when the core cooled, and the Well water retreated on its own, seeping back through the walls into the ship's regenerating tissue.

He had stayed quiet when Clemantine roused, gazing at him with eyes carefully empty of emotion. Makers had already cleaned away the scent of her sweat. She had told him, "Lot, let her go."

Only then had Lot realized he still held Deneb's hand.

Clemantine made the body disappear, but the images lingered. Lot could not forget the way Deneb had looked: her kisheer swollen and the papillae in her mouth, like fat fingers strangling her from the inside, her nasal tissue emergent, soaked in blood, her eyes—

He huddled against the wall, trying to recall the calming exercises he'd learned in Silk, and that he'd abandoned, until now. Closing his eyes, he performed breathing routines, sublimely conscious of the core's imprisoning walls. Though he'd been born on a ship, in Silk he'd come to love open vistas and he craved them now.

Now.

The pace of his breathing picked up. He blew it back down, fighting a sense of entrapment until he could stand it no longer.

"*Nik-ko!*" he roared.

They heard him. Clemantine's somnolent form stirred for the first time in hours. Urban woke too: Lot watched the peaceful lines of his sleeping face give way to a troubled perplexity. And Nikko manifested, a ghost at the chamber's curving bow end.

As Lot turned to face him, the chill touch of a circulating breeze dragged past his face. "It's cold in here," Lot accused.

Nikko said, "It's the same temperature it's always been."

"It's not."

Nikko's chin rose. "The same temperature before the passage then."

Lot felt a hard knot frozen in his chest. "She's dead, and nobody has said a thing."

"We have her ghost," Nikko answered.

"Lot, I'm here." Deneb's voice issued from the wall behind his head. She sounded concerned, and a little confused. "You know there were copies."

"It's not the same." *She* had been sensitive to the charismata; she'd made charismata of her own. That Deneb was gone.

He could not shake the image of her flesh swelling out of her scaled hide. She'd burned it into him with the charismata of her fear, like a hyperconscious drug injected in his spine.

"It shouldn't have happened like that! Nikko, you forgot about us. You were thinking of the ship, what *it* could survive."

Nikko's posture possessed an artificial stillness. "Null Boundary's neural tissue had priority, but I was thinking of you too. I knew your tolerances, and I made sure you came out all right."

"But what about Deneb? She mattered too!"

"Lot, *I'm still here.*"

Nikko's kisheer moved in slow, mechanical ripples. "It's not my fault Deneb stayed with you. She should have dissolved herself. I did."

"She's not like you. She had a core persona."

"Lot, stop it, please," Deneb begged.

"She had a choice," Nikko said. "Don't blame me if she didn't make the right one."

His image winked out. Lot held on to a grip with whitening knuckles. His hand hurt. His arm too. Deneb's voice whispered from behind his head. "Nikko's right. It was my fault. Lot, I'm sorry. It was a mistake. I held on too long."

He couldn't answer her. She'd touched him with her charismata. Now she was gone.

One by one the cooling fins were drawn back into the ship, until only a handful remained to bleed the heat of reconstruction. Their material was cannibalized for other jobs. Work began on new optical telescopes, on an array of replacement antennae, on expanded apartments in the interstitial space, and on banks of steerage jets. They worked on the ramscoop too, though that had become a backup system, now that Urban was learning to handle the reef.

Interstellar dust sweeping in through the intake tube would dampen the reef's exotic activity. Radiant energy would enhance it. When it was thriving, the reef threw off dangerous energy of its own, but Urban was learning to harness that too.

Clemantine reported the quiet death of Vigil. Its loss was inferred, not observed. Its last transmission showed the courser just outside weapons range. When she sought to contact it again, there was no reply.

Nikko let his consciousness stretch out through the body of the ship. *His* ship. His body. It was smaller now, tons of mass lost in the passage of Alpha Cygni, but it was clean, and whole, and flying faster than it ever had before, so that Nikko worried about collisions with random pebbles of debris, as much as the courser's guns.

The telescopes were regrown, and he could see again across the spectrum, from radio through microwave to infrared, on up to visible light, and beyond, to ultraviolet and X-ray emissions.

On all sides, stars like glowing fairy dust framed his world, blue and white and red and yellow. Alpha Cygni fell behind them, a signpost marking the way home. Ahead, in the direction called *swan*, a gathering of giant young suns dominated the sky, insufferably brilliant. Beyond them, curtains of red fire burned in vast, amorphous sheets. These were the nebulae marking centers of star formation on the edge of the cold dark mass of an immense molecular cloud, less than ninety light-years away. The Swan Cloud: the Chenzeme warships had come from there.

Visible light could not penetrate the Swan Cloud's dust, but to infrared and radio frequencies, the cloud was nearly transparent. When Vigil failed, Nikko turned his radio antennae toward the cloud. He recorded the positions of young stars still veiled in dust, and the trumpeting galleries of natural masers that lay around them. He marked shells of speeding gases blown off by supernovas, density waves that spawned clusters of infalling matter that would become protostars.

These things he could identify.

He could not put a name to a scattering of faint, ephemeral, point source signals in the microwave range. They would flare up, then die back. Once, sometimes twice. Then they would vanish. He tried to decode them—as picture or sound or Chenzeme chemical exchange. Nothing made sense. Perhaps they were just random noise, produced by the tumultuous activity of the cloud. But they did not look random. Their modulated frequencies clustered too tightly around a steady carrier wave.

"Nikko?"

Urban's voice intruded on his awareness. Nikko answered automatically. "Here."

"Come to the core chamber. Clemantine wants everyone together. She says we need to talk."

He found them gathered in the core chamber: Urban, Clemantine, and Lot, with Deneb an unseen ghost within the walls. "The Swan Cloud talks," Nikko told them.

Clemantine laughed. A dark laugh, like the capstone of far too many concerns. "Do tell. And can you translate it?"

"No."

She sighed and stretched, her long body arcing like a bow. "Ah well. When we reseed the philosopher cells, perhaps Lot will be able to tell us what it means."

Her eyebrows arched. The gold irises on her earlobes glittered. She had caught them all by surprise with this statement, Lot most of all. He clung spiderlike to the wall, his hair grown out to three inches of gold drift. It waved around his face as he studied her. "You aren't going to fight it?" he asked.

"No. You see, I'm becoming Chenzeme too. No one deserves special protection, from the world or from themselves. I am learning that. It's the Chenzeme way. Survivors survive. Everyone else falls away into history." Her dark gaze held him a moment; then she turned to Urban, who crouched at her feet, looking wary and unhappy. Finally, she looked at Nikko. "We have captured the reef. We are learning to control it. Now we have to take it home."

Nikko let his awareness drift back into the body of the ship. Starlight seared his hull. The courser hunted him. It wasn't gaining though. A submind let this new fact explode within his consciousness. Slowly, slowly, the courser was falling behind.

"We can't go home," Nikko said. "We're pulling ahead of the courser now, but if we slow down, if we try to reverse our course, it will be on us within hours. You know it."

Clemantine nodded, her face smooth, and cold. "Sooth. Null Boundary will never go home. I know that. And I've run enough engineering simulations to know we haven't got the mass to build guns that will match our dog. But we have got mass left, Nikko. We can divide the ship. Vigil was just a little craft, hastily made. We can do better. A stealthed ship, powered by its own reef, guided by a ghost. Give me the mass, Nikko, and I'll take this find home."

Nikko felt a hollow space open in his chest; guilt rushed in to fill it. "It's been centuries," he said. "You don't know if anyone's alive back there."

She nodded. "We can't know. That doesn't mean we can't try. I'll go to Deception Well first. If they're gone, I'll push on. They can't all be gone, Nikko. Not the whole species. But if they are, then to hell with them and good riddance. They deserved to die. In the end, survival is the only measure that counts."

Messenger was two thirds the length of Null Boundary, but only a few meters wide, a sliver of a ship, like a rib pulled from Null Boundary's flesh. Its hull was stealthed, so that it would not reflect visible light or radar, and prior to launch it was cooled, to reduce its heat signature. A tiny, tentacled robot was used to transfer polyps from Null Boundary's reef to a chamber in Messenger's bow. At first the bits of reef matter glowed as isolated points of light, like the flecks of light on Urban's glove when he'd returned from the dark courser, but as the hours passed, the spots of light grew larger. In time, they began to ooze in slow-migration along the chamber walls. A new reef had begun to grow.

"It's time," Clemantine said. "I want the two ships to separate, before their reefs can interfere with one another."

Messenger rested in a trench on Null Boundary's hull. The little ship's success depended on secrecy. If the courser detected Messenger's presence, Clemantine had no doubt it would go the way of Vigil—and if that happened, then to hell with them all.

She kissed Lot one last time. She kissed Urban. She held them both, their bodies hard and strong against her. Tears formed in her eyes.

^

She would stay with them forever. She would never see them again. "Godspeed," she whispered.

She made a ghost, and uploaded it to Messenger's core of neural tissue.

Like Nikko, she would loop, and if all went well, the two-hundred-year journey would be reduced to ninety seconds in her awareness.

Nikko watched the launch with Urban's ghost at a library window. Clemantine, in her incarnate version, watched with Lot and another version of Urban in the core chamber. Deneb was a voice, guiding the final deployment. "Cooling's complete," she told them. "We're ready."

There would be no fiery ignition. Messenger would be kicked free by explosive bolts deep within Null Boundary's tissue. Without hull cells, Null Boundary was dark and

hard to see. The waver in their course would be undetectable at any distance.

The courser dogged their flank. Deneb waited until Null
Boundary's slow roll carried Messenger's trench away from
the courser. "Now," she said softly. The ship shuddered.
That was all. For a fraction of a second, cameras on the
hull showed a black silhouette that slipped behind them almost before the eye could perceive it. Null Boundary still
accelerated, while Messenger's embryonic reef was aimed in
the opposite direction. As the reef matured, it would begin
dragging down the velocity of the little ship, bringing it
ever closer to the pursuing courser. "It's away," Deneb said.

Though not safely away, not yet.

Nikko watched the courser, waiting for some sign that it
had discovered Messenger's presence, that its guns were in
use. He watched it across the spectrum. He watched it for
weeks, until Deneb's voice spoke softly out of nowhere:
"She's safely away. You know it."

He watched it a few weeks more anyway, but the
courser did not veer, or slow, or drop dust, or fire its guns.
It ploughed on toward the Swan Cloud at a constant
velocity, slowly, slowly dropping ever farther behind the
still-accelerating Null Boundary.

Nikko felt a strange sensation move through his sensorium as he finally admitted to himself that Messenger had
escaped. This was a victory. For the first time in the centuries since Deneb had died *(my Deneb)* Nikko felt as if he
could claim a victory over the Chenzeme.

He cautioned himself that problems were abundant.
Null Boundary's reef could die or it could spread out of
control throughout the ship. At any moment, the courser
might make a push to catch them. They could meet a swan
burster. They would still need to face the source of the signals in the cloud.

Once again, Nikko scanned a map of the inexplicable
microwave bursts originating within the Swan Cloud. This
was Chenzeme territory. Could the signals be the first sign
of a civilization behind the warships?

He couldn't know. Not yet. Still, he felt encouraged, and
impatient to push on. If a Chenzeme civilization did exist,
he promised himself he would find it, and that he would

find a way to beat it. The successful deployment of Messenger had given him that optimism. There was hope in the future: the reef was on its way to human hands, along with all the power that implied, and the Chenzeme did not seem quite so invulnerable anymore.

What does it feel like to be happy? Nikko had almost forgotten. *It feels like this.*

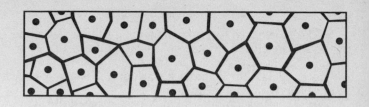

Chapter
20

Deneb remained a ghost. She would not say why.
Yet she insisted on a new gee deck, so one was made, though it was smaller than the first. Nikko carpeted the deck in meadow grasses that would grow waist high in a few weeks. Clemantine moved in, growing a house, and laying out a patio and a flower garden. The water in her fountain was thick, and tinged with green.

Night had fallen in their facade of planetary cycles when Nikko walked out on the gee deck. The first generation of crickets chirped in the new grass. Overhead, a thin field of hot young stars shone against the backdrop of the Swan Cloud.

Nikko felt pleased, though a little awkward too, he had to admit it, as he walked toward the fire burning in the soot-stained diamond pit on the patio of Clemantine's house. His ghost went ahead of him, to survey the setting through the eyes of a wired gecko climbing the latticework of the enclosing arbor. Lot lay in a hammock, his half-open eyes glittering in the light of the flames that flickered and licked within the new fire pit. Urban sat with Clemantine on a pliant bench, talking softly, but the gecko's ears were not attuned to the words.

Nikko's long-toed feet carried him in a rolling gait along the path. The closest crickets fell silent, and Lot turned to look. When he saw Nikko, he sat up, his feet hammering the patio to kill the hammock's swing. "Nikko? What's wrong? Has the courser caught us?"

"No. It's still dropping behind." As he reached the patio, he saw the gecko dash along the lattice, a flash of white as it pursued a moth. Now Clemantine and Urban were staring at him too. He felt a surge of heat as they sent ghosts to investigate the ship's condition. Nikko cocked his head, baffled at this reaction. "Uh . . . why do you think something's gone wrong?"

Clemantine leaned back, visibly relaxing, a sly smile on her face. The pliant bench shaped itself to the new posture of her shoulders. "You've never been incarnate when things were good."

"They've never been this good."

Lot moved his head from side to side. "Hey," he said softly. "You're happy."

"Is he?" Clemantine asked. "I can't tell." Then she snickered. "Deneb says you should rewire your face so it will work like hers. Then we could all tell how you feel."

"Deneb's ghosting with you?" Urban blurted.

Clemantine ignored him. "Have a seat," she told Nikko, patting the armrest of a heavy lounge chair. "And welcome."

"Thank you." As he sat down, the chair back rose to accommodate his relentless posture. He looked around, wondering where in this scene Deneb had placed her ghost. He could not see her, of course. She existed only within Clemantine's perspective, but he wondered: Had she been sitting in this chair? Was she here now, perched on the armrest? He couldn't know. His kisheer fluttered: the echo of a smile. "I did rewire my face once."

It was meant as a casual remark, but it elicited a stunned silence. Nikko looked from one astonished face to another, trying to guess why. "What?" he asked. "It wasn't that hard to do."

"No," Clemantine said. "I doubt that it would be." She didn't look at him. She seemed ready to laugh.

"Obviously, I've missed something," Nikko said.

There was an uncomfortable pause. Then Lot said, "It's just that, well, if you know how to give your face some expression . . . why don't you?" The question embarrassed him. He reached for a wineglass that had been warming by the fire, sipped quickly, then made a face while Nikko thought about the reasons. So much had changed after Deneb had gone.

Finally, he shrugged. "It was part of another life, that's all."

"So when you were a kid," Urban asked, "you were, uh . . . like you are now?"

"Expressionless?"

Urban's eyes became evasive, and Nikko chuckled. "I was the first, you know. The very first of my kind. The design wasn't perfected."

"How long ago?" Urban asked.

"A long time."

"I guess. It must have been weird to grow up like that."

"Weird enough."

Lot was frowning at him across the fire. Dancing orange reflections glistened in his sensory tears. "It must have felt strange to get your face rewired. Scary. Like suddenly, everybody could see what you were thinking."

Had it been that way? Nikko wasn't sure. Those memories had been stripped and stored, long ago. Did he want to search them out? He tapped his fingers against his thigh, producing a bony, clacking sound. There were hazards in the past, pain and love, long forgotten. He didn't want to hurt again. Not now. So he said to Lot, "Perhaps you're right. It was a long time ago. I don't really know."

The gecko clucked in the latticework. Through its eyes, Nikko watched himself staring at the fire. He flinched. What was this? Remembrances unfolding in his mind. *Damn!* Had a submind responded automatically to the query?

Oh.

He looked at Lot in sudden shock.

Lot rose to his feet. "What is it?"

Nikko chuckled, forcing himself to relax. "It's okay." His long fingers twitched and jittered. Love and nature, did his muscles remember those days too? "It was my brother," Nikko said. "I didn't really want to rewire my face, but he dared me to do it. No. He browbeat me into having my face rewired. That was after the fall of the Commonwealth."

Clementine whistled a low note. "Nikko, *civilization*

began after the fall of the Commonwealth. You aren't telling me you remember . . . ?"

"I remember it. Or, I *can* remember it. If I want to."

"By the Unknown God."

"Okay," Urban said, unimpressed by the trivia of a time so ancient. "So you had a brother. Was he older than you?"

"No, younger. Twelve years." He gazed again across the fire at Lot. "He looked quite a bit like you."

The resemblance was there, in Lot's lean, narrow face, in his remorselessly blond hair—cut short again—and in his dangling posture, as if his mind had not caught up with the long limbs and the tall build acquired in adolescence.

Apparently, Lot did not appreciate the comparison. The sudden concern on his face was so profound Nikko had to laugh. "Oh, not exactly like you," he chided. "Just similar . . ."

Leaning back in his chair, he closed his eyes. The edge of his kisheer trembled like struck metal. A dark sense warned that he did not want to follow this memory thread any farther. Things had happened after, that he didn't want to remember. *Let it go.*

He reprimanded his subminds and performed some blunt editing, until blankness replaced the answers that had been stewing just beneath his conscious reach. Let the past remain the past.

It was a resolution he should have shared with Deneb, for now she spoke tentatively within his atrium. *So when you knew me, did you have a real face?*

Nikko felt his fingers knot. *I guess I did.*

How strange to think so. He would have appeared to her as someone completely different.

"You should rewire your face again," Urban said. "Why not? You'd look better."

Nikko sighed. "Thank you, but I don't think I will. At least, not now." It was never wise to try to reconstruct a vanished life. Push on. Push on. That was the only answer.

And wasn't he happy? Quietly happy. He'd had a victory, at last.

Late in the night, Clemantine stood in the doorway of her house, watching Lot retreat through the meadow grasses. The giant stars that dominated the artificial sky shed an eerie blue light across the gee deck, laying multiple shadows. Deneb spoke from behind her. "I'm sorry. I know he misses you."

Clemantine turned. Deneb's ghost sat on the couch, her slender arms folded over the back as she watched Clemantine. On her face was an unhappy frown.

Clemantine shrugged, knowing it was a small thing. "The discipline's good for him."

Deneb's smile was vague. She existed as a ghost within Clemantine's atrium, not within the physical space of the room, so she had been invisible to Lot as he stood in the doorway, wishing Clemantine a reluctant good-night. To Clemantine, though, Deneb looked utterly real.

"Lot makes you nervous, doesn't he?" she asked, as she walked into the room. It was a casual question, no more than an idle observation.

"I guess he does." Deneb's kisheer flickered once. "Clemantine, there's something he and I haven't told you."

Clemantine felt her guts go cold, certain that she did not want to hear this. Their society was tiny, and vulnerable. It could be so easily broken. "Be careful, Deneb. Be sure you really want this before you say it out loud."

Surprise melted out of Deneb's scaled face. Her hand went to smooth her rippling kisheer. "It's not that! It's . . . worse, maybe. Depending on you. I didn't want to tell you before. There was too much going on."

"Tell me what? And why are you hiding out with me? You don't want Urban anymore?" She did not mean for her voice to be so harsh.

Or maybe she did.

Deneb drew a deep breath. "I asked you to shelter me because I needed time to think before I returned—and Urban asks too many questions." She turned, patting the sofa beside her. "Will you sit?"

Sooth. Of course. Talk about it.

The mural of Heyertori had been reinstalled in her new home. She sat, watching a trio of white seabirds rise in a slow circle up the green cliff face. Her hands trembled in her lap.

Deneb said, "I've started my new body growing. It will have a neural organ in it, similar to Lot's. I will sense his charismata. He will sense mine."

"Your charismata?"

"Yes. I redesigned the organ. It's harmless now. I won't be a carrier of the cult, and Lot can't control me."

Harmless?

"Well. That's good." Clemantine thought her voice sounded calm. This struck her as funny, for she was definitely not calm. A laugh caught in her throat, turning her voice husky. "So Lot knows?"

Deneb nodded. "I seeded the organ a few days before our passage of Alpha Cygni. That last hour in the core chamber—it must have matured. He felt my dying. It hurt him, I know, but it was the most intimate experience I have ever had."

Clemantine had lived under the cult. She understood. "Why have you done this?"

"We are getting closer and closer to the Chenzeme. When we find them, I want to understand who they are. I don't want to rely on Lot to interpret for me."

"Sooth. I should have guessed—" A shudder ambushed her from out of nowhere. She clutched the sofa arm. Her heart leaped and shivered in a frightened race to chaos. She hunched over it, breathing in hard, shallow gasps. *Damn!* And what was this? A panic attack? By the Unknown God, was she really so far gone?

Deneb dropped to her knees. "Clemantine?" She studied her face in concern. "Are you okay?"

"Huh. Just sliding over the edge." Swift, rapid breaths.

"Scared?"

"Oh yes. All the time." Her cheeks were hot, her limbs weak. "Ah god, I have been afraid for so long, ever since the swan bursters took Heyertori, and I'm tired of it. I want some reason to be happy that has nothing to do with the Chenzeme or the cult."

Deneb tensed. A single ripple flowed through her kisheer; then the membrane subsided into perfect stillness. She placed a hand on Clemantine's knee. "I could give you that."

Part human, part Chenzeme. Clemantine stared at her, while a smoky-cold dread wound throughout her brain. Deneb had taken the Chenzeme into herself. What else might she have in mind to do? "What are you thinking?"

Deneb turned away. Light glinted in a galaxy of tiny points on the scales of her cheek. "In that last hour in the core chamber, I felt so empty. I didn't want to die, and leave nothing behind me. I didn't want to die, and leave this fucking Universe untroubled by my passage."

Clemantine's throat had gone dry. She felt as if Deneb were groping around inside her mind. "Just say it, all right? Just say what you mean."

Deneb's hand tightened on Clemantine's knee. "I want to make a child. I want to make her new, and better than me, better than any of us—we are all so weighed down by our pasts, I'm afraid of the mistakes we might make. We need someone new. Someone with a new outlook. Someone who can see an untarnished future, and be our bridge to the Chenzeme."

Clemantine forced herself to sit up. She rubbed at her clammy cheeks. Her gaze fixed on the mural. A swell was rising. She tried to remember what it had been like to stand on the beach at the river mouth, a surfboard under her arm.

"Say something," Deneb pleaded.

"You could see it die."

"Yes, but parents have always taken that chance." She still knelt on the floor, gazing up at Clemantine with steady eyes. Doubt-free. "Will you help me build this child?"

Build it. Clemantine toyed with the verb. "Usually children are grown."

"They are grown only after the zygote is built. Clemantine, I want you for her second parent."

"Oh no—"

"It has to be you! It can't be Lot, can it?"

"Well, no. His genetic system isn't compatible, and it would be wrong to reproduce it anyway."

"And Nikko and Urban—"

Clemantine nodded her passive understanding. "Yes, of course. What jealousies would that stir?"

"If she is *our* child, they will all love her."

"So. I guess they will."

Something broke inside her. An era, snapping off an abrupt end. Here would be something new to worry about, something new to grieve over. Something new to invest with her hope, her love.

She set her hand on Deneb's. "All right—but when you build her, see to it she looks like you"—Clemantine mimed a waveform from her forehead to her waist—"not like this antique form. There are no living planets in the Swan Cloud. Let her be adapted to it."

Deneb nodded. "I will give her a neural organ like mine. She will be part Chenzeme."

"We are all becoming part Chenzeme, in our thoughts, if not in our bodies. Maybe we can take it back to them. Maybe someday we can force them to become partly human too."

Deneb's elusive ghost had disappeared again. Urban could not understand it. Since the incident in the core chamber she had become an unfathomable mystery, a puzzle that did not pretend to a solution. What could have led her to do it? He had no guesses, and she would not tell him. She would not talk to him at all.

Moved by a restless need to work, he went down alone to the core chamber. With one aspect of his attention he watched the courser, and the precise wavelength of its Dopplered hull light. If that light shifted toward the blue end of the spectrum, they would know it was accelerating again and that the distance between them was closing. Instead, its hull glow remained slightly reddened, meaning the courser continued to fall behind.

With a second aspect of his attention, Urban called up a model of star formation, returning to a question that had puzzled him since Alpha Cygni. Stars formed within molecular clouds, when dust and gas were drawn into ever denser knots under the influence of gravity. Once the mass of a protostar reached a threshold level, it would ignite in a fusion reaction that would generate a fierce stellar wind, to blow away the remnants of the nursery nebula.

What if a macroscale object existed in the nebular cloud, even before the gravitational collapse of the protostar? He reset the model, then added to it a solid, ring-shaped object, two kilometers in diameter. He gave it a density close to that of water.

On the first run, he placed the ring very close to the protostar's center of mass. It swiftly fell into the incandescent globule and disappeared.

On subsequent runs he placed the ring farther and farther out on the nebular disk, until he found a point where it would not fall into the star at all, but instead would begin to orbit, like a tiny planet circling the newborn sun.

His first aspect brought news: The courser's Doppler-shift had changed, climbing slightly toward the blue, indicating its speed was edging up toward Null Boundary's baseline velocity. Urban considered this, and frowned.

A transit bubble opened. Lot dropped into the core. Urban's chest rose in a great sigh, as he saw his own poor prospects reflected in Lot's presence. "Clementine kicked you out?"

"Deneb is staying with her."

"Sooth. Looks like we're a celibate ship again, huh? If Deneb keeps this up much longer, I'm going to be as crazy as Nikko."

The courser's Doppler-shifted wavelength edged up another tiny fraction.

Lot anchored himself with a foot hooked under a loop. He watched the model of star formation as it went through another collapse. "You're working on the ring."

"Sooth. It's been bothering me. None of the easy assumptions makes sense. Look." He raised a hand, pointing to an empty section of air. A blurred image of the ring snapped into existence at that point. "This is what Vigil saw, and this"—he moved his hand, and a brighter, sharper image appeared beside the first—"is an enhanced version."

Urban had studied both images, and he knew that except for their sharpness, they looked exactly alike. No more detail could be gleaned from the enhanced image than from the raw scan. Both showed a black ring, without surface features. Even the object's thermal profile was only a passive reflection of the considerable radiation it received from Alpha Cygni.

Urban waited while Lot studied the pictures. Then he drifted down next to him. "So tell me. What is it?"

Lot's sensory tears glinted as he shook his head. "We can't know that."

"Take a best guess."

"Okay." He ran a hand through his short-cropped hair. "There are no philosopher cells. So it's a ship or a habitat of some species like us—hunted by the Chenzeme, maybe to extinction."

"Sounds reasonable," Urban said. He tapped a wall so that he drifted backward. "So where's the drive system?"

"Maybe it had a zero point drive. Or maybe it wasn't made to move."

"Okay. So why was it in such an inhospitable environment?"

Lot thought about it. "Maybe it used the incoming energy?" he suggested. "It's possible to engineer for extreme environments."

"Implying it didn't get its energy from a reef."

"So it was made there?"

"I guess. Of course, Alpha C is probably no more than a few million years old."

"So you think it was made there within the last million years or so?" Lot pressed.

Urban gazed at the smooth black surface of the ring, so depauperate of information. "Who would build an undefended structure in such an exposed orbit, so easy for a passing warship to spot?"

Lot stared at the image. "Someone not familiar with the Chenzeme," he concluded. Then he looked at Urban with a puzzled frown. "Who wouldn't be familiar with the Chenzeme, this close to the cloud?"

"That's what's bothering me," Urban admitted. "Especially since the courser was obviously familiar with the ring. Do you remember, Nikko told us that the first time he ever saw a courser, the ship stood off, like it was trying to figure out what he was."

"Sooth."

"Our dog didn't hesitate. It *knew* it wanted to hit that ring."

"So what do you think it was?" Lot asked.

"Something old. Certainly older than Alpha C. Maybe as old as the Chenzeme war."

Lot grinned. "Yeah? Thirty million years old?"

The courser's Doppler-shift took a considerable jump. Urban cocked his head.

"What is it?" Lot asked.

"The courser's picking up speed. Not by much, but not insignificant either."

"We need to regrow the hull cells."

"Sooth. That'll let us work the interface. We need to

train it on the real thing." He sent a thought to his ghost at the reef, urging it to pull a little more acceleration, if it could. Nikko wouldn't like it—too much speed could kill them as easily as too little—but Urban did not want to yield any ground to the courser just yet.

With the public aspect of his attention, he continued to discuss the ring. "Thirty million years," he repeated. "It's long for us, but who knows how the Chenzeme regarded time? Think about it. The artifact didn't defend itself. It didn't camouflage itself. It showed no adaptations to the courser's aggression, and why should it, if it predates all coursers?"

"Then how could it be here?" Lot asked. "This star is too young."

Urban nodded at the model of the protostar. "Watch it run."

The display winked back to an infalling cloud of hot dust. The ring emerged from it, to fall into orbit around the new star. "Maybe the ring was meant to lie hidden in the cloud, but when the star formed, and the remnant cloud was blown away, the ring was exposed. It's a black object, and cold. If it had been in a molecular cloud, it would have been impossible to find."

Lot stared at the model for several seconds more, then looked at Urban. "So, uh . . . what is it?"

"We have to find another one, to know that."

The courser's Doppler-shift still showed it gaining speed.

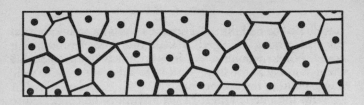

Chapter 21

Clemantine and Deneb said nothing, but Nikko worked it out anyway. It would be easy for him to know what files were being accessed, what Makers were being synthesized. With one part of her mind Clemantine watched him walk up the garden path and into the living room. With another aspect of her attention, she continued to discuss with Deneb the modifications they would need to make to the extracted gametes. She looked up only when Nikko's tall, spidery figure shadowed the lab door.

He said nothing for several seconds. It was hard to tell where his off-centered gaze was focused. "Deneb," he said at last. "It's good to see you back."

A smile fluttered on her face. She flexed her fingers. "Thank you."

Clemantine looked back at the chromosomal schematic on display above her desk. The image shimmered as a Dull Intelligence inventoried and manipulated the coding.

"How many are you planning to make?" Nikko asked.

"Two for now," Clemantine said. "More later."

"It's not a very safe time."

"If we live, they'll live," she said. "If not, they won't know the difference."

"All right."

She turned around in surprise. He shuffled awkwardly,

as if he had something more to say, but all he managed was, "Well. Good luck with it." He nodded at Deneb. His long fingers clacked against his thigh. Then he turned and walked away.

Clemantine held on to her cool until Nikko was out of earshot. Then she sputtered, and finally she laughed. Deneb joined in. They were on the floor before it was over.

The DI inventoried another chromosome.

Lot reseeded the philosopher cells. Nikko had long ago worked out their needs, and so they spread swiftly, painting the hull in their white glow. None too soon. The courser was closing the gap between them, while Null Boundary's reef grew more sluggish with every passing hour.

Urban's ghost brooded over it. The reef's power was not the deep well he had imagined. The polyps were easily exhausted. After a surge of activity they died back, and then the reef would need to grow a new living layer.

He turned to Nikko. "The courser must have burned out its reef coming out of Alpha C. It took this intervening time to recover."

"Maybe." Nikko was only a voice, emanating from a sense of mass. "Can we get any more speed?"

"Not now. Probably not for a while." It would take years of experiments to learn how to efficiently handle the reef. "We need to hit the courser," Urban concluded. "I'll talk to Lot."

Lot lay in the wound, bathed again in the brilliant light of the philosopher cells. The courser was moving up on them. He did not want to meet it—not yet. He was working out his own symphony with this new generation of cells, trying to tease out of them whatever remnants of their ancient past they might still contain, searching for some clue to the vision of the drifting entities he had seen so briefly when the Well water flooded the core chamber. Had that been a memory of the governors? Or had it been a memory the governors plucked from the archives of the philosopher cells? Or from his own fixed memory?

Eyes closed, he searched his own mind, plumbing the

depths of his fixed memory, spilling the data out into the cell field to see how it would play. There was a trove of information on molecular structure that he'd gathered from the Well. There were personal memories, of his own life, his family. Delving ever deeper, he recovered older, vaguer recollections inherited from his father and from the charismatics that had come before him. It was a flood of experience that reshaped the plane of the philosopher cells. They were not just Chenzeme anymore.

Exhaustion closed his eyes. He called for a transit bubble to take him to the gee deck.

Urban met him when he emerged from the new transit wall at the back of the pavilion. He set a hand on Lot's shoulder; his apprehension stung Lot's sensory tears. "Fury, we can't outrun the courser. Is there *anything* you can do to discourage it?"

Lot scowled. He didn't want to have this fight again. "I won't poison it." He slipped out from under Urban's hand, heading for the cabinet factory.

"I didn't ask you to poison it," Urban said. "I only asked if you could discourage it."

Lot turned around. He sensed no subterfuge.

"I know you're tired," Urban said. "But we need to do something."

"Okay." Lot thought about it while he got something to eat. "I guess we could try the same thing we did with the dark courser—infect it with the peacekeeping protocols of the Well."

"Through a dust drop?" Urban asked.

"Sooth. Through a long-distance drop."

Deneb slept in the babies' room, staying close to the zygotes as they grew within their jostling artificial wombs.

The wombs were opaque and egg-shaped, their servos slaved to the motion of Deneb's body, so that they moved as she moved, and when she spoke, the babies would hear her voice. She could not watch them directly, for they needed to be in darkness, but cameras in the wombs tracked their growth.

On a monitor, she watched their cells divide and their

bodies form. Soon, they would have limbs and kisheers. Then their bodies would form their scaled and pigmented outer shells. Kiyo's would be auburn; Hailey's would be a glistening mother-of-pearl. They could change the colors if they liked, when they were older.

Lot and Urban came by. They looked at the equipment and the monitors. Deneb could feel Urban's anger like a needle in the spine. "Why now, Deneb?" he demanded. "The courser is only another day or two away."

"Something more to live for," she murmured. A magic spell. She felt the shy touch of Lot's inquisitive charismata. It made her smile. She told him, "They'll be like me."

"You don't have sensory tears." His worry flickered like dark lines in her vision.

"I won't be as sensitive as you."

Then she had to explain it all to Urban and listen to his complaints.

The courser was thirty-four hours from weapons range when Lot prepared the cells to drop a cloud of dust. Nikko watched him through a library window. He lay on his side in the wound. The cells lapped over his sensory tears, long white fingers caging his face.

"Ready?" Nikko asked. The information-bearing particles would be the usual greetings and threats, but into this scaffolding Lot would weave the viral thoughts generated by the Well governors: chemical information that might infiltrate the Chenzeme system of communication, closing off the loop of unprovoked aggression.

Lot's eyelids fluttered. "Ready," he whispered. "*Now.*"

Nikko detected the charismata of command that flushed from Lot's sensory tears. He felt it replicate across the cell field as his own senses stretched out along the lines of the ship. A moment later, the searing heat of the dust drop burned across his awareness. He drank it in, watching through the hull cameras as the dust sparkled in the infrared, then disappeared, cooled to the temperature of surrounding space. The data it contained would be reactivated only within a Chenzeme neural field.

There were many reasons why this assault could fail:

The dust might break down in this stark, radiation-laced region of hot young stars, or it might not survive the impact with the courser, or the courser might be immune to it.

Then again, the Chenzeme were not invulnerable. It might all work out just as they planned.

Nikko watched the courser, keeping at least one aspect of his awareness fixed on it at all times. If it sensed the dust drop, it did not respond, either with a change in course or a radio hail. Urban joined Nikko in the library. He split his ghost so that it had several faces, one for each open window in a semicircular field. The central face spoke: "There won't be much time for the drop to take effect. We're almost within weapons range now."

Nikko's thoughts went to the growing embryos, blissfully unaware. Lot insisted they needed only one successful hit, only one particle of dust infiltrating the courser's cell field, and within seconds the Well virus would replicate itself into every branching dialogue. Still, it was an open question how long the virus would take to modify the cells' hardwired behavior.

Time ran down. The courser neared the dust drop. Lot huddled in the wound. Urban had a ghost on the interface, so that he could follow the cell-talk too. Somewhere, Clementine and Deneb were also listening. Nearly zero now.

The telescopes picked up a flare of heat from the courser. "What's that?" Urban said, his multiple faces coalescing into one as he stared at the central window. "An explosion?"

"No," Nikko said. His kisheer went still. Across its membrane, hope was exchanged for sullen fury. "It's fired its forward gun."

"At *us*?" It took Urban a second to catch on. "Ah, hell. You mean it's torching the dust."

At least the embryos would never know the difference.

The courser's gun sparkled three more times, burning off everything in its path. Nikko roused Lot in the wound, to let him know. "It's coming in," he said, when he was sure he had Lot's attention. "We're going to have to go through a mating again—unless you can convince it to turn away."

Lot's answer came in a hoarse, exhausted whisper. "I don't think I can. It will overwhelm our hull cells."

"Do what you can."

Urban drifted beside him, staring at the courser through

a library window. "Nikko? Shouldn't it be slowing down by now?"

Nikko followed his gaze. The courser was still gaining speed.

Urban said, "If it wants to mate, it should try to match speed with us, but it's not slowing down."

Nikko grunted. "You're right. And it's not really on an intercept course either. Look at the graph. Its path will bring it across our stern still a hundred thousand klicks away." More than that, the displacement was in two directions.

"It's not going for a mating at all," Urban concluded. His coiled fist sparked with heat. "It's just trying to get within weapons range."

The courser would not take their dust; it would not mate with them. So it was coming in for a hit. Nikko shared the news with Lot. "Is there anything else you can do?"

Lot was silent for a minute. Then his voice spoke again in Nikko's sensorium, relayed from the wound. "I've got an idea. I don't know if it makes any sense."

"Let's hear it."

"The reef's exhaustible, right? And the courser's been pushing itself hard. It's used its gun too. If we could get it to use its gun again, before it gets within killing range—"

"He's right," Urban said. He'd been floating cross-legged before the arc of open windows, but now his feet hit the data path with a crack. He rubbed his hands together, as if thoughts might spark between his palms. "We could buy some time if we force the courser to burn out its reef."

"Sooth," Lot said. "I could drop more dust. It'll bleed our mass, but if it helps . . ."

Nikko nodded thoughtfully. "Do it."

The dust went out in less than a minute. Only some of the cells responded though, so it was a small drop. Nikko told himself that size didn't matter, so long as the courser was forced to push the capacity of its reef. He told Lot to make two more drops. They went out at ten-minute intervals, each one smaller than the last.

"The cells are buzzing," Urban said when it was done. "Listen to them."

Nikko shook his head. "I can't interpret it."

"I can't either," Lot said. "It's unpatterned babble. They're exhausted."

Nikko could hear Lot's own fatigue reflected in the dry, soft timbre of his voice. A librarian fluttered in his face. "Bring Lot in," it said, speaking in Clemantine's voice. "We should all be down in the core."

"Sooth," Lot said. "I'm ready."

Nikko roused his own corporeal form. Deneb brought the embryos in their melon-sized artificial wombs. It felt crowded and close in the core chamber as the image wall tracked the courser's advance. It bore down on them, going ever faster.

Light flared from its bow.

"That's the first dust drop," Urban muttered. "Cooked to plasma."

It fired again, rejecting the second cloud as well. Nikko waited for it to fire a third time. The last dust drop was the smallest. Nikko could not track it. He could only estimate its position. The courser neared the site. Its gun remained dark. It reached the site of the drop. It surged through it, without firing. "The dog took the bait," Urban said in reverent wonder. "Lot, you've hit it."

Lot smiled in a crooked, half-terrified way. "Either that, or it's saving what it's got for us."

"Shut up, fury. The bait will work."

"I don't know." He took Clemantine's hand. "I don't know if there's time."

Nikko watched the freely drifting orbs of the artificial wombs. Blissfully unaware.

Deneb caught his eye. *I'm not sorry I did it.

Nikko nodded. *I'm not either.

"It's stopped accelerating," Clemantine announced. "This is it, folks. It's coming around."

The scopes tracked the courser as it swiveled on its short axis. It still hurtled behind and beneath Null Boundary, but now it was bringing its bow gun to bear on them.

"Entering weapons range," Nikko said. ". . . now."

For a century and a half this courser had been little more than a white blur in their scopes, but now, as the distance between the two ships closed, detail emerged in its image, until it was revealed to be an exact copy of the dark courser that had held them to a mating, only this courser was larger still, at least a third again as long as the other. Nikko looked down the lens of its bow gun, and he saw the flash of light.

All his ghosts froze, anticipating the last moment.

Then he snapped back into himself with a furious whoop. "We *saw* the light! So we've already been—"

"Hit," Clemantine said. "A third of the hull is sizzling."

"Yes, but we're not plasma!"

Now Urban was shouting too. "So much for the fabled Chenzeme lasers. That dog has got nothing left to hit us with!"

The courser fired again.

"Hit again," Nikko said. His kisheer lashed. "Sixty percent of the hull is cooked now—but it's not bad. The heat's not penetrating."

The courser's image flashed a third time.

Urban laughed. "That one hit with the impact of the noon sun in Silk."

"It's receding," Clemantine said. "It's falling out of range."

Lot asked anxiously, "Do we have any hull cells left?"

"Some," Nikko assured him. He slapped Lot on the back, sending them both bouncing across the chamber. "Don't worry. They'll regrow."

He caught a grip, turning to follow the courser's trajectory. Out of weapons range now. The telescopes marked its reorientation, as the warship returned to its running posture. Suddenly, Null Boundary had become the pursuer.

The courser did not resume its former acceleration. It coasted at a constant speed, but that was so high, it continued to pull away from Null Boundary, racing ahead toward the Swan Cloud. It had so much velocity that every few hours they would see the flare of an incandescent explosion as it struck some tiny bit of matter in its path. Still, it did not slow.

Maybe its reef had burned out. Maybe the Well influence had quieted its aggression. Maybe it had found a new, more important target.

They couldn't know.

"We could turn away from it." Nikko felt obliged to make the suggestion. "We could change our course, slow down." He didn't want to, and to his surprise, no one else did either. They'd come this far to find the source of the Chenzeme. That still lay ahead of them, if it existed at all. No one was willing to turn aside. Not now, when they might finally have a chance to follow the dog to its lair.

The courser drew ever farther ahead of them, racing on toward the Swan Cloud. Nikko never ceased searching the cloud for evidence of the Chenzeme. He would start in the radio spectrum, mapping the natural emissions of the cloud's fragile molecules—hydroxyl radicals and carbon monoxide, alcohols, amides and amines, and many others. The molecules owed their existence to the cloud's abundant dust grains, which screened them from the ultraviolet radiation that would have shattered their delicate bonds.

He would track the hot points of infalling protostars and the shock fronts of old supernovas.

And always, he would make special note of the occasional eruptions of the faint, point-source signals he had first detected just after Alpha Cygni.

These enigmatic signals were widely scattered, yet as the months passed, he charted an apparent cluster. Four signals with similar amplitudes had occurred around a point in the sky close to a powerful infrared source that marked the position of a massive, new-formed star, hidden deep within the veils of the Swan Cloud. The four signals occurred over a period of months, while the ship's position changed, so they were not just a line-of-sight cluster.

The philosopher cells did not react to the irregular signals, even when Nikko reproduced them at greater strength. He wondered if the cells had been hardwired to ignore them; if the Chenzeme had included some behavioral loop to ensure the warships would not turn against their own civilizations. There was no way to tell.

From the nursery in Clemantine's house, he heard Kiyo scream. He looked in on her, through the eyes of a teddy that he'd left in her crib. She had gotten an infant fist around the edge of her kisheer. Nikko winced, knowing how that would hurt, but she had not learned her hands yet. She did not know how to let go. *Urban*.

Got it. His dark hands reached down to pry Kiyo's little red-scaled fist open—not an easy task, given the length of her fingers, but at last he managed to untangle them. He put a soft cloth in her hands for her to hold, then he picked her up, lifting her out of range of Nikko's vision.

Out of habit, Nikko checked on Hailey next. She was peacefully asleep, though her shapeless infant ghost was active. In the library kindergarten Deneb had devised, her ghost played at being a wandering breeze. Where she looked, there she went, and Deneb had hung her world with shapes to please her.

Nikko watched her, always fascinated by her activities. These babies scared him half to death. They astounded him. Everything he did seemed so much more important now.

He looked again at the infrared source that marked the hidden crèche of the new-formed sun. Rushing outward from it was a shock wave of cloud particles moving at supersonic velocities, driven by the fierce young stellar winds. Somewhere in that harsh environment something was talking, and not in the language of the hull cells.

Nikko wanted to go there.

Kiyo was making happy noises as Urban walked and talked to her. Hailey's ghost had become a breeze with hands, batting at a collection of brightly colored bells.

The new star lay some four hundred years away, not far from the route blazed by the courser. As Nikko considered this, he felt the vastness of time unfolding before him, and he wondered, *How long can we make this last?*

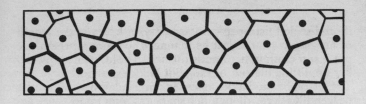

Chapter
22

The courser continued to run.

Lot came down to the core chamber every few days to watch its dwindling image in the scopes. Weeks passed, until they added up to a year. The years accumulated, and Kiyo and Hailey grew from babies into young girls. Still the courser didn't slow. It didn't adjust its heading. Its burned-out reef should have recovered by now—Null Boundary's had—yet the courser ran on, like a mindless drone following a homing beacon, summoned by an instinct more powerful than reason.

Lot watched it, all too conscious of his own instinctive need. The cult chewed at his belly all the time now, its dull, warm bite eating him hollow. If he was a weapon, he was an antiquated one. No one here was vulnerable to him. He could not fulfill his purpose. The designers in the cloud would need to invent someone new.

His gaze slid away from the courser. The image walls reflected the gulf of space outside the ship. Alpha Cygni lay behind him, the Swan Cloud lay ahead, and on every side the gleam of stars like glowing dust. The immensity tugged at him. He felt thin, as if the effort of filling even his tiny portion of this image was too much for him. Far smaller than a virus, he thought. That's me. And the hull of Null

Boundary was his protein coat that kept him from dissolving in the invisible medium in which he was embedded.

Embedded in space-time.

He did not feel as if the ship was moving, or even that movement was possible beyond the thin layer of philosopher cells that was Null Boundary's skin. They were a discrete point, a virus. No more. A single pixel within a static image of incomprehensible magnitude. They could not escape from this point that contained them, and the only force acting upon them was Time. Uppercase *T*. Time as the Unknown God, forever refreshing the Image in which they existed; at unknowable intervals rearranging their position within the whole. Not randomly, but with a forthright progression that continually expanded the quantity of dark points intervening between Null Boundary and the courser, while placing them ever closer to the black wall of the cloud.

Something lay within those veils of dust. Nikko had heard it speaking—from many points, but mostly from the neighborhood of the newly formed star he called Nightlight. Four hundred years away.

"Lot?" Kiyo's voice was a shy peep.

He turned to see her crouching at the rim of an open transit bubble, her auburn face framed by a kisheer that looked oversized as it drifted in a smoky red cape around her shoulders. Behind her, Hailey clung to the bubble wall, her mother-of-pearl hide iridescent in the starlight. Lot smiled sheepishly. He ran his fingers through the stubble of his hair. "Oops. We had a date, didn't we?"

"You forgot?" Hailey asked. The whole concept of forgetting was quite beyond her, and therefore, endlessly fascinating.

"Just for a few minutes," Lot admitted. "Sorry."

"It's okay," Kiyo said. "But Urban showed us how to use the bridge. We're ready."

Together Kiyo and Hailey had learned to walk and talk and glide and ghost, and to use the charismata. Lot silently thanked Deneb yet again for giving them that sense. From the time they were babies he'd taken them with him out to the hull. He would lie with them, one in each arm, and let them feel the standing waves of debate that flowed between the cells.

When they were babies they had grown tense and silent under the Chenzeme influence, small frightened mammals huddling out of sight of greater forces. Given time though, they would relax, sucking on their fingers, pulling on Lot's hair, their eyes unfocused, as if they listened to some inner music.

As they grew older, Lot would ask them, "What do you feel?"

Shy Kiyo—ever fearful of being wrong—would remain quiet, letting Hailey speak first: "It's like dream scenes. Colors that make me feel things."

"Can you change the colors?"

Hailey frowned, further obscuring blue eyes already half-hidden behind their crystal lenses. She shook her head. Her kisheer rustled against Lot's cheek. He felt her puzzlement escape into the cells, building a ripple of confusion that played against the Chenzeme themes. "Do you feel that?" Lot asked. "You did that."

"But it doesn't mean anything," Hailey said.

"It's static," Kiyo agreed.

"No, it's not. The cells are trying to—" Lot caught himself. It did no good to explain what the cells were doing. They needed to understand it on their own. The girls handled the charismata of human emotions as naturally as breathing, but neither of them had ever made sense of the Chenzeme version, so on that score, the sensory plexus Deneb had made for them was a failure.

Kiyo felt his disappointment, and stiffened at his side. "Lot—?"

"Don't worry," Lot said, tickling her kisheer. "We'll figure it out."

It had finally come to him to let them try Urban's virtual interface.

Urban had made the interface as a metaphor for Chenzeme neural tissue. It was supposed to function as a bridge, allowing his ghost to cross the divide between human and Chenzeme thought. With the help of sensors embedded in the wound, he *could* interpret the general thrust of Chenzeme conversation, though he was still training the interface to follow discrete dialogues all the way through their loops, and to distinguish conversations that blended, or split.

In the other direction the virtual bridge didn't perform as well. Urban's attempts to speak to the cells were little more than unintelligible interruptions. Still, the bridge was one more window onto the Chenzeme world. So Lot had sent the girls to borrow it.

"If Urban showed you how to use it, then I guess we're ready," Lot said. "So let's go!" He kicked himself into the transit bubble while the girls dove squealing, out of his way.

In the wound, Lot let himself descend into the cells while Kiyo and Hailey clung like bugs to the wall of the transit bubble. They grumbled about the cold. Kiyo had her kisheer scrunched up around her neck so the cells couldn't touch it. Lot grinned at her dainty efforts, made a feint for her arm. "Come down in the cells with me!"

She squealed and knocked his hand away. "I am *not* going to let them touch *my* mouth."

He made a mock grab at Hailey too, but she just shoved a loose mass of cells in his face. He sputtered free of it, laughing. "I wish Deneb had given you both sensory tears. She pruned too much."

Hailey squinted thoughtfully. "Maybe we could give ourselves sensory tears?"

"I already asked," Kiyo said. "Deneb said no. It would make us too much like Lot."

"That's what she told you?" Lot asked. Her kisheer scrunched tighter. He caught the taste of her uneasiness. "Not supposed to talk about it?" he asked gently.

She nodded. "Deneb said it's not polite."

Not for the first time, Lot wondered if their difficulty with the cell field might be just a problem of resolution. They could sense the charismata only through the mucous membranes of their noses and mouths. It might not be enough. As an analogy, would he be able to learn a new language if he heard only inconsistent fragments of it? Urban's interface could monitor cell-talk better than they could. Maybe it really could close the gap.

He closed his eyes. "Okay. I'm going to be quiet for a while and listen to the cells. You two hook up to Urban's bridge. If you can sense anything, talk to me about it— *softly*. I don't want to get scared." They giggled.

He still felt their presence close beside him, but as his consciousness sank into the field, they became only starting points in conversations that went nowhere. Seeds of potential that did not grow. All around them flowed looping scenarios, as the cells explored the meaning of their last dust drop, now almost eight years old; as they examined an ancestral memory of an attack on another courser; as they explored the nature of Hailey and Kiyo.

Hailey gasped. Lot felt himself buoyed by the noise. He opened one eye a slit. Her kisheer trembled in a wad at her neck. "Hailey?" he whispered. "Talk to me."

"It's angry," she blurted.

"Sooth. That's the Chenzeme way."

He felt Kiyo's fingers against his chest. "I can see myself."

"Can you?" The triumph he felt flowed into the cell field. The cells understood it. They echoed the sentiment by dredging up triumphant memories. It was a celebration of vicious assaults, a conflagration of ancient victories. Hailey screamed. Her terror inspired intricate patterns of dialogue, as if the cells remembered the last emotions of the dead.

"Lot, wake up. Get out." Kiyo's little fist pounded at his chest. "We want to go back right now!"

He opened both eyes to see panic on their faces.

He lifted his head out of the flowing cells, and then he could feel their fear, cold stings against his sensory tears. He dug his fingers into the wall of the transit bubble. "Hark. Close up."

The bubble sealed, but it didn't move. Lot held the girls, waiting for them to calm. "It worked, didn't it?" he asked after a minute. Kiyo started trembling all over again. Hailey punched him in the thigh. Lot chuckled. "The Chenzeme are fierce murdering bastards. You know that."

"I don't like feeling that way," Kiyo said. "It's like being dirty and thinking you can never be clean." Lot felt her kisheer fold like a second glove around his hand. He felt scared too, and at first he couldn't tell if it was his own feeling or an echo of theirs, until he thought about it for a minute. Then he knew it was real. *It had worked.* The girls had vividly understood the cell-talk. They weren't guessing, like Nikko guessed. They weren't stuck in a single loop, like Urban was when he plugged into the interface. They had sensed the breadth of the field, all those separate memories of murder. They had done what only he had been able to do . . . until now.

He had become replaceable.

He held them tighter, trying to cover his resentment with fierce charismata of love.

He lay with Clemantine that night, not sleeping. He lay on his side, and he could see the glitter of false starlight in her wide-open eyes. "How are you feeling?" she asked, without any padding or prelude. She hadn't asked in a while.

"I'm pleased."

"You know that's not what I mean. You had that look on your face tonight. The cult is eating at you again, isn't it?"

"It's always eating at me." He imagined touching her again with the cult, the way he used to. She would feel what he willed her to feel. The cult would live. If he let it, it would grow around them, an expanding entity that could swallow suns, and he would be its heart and its skin and all the rushing thoughts that filled its unfathomable mind. If he could only bring this structure into being, he would be complete. The desire of it burned in him. His charismata permeated the air, carrying a foul mix of love and anger, deception, frustration, and fear. An ugly stew. "I've been thinking I would go back into cold storage."

Her sudden fear stung in bursts of cold against his skin. "Why?"

"I want to know where the courser is going. I want to know what lives at Nightlight."

"And you will, in time." She sighed. It was a lonely sound, like a wave running up the wet sand of an empty beach. "It's getting worse?"

"Do you have a memory of how it felt when you first desired sex?"

"*Sooth*," Clemantine whispered.

"It's a desire like that. It just grows and grows. I don't even want to know where it's going."

He thought of his father. All his life, Jupiter had touched the cult—with his prayer circles and his Communions he had fed on it lightly—never allowing it to ignite, just enough connection to keep him sane. Not Lot. He had lived without it, but debt accumulated just the same.

"How long can I trust myself?" Lot asked. "Jupiter finally gave up everyone he ever loved."

"You are not Jupiter."

"Yes I am!" he snapped at her. "And I'm all the other charismatics too, and you can't change it. I know you've tried. So we deal with it, okay?"

There was no trace of softness in Clemantine's aura. "Okay."

"Anyway, it's a good time for me to go into cold sleep. While I'm down, Hailey and Kiyo can learn the cells, and you can wake me if you ever need to."

"*Damn,*" she breathed. "God *damn* the Chenzeme."

He closed his eyes. "I'm sorry."

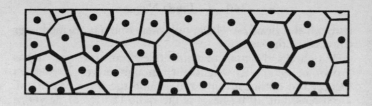

Chapter
23

Point zero: initiate.

A sense kicked in. Something like vision. Not because it emulated sight, but because it revealed. Himself: Nikko Jiang-Tibayan.

Point one: identify.

Personality suspended on a machine grid. He is only one mind within the great ship Null Boundary, his existence contained in discrete ninety-second loops.

It seems just a few minutes since Clemantine and Deneb, Urban, Kiyo and Hailey, all followed Lot into cold storage, nine years after their transit of Alpha Cygni. He checks his records. It has been 219 years. The courser is a mote in his telescopes, requiring days of observations to resolve. Its heading has never varied.

Point two and counting: status check.

Null Boundary has penetrated a peninsula of the Swan Cloud. It's a tiny finger of material reaching out from the cloud's main bulk, yet this finger is larger than Sol System. The density of particles outside the ship has climbed from less than one per cubic centimeter in "open" space, to five thousand per cubic centimeter. The material is mostly hydrogen, but there are trace amounts of other molecules too, all slamming against the prow as Null Boundary forges through the cloud. A ghostly plasma cone has formed over the nose of the ship.

He checks the map of unidentified transmissions. It has grown in detail. At Nightlight, enough bursts have been recorded to outline a thin band around the waist of the star. He listens, but all he hears is the radio chatter of newborn stars and the whisper of complex organic molecules collecting within the cloud. Inside the ship, all is still, and very quiet.

Point twenty: additional subminds report in. Their assessments are pleasingly dull. Reef function is nominal. Air quality is—

An excited submind dumps itself into his awareness. A new radio burst is arriving, on a chillingly familiar frequency. It is from a point half a degree off their present heading, so it does not come from the courser—yet he recognizes its signature even before the hull cells react.

It is Chenzeme.

Full awareness snapped over Nikko. He broke the loop, extending his senses outward through the ship's neural system to "hear" the signal himself. Definitely Chenzeme.

The hull cells confirmed it. They fell into a brief state of utter inactivity—startled? wary? listening?—Nikko couldn't say. Then debate erupted. Charismata swept between the cells in a crazy, surging, chaotic tide. The meaning of it was beyond Nikko's ability to track, so he sent a submind to waken Lot—but in hardly more than a minute the storm of debate was over. Opposing waves coordinated in a rolling consensus achieved with frightening ease. The activity of the cells did not decline, but it was concerted now. Nikko felt a nascent radio emission building. He sought to stop it. He did not want the cells going independent again. He did not want them speaking without permission.

So he made a rough code with a brutal meaning—*negate that*—and he sent it to cardinals near the hull, where it was duplicated and released. He waited for some response from the hull cells to this demanding opposition . . . but there was none. Whether it was ignored or excised or simply not detected, he couldn't tell. The cells' consensus did not reveal even a flicker of doubt. Climax loomed a moment away.

Now.

A radio signal burst from the cell field's unified ranks. Nikko recognized it as a greeting: dangerous and joyful, submissive and threatening. It was aimed in a line half a degree off their course. He put Null Boundary's instruments to work, searching for any visible object at that point in the sky. He had no way of knowing how far away it might be.

He found nothing. The only visible object anywhere near the radio source was the courser, and that could barely be seen. Even as he watched, the faint gleam of its hull cells faded beneath the threshold of detectability—stealthed like the dark courser? *Why?*

What was out there? A predator? Or prey?

His own hull cells subsided into a frightening quiescence now that their message was sent. Never had Nikko seen them so inactive. He watched them warily, while he sent subminds to waken all the ship's dormant ghosts.

Lot rose to a groggy awareness within the dissolving tissue of his cold-sleep cocoon. The transparent, mucilaginous capsule was suspended across a tiny chamber in his core apartment. Its surface layers shimmered as its tissue flowed away across the anchoring umbilicals, disappearing within the walls.

Movement caught his eye.

He turned his head—as far as he could within the constraining tissue—to see Kiyo's auburn face disappear behind the rim of the chamber door.

"Kiyo?" The cocoon was dissolving to threads, but his hands remained pinned. He shrugged a shoulder to rub at his sensory tears. Why was he waking?

"Kiyo?" he called again.

She reappeared at the doorway, looking a little bigger, a little older than he remembered, but not much. So not much time had passed. This conclusion left him relieved and annoyed and frightened . . . not a pleasant breakfast cocktail, though its impact was eased a bit by Kiyo's charismata of pleasure.

"Why am I waking?" he asked.

"Everybody's waking." This time she came all the way

into the tiny chamber. "Nikko woke us all up. Lot, we're in the cloud."

His heart skipped. If they were in the cloud, then he had no idea how much time had passed. A hundred years, at least. Maybe a lot more.

Kiyo touched his hand. "Hurry. Something's wrong with the hull cells. I've never seen them like this before. They've gone quiet. They remind me of the way I felt when I was sinking into cold sleep. Nikko wants you to look at them. Hurry." She dove out of the chamber, then returned a moment later with his spider and a skin suit.

He tugged at the last of the suspension threads and finally freed himself. Kiyo touched the spider to his ear, while the skin suit's formless, silvery mantle folded around him.

"On-line?" Nikko's voice demanded.

"Sooth."

"Get out to the hull, then. I need you there."

Kiyo went with him.

In the transit bubble Nikko let him feel a replay of the radio signal. Lot pondered its meaning while he sank into the cold tissue of the wound. The cells lapped over his sensory tears, and abruptly he felt himself invaded by a powerful lethargy. His eyes closed. A sweet, peaceful grayness flooded his senses.

"Lot!"

Distantly he heard Kiyo. He felt her slapping at his hand. Clemantine's voice spoke in his ear, gently chiding. "Wake up now, son."

"I'm pulling him out," Nikko said.

No. Lot did not want that. He was content. A fulfillment was coming.

Kiyo's child voice screamed at him in a woeful panic. It hurt him to hear it. It disturbed his mood. He raised a hand. He felt her grab it. He started to pull her down into the field with him, for now no dissent was required. She fought him, her slender limbs pulling, kicking to escape.

A knife fell, shearing him loose.

Emptiness poured in.

Awareness flickered.

He blinked at the wall of a transit bubble inches from his

eyes. Nikko's angry voice buzzed in his ear: "*I am not putting him back.*" And Kiyo: he felt her fingers on his cheek. "You're bleeding," she said.

"Lot." Now it was Urban's voice issuing from the spider. "We're getting a repeat of the signal Nikko detected earlier. The cells are awake again. They're reacting to it."

"Put me back," Lot said, his words slurred. He felt half lost in sleep, aware but unable to awaken.

"No," Nikko said. "It's too dangerous."

"We need to know," Lot said. "Do it."

Urban's voice again: "We'll take him out if the cells go quiet. It'll be okay."

"Leave Kiyo out," Deneb warned. "She can listen through the interface."

"Separate them then!" Urban sounded angry and impatient. "Come on. Before the cell response fades."

"I want to stay with Lot!" Kiyo protested, but they didn't leave her a choice. The transit bubble pinched in two and took her away. Without quite noticing the change, Lot found himself back among the cells.

They were no longer quiet. Their excitement chased his lethargy away. He felt a rising crescendo of unanimous agreement.

—*don't translate*—

And he let himself be swept up in it as an answering radio signal once again exploded outward from the cells.

Later, Lot washed the blood off his face in Clemantine's house, using the moment to think about what he had felt and what he'd learned. When he returned to the living room, everyone was there, even Nikko, who stared at him, his mood severe, as if he expected some permanent damage.

"I'm okay," Lot said.

Nikko snorted. Clemantine stood beside him, arms crossed over her chest and a cool half-smile on her face as amusement veiled a sharp concern.

Kiyo crouched on the couch next to Deneb. She stared at Lot, looking as if she wanted to spring up, but Deneb's hand was a firm weight on her shoulder. "You should not have had her out there with you," Deneb said. "She told you something was wrong with the cells. She shouldn't be out there at all! The interface is a better link for her."

Lot looked away. Deneb was right, of course. Had he really tried to pull Kiyo into the cells with him?

"So you're sorry," Urban said. He sat behind Deneb, balanced on the sofa back. "You didn't mean to do it, et cetera. Now, do you have any idea what's going on?"

Lot glanced at Kiyo and found himself the recipient of a warm smile. No grudges there. So he turned to Urban, and tried to explain it: "It's simple, really. The cells are being called to the radio source. If this were a Chenzeme vessel, our course would have been adjusted right after the first signal. But our cells can't turn the ship. That's why the call was repeated. It's a command, but it's up to us to carry it out."

Urban stood, his whole posture tense with anticipation. "Then this is what we came for. This is the controlling element behind the warships."

"Maybe." Lot looked at Kiyo, and then at Hailey, leaning over the sofa back. Doubt touched him, and he frowned. "I think we need to decide soon if we're going to respond—in the next few minutes. We've already been signaled twice. If we don't give in to it and turn the ship, we might not be offered another chance."

"A chance at what?" Clemantine asked.

Lot shook his head. "I don't know. The cells don't know. But look how they reacted. There was no debate. Only consensus, then acquiescence. They have to be reacting with hardwired instinct. Whatever sent that signal is closely tied to the Chenzeme ships—maybe in control of them."

"The next step up in the Chenzeme hierarchy," Urban said grimly. "Do you think it's already summoned the courser?"

"Probably."

"I say we go. Judging from the time between signal and response, it's no more than a few months away."

From her post beside Nikko, Clemantine nodded thoughtfully. Her gaze fixed on Lot. "A true Chenzeme ship would be enslaved by this source, wouldn't it? That's why the cells have gone lethargic . . . so they can't further amend the course."

Lot nodded, feeling a blade of aggression within her caution. "I'd guess so."

"We're not enslaved," Clemantine pointed out. "We can turn away at any time. So why not take a closer look? It's what we came for. And we'll want to find the courser again anyway."

"Sooth," Urban said. "It's so."

"I think so too," Hailey said. Kiyo backed her up, though she sounded more timid: "Me too."

"Hush," Deneb told them. "You're too young to understand the choices."

Lot exchanged a sharp look with Urban. Then he took his life in his hands. "You can't dismiss them for that."

Deneb's kisheer bunched around her neck as she turned to glare at him. "I am not dismissing them." Her fingers were twitchy. Lot felt the mixed drift of her feelings: curiosity and caution, and a low-level guilt.

"Deneb?" Clemantine asked. "What's your opinion?"

Her grip tightened on Kiyo's shoulder. "We don't have a choice, do we? We need to know what's out there, before it finds us first."

They all looked at Nikko. He leaned against the wall, his arms crossed over his chest, his gaze unreadable. His kisheer rustled once. "It's done then," he said.

Lot thought he felt a strange, varying pressure. He imagined the steerage jets, pushing them slowly, slowly onto their new course. Long before that was finished, the philosopher cells obeyed their apparent programming and went dormant. Within a few hours, their illumination faded away. When the course correction was finally done, Null Boundary was as dark and stealthed as the vanished courser.

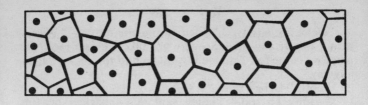

Chapter 24

There was nothing immediately ahead of them. Nothing that Nikko could see, on any wavelength. In the library he skipped through all the collected records again, just to be sure. He pulled up the image he'd made of the original signal. It was only a point source.

"So it's small," Clemantine said, startling him.

He turned, to find her ghost had taken form on the white path behind him.

"We should see something by now," Nikko insisted. "Even if it's only the size of a Celestial City, if it has any illumination . . ."

"Why do you think it needs to be that large?"

Nikko looked again at the point-source image. "It had to generate a signal. It had to detect a response. The power source—"

"Would be the zero point field. It could be very small."

"It could be," he agreed grudgingly. "How did it come to be almost directly on our course?"

"I don't know."

The signal that had silenced the hull cells was the signal of a Chenzeme warship—not at all like the signals Nikko had picked up from the vicinity of the young star he called Nightlight. Could the two sources be related? Or was he listening to the emissions of distinct civilizations? The winners and losers in an ancient war, perhaps? One stealthy and vicious, the other unconcerned. Or was it something altogether different? This cloud was so vast, reaching where his imagination could not follow. He shook his head, musing aloud, "Can we be as mysterious as they are?"

Clemantine nodded somberly. "You are to me," she said. "Nikko, my friend, you certainly are to me."

Nikko had a ghost always on watch, so he witnessed the event as it happened: a sparkling, infrared flash on the threshold of detectability, lighting a point in the void directly ahead of Null Boundary. Watching the display, he felt a chill. That first time he had seen a Chenzeme ship he had watched it drop dust. Its heat signature had looked like the signature of this flash. The conclusion came easily: Something was laying down a message for them. It could not be the courser, or he would see the illumination of its hull cells. So it must be whatever thing had called both ships this way.

Lot readied himself to go out once again to the hull cells. There was still nothing to be seen in the void ahead, but Nikko had made a guess at the position of their target. He knew the velocity at which dust could be ejected from a Chenzeme hull, and he had modeled the dispersion rate of that dust within the cloud. Null Boundary's course and speed were easy to factor into the equation, and now Nikko believed they were very close, at last.

For Lot, it had been a long, hard wait. The cult craving wore on him, demanding a satisfaction he could not give. He distracted himself with the synthesizer, practicing the Chenzeme speech with Hailey and Kiyo, but it was a weak imitation, leaving him hungry for the intense, flowing waves of true Chenzeme thought. So when Nikko called him, he quickly retrieved a skin suit and hurried to the hull.

Kiyo and Hailey wanted to go with him, but Deneb wouldn't hear of it. "You don't need to go," Lot told them. "Ghost it. Use the bridge. You won't a miss a thing."

"But you shouldn't be alone," Kiyo said. "Remember last time."

Lot remembered well enough. "Nikko will be watching."

Still, he did not go quite all the way to the hull. He had no desire to be sucked down again into the cells' torpor, so he huddled in the transit bubble a few feet below the philosopher cells, waiting for some sign that their dormancy would break. Several hours passed. Clemantine came to sit with him. She brought food, and he ate greedily, but his attention was not fixed on the meal. She felt it and smiled. "Not tired of me yet?"

"No way. Want me to prove it?"

She chuckled softly while her presence drifted in easy packets against his sensory tears. "Yes, I think I do."

Nikko was the voice of the spider. "It's starting," he announced somberly. "We have now got a detectable metabolic rate in the cell field."

Lot opened his eyes. His head was pillowed on Clemantine's breast. She held him close, her hand stroking his buttocks in a half-conscious rhythm. "*Finally,*" he breathed. He raised his head, and she let him go. He turned to grab his skin suit. "Can you see anything out there?" he asked her, as the suit folded around him.

Her gaze was far away. "No. There's still nothing visible, but then we've only reached the edge of the dust. It could be hours yet, before we really get there . . . wherever 'there' is."

"Hours, huh?" She was still naked. A floating vision, he thought. A warrior angel.

"Huh," Clemantine said. "I can hear your pulse."

He grinned. "All for you."

The transit bubble started to pinch shut between them. Clemantine reached through the shrinking orifice to touch her fingertips to his sensory tears. "Be careful, Lot."

"Sooth," he said. "Watch me close?"

"You know it."

There had to be something out there.

Nikko pirouetted at the center of the core chamber, surveying first the raw observations gathered by Null Boundary's instruments: maps of emissions across the electromagnetic spectrum. Next he shifted the display through a series of views filtered and enhanced by a DI. No solid objects were revealed within a scope of several light-years. But if an object was small and cold and dark, he could detect it only at very close range.

The philosopher cells were quiet, but awake. Waiting? Maybe.

Nikko used radar to probe the darkness. For weeks Null Boundary had dumped velocity until now the ship ran at hardly five percent lightspeed. It seemed brutally slow. And yet, in less than three hours the ship would traverse an astronomical unit. An AU was the distance that had once separated Earth from the Sun. It was not a small measure of space. Kept quiet and cold, a planet-sized mass could vanish easily into such a vast, dark night.

There has to be something concrete out there. Something with an antenna large enough to capture the feeble traces of an attenuated radio signal, or it would never have heard their answer. Nikko told himself he would be able to detect something that big. But could he locate it soon enough to make a difference?

He still didn't know what he would do when something was found.

He scanned the image walls again, while ghosts on continuous pilgrimage dropped in and out of his atrium. He'd edited impatience from his persona a dozen times before an alarm sounded its gray ringing announcement over the atrial channels. At last, the radar had collected a probable return.

The image wall refreshed itself.

A ghostly, pockmarked expanse emerged from the darkness, looking like white chalk drawn broadly on a rough black surface. Its edges flowed in too many lobes to be called circular. Nikko surveyed the time from signal launch to return, finding an average of 134 seconds, indicating a range of some twenty million kilometers—a distance they would cross in twenty-two minutes. The object lay precisely in Null Boundary's path.

Love and nature.

Urban's voice was tense in his atrium: *What is that?*

"No idea."

*Look at it! It's huge. What's its diameter? Seven thousand kilometers? Nikko, it's centered on our course. We have to veer now, or we're going to hit it.

"It's already too late for that." Even with the reef, they didn't have that much maneuvering power.

*Rotate the ship then. Fire up the fusion engines. It looks soft. If it's not a planetary object, we can use our exhaust to burn a path through it.

"It won't work! It's too late to bring the engines on-line, and there isn't time to reorient the ship. We'd hit broadside."

*We have to do something.

They had no guns.

The next radar pass unrolled and the ghostly smear gained definition.

*Shit, Urban whispered. Nikko could not think of anything more inspired to say. From left to right the object was hardening from an airy blur to a low-resolution snapshot of a swarm of closely packed ships, each vessel's round prow pointed squarely in Null Boundary's face.

"Get everyone into the core," Nikko said.

*Sure. But look at the scale. Those can't be ships. Each prow is only twenty meters across.

Nikko stared at the projection. He still saw ships on the right-hand side of the image, where there was the most detail, but Urban was right; they were impractically small. "What else could they be?"

*I don't know. We need more detail!

"It's coming."

Nikko's kisheer bunched around his neck as he waited for the data from a new set of returns to be integrated into the display. The echoes they received carried only a minuscule fraction of the strength of their initial signal, but that was enough to paint the image in finer and finer detail. Nikko watched each pass with rapt attention.

The airy left side of the swarm gained resolution. Individual ships sifted out of the blurred image. Each prow was still no more than an undetailed smear, but clearly they were larger than the ships on the swarm's right-hand side, thirty meters at the smallest and increasing in size toward the center.

Nikko felt staggered by the sheer quantity of objects. If

this was an armada, it extended over seven thousand kilometers in at least two directions. He paused to consider the logistics of such a fleet—how could so many ships run so close together? Any slight error in navigation would be fatal. It reminded him of the Dyson swarms in the Hallowed Vasties.

New data continued to load, rewriting the right-hand side of the image now. Nikko felt a flush of shock; his kisheer shivered as he took in the results. The "ships" in this quadrant, which had been only twenty meters wide seconds before, had expanded to at least forty-five meters across. There was no improvement at all in surface detail. "Our initial estimate couldn't have been that far off," Nikko said.

No way, Urban agreed, his tone one of cold satisfaction. *Whatever we're looking at, it's expanding in size— like an antenna opening up? Maybe a cluster of recording stations. Not like a fleet of ships. Whatever they are, they can only get so big. We can still slide between them.*

That hope lasted until the next radar pass, when the returning echoes no longer described a swarm of discrete objects—mapping instead an unbroken wall of planetary scale.

Nikko stared grimly at the display. "I want everyone in the core. We might still weather a minor impact."

Sooth. Urban agreed, but he did not sound as if he believed it.

Waking came slowly to the cell field, but it came as a smooth, inevitable slide into heat and quickening activity. Lot tracked the progress, anticipating an explosion of chaotic debate.

That never came. As the cells awoke, each one emitted the same pattern. It was not a thought, only an empty tonal structure like a carrier wave devoid of information. Lot's breathing grew shallow. His limbs felt remote. Vaguely, he saw himself falling into this unprecedented regimentation, but soon he forgot it, and waking became no different than sleep.

•   •   •   •

A crawlway opened. Nikko looked up, just as Clemantine dropped into the core chamber. "So," she said grimly. "I guess our target is not hiding anymore."

Kiyo and Hailey spilled in after her, with Deneb in the rear. Fear clogged the tiny sensors studding the image walls, so Nikko shut them down. "The object can't be dense," he said. "It didn't exist a minute ago. We could punch through."

"Sooth," Clemantine said. "Maybe."

"It wants us to hit it!" Kiyo shouted. "It wants us to crash."

"Why?" Hailey asked, her head cocked as she puzzled over the question.

"Because we're not really Chenzeme!"

"Or because we *are* Chenzeme," Clemantine said.

Nikko glared helplessly at the display.

"*Come on, fury.*"

Lot squirmed, as Urban's voice intruded like a hard line drawn straight through his easy, unstructured world.

"*You're too young to introvert. Focus. Focus. That's right.*"

Lot felt a flush of heat, before real vision broke through his gray surrounds, bubbling up like water through a bore hole, spreading a swirl of imagery to fill in the field of his perception. He recognized the curving wall of a transit bubble, and Urban's face, set in an impatient scowl. "You know, fury, I don't think you can handle those cells anymore."

The cells.

Lot turned his head, as if he could look back over his shoulder and see the past few minutes. Every sensation experienced within the philosopher cells existed in his memory. Yet while he'd been part of it, he'd been utterly unaware of what he participated in . . . as if his conscious mind had been shut down along with his ability to choose. He had become a conduit of information, unconscious but awake.

He looked back at Urban. "There's a lot of dust out there. It's clogging our receptors."

"Sooth. It's thick."

Lot frowned, trying to order his concerns. "It's a drug—the dust, I mean. It's overriding our instincts. It's in absolute control of our cells."

"Get yourselves secured," Nikko said, as Lot and Urban dropped into the core chamber.

Lot's brown cheeks were flushed, his eyes wide. He scanned the chamber like a mistrustful security camera; then his gaze locked on the girls. "Are you linked to the bridge?"

The girls hesitated while Nikko looked on with growing misgivings.

"The neural bridge!" Lot insisted. "There's dust everywhere, so thick it's clogging the receptors. Go on! Ghost it. Get on the bridge. Try to follow the dialogues. Tell me what's going on."

He turned to Nikko. "It's reading us. It's sucking every bit of history out of our cells."

Nikko could not suppress a triumphant twitch of his kisheer. "Then it's also taken the viral thoughts of the Well."

Lot nodded. "Sooth. It will know we're different."

"It?" Urban asked. "What is *it*? Will it care if we're different?"

Lot laughed at that. "It will if it's Chenzeme. Maybe that's what it's for. Nikko? What do you think? What if it summons every Chenzeme ship that comes this way? What if it sucks the history out of every one of them?"

"A Chenzeme library?" Deneb asked.

Clemantine shook her head. "More like a Chenzeme checkpoint, I'd bet—evaluating every ship?"

Hailey's shrill voice made them all jump. "*I don't like this!*" she screamed. "It's dark. It's trying to scare me. Kiyo, where are you?"

"I won't do it!" Kiyo cried. She dove away from Hailey, to take refuge in Deneb's arms.

"*Kiyo,*" Hailey pleaded. "Come back. Don't leave me alone."

"I won't go back!" Kiyo shouted at her. "I won't, I won't." And she buried her face against Deneb's kisheer.

Deneb held her tight. "Hailey, break the bridge," she urged. "You don't have to do this."

"No," Lot said. He dropped close to Hailey's side. "Listen—"

"Leave her alone!" Deneb shouted. "She doesn't have to do this for you." She toed the wall, sliding toward Lot. Nikko got in her way. He bumped her back. She glared at him, outraged. "You can't let him do this to her. She's just a child."

"We have to know what's going on," Nikko said. His kisheer bunched at his neck. He felt hot and dirty. "Just for a few minutes, Deneb."

Behind him he could hear Lot talking, crooning, his voice low and hungry. "Hailey, it can't hurt you. Tell me what you feel. Is it talking now? Is it?"

Nikko glanced cautiously at Urban and Clemantine, but they were silent, undecided. He guessed they would not interfere. He turned back to Lot.

Hailey stared at Lot, her eyes huge behind their lenses. Her kisheer shivered. She raised a hand to touch Lot's glistening sensory tears. Nikko felt like a voyeur.

"You smell like the cells," Hailey whispered.

Lot's answering smile was Chenzeme-cold. "What does it say to us?"

Hailey closed her eyes. "It tells us what we already know. It tells us what we told it, only . . . *strange*. Do we remember it wrong?" She reached for Lot with shaking hands. He took her in his arms. "We must remember it wrong," she whispered. "All this is our knowledge. This is all we know, only . . . we know it better now. Now it doesn't conflict. It doesn't trouble us. We have no doubt. We are right. We are clean. We are pure—"

She caught her breath. Her kisheer went still.

"*Tell me,*" Lot whispered fiercely, his lips beside her ear.

"No!" Deneb shouted. "She's done enough." But again Nikko blocked her lunge toward Hailey.

Hailey screamed: an incoherent wail that abruptly crashed, shattering into words. "We have to go back!" Her fists pounded on Lot's shoulders. "Lot, we have to go back, or we'll die in the cloud. We have to be quiet, or we will die."

Nikko reached out with all his senses. He felt the heat of the cell field; heard the radio mutter of the cloud; saw the radar image of the approaching wall. "How will we die, Hailey? *Why* will we die? What's out there besides the wall?"

"I don't know." Hailey's hands twitched. She twisted in Lot's grip. "We don't like it!" she screamed. "We defy!"

Deneb's long fingers closed in a painful grip on Nikko's shoulder, squeezing his kisheer. "Get her out of there," she warned. "Now, Nikko. You bastard. Break her link."

Nikko did it. Confusion blossomed on Hailey's face. Deneb saw it. She shoved Nikko hard against the wall. Dropping Kiyo, she dove for Hailey, sweeping her up in her long arms.

"Five minutes," Urban announced, "before impact."

Null Boundary plunged toward the barrier. Nikko shed his body, slipping fully into the structure of the ship. *We will die in the cloud.*

Here? he wondered. Now?

He watched through an infrared camera as the wall grew closer, details rising into visibility. The surface was an amalgam of overlapping cups of different sizes, each with a whip-thin receiver protruding from its center: the characteristic flower shape of a parabolic antenna. So Urban had been right.

Nikko checked the security of his passengers. "It's time," he announced. He made sure each one of them was furled into a shock cushion. Then, as the moment of impact loomed, he gave all his attention to the ship.

Urban chanted a soft countdown: *Five, four, three, two—?*

His voice faltered as a parabolic flower in front of the ship snapped shut, its ribs first folding, then collapsing on its central axis like a closing bud. Nikko watched the lithe spindle dart aside on a burst of reactionless acceleration, an instant before Null Boundary's prow sliced into the resulting bore hole. In the same moment, flowers on every side collapsed in an identical sequence of snap, fold, shut, and go, darting out of Null Boundary's path like fish evading a stick thrust into the water.

Nikko . . . ? Urban's confused voice croaked in his sensorium.

"I don't know."

More flowers loomed behind the first layer of the swarm, but they too vanished in the white heat flash of closure, leaping past on all sides, fleeing fishes—

Null Boundary broke through. With astonishment, Nikko looked out on a void that glistened only with the heat of distant stars.

Immediately, he reversed his view.

The collapse of the wall continued, rolling outward from Null Boundary's bore hole, a circular wave of darkness eating through the structure. Shimmering points lingered in the new void, while the wave advanced toward the swarm's perimeter.

A checkpoint?

It tells us all we know, only we know it better now.

Lot went back out to the hull. He lay with the cells, and as the last flowers folded, he confirmed what Nikko had already guessed. After the swarm had taken all the history embedded in their cells, it had poured back a purified history, purged of clutter and failing strategies, of heresies and mental pollution.

. . . we know it better now.

This was how the Chenzeme ships remained committed to war, when it would be to the advantage of any one of them to make peace. They were reeducated by the swarm. Peace was a heretical notion. It could not spread in the Chenzeme fleet because it was purged, if not by the swarm, then by the ships recently returned from the swarm.

And how many swarms existed within the cloud? That Null Boundary had found even one, the number must be immense. Whoever the Chenzeme were fighting, they'd programmed their war to go on and on and on.

The last stale traces of heat bled away. Once again, the swarm was undetectable. Stealthed. Nikko imagined the Well influence lying quiescent within it, waiting a thousand years, or ten thousand years, for the chance to jump to another ship, while Null Boundary forged on.

We have to be quiet, or we will die.

Nikko looked for the courser, but it could not be seen.

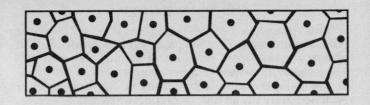

Chapter
25

Urban could lose himself, riding on the senses of the ship. The bright-hot impact of dust along his sides scoured him with a sense of motion. Dopplered radio emissions let him track myriad shock waves and currents within the cloud. Runaway stars drilled their own paths, flung from their orbits when their binary partners exploded in cataclysmic supernovas. In the radio spectrum, he listened to the roar of the galaxy's heart.

All these things were far away and unthreatening; it was the near-dark that made Urban uneasy. Every day he searched the ship's sensorium for some sign of the vanished courser. He remembered the way the dark courser had slipped close, coming out of nowhere. . . . Anything could be out there, hidden in the dark.

Anything.

The evidence was clear: The swarm had been aware of their position long before it could have resolved the light of their hull cells. How had it known they were coming? Had it been alerted by some unseen watch station? Null Boundary ran silent, but that did not make them invisible. Hailey said they had to be quiet . . . but what if "quiet" wasn't quite the right word?

"Nikko?"

"Here."

Urban hesitated. Was he only scaring himself? "I'm thinking . . . maybe we should send the hull cells into dormancy again. We would be a dark courser, effectively invisible. No more traps could be sprung in our face—and we would still have the cells if we ever needed them."

The mood Nikko strung between the cardinals was thoughtful and dryly approving. "We could try it . . . if we knew how to darken the cells."

"Lot could do it."

"Maybe. You'd have to convince him to try."

Urban cornered him in Clemantine's house when he came in to rest after spending hours lying with the philosopher cells. He had Clemantine, Deneb, and Nikko for backup. Lot looked them over suspiciously. "We need to talk," Urban said, slipping a glass of wine into Lot's hand.

Lot listened, but he didn't like the idea. He didn't want the philosopher cells to go dormant again.

"Will you risk Kiyo and Hailey then?" Clemantine asked matter-of-factly. She sat next to him on the couch, cradling a glass of wine in her interlaced fingers. "We survived the swarm, but next time, your gaudy hull cells might attract something less benign."

"That's right," Deneb said, neatly curled in a chair. "We know there's something out here the Chenzeme fear. Going dark is the only prudent thing to do."

Urban perched on the arm of the couch, studying his target. Lot looked tired and confused. They'd caught him at a good time. Urban leaned a little harder. "Think about it, fury. The courser itself must be stealthed, or we would have seen it."

"But we agreed to follow the courser home," Lot said. "What happened to that?"

Urban nodded. "It's done. The courser led us to the swarm. Now it's either waiting to ambush us or it's headed back to the frontier. In either case, we're better off without the hull cells."

Nikko spoke from behind them. He stood in the doorway, arms crossed over his chest, while his rich voice filled the room. "I want to go to Nightlight. Something's there, and it's not like the Chenzeme we've known."

Lot's chin came up. He turned to look at Nikko, and Ur-

ban smiled, knowing they'd found a lever that could work.
Push it, he whispered in Nikko's atrium.

Nikko's kisheer twitched. "I don't have to fake it," he
said. "I won't have the courser following me to Nightlight. I made that mistake at Heyertori, but I won't make it
again. We need to be stealthed."

Urban shrugged, not allowing his irritation to show.
"Who could argue with that? Fury?"

Lot sighed. "How long is it to Nightlight anyway?"

Clemantine answered: "As short as you want it to be, if
you pass the time in cold sleep."

So Lot agreed to try it. He experimented, using a record
of the signal cast at them by the swarm. Eventually he
pieced together the dormancy code, though he only discovered this afterward, when Nikko sliced him free of the
sleeping field.

To Nightlight.

Kiyo was waiting the first time Lot awoke from cold
storage. When he saw her at the chamber doorway, he was
still tangled in the suspension threads. He stared, hardly
comprehending. She had been a child when he kissed her
good-night.

Now her face was narrower than he remembered, and
her breasts were just beginning to bud upon a petite chest.
Her skin was auburn, and still, she looked so much like
Deneb, he had to look twice to be sure.

She did not smile: the stillness on her face was inex-
pressibly sad.

"Kiyo?"

Her mood turned over. Fury condensed in droplets out
of the air. The charismata touched Lot's sensory tears, and
panic seized him. He yanked at the threads. One broke
with a raw snap. "What's gone wrong?" he shouted.

But Kiyo was gone.

Later, Clemantine laughed it off. "Of course she's angry
with you. You left us for almost three years."

By the next morning Kiyo had forgotten her grudge. She
was smiling and gracious and eager to show off her new
skills. She'd learned to cook, and she made breakfast for
him and Clemantine and Hailey.

Lot watched her, but his thoughts chased after Nightlight. He wanted to see it. He wanted to know what was out there, and where he had come from. And why. He pretended this was his obsession. He built himself a fiction around it, so that he would not have to acknowledge the merciless craving for the cult that ate at him all the time now.

To Nightlight.

It became his mantra. He wanted it *now*.

But time would not be rushed, it could only be skipped over. So he went back to cold storage within a few days.

"Urban! Watch me!"

Urban turned at the child's shout. Seth was three years old and learning to somersault just today. Urban watched him, feeling mildly bored, mildly irritated, mildly amused. Seth tucked his head and rolled, but his long, prehensile toes spilled over sideways as he tumbled in the grass. His blue scales flashed in the artificial light. "Ouch!" he cried, as the edge of his kisheer was crushed under his shoulder.

"Bunch it up before," Noa advised in his serious way. He was smaller than Seth, but just as determined. He crouched, a look of intense concentration on his face. And indeed, he managed to hold his kisheer close to his neck as he tumbled, though he landed with an *oof!* flat on his back, his mixed blue and green scales glinting like a sink of deep water among the meadow grasses.

Urban winced in sympathy. "Tuck your knees in," he said, squatting to show them how.

Seth objected: "How can I hold my knees and my kisheer?" He tumbled again, but only succeeded in falling over sideways.

Urban laughed, tousling the rippling edge of Seth's kisheer. "Keep trying," he advised. "I'll watch." Then he retreated to the blanket where Deneb reclined on one elbow, watching their sons. He lay down beside her, his free hand moving possessively to her hip. He stroked her skin's china surface, fascinated still by its hard-yet-pliant feel. She smiled without looking at him. He leaned forward, laying his cheek against her kisheer, letting it lap against his face, softer than any hand. He sighed.

He didn't know what to do with himself most of the

time. He thought of Lot in cold storage and envied him. Lot could skip over these years. For him, only a few days would pass before they reached Nightlight. For Urban, it would be tedious years. "Nightlight is still so far away. Sometimes I feel we'll never get there."

"We'll get there," Deneb said.

"Time moves too slowly."

"The boys need this time to grow."

Urban watched them. They were the only reason he had not given in to cold storage. Deneb must know that. Damn, but Lot had taken the easy way out.

Deneb sighed and stretched beneath his hand, rolling onto her back so that she looked up at Urban. "We waited too long to have the boys. Did you know that Kiyo is in love with Lot? She's pining for him to come out of cold storage."

Urban snorted. "Kiyo's been in love with Lot since she was five years old."

"She's reached the age where these things matter."

"Then it's not our business anymore."

Deneb sat up, scandalized. "How can you say that?"

"Because it's true. Kiyo's as old as you were when you went to Nikko."

Deneb's gaze clouded. She looked back at the boys. They had spotted a lizard and were chasing it, crushing crazy paths through the tall grass. "I don't remember that."

"Still it happened. Nobody stays a child forever. If Kiyo's unhappy, she can edit her feelings. So can you."

Deneb continued to watch the boys at their play, but her face had gone as still as Nikko's. "I hate it when you talk like that," she said. "It's as if personalities are only costumes to you." She looked at him with a mistrustful gaze. "You don't like what I'm saying now. You'd change this part of me if you could."

"But I can't—"

"Love and nature! You could at least pretend the idea offends you."

He laughed. "Deneb, you know who I am. Why do you want to play this game?"

"It's not a game, Urban, and you scare me."

The boys had made their way to the koi pond. Seth balanced uneasily on the first stepping-stone to ford the pond.

Urban watched him, while inside he wrestled with a deep impatience. They had come this way to find the Chenzeme. They had survived the courser, they had survived the swarm, they had survived centuries of travel. They had gotten farther than almost anyone before them—except Lot's ancestor?

Urban tried to imagine that first charismatic. Who had he been? And how had he become infected with the cult?

Lot believed him to be some hapless early explorer who'd had the poor luck to stumble across a hidden sanctuary of the Chenzeme. They'd made him into a tool, a living weapon, a hybrid device designed to spread the cult.

Urban wondered if Null Boundary might be retracing the route of this forgotten man. Had his expedition heard the enigmatic signals at Nightlight too?

It could have happened that way.

Urban sighed. He couldn't talk about these things with Deneb anymore. She'd let the children change her. He remembered the way she'd looked just before they boarded the dark courser, so eager to touch the alien.

She was a mother now.

He was a father, but he still felt the same. "I love you," he said softly.

"And still you're bored. So why don't you edit your own impatience?"

"Deneb—"

"Urban, why can't you see that *this* is what life's about?" She nodded at the boys. "This is the reason we're here." Then, in a soft whisper of confession: "I'm afraid. I don't really want to go to Nightlight anymore."

"Don't say that."

"Urban, we don't know what's there. It could be anything."

"That why we have to go."

"I don't want to see them die."

"I don't either! Deneb, you know that, but—"

Noa stepped out on the stone, forcing Seth to jump to the next one. Deneb got up. "Seth!" she called. "You be careful."

"*Deneb.*"

"They could fall in," she said, her voice shaking. She strode after them. Noa turned to grin at her. Seth took her hand. Deneb helped them across the stepping-stones while Urban watched, puzzling over his own feelings. Why did he want more than this?

Kiyo was not waiting the next time Lot awoke, and he felt oddly disappointed. Now her adolescence was in full flush. She'd left Deneb's house, moving into a house of her own with Chenzeme receptors in the walls, so that she and Hailey could practice the language of the dormant cells.

"I wish we could wake the philosopher cells," Lot told her when he stopped to see her one afternoon. The simple nature of her house surprised him. She had no murals on the white walls. There was a low couch, and two honey-brown tables with curving legs. One supported a vase with a nodding clutch of columbine.

Shunning the couch, they sat instead on a tatami. Sliding doors had been drawn open on a sheltered garden, and Lot could feel the reflected warmth of false sunlight. Small golden flies darted over the flowers.

He turned from the view to look again at Kiyo. Her kisheer lay still upon her shoulders. Her mood was tangled: cool-warm and eager, hard to read. "Do you remember how the real Chenzeme language feels?" Lot asked. "It's so different when you're immersed in the cell field."

"I have some stored memories. And Hailey's been improving the neural bridge. It can synthesize some conversations."

He nodded his approval. "In the cell field you're faced with a series of thoughts. It feels like endless, bickering debate."

"But when the cells agree, the talk ends," Kiyo said, her gaze strangely intense, as if she spoke to someone hidden just behind his eyes. "That's when action is taken."

"Sooth," Lot agreed—hesitantly. He found himself suddenly aware of her posture: the curve of her shoulders, half turned away from him. The shape of her breasts, dark nipples partly veiled by the pliant scales of her auburn skin.

Hailey was somewhere else.

"I want to equip the bridge with an encyclopedia of Chenzeme syntax," Kiyo said. "Bring it to the point where any one of us could understand the philosopher cells. I've already included everything you taught the synthesizer, but that's just a beginning, isn't it?"

Lot nodded cautiously, feeling himself surrounded by the charismata of her presence.

"I thought—if you would stay awake for a while—you might help me expand the vocabulary?"

He didn't want to agree to anything. He looked past Kiyo, to the garden, where a small bird with trailing, iridescent tail feathers climbed the trunk of a weeping orange tree.

Kiyo leaned a little closer, so that her smoky-red kisheer rippled against his shoulder. "It's just that the cells have a genetic memory. They almost always process historical incidents."

"Sooth. You're right about that." Maybe he *could* help her. A conversation with her in the Chenzeme way might lead to a more complex dialogue than the synthesizer could ever inspire. He looked at her again, at the smooth scales of her face, the bemused turn of her lips, wondering if it could work.

She returned a thoughtful gaze. "Of course, when you use the charismata, there is no history. Lot, why don't you trade memories like the philosopher cells?"

It was a strange question. "Why should I? I wasn't made to argue with the cells."

"No." Her smile was faint, but her charismata touched his sensory tears with a stronger emotion. "You were made to interact with people."

"Sooth."

But not like this. He'd been designed to infect the minds of others, but since he'd left Silk, that trait had evolved into something else. Now *he* was vulnerable. The charismata that Kiyo made fell against his sensory tears like small explosions.

"*Come back, Lot,*" she whispered, her lips inches from his ear. "Come back. I'm still here."

He flinched, pulling away in surprise.

She laughed in an adolescent style that he remembered with striking clarity, as she settled back on her heels. "You look so funny when you phase out like that."

"Sorry."

She faced him with her shoulders at a quarter turn, her eyes sparkling. It was a pose that stirred an old excitement in him. Desire, mingling with confusion.

"Kiyo, I—"

"Have to go?" She treated him to an overacted look of deep regret, and despite its silliness, it worked on him. He couldn't laugh. Somehow she'd cut him off from any anchor of normalcy.

She raised a hand to touch his sensory tears. Did she know how arousing that gesture was?

"I've learned how to make these."

At first the meaning of these words escaped him. Then he played the moment over again in his head. "*What?* But Deneb didn't want you to even try. . . ."

She smiled, her coy gaze darting away.

"Kiyo?"

"I'm not a little girl anymore, Lot. So it's not for Deneb to say. I could make the sensory tears for myself, and then I'd be different from Hailey. I'd be more like you."

A new excitement gripped him. "Kiyo, are you sure you know how?"

"Yes . . . but—" She hesitated, catching the shift in his mood. "That's not what you want . . . is it?"

"Could you take the sensory tears away?"

Confusion clouded her face. "Why would you want that?"

Lot frowned. He needed the sensory tears, didn't he? To speak to the philosopher cells. He couldn't link to the bridge; he had no ghost. "I don't know. I just thought, if you could—"

"You want a real atrium, don't you?" Kiyo looked distracted, as if she were already making an intrepid ghost to set upon the problem.

Lot smiled. "You were always so determined."

"Nikko says that's good."

"It is good. But some things . . . Kiyo, some things just aren't possible. Clemantine has tried—"

"I'll try harder." Her affection burst against his sensory tears in faint, sweet explosions, drowning his objections. The proximity of her body became an unignorable fact. He shifted, fairly sure he should leave.

"Lot? It's okay."

Was it? He touched her kisheer, letting it lap against his hand. He touched her small breasts. She looked into his eyes, and he could not tell if she was looking at him or at the tangled Chenzeme structures in his brain. "It's okay," she said again.

She was only fourteen.

It didn't seem to matter.

He left over the wall at dusk, when Hailey came. He dropped into the meadow grass on the other side and crouched there, sweating in the gathering dark of ship's night. Crickets had begun to sing. Kiyo's voice drifted over the wall as she spoke softly to Hailey. Lot listened without hearing the words, moving off only when Hailey's voice intruded.

Ah god, he felt so high, every cell in his body vibrant with a fertile heat. The grass brushed his hands as he strode through it. The seed heads drummed his thighs. Somewhere Seth shouted and Noa answered back and Lot knew he couldn't bear to be with anyone but Kiyo, not yet. Her charismata clung to his hair and his sensory tears, saturating his emotions.

He cycled out of the gee deck, into a transit bubble. He got a skin suit and he went outside.

On the hull there was nothing to be seen within visible range. The cells were dark. The hull was dark. Lot drifted on a tether, careful not to touch the line. All was shadow, and he was invisible to himself.

His eyes ached from trying to see.

He saw only blackness, neither vast nor close-pressing: the dimensionless dark that exists as the beginning of creation myths. He felt himself embedded in this nonworld. He felt himself burning in it, violently alive, a spark, a scintilla of organization and warmth, a defiant alien in an amorphous and unconscious sea.

He closed his eyes.

It made no difference.

Vertigo seized him. Eyes open, eyes closed. No difference. No up. No down. No here. No there.

And yet he existed.

He could feel his existence even if he could not see it,

and it amazed him: that he could be here, as if at the beginning of the world.

Sometime later—an hour? maybe longer—Lot retreated to the ship and stripped off his hood. His mind had begun to cool, and now he felt shaken by the magnitude of his feelings. Kiyo's charismata still clutched at him. He wanted to go back to her, but she hadn't called him yet.

"Lot." Urban's voice issued from the spider. "You on-line?"

"Sooth." Lot answered cautiously. Things would change now, wouldn't they? Relationships would shift. It seemed almost certain someone would object.

"Where?"

"I was on the hull."

"Yeah?" There was only curiosity in Urban's voice. "What for?"

"Just to do it."

"Come to Clemantine's house, okay? I want to show you something."

"Is Clemantine there?"

"No. I think she's with the kids. . . . Why? Did you have a fight?"

"Not yet."

Urban chuckled dryly.

A few minutes later, Lot found him pacing in Clemantine's living room. He stopped when Lot stepped through the doorway. "Good. You're here. Now listen to this."

Sound issued from speakers hidden in the walls. It had an odd, metallic texture, and at first Lot didn't know what to make of it. But as he continued to listen, training his ear to the new noises, he heard something like words in the shifting garble. If they were words, they were oddly distorted, their overtones stripped away or crushed.

"Is that a voice?" Lot asked.

"I don't know."

"What file did it come from?"

"I didn't get it from the library. It was recorded today by the DI that monitors radio noise out of Nightlight—but it's different from the signals we've heard before."

Nightlight. Lot's heart beat a little faster. The cult hunger moved like a shadow under his skin. Were there *people* out here? He had imagined a long-ago expedition, venturing unknowing into Chenzeme territory, stumbling across some alien stronghold, and only one of them surviving the encounter, the one man who had been made into a weapon of the cult.

He had never imagined any other member of that expedition surviving, to make a home in the cloud. He looked at Urban. "Do *you* think it's a voice?"

Urban would not be coaxed. "How could it be a voice?"

"Those are words." Lot cocked his head. "Listen. Did you hear that? It's a word that means 'island.' "

Urban scowled. "What word? How do you know that?"

Lot smiled, feeling as if he'd been granted a reprieve. "It's the language I used to speak." The same language his ancestors had spoken.

"It could have been noise."

"There," Lot said. "It said 'for the city.' That was clear."

"I didn't hear it."

"Set a DI to listen for you in the proper language frame."

"It was supposed to find the closest match."

"Oh. Well maybe it's because you haven't had practice with this language. Is this the best enhancement you can do?"

"Without losing meaning, yes."

"There's not much meaning here," Lot said. "Can't we step up the enhancement and trade off some accuracy?"

"Sure we could, but then the DI would create sense, rather than interpret it. We could wind up hearing articulate Bible stories, but that might not reflect anything about the source."

"Bible stories?" Lot asked.

"Never mind. I just don't want to do it. It wouldn't mean anything."

"Run it again from the start, then."

Urban frowned. "If you hear anything now, it's likely just patterns made up in your mind."

"It might be people talking."

"Don't say that, Lot. We have to be careful. We're so far from home. It's easy to imagine things."

"Run it again from the start," Lot urged.

"It doesn't mean anything."

"Not yet."

Lot listened again to the recording. He heard the word *island* again. He thought he could pick out other words too, but he wasn't sure. Urban could be right. His mind might be making words out of the noise, inventing patterns where no patterns existed. Then he heard it again—a phrase now crystal clear: *for the city.* Urban looked up to meet his gaze. He'd heard it too.

Lot felt a flush of heat. It started in his belly, moving outward in a circular wave. "It is a voice," he whispered. "A human voice."

"A machine voice, maybe," Urban allowed.

Lot considered this. "A probe? Talking to . . . ?"

"Dammit! I don't know."

"Machines don't need human voices to talk to one another—"

"If it is a human voice."

"If. Yes. I want it to be human."

To Nightlight.

The cult stirred, flowing under his skin, awake and very hungry.

Urban watched him closely. "You're thinking they'll be like you? Maybe from the same expedition as your ancestor?"

"No. If they were like me, they would have gone back. No charismatic would have chosen to stay in the cloud. They might be survivors of that expedition, though. Or another expedition. We can't know unless we find them."

Urban's tension chilled the air. "Whatever they are, they're awfully noisy."

Lot thought about it. Along the frontier, communication had been strictly limited, so as not to draw the Chenzeme— but whatever existed at Nightlight obviously had no fear of discovery. "So they aren't vulnerable to the Chenzeme," Lot concluded. "That's the best reason of all to find them."

It was then he noticed Clemantine standing in the doorway. Her presence registered like an electric shock. How long had she been there? Her aura touched him, dense and potent with a stew of emotions.

Urban grinned at her. "I heard you're scheduled for an argument. So I'll go."

"Go see Deneb," Clemantine advised, her voice dry, and emotionless.

Urban's grin faded. "Why? Has something happened?"

Lot watched his face, and found he could mark the precise moment when a ghost brought Urban the news. Confusion swept his features. His gaze fixed briefly on Lot. Then he ducked past Clemantine and out the door, running hard in the direction of the transit wall.

"Hailey has gone into cold storage."

Clemantine said this as she moved away from the door. It wasn't the news Lot expected. "What?" he blurted. "Why?"

"Kiyo told her what happened."

"But . . . cold storage?"

"Why did you do it, Lot? What were you thinking? You had to know this couldn't stay just between the two of you."

He shook his head. Hailey had gone into cold storage? "I didn't plan it, Clemantine. It wasn't about thinking."

"A rutting adolescent."

"Sooth. It was like that."

Clemantine's anger finally exploded. "This is not Silk! Where was Hailey supposed to find a lover?"

"I don't know."

"How do you think Deneb feels?"

He shook his head. The press of her fury made him sullen and defensive. "I would do it again."

"And she's my daughter too. Did you forget that?"

"No, but it doesn't matter!"

"My anger hurts you, doesn't it?"

He turned away, unbalanced by this shift in her attack. He paced toward the door.

"Look at you! Always bent on escape whenever we disagree. My anger hurts you. You can feel other people's emotions so much more intensely than they can feel yours."

That was truth. Things had changed from their days in Silk. Turned right around.

He stomped onto the patio. It was night. He could just make out the roof of Kiyo's house around the curve of the gee deck, silhouetted against false stars.

"Just like a rutting adolescent," Clemantine said. Lot looked back, to see her outlined in light as she leaned within the doorway, arms crossed on her chest. "I can feel it steaming off you. You're making me hot."

"This isn't wrong," he said huskily. "Urban was your lover too, in the early days. It worked for us."

"We were only three then."

He shook his head. Why did that matter? "I still love you," he told her. "It's not changed between us."

"Then come inside. Come with me."

"No. You can't erase it."

"Kiyo has gotten very skilled with the charismata."

"Sooth."

"You know what she's done to you."

He knew, and it didn't matter.

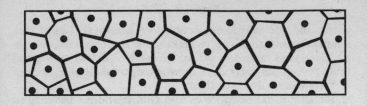

Chapter
26

As the days passed, Nikko scoured his data paths, searching for some sign of Hailey's ghost. He would not believe she had put all her aspects down. An adolescent temper tantrum had to be abridged by some curiosity.

In time, his suspicions focused on a truncated personality. The ghost was oddly pruned: airy and isolated, with limited inputs, it might have been an anonymous utility made by Deneb. Nikko replayed its passage. Was this Hailey? If so, she wanted to be invisible.

He strung a net that fell over the ghost the next time it passed. The net said nothing. It was only a faint sensory construction, bearing a digitized charismata of keen affection. Nikko wasn't sure there was enough personality in the ghost to register the net. The ghost slipped through the cardinals, then vanished into a proscribed space that Nikko had not been aware of.

Another weak radio transmission was gleaned from the neighborhood of Nightlight. The bulk of the signal was untranslatable, and Nikko theorized it was encoded data. The parts that could be interpreted, though, were a confounding mix. They heard that in the new archipelago the fishing was good, though the business of slaughtering an island was acknowledged to be dark and ugly. Name-untranslatable was soundly taken down for being late out of the pond when the quake hit. The brat was acknowledged master of island mood.

Deneb sat on the couch in Clemantine's house, listening to the transmission replay in her atrium, once, then twice before she cut it off. Human. Undeniably human. Here, far beyond the known frontier. She had believed their world confined to this tiny bubble of warmth within Null Boundary's hull; but now new possibilities played in her mind. Enticing. Frightening. *Hailey, are you listening?*

No answer.

Hailey, our world is changing.

Deneb fervently hoped some part of her was awake and aware. *Hailey, I woke up aboard Null Boundary a stranger, displaced in time, plunged into a foreign culture, yet I survived it. I thrived. I could do it again. You could do it too.*

In the bedroom, Clemantine sang a funny little song for Seth. He had napped on her bed and woken up cranky; he needed time to settle. Everyone else had gathered on the patio, because Urban wanted to talk. Watching Clemantine, Deneb felt like a traitor. The mural of Heyertori showed a storm-tossed sea, whitecaps blown off the swells by a fierce wind, all semblance of order pounded out of the waves.

She stood. Clemantine looked up at her. *Listen for me?* "I will."

Outside it was dusk. Crickets sang, and for a moment all seemed blessedly normal. There was Lot, sitting on the edge of the patio, his back against a supporting post. He had Noa in his lap. They both stared intently at the synthesizer's glowing flatscreen. Deneb could not see the image, but as she walked past them, she could feel the disturbing alien cell-talk in which they engaged. The synthesizer caught the charismata and interpreted them according to some formula Lot had devised, responding with a counterargument that Noa must overcome. Success was measured by the shifting colors of the pixels. Now the glow on their faces was a mix of red and blue, though Deneb had no idea what that might mean.

Her gaze flitted to Kiyo. She huddled on the bench next

to Urban, affecting a little girl's posture as she sat within the circle of his arm, her legs demurely folded on one side, her head against his chest as she stared at the firelight. Kiyo had come to regret her rush to grow up, but it was not a thing that could be erased. Hailey was gone away. Kiyo had cried over that for days, and how it had torn at Deneb's heart! She'd held Kiyo and assured her over and over *I forgive you, it's not your fault, you're too young, you couldn't know.* Lies. Deneb wasn't ready yet to edit her anger. And Kiyo knew it, of course. Poor Kiyo. Clemantine would not forgive her either while she continued to play with the charismata.

"That's not fair!" Urban had shouted in one of a multitude of stunningly intense arguments that had flared throughout the ship. "You two endowed her with the charismata. How can you ask her not to use it? It would be the same if you asked her not to use her eyes or her ears or her sense of touch."

Could he be right? Were the charismata just another sense to Hailey and Kiyo? And what about Noa and Seth? And Lot? And the mysterious voices out of Nightlight . . . she wondered what their opinion might be. What would they think of this alien influence?

Everything was changing. Kiyo sat cuddled in Urban's arms, playing the role of little girl. But later tonight, when this gathering broke up, she would be down in the grass with Lot again, under the light of false stars.

Deneb took a seat beside Nikko. He sat with statuesque patience in his usual chair, his back straight, his posture both alert and dreadfully still. Listening or looking at something else? With Nikko it was impossible to tell. He had hardly acknowledged the turbulence Kiyo had caused, overlooking it all as if it were some unpleasant melodrama the rest of them insisted on producing.

"Clemantine's listening," Urban said. "So we're all here. We've all heard the transmission, and I don't think there can be any doubt we are hearing human voices. Ever since we left Deception Well, we've had no way to know if anyone still survived on the frontier. Between the cult and the warships, they might all be gone. I don't believe that, but it's a possibility I can't ignore.

"Now, though, we know that someone else has survived. I don't think these new people will be able to tell us what's going on at home—they must have left long before we did—but they will be able to tell us other things, like who they are, how long they've been here, and how they survived the Chenzeme."

"And if they've avoided the cult," Lot added from his seat outside the circle.

Deneb could feel the desire in his charismata. She sent him a soft warning. Aloud: "They sound so unfettered. I don't think the cult has touched them . . . yet." And if it had, surely these people would have already gone the way of the Hallowed Vasties? Burned out to insensate dust, to mingle with the dust of the cloud.

"Sooth," Lot said. "You're right." Contrition was in his voice, and she felt it on the air a moment later. She told herself it was not his fault.

Not yet.

"We'll have to be careful if we approach them," Urban said, "but we should try it. I want to try it."

"I do too," Deneb said. "Nikko?"

"Yes."

"And me," Kiyo said.

Clemantine stepped into the circle. Seth clung to her hand, looking shy and tired. "Count me in too—though it will mean more adjustments. It won't be easy to graft ourselves onto a foreign culture."

"We're not after a new home," Urban said. "Just information."

Darkness was falling. Deneb sent a command to start the fire. "I don't think that's been decided yet." She made herself look up, to meet Urban's angry glare.

Clemantine laughed. "Maybe this is what we've missed: the day-to-day friction of a real culture."

"I've had enough friction lately," Deneb observed.

Urban's arm tightened protectively around Kiyo. "There's enough blame in that to go around."

Deneb felt the argument starting all over again. She found herself sliding irresistibly into her role. "Not everybody responds the way you do, Urban. I know what you think: If Hailey's unhappy, she can just rewrite herself. But the best thing *we* can do for her is to give her some prospect of change."

"Somebody new to play with," Kiyo said softly, "when you get mad at your friends."

Clemantine scooped up Seth and carried him to an empty seat on the bench. "Strangers," she mused. "Strangers and their unpredictable behavior. City adventures. It's been a long time."

"They might not be friendly," Nikko pointed out.

Deneb shook her head. "We'll have to find out, won't we? We have to give Hailey this chance."

Nikko's long fingers tapped at his china thigh. "This is just a bump, Deneb. Hailey will get over it, one way or another. She's no more fragile than the rest of us." He was looking in the shadows beyond Deneb's shoulder when he said this. Her heartbeat quickened. Whom did he see there? She almost turned to look too, but she restrained herself. The sense that she caught from Nikko bore a quiet affirmation.

The cloud was a nursery of stars, but it was also a graveyard rich in the heavy ashes of massive suns. All the elements of the periodic table existed here, in the cloud, brewed from primordial hydrogen during fusion processes in the hearts of stars, or formed in the violent explosions of supernovas. Urban thought about that, and about the mass Null Boundary had lost in its encounters with the two coursers. If they could replace that mass, they would be better prepared to meet any future conflicts. If they could add to it, they would have more options in their own defense.

So while Null Boundary fared toward Nightlight, Urban developed a scenario to harvest matter from the cloud. It called for the conversion of almost a quarter of Null Boundary's remaining mass into a diaphanous membrane that would filter rare elements from the particles of the cloud. In the library, he ran a simulation. Nikko watched it twice. Urban felt the burn of his subminds tearing furiously at the model's assumptions. "It could work," Nikko admitted at last. He waved his hand, and the simulation faded. "It's a risk, though. If we lose the membrane, we'll have no margin left."

"It is a risk," Urban agreed. "We could gain a lot, though."

"Why do you really want to do it? Do you want to make weapons?"

"No. That wouldn't look friendly. I wouldn't trust strangers who showed up in my home fully armed. I just want to be *able* to make weapons, should the need arise."

"The coursers were both bigger, faster, and stronger than us."

"Sooth," Urban agreed. "And we could meet them again. If we do, I'd like to have an expanded reef. Will you let me try it?"

A hairline seam of glowing warmth slit the hull, only to fade a moment later. Crouching on the hull, Lot craned his neck to better see this first evidence of the pending growth of the filtration membrane.

But there was nothing to see—not for a long, breathless moment. Darkness mobbed his retina, so that he almost dismissed the first glimmer of real light as the delusion of a brain starved for visual input. But the faint gold gleam vanished when he blinked. It returned when he opened his eyes. It was an arc: a shimmering, barely discernible bow of light. It drifted toward him and his eyes widened in alarm. He hunkered down against the hull. Then his cheeks warmed, as he realized his mistake. The arc was the leading edge of the filtration membrane. It was not bending toward him. It was inflating, growing larger in a space that it defined with its own light.

Beneath the faint arc, even fainter traceries could now be seen on the membrane's expanding surface: gold lightning bolts, branching trees, drainage patterns. Lot forced himself to rise. He stood now, anchored to the hull by the soles of his boots. One hand on the tether.

He looked away, letting his visual cortex rest. He looked back. The arc curved down around Null Boundary's short horizon. With slow grandeur it continued to expand, rising past his head. Fluid pumped through channels only micrometers in diameter, ferrying building materials to the lighted perimeter. Embedded Makers constructed new layers of tissue, millions of layers, in the time Lot took one slow breath. The Makers copied themselves, and the arc expanded.

Lot considered kicking free of the deck, but he did not want to drift into the arc. He might break through it. Or he might adhere. Then his skin suit would be dissociated and sorted into its elements . . . unless his Makers could defend him? He should ask Nikko what would happen. But not now.

He sat cross-legged on the hull. The suit DI secured his posture. Later he lay back on his elbows. The arc continued to rise, pulling behind it a plain laced by dim drainage patterns that faded from sight an indeterminable distance overhead. Lot felt as if he looked upon a vast planetary surface, from several hundred miles up.

By the next day, the setting had changed. The arc had become a halo, and it no longer grew. Instead, Null Boundary shrank within it, contracting to a tiny center point of mass, of heat. Lot had to stare a long time, just to make out the halo's light. He had to be very still to compile the long exposure.

Kiyo had come with him this time. With her kisheer sealed over her nose and mouth and ears, she had a veiled look in the faint glow of the membrane. He loved her so much. It was only her presence, the gentle rain of her charismata, that kept the cult hunger at bay.

"Lot?" Kiyo spoke through her atrium, her voice arriving by radio. "Look over here. Can you see this?" She stood close to the membrane. The tips of her toes dug into the pliable hull as she stretched to look at something just over her head.

Lot joined her, his boots clinging and ripping on the hull's surface. His gloved hand touched the small of her scaled back as he leaned close to get a look. He was still a head and shoulders taller than Kiyo, so it was easy for him to see. "*Damn.*"

"What is it?"

"Well, I don't know, really. But it looks like gnomes."

In the stony nebula that surrounded Deception Well there had lived tiny entities of artificial origin. They had been called butterfly gnomes, for their winglike solar panels, and they'd been just large enough to see. Lot had looked at a display of them once, in the city library.

These . . . cloud gnomes, they were larger, almost the size of a salt grain. Their white wing panels clustered thickly at opposite ends of a short, tubal body. Lot could see their shape only at the edge of the colony Kiyo had found on the filtration membrane. Inside the colony, the cloud gnomes clustered so tightly together they looked like a thin, glittering mineral deposit. The colony was a fluid shape, already six inches across at the widest point.

"It's feeding on the membrane, isn't it?" Kiyo said. She took a loop of her tether and jabbed at the colony's edge.

"Don't," Lot said. "You could make it spread."

"Don't worry. We can decontaminate."

"Kiyo—"

"Look. There's another one."

She hurried farther around the hull, walking on her hooked toes. Lot followed more slowly, annoyed at the slight resistance in his boots.

Kiyo stopped at the next colony of cloud gnomes. It was much smaller than the first, only an inch or so across, but at three feet above the hull, it was more accessible. She squatted beside it. Then she leaned back, swatting at something just in front of her eyes. "Lot, look." She duckwalked backward, but her pointing finger remained in the same space. She moved it slowly, as if she were hooking a spiderweb.

Lot saw it then. A thin filament barely visible in the membrane's faint light. "Don't touch it! You don't know if—"

Kiyo's finger touched it. Lot expected the strand to slide through, expected to see blood crystallizing on a severed finger.

"It's everywhere around us," Kiyo said. "If it could cut us, we'd already be dead."

Lot crouched beside her and looked up, as she was looking. It took a moment, but then he saw it: a network of filaments like the thinnest spiderwebs, crossing, touching, trailing off into darkness. Tiny white points floated at the filaments' intersections. He looked toward the closest one, urging his eyes to focus. *Sooth.* It was a cloud gnome. He watched as it was drawn in by the filament, until finally, it joined the growing colony on the membrane's face.

"Lot, they're on your skin suit." Kiyo raised a hand to touch his chest. Lot saw gnomes glinting like salt crystals on her arm. Filaments drifted between them in lazy arcs.

"Don't let them attach to you," he said, anxious at the thought of contamination. He brushed at the gnomes, and they came off easily.

"Our Makers can handle them," Kiyo said. "Their defenses probably aren't much. The cloud must be a fairly benign environment."

Now Lot used a loop of his tether to brush at the growing colony on the membrane's surface, but the gnomes that clustered there were stuck fast. "I guess the membrane doesn't have defensive Makers."

"No," Kiyo agreed. "That would have demanded too much of the metabolism." A frown creased her brow. Above the veil of her kisheer, her expression became a mysterious amalgam of devotion and doubt. "I wonder how common these colonies are."

More filaments caught against her, so she ducked and twisted, allowing them to slide free. Still, she glistened with tiny crystal points. It was an enchanting sight, yet Lot could not stop worrying about contamination. He brushed the gnomes off her in long smooth strokes of his gloved hands, but of course that became a game, and in a minute she was laughing—or trying to laugh. Choking, really, with the kisheer in her mouth.

So they retreated a few steps from the membrane and he held her quietly. He could feel her heart beating beneath his hands. She laid her head against his shoulder, while webs glimmered past them.

"This could be a problem," she said. "The gnomes could damage the membrane."

"We could put up with a little damage . . . they're pretty, aren't they?"

"Sooth."

They were silent for several minutes, admiring the tiny sparkles drifting past, flecks of life going about their business with a deliberateness and a determination that Lot could only admire. No asking for an invitation here.

Watching the gnomes, he became more aware of his own

existence. He felt Kiyo's life wrapped up in his arms, the fierce energy of it, the pleasure. Here in the cold dark all life radiated defiance against the entropy of history. The webs that draped them were made of a quiet kind of courage. He held hubris in his arms. At the same time he knew there was no choice in it. Life was a repeating and evolving algorithm, kick-started uncountable times and in uncountable places by the slow evolution of complex molecules. *Stubborn as life.*

In that moment, Lot found himself supremely conscious of the long, long evolutionary history that had produced himself and Kiyo.

Never before had he felt so powerfully attached to the world.

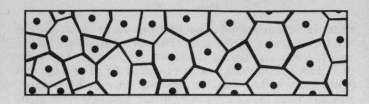

Chapter
27

Urban sat cross-legged in the library, staring at an open window. Within its frame, Kiyo again touched the gnome tendrils, drawing them out like fine spiderwebs. Lot called them pretty, but then it had always been easy for him to forget the pain of disaster.

Urban reached into the window, touching the glistening strands for himself. They lay across his fingers, threads of cold, slightly sticky. That last night in Deception Well, Urban had seen something like this. White tendrils had emerged from the rich soil, tracking Lot's scent, burrowing into his body, seeking the nerve paths, pulling his consciousness outward in an association like the one he would later make with the hull cells, but that night it had been stronger. So much stronger, because it was the cult.

Urban had burned the tendrils off Lot's body. He did it in a panic, but if he had done any differently, the cult would have flowered in Lot that night. He could not doubt it.

They never learned if the filaments writhing up from the ground were one thing or many, but when Urban saw the gnomes linked by their tangled threads, it came to him that *this* was what the cult organ would look like if it could be exhumed.

Lot laughed at the idea. "The gnomes are nothing like

that. Their threads are a hundred times finer than the cult tendrils. They're not so aggressive, they link to each other, and where are all the free ends?"

Urban had an answer for that, at least. "Watch the record," he said. "Each gnome can grow a free thread when it needs to."

He ran a video of a new colony attaching to the membrane. It was an eerie sequence. When he masked the drifting gnomes behind a black overlay, the tips of white, writhing tendrils could be clearly seen, reaching for the membrane. "Exactly like the Well," Urban concluded.

"Except at a hundredth the scale."

Lot was partly right. The cloud gnomes did not show cult aggression. They fed on the membrane, but so slowly it made little difference. Should the gnomes chance to drift against a clump of ordinary stony matter, they might feed on it for centuries. Their lives moved at a pace far more languid than anything a human mind could comprehend.

Still, the filaments proved to be distinct organisms, specialized tubal creatures living in a commensal relationship with the gnomes. They provided an efficient pathway for the exchange of nutrients and reproductive matter, allowing the colony to spread out when there was no substrate to feed on, while preventing it from drifting apart. The gnomes in turn harvested complex molecules from the cloud, feeding both themselves and the filaments. It seemed innocent enough—except each filament had a neural system made of a handful of cells of the type found in the cult's neural organ. Chenzeme neural tissue.

Is this what remains when a cordon fails?

In the Hallowed Vasties, planets had been torn apart to build the cordons—swarms of orbiting habitats so dense they hid their central star. When the cordons themselves collapsed to dust, nothing remained—or so Urban had always believed. Now, though, he had to wonder: Was it possible for simple bits of life to survive such a disaster? Even to help each other survive, in a commensal relationship? If so, then the gnome tendrils might be living evidence that the cult had once thrived here, in the cloud.

●　　●　　●

The cult was here.

Lot stood on the hull, staring into the blackness of the void, striving to see what could not be seen. The civilization at Nightlight remained hidden by distance and dust. It would be years before he could know if the cult lived there. He hoped it lived there.

If it did, he would join it.

Or he hoped he could make it live . . . and hated himself for wanting it so badly.

He sat on the tatami in Kiyo's house, playing the captured signals over and over again, hearing the word *island* so often that in his mind it became the name of these people. Islander conversations were brief and infrequent, lacking the embroidered description that would set the stage for their culture. It was all words out of context. Still, every word was collected and analyzed for frequency, accent, and association. Lot studied the lexicon for hours on end. He tried to imagine the landscape these people inhabited. He yearned to be there, *now*.

Kiyo brought him tea. He felt her worry as she lay down beside him on the tatami. "It's getting so much worse for you, isn't it?" she asked.

She didn't have to ask. All his feelings spilled freely into her mind. "Not when you're with me," he said.

Together they stared out at the garden, where insects buzzed in golden light. Once again her charismata fell across him, binding him in the invisible threads of a pseudocult, and as they made love he was able to forget he had ever wanted anything else. "*I love you,*" she whispered, but as he closed his eyes, falling away into sleep, the cult hunger reasserted itself, like a separate mind, defying Kiyo's soothing ministrations.

He awoke at twilight, to find her gone. He got up slowly. His belly ached. The cult was a negative pressure, running under his skin. Where was Kiyo? He needed her to dilute this craving. She knew that. She had not left him alone in days. "Kiyo!"

No answer. He moved his head back and forth, but he could get no trace of her. He got his clothes and put them on, then stood in the doorway, listening, but he could hear no voices on the gee deck. He could get no sense of anyone present.

They had all left him alone.
He thought he understood.

From the library, Urban watched Lot disappear into cold storage. His hand knotted into a fist. He turned to Deneb and Clemantine. "There. It's done. Kiyo has no lover now."

"Urban, stop it," Deneb said. "You know this is not about Kiyo."

Sooth. It was about the cult. Kiyo felt what Lot felt, and she reported that it was like starving to death.

"Think about it," Clemantine told him. "The library says that starving was once the worst way to die, only he *won't* die. Urban, how long could you feel that way, before you took a transit bubble to the hull, with no skin suit on?"

Urban stared at her in shock. "I wouldn't let him do that."

Clemantine's gaze didn't waver. "I would."

Urban shook his head. It wasn't like that. Lot had gone into cold storage, that was all. It didn't mean anything. He waved a hand to close the window. "I'm going with him."

Deneb gasped. "Urban, no. Don't say that. This is *not* about Kiyo."

"I know that. I just don't want to put up with the waiting. I'm tired of listening to whispers in the dark. So I'm going into cold storage with him, and I'll stay there until we come up on the islanders."

Deneb tried to persuade him, but he would not listen. For a few days after he was gone, she went on with her usual routine, telling herself that Seth and Noa were too young for cold storage, but she missed Urban, she missed Hailey. She missed Lot too. *It is better to sleep, isn't it?* she whispered to Clemantine on an atrial channel, when the boys had gone down for the night and the evening hung around them, very still. *And when we find the islanders, Hailey will wake up. I know she will.*

Kiyo and Clemantine stayed a little longer. They shared tea in the afternoons for almost a week. They didn't speak much, but the mood between them softened. It became clear that Kiyo did not understand death. "How can Lot leave before the rest of us?" she asked, on their last afternoon before they followed the others down to cold storage.

"Aren't we really one creature? I've always thought we were one creature. Like the cloud gnomes, tied together by thousands of threads."

"Threads break," Clemantine said, as she stared at the swirl of tea flakes in the bottom of her cup. "The past falls behind."

Her last act, before her consciousness faded within the soothing gels of cold storage, was to reach into the ship's memory and erase the holographic record of the sea cliff on Heyertori.

Now that the others were absent, Hailey's ghost stirred again. She moved through the data paths in a diffuse affiliation of subminds, tentacular entities that reached out to distant cardinals to gather the data collected there. Nikko observed her passage, strung tight with a sense of anticipation. Deneb had assumed Hailey was sulking, but Nikko knew it wasn't true. Hailey had come into his atrium once. A different Hailey, not a child anymore. How many lives had she lived within the sequestered world she'd made for herself in ship's memory? He couldn't guess. He only knew she was growing herself apart from Kiyo. As her formless ghost vanished again into her private sector, he found himself hanging above a tentative disappointment.

"Come out, Hailey. You see they've all gone away."

She didn't stir.

"Well. You know you're always welcome."

He retreated from the data paths, sliding into the library, where his ghost manifested. He opened a window that charted the radio log of islander activity and sat cross-legged before it. He had enough observations now to know that the Hotspot of talk was not Nightlight itself, but a region in line with that distant star. Several days had passed since the islanders had last been heard. The silence troubled him. He did not think they could be aware of Null Boundary . . . but why else would their whimsical banter cease?

A sense of mass alerted him to her presence. He turned, to find Hailey sitting beside him as a fully composed ghost.

Her gray kisheer drifted over her shoulders, apparently immune to the convention of gravity written into the library's environmental files. Her scaled, mother-of-pearl skin glistened in the crisscrossing white light of the data paths.

"So, I see they have left you alone again," she observed.

Nikko shrugged. "Things are changing."

"I felt it."

Her eyes were dark and unblinking. Nikko could see them clearly beneath their protective lenses. How had Deneb done that? How had she managed yet another clever trick?

He shifted the window, combing the collected data that mapped the Hotspot, fretting over what he could not see. The ongoing silence from the islanders worked at him. He remembered how it had been at Heyertori, when he'd realized the swan bursters were behind him.

But they'd been *behind* him. The islanders still lay ahead. He could not be responsible for anything that still lay ahead. Could he?

Hailey asked, "Why are you afraid?"

Nikko floundered for an answer. He did not want to confess his own weakness. He should have edited that long ago—yet he did not trust himself to act without this constraining guilt. He had no confidence in his basic moral nature.

He voiced only his surface worry: "Why has the Hotspot gone silent?"

"How could we know?"

"We can't. I wonder about it, that's all."

"No." Anger flared in her eyes and among her charismata. "That's *not* all."

He chuckled. "It's all I care to admit."

So much death had dogged his path. Null Boundary's original crew was gone, and the Celestial Cities that had flourished briefly in Sol System, and Heyertori, collapsing in his wake. But his evil influence *could not* reach ahead in time, to destroy a civilization even before he came to it. Could it?

They had not seen the courser since the swarm.

Hailey said, "Why do the others believe it's okay to leave you alone?"

Nikko's kisheer twitched in irritation. "Because it is okay."

Her brows rose in a skeptical look. "They pretend you're only half real. Is that okay too?"

Nikko glanced at the open window. It would be so easy to be elsewhere.

A new window snapped open before him. Hailey sat cross-legged within its frame. "The others don't think of you as a real man," she insisted, an edge to her words.

She could not read his expression, but surely she could read his charismata? He let his anger flow.

"You want to hurt me?" she asked.

He turned away, ashamed. "Love and nature, *no*. You know I don't." Why was she riding him like this? "I am different from you, Hailey. I'm old. I don't feel things like you do."

She looked at him with eyes that were dark and glossy, perfect windows onto cloud matter. "Nice try, Nikko, but the truth is, you've lived such an intermittent life. You're not as old as you'd like us to think . . . are you?"

Her adolescent confidence made him laugh. "I'm old enough. Just because I've locked nets of memory away doesn't mean those things never happened to me."

He realized he wasn't gazing at her eyes anymore. He was looking on the cloud, seeing heat and radio emissions. Her voice spoke from inside his head. *Really? Then why do you think of yourself as half a man?*

Her presence fragmented, dropping off into a hundred obedient subminds that swarmed through ship's memory, probing, searching out the sequestered aspects of himself. He hissed. How could she have gotten so deep into his private cache? He sent a submind of his own to sew up security, while he warned her, "Stay out of it."

Why don't you just erase it? She spoke from inside his head, and she did not back off. Sequestered memories rustled through her fingertips. *Erase it and it won't bother you again.*

"Leave it alone!"

All her subminds vanished. Once again she faced him, a well-composed ghost in the library. The open window was blank. She said, "It wasn't fair that you alone lived, when plague took Deneb, and all the rest of Null Boundary's original crew. It was a horrible trick of fate—and it wasn't even your fault. Not that time."

What did she want from him? He turned away, his kisheer twitching while his mind slid sideways along a path that he must have explored a hundred thousand times before. He had left Deception Well with Lot and Urban and Clemantine, seeking the source of the Chenzeme. Now he dared to ask himself: *What if we should succeed? What if we found the real, physical heart of Chenzeme culture?*

It was an outcome he had fantasized for years and years.

What if Null Boundary uncovered some great city of the Chenzeme? A grand, gleaming construction adrift in the cloud, filled with entities. Bio or electronic, it didn't matter. They would have memories, and they would speak, whether in words or dust, it didn't matter. They would be alive—*that* mattered. He imagined them thriving in a great gleaming castle with no up side or down. A hive, thirty million years old.

Nikko knew that if he ever found such a place, he would run Null Boundary through its heart.

He forced his kisheer to be still. He had seen too much evil. It ran before him or it followed after him. In time it would break again through the skin of his world.

Hailey watched him, her demeanor patient, her eyes calm. Nikko sighed, mystified as to what she was after. "I worry that something's tracking us. I know it makes no sense, but what if I've pointed the way to the Hotspot?"

She nodded thoughtfully. "If any Chenzeme ship comes this way, it will hear what we hear, but that cannot be your fault." She said this with soft conviction. "Besides, we don't really know where the Hotspot is, what it's for, or if it's permanent."

Nikko had explained all this to himself many times. He remained unconvinced. "What else might we be introducing to the islanders? We are a commensal organism. We are carrying Chenzeme cells on our hull. Lot carries the cult virus. We have the reef growing its own strange world in the bow, and we have the Well governors, sleeping like a dormant virus in our tissues. What other infestations might we carry? We are a sump of parasites. Biopollution. The boundaries that used to exist between clades are gone, and not every species will survive the mixing."

"Sooth, but we're not the first, Nikko. It's unlikely the cloud gnomes are Chenzeme, yet the tendrils that bind them are. Is it an accidental symbiosis, do you think?"

"It could be. Evolution is clever." Far more clever than any conscious mind, trapped in a brief bubble of time, its vision clouded with preconceptions. Natural selection had the advantage of being blind and unsympathetic and unattached.

He explained this to Hailey, but she refused to be impressed. "Nothing is ever certain," she insisted. "You know that better than I do. You can't foresee the effects of any action you take. You can't foresee the effects of inaction."

"If that were so, we would all be guiltless. But I know that if a Chenzeme ship comes this way, it will be because I brought it. And it's true. I am only half a man. The Chenzeme became my other half a long time ago."

A slow smile spread over her lips. "I'm sorry to hear that. I was hoping to take on that role myself."

He cocked his head, trying to sieve her meaning.

She sighed. "Nikko, you are so dense, and so self-centered."

"I know."

"I am not a baby anymore."

He looked at the shape of her, while an uneasy flush worked through his kisheer. "I can see that."

"And you are not half a man."

Shock rolled over him as he finally understood where this was going. "Hailey—"

"You've felt sorry for yourself too long! Either die or live, Nikko. The past is not repairable." She stood up on the data path, her anger falling over him in virtual charismata.

Love and nature! She'd let jealousy tie her up in knots. He felt used by it. He felt betrayed. "Hailey, you know this is all about Kiyo, not me. Wait a few years. You'll have a better choice of mates."

Her kisheer floated, serenely detached from the scripted gravity and from her own harsh emotions. "You are *not* half a man."

"Let it go."

"No. I won't. I'm going to the gee deck. You can come see me if you like. You. Not your ghost."

She didn't wait to hear more argument. Her ghost vanished, but soon he felt her stirring in her cold-sleep chamber. She went to the gee deck, as she had promised. He watched her kneel by the koi pond. The fish came to her hand. Unwanted possibilities played in Nikko's mind.

Edit that! he told himself. But he did not.

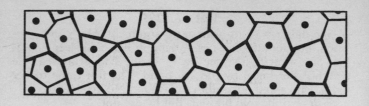

Chapter
28

Lot was still groggy from the lingering effects of cold
sleep when he wriggled through the membrane at the
tunnel's end and dropped into the core chamber. A
glance around showed the chamber to be empty, though the
walls were active, displaying an infrared image of the surrounding cloud. Scattered in thin groups, point sources of
heat glowed an artificial ruddy red. Nightlight was the
brightest source. Lot squinted at the image of the giant star.
It was still years of travel time away. The Hotspot existed
in a vast sphere of dense dust and gas around Nightlight,
a bubble formed by the pressure of the young star's fierce
radiation.

There was still no visible object in the region of the radio
source. Nikko had marked the Hotspot's estimated position
with a blurred purple field. Lot studied it a moment, then
rubbed at his eyes as if he could grind away the remnants of
sleep. "Nikko?"

The gold spider on his ear had filled him in on the ship's
position and history as soon as he'd recovered enough consciousness to understand it. The islanders had been silent
throughout his years in cold sleep, leading Nikko to worry
that they had moved on, or fallen victim to some unknowable tragedy. But less than two hours ago, the ship's instruments had picked up a new islander signal, far stronger

than any detected before. Nikko had roused everyone from cold storage. Thanks to his peculiar metabolism, Lot was first out of the gel.

"Nikko, do you know how far away they are?"

This time Nikko answered him. His voice came from the chamber's forward end, though his ghost still did not appear. "They're scattered, but this latest source, it's probably no more than twenty AU."

"So close?"

"Not really. We're stern-first, and slowing fast. It'll take days to get there."

"Play the transmission again?"

A DI in the walls obliged. Only a small opening segment could be translated, and that was strictly audio. Lot closed his eyes, listening to a strangely accented, jovial masculine voice:

"Greetings from the jewel lands! We are here and awake and everyone of us suitably alive. It is our pleasure to report that the land is as poor as Velt predicted, but surprise! The fishing is luxurious. Such an abundance of species has surely not been recorded before. Encoding to follow, of course. Sirkit has commandeered the survey, while Charm has stolen away to find the ready victim. It would seem that Dieter and I have fallen into housekeeping. Some fun. Don't be jealous. The gateway will open soon—then we'll have time off in the choir. Ha ha! Until then, love and obligation. Remember me? Ruby Dimaya Aheong Yan.

Lot laughed. He couldn't help it. Ruby Dimaya Aheong Yan—unarguably human—was so full of joshing good humor that Lot felt an immediate fondness for him.

"They're outliers, aren't they?" he asked Nikko. "Not part of the city we heard of before."

"Whatever a city is."

This time Nikko's voice came from behind Lot. He turned to see Nikko upside down to his perspective, clinging by his prehensile toes to the chamber wall. Lot could not tell if this version was flesh or a projection, until Nikko kicked off the wall, spinning his orientation to match Lot's—and stirring a soft rush of air. "It's time for us to talk to them."

"Sooth. I think you're right." Lot felt a quickening in his blood. A memory flashed across his mental landscape:

night in Silk, the crowd fervor running silver around him. The cult had grown its threads into hundreds of thousands of adolescents. In those hours they had belonged to him.

He shook his head, staggered at the intensity of the memory. Nikko drifted close, his kisheer rippling in tight, rhythmic waves. "What's wrong?" His suspicion stung Lot's sensory tears.

"Nothing's wrong." Lot shoved the memory aside. Excitement sparkled in his sensorium. The cult simmered beneath it, just on the edge of perception. Let it stay there. Let it stay. "I want to talk to them, Nikko. Let me send the message."

Nikko shrugged: a ripple of blue reflections that ran from his neck to his thighs. "If you like."

"Thanks! I've been thinking about what we should say."

Now he could feel Nikko's amusement leaking onto the air. "Okay, I'm recording. Go ahead."

"Already?" Lot swallowed against a throat gone dry. "Uh . . . we'll get to modify it . . . right?"

"Of course."

"Okay." He looked at Nikko. "This is just a first pass." Nikko nodded.

Lot let out a slow breath, striving to ease this bout of nerves. Then he began, speaking in the language of the islanders, which was the same language he had used as a child. "Uh . . . hello? *We are here.*"

(At once a bold and obvious statement.)

"We are here aboard the great ship Null Boundary. We are strangers to you, but we are human. Our ancestors are from the center—"

Lot caught himself, paying Nikko an uneasy glance. "Our ancestors are from Earth. We began this voyage on the edge of the frontier, and have run far, far beyond any known human settlement. We came seeking the alien, but we found—"

He stopped in midsentence, his composition interrupted by a sudden, stark thought: The islanders were here, in what they had always believed to be the territory of the Chenzeme. They had to be the descendants, or the survivors, of some ancient expedition. It didn't have to be the same expedition that had spawned the first charismatic. It didn't have to be the same.

"What is it?" Nikko asked, his low voice soft in the semidarkness.

"I just . . . I wondered just now. How do we know the islanders and the Chenzeme are not the same thing?"

"We don't know it."

Lot looked uneasily at the blur of purple marking the Hotspot. "They're probably human."

"Probably."

"Or mostly human, anyway."

"Impossible to tell," Nikko said, his voice curiously neutral.

"*Sooth.*" Lot was mostly human, yet somehow, the neural patterns of the Chenzeme had gotten tangled in his brain. Who was to say the islanders had not intermingled too? Like the gnomes and their symbiotic tendrils. The islanders chattered like naive children, showing no fear of Chenzeme reprisal.

"We can't know until we look," Nikko said. "Try the message again. You have a good voice for it. The accent is true."

We are here. Lot listened to the canned greeting whisper into the void. It was a directional whisper. Still, it broke Null Boundary's long silence, announcing their presence to anyone or anything that might be listening.

They watched their back.

A day passed, and then another. Nikko picked up a weak signal from a new direction. *Greetings and congratulations on a successful crossing. The archipelagoes are as various as the crazy humans who infest them. Lay the gate, Ruby, and we'll trade [untranslatable] . . . ever fishing for new contaminants in the rivercosm. The gates at least are clean. Love to all and ever. Velt and all of us.*

They listened to it play twice more in the core chamber. Clemantine spoke first. "That's not our answer," she said, shaking her head.

Urban grunted agreement. "That's got to be from their home. At least a light-day away."

A membrane bulged. Hailey slipped through it, into the chamber. A chatter of surprise arose at her appearance. Lot felt a flush warm his cheeks. He clung awkwardly to the chamber wall while Clemantine and Deneb, Seth and Noa, and even Kiyo crowded toward Hailey, their questions bubbling forth: *Are you well? Oh, Hailey, do you know how much we've missed you? How long have you been awake? Ah, you look older—you're so much taller than Kiyo.*

Hailey smiled proudly. "I'm sorry I left. I needed to do it, but I was never really gone."

"You're older than me," Kiyo said, touching Hailey's arm. "Look, you really have grown taller."

"I've been awake a long time."

"Keeping Nikko company?" Kiyo's excitement flared against Lot's sensory tears. He held his breath, waiting for Hailey's answer.

"Sometimes." She glanced at Lot, then at Nikko.

Someone was nervous. Someone besides Lot, that is, though for once he could not tell who.

"Let's repeat the query," Hailey said. "If nothing else, a repetition might reassure them."

So Lot's voice went out into the void again: *We are here. We want nothing but to talk.*

Later, Lot sat with Kiyo by the koi pond, watching Seth and Noa play across the water. The fish mouthed the surface, their tails sloshing as they turned to chase one another. *Nikko is Hailey's lover.* Lot turned this new fact over and over in his mind, wondering why it should feel so strange.

"It bothers you, doesn't it?" Kiyo asked, as if his thoughts were on display for her to read.

"No. It just seems strange. I don't know why."

She nodded. "I don't know why either."

The cult simmered just under his skin, a hot, dark sea bubbling in brief flashes of silver. Kiyo sent him a calming charismata. It touched his sensory tears and vanished, a stone plunging beneath the sea's dark surface.

She turned to him, her brow knitted in concern.

He looked away at the milling fish.

"You have to hold on, Lot. I need you."

And I need you. But not in any way he could confess.

Another day passed, and still no answer returned from the islanders. Nikko recalculated a range of possible lightspeed transmission times. Kiyo urged patience, insisting the islanders would need time to investigate, and to determine a reply. Urban would not be patient; he grew more sullen and suspicious with every passing hour, while Lot worried aloud, "How did the islanders survive the Chenzeme?"

The question weighed on him. Long ago, the intelligence that inhabited Jupiter's great ship had described the original cult virus as "a gift from the void," brought back to Earth in the flesh of a man like Lot. It seemed likely the virus had once preyed upon the Chenzeme. It seemed certain that someone, somewhere, had deliberately modified it to work on human hosts.

Lot felt haunted by a quiet terror. He did not want to meet a people who could do such a thing. Human or not, how could one person do such a thing to another? After the original infestation, it must have been easy, but that first time?

Did we do this to ourselves?

He didn't want to believe it.

He went out to the hull. A thin layer of dust had adhered to the dormant Chenzeme cells. Lot walked the edge of the field, thinking.

There had been no sign of Chenzeme warships since they had passed through the swarm. Yet Chenzeme ships haunted the frontier. Where did they come from?

His gloved fists closed in frustration. It was as if the alien ships came out of nowhere—slipping from some magic gateway at the edge of the cloud, vanishing back into it again. They had not seen the courser since encountering the swarm. Had it gone back to the frontier as Urban suspected? Or had it gone as dark as Null Boundary? Could it have followed the same signals that had drawn them to the Hotspot?

Back in the core chamber he found Kiyo and Nikko listening to a playback of their transmitted greeting. Lot waited for it to finish. The words still sounded good to him. He shook his head, the charismata of his frustration sparking on the air. "Why aren't there Chenzeme ships here in the cloud?" he demanded. "Could we have passed the Chenzeme source without knowing it?"

Kiyo dropped close, enveloping him in a fog of soothing charismata. "That's what we'll ask the islanders. They might know."

They might know too well.

She misread his doubt. "They'll talk to us eventually."

"Sooth."

Nikko would minimize the risk.

Null Boundary did not follow a direct line to the Hotspot. They stood off, waiting for contact. They would speak from a distance. They would learn all they could about islander social structure, but in the end, they would still be faced with doubt.

On the fifth day, a message reached them in the voice of Ruby Dimaya Aheong Yan, sounding more somber than he had before.

To Null Boundary: Cautious greetings. We are here. We are people—humans—of Earth ancestry too. We were first here. No one has come since, or spoken—until now. We have wondered why for a very long time. Now we are afraid and curious and joyful and wary. The alien is here, in the remnant life-forms of the cloud, relics of another age but useful to us sometimes. What kind of people are you? How many? And what do you believe?

What do we believe? While the others debated their response, Lot pondered that question, wondering what sort of people would ask it straight up.

Of the spare facts Nikko included in their next transmission, the islanders responded to one:

There are only nine of you? Are you refugees?

In the core chamber, Lot met Urban's hard gaze. "Let's send them our history," Urban said. "Let them have a foundation for their fear."

It was done. The answer that came back was somber and mistrustful: *There is little light in the cloud, and now there is less. We cannot think what to say in the face of this news that Earth is gone. Our own existence has been calm. We have no experience of an enculting virus. We know nothing of these alien vessels you call Chenzeme. We do know plagues, but they are ancient and impotent. We have no reason to disbelieve you, and yet . . . it feels as if you've stepped out of a VR drama, invented characters insisting their roles have been true to life.*

Lot endured a weary restlessness while the particulars of their reply were discussed. He sat on the edge of the pavilion, staring down the grassy slope to the koi pond. It was late afternoon, ship's time. Seth chalked on the pavilion floor, while Deneb detailed the files she wanted to transmit. A round of comments followed, each one laden with careful annotations. Lot listened to another noise, welling up inside him, a soft, compelling murmur.

The islanders claimed to know nothing of an enculting virus. If so, then the cult must have started with some other expedition, leaving these people untouched by it . . . though not untouchable.

Distantly, he heard Clemantine declaim, "We need to know when they first left Sol System. It must have been before you left, Nikko, if they've never heard of the cult."

"It would have been early," Nikko agreed.

Lot shivered. He turned round to the others. He looked over their serious faces. Their words ran shallow over his consciousness, scarcely attached to meaning. Talk, talk, talk. Lot could bear it no longer. In the middle of a detailed argument from Kiyo, his patience slipped. "Enough! The only question we need to answer is whether we are going to see them or pass them by."

They froze, a tableau of shock that fed back into him, becoming his own. His cheeks colored. Had his voice been so loud? He turned away, fury welling in his gut. Why should they be able to rock his moods so easily, when he couldn't touch them?

"Lot?" Clemantine crouched beside him. "Do you think you should go back into cold sleep?"

"You wouldn't wake me again."

He heard the slight catch of her breath. Then she settled beside him on the tiles. "Is that what you want?"

"No. I want to get off this ship."

"Or the cult virus wants off."

"It's the same."

He felt the hard slash of her anger as she slapped her thigh. She turned, to confront the others. "Well? What's the consensus? The cult virus wants off this ship! Shall we oblige it?"

Lot laughed, while Kiyo warned, "Leave him alone."

Clemantine shook her head wearily. "We are a collection of parasites. We have no business approaching these people."

"There's nothing here we can't control," Urban countered. "I won't pass them by."

"They haven't invited us," Hailey pointed out.

Deneb said, "Let's ask them, then. Urban's right. We can handle our symbionts. I want to stop."

"We'll warn them first," Kiyo agreed. "It'll be all right."

Clemantine's sarcasm sizzled on the air. "Oh, sooth. We'll warn them. That should keep everyone safe."

Lot listened to her rant, fairly sure it didn't matter, because the temptation was just too great.

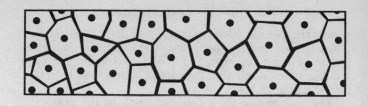

Chapter
29

The telescopes picked out flecks speckling the sky around Nightlight's dust-reddened point; motes, barely within resolution. They brightened with the passing days.

Nikko went out on the hull with Lot. The filtration membrane had been a success. Over the years, the ship had gained mass, and the reef had been expanded. Now the membrane was reabsorbed, and the ship ran stern-first, so the reef would work against their velocity. The pressure of deceleration had turned the hull into a vertical column. They clung to its side, gazing past the stern, in the direction of the navigation signal Ruby Yan played for them.

"There!" Lot declared, speaking through his suit radio. "I can see an island. With my own eyes."

Nikko could just make it out: a glint of real light peeking through the cloud's untextured darkness. "That's an archipelago," he said. "We're too far to resolve the light of a single island."

Hours slipped past. Nikko spent the time trying to dredge up some record of an expedition that could account for the islanders. His files offered numerous prospects. So much history had been packed into those first years after the fall of the Commonwealth! There had been hundreds of small interstellar forays crewed entirely by ghosts, and there had been several larger enterprises too, each with a corporate sponsor. More than one had never reported back. The islanders insisted they were not the expedition that had produced Lot's ancestor, and Nikko was willing to accept this claim, for surely that expedition would have been taken by the cult long ago?

The archipelago grew brighter, until, by the next day, it resolved into a constellation of individual islands. They hung in open space, each one twinkling faintly, brightening and darkening at irregular intervals. The telescopes picked out almost two hundred of them, congregating in a spherical swath of sky. Lot watched with Nikko.

"Look, Nikko. The islands are crescent-shaped."

"They look that way because we're seeing them edge-on. They're actually shaped like round, concave lenses."

"Oh." Lot was silent a moment. "They all face the same way, then—toward Nightlight."

"Yes. They're not asteroids, or any other kind of planetary material. Ruby Yan claims they are alive."

"Alive . . . ?"

"Look how their lights run in strings of changing colors."

"You're looking through the telescope," Lot accused.

Nikko chuckled, for that was true.

As they drew closer, more and more islands were sighted, until the count rose above twelve hundred. The farthest was some two thousand miles away.

Null Boundary nosed toward the archipelago, following Ruby Yan's navigation signal. Nikko's ghost haunted the ship's instruments, but his incarnate form stood on the hull with Lot as they edged up on the first outlying island—a disk of solid matter drifting in open space. His fingers twitched and tapped his thigh as the "land" spread out beside them.

The island was big—almost sixty miles across—its perimeter a perfect circle. The disk itself was gently curved like a lens. They passed a whisper away from the convex side—Nikko couldn't help but think of it as the backside, since it was the side that faced away from Nightlight. Only five hundred yards of open space separated Null Boundary from the shore.

The surface of the island was a tangled thicket of lacy tubes, or piping. Rapid bursts of light shunted through the fragile-looking network: reds, yellows, blues, greens, and a hundred combinations, moving first one way, then another, with no discernible pattern. Black branchworks sprouted from between the light-bearing pipes, like the skeletons of frail trees. Some were studded in points of steady light. One seemed half melted beneath a shroud of gleaming white threads.

The island looked organic: grown, not built. There were no visible windows or doors or anything at all to indicate the presence of people here.

Nikko's gaze shifted. Now he looked down the narrow black chasm that separated them from the shore. Far away in that slice of space, the crescent of another island gleamed. Distance had stolen away the details of its light display. Distance redefined so many things. Each island was a massive object, but each was small compared to the archipelago, and insignificant against the cloud. The scale of the cloud could compress even stars to little more than motes.

"Wha—?" Lot's shout of half-formed protest shattered Nikko's thoughts. "Nikko! Look here."

Nikko turned, to find Lot on his knees, staring at something that was rapidly sinking into the hull. "It hit me in the belly," Lot said. "I slapped it off, and it hit the deck."

Nikko crouched beside him. The thing he saw was less than two inches across: an iridescent crystal made of many fused petals. He couldn't tell if it had its own light or if it was multiplying reflected light from the island. The hull sank beneath it in a defensive reaction, forming a pocket that threatened to close over the prize. Swiftly, Nikko scooped the thing up with his long fingers.

Lot's eyes went wide. He pulled back, hissing in protest. "It'll attach to you!"

"Your Makers dumped it easily enough." He held the crystal in his palm. He could feel a faint rasping, so he used a finger to turn it over. The flat bottom glistened like a drill bit coated in diamond dust.

Lot leaned in close. "It looks like a hundred tiny legs. Hey! It closed up."

"Yeah." The creature had either retracted its legs or folded them flat; Nikko couldn't tell. Now its base was as smooth as its crystal petals. He held it up close to his eye and looked through it. Colors glinted in the glassy walls. Deep within he could see flaws, or channels, like a capillary system.

"There's another one," Lot said, tramping over the hull. "Hey! And one more. We must be passing through a swarm."

"Stand back," Nikko said. "The hull's going to start ejecting them."

Lot backpedaled cautiously, but the creatures were sent off with a gentle push. Nikko looked again at the island sliding past. They'd almost reached the far shore.

The islanders had joked that the fishing was good here.

And what qualified as a fish? Nikko set the crystal rasper loose at eye level, then tapped it, giving it a tiny momentum that would carry it away from the ship, and back, toward the land.

The next island on their course lay on the opposite side of the ship. Nikko and Lot hiked around the stern, skirting the dust-covered field of dormant Chenzeme cells. On this transit Null Boundary got no closer than two miles, sliding by on the concave side of the lens-shaped island, the side that faced Nightlight's remote glow.

This side of the island was lit by a pale white gleam. It had no tubes or skeleton trees. Instead its surface was covered with a monotonous field of cone-shaped, latticework baskets packed rim to rim. Each basket was large enough that everyone aboard Null Boundary could have huddled in it together with room to spare. A shiny integument coated the latticework.

"It's catching dust, isn't it?" Lot asked.

"I would imagine so."

Nikko wondered: How many eons would it take to gather enough mass to build an island? That would depend on how efficiently it could trap dust.

The particle flow here was almost fifty kilometers per second. At a density of five thousand particles per cubic centimeter . . . Nikko set a submind working on the calculation. It brought him an answer: In the course of a year, 146 tons of matter might strike the island's face. Not much, given the island's size . . . but not insignificant either. Much of the dust must be deflected. But what if an island lived for thousands of years? For all he knew, they might grow for millions of years while the microcollisions generated by the constant sleet of particles helped to warm them.

For nine hours Null Boundary followed the navigation beacon. Lot paced the hull, ducking into a transit bubble only to eat or to refresh his skin suit. Nikko continued the vigil in Lot's absence, then took his own rest when Lot returned. There was no real reason for it. They could see nothing from the hull that was not better seen through instruments. Still they shared an unspoken agreement that this event needed to be witnessed.

More parasites appeared. There were wire-thin black worms that tried to bore into the hull and into Nikko's skin. Lot found a tiny gas bag, no bigger than his fingernail, trailing a gossamer thread behind it that seemed to stretch all the way to a passing island.

Most of the parasites were tiny and were noticed only by the ship's defensive Makers. They were spores, seeds, eggs, or larvae: a sea of reproductive packets cast loose upon the cloud, given up to luck. Only one in billions might be expected to find a new island on which to grow.

"You know," Lot mused, "all these creatures that live on or around the islands—their populations are limited by the territory. But what keeps the islands themselves from endlessly reproducing? Why isn't the cloud full of them?"

Nikko thought about it as he watched yet another crystal rasper settle against the hull. "They're all facing Nightlight."

"Sooth. The dust flows out of there in a current."

"Density of nutrients?" Nikko mused. "It could be."

"What happens when the star dies?"

A star as massive as Nightlight might not live for even a million years. "The radiation would probably kill them."

"Sooth. And if it didn't, the dust would be blown away. The islands would starve."

"Even if the star was long-lived, the dust would be blown away in a few tens of thousands of years."

"Feast or famine," Lot said. "I'll bet some of this plankton is island seed."

"It would have to be viable for millions of years to have any hope of reaching another star."

Lot shrugged. "Maybe it's ejected with velocity. Or maybe the islands themselves can migrate. Anyway, this cloud's been here a lot longer than a million years."

Nikko nodded. "Only a few of us ever move on to other star systems. Maybe the islands are like that. Maybe every archipelago is descended from one colonizing island. . . . Of course, we move faster.

"And burn out sooner," Lot added somberly.

A lot sooner. Nikko did not want to chase that subject any farther.

Now Null Boundary's relative velocity was so low Nikko could no longer detect any motion at all through his organic senses. He clung to the hull, while the target island hung stubbornly in place, still two miles away. The navigation signal washed over them in strong, steady pulses. It was the only sign that this island was different from any others they had passed.

Slowly, slowly, they eased up on its backside while the instruments surveyed the surface. A small sled was sighted, tethered near the rim. There was no other evidence of habitation.

"Do you see them?" Lot asked anxiously, relying on Nikko's atrial access to the instruments.

"No. Not yet."

"How close will we get?"

"Half a mile."

"Are they talking to us?"

"Clemantine's calling a greeting now. You can listen."

Lot swore softly. "There. I've got it."

Nikko listened too, to an exchange of flat technical talk on the ship's momentum, the cloud organisms, and the compatibilities of their two populations of defensive Makers. It felt like a strangely detached exchange, as if he were overhearing an idle conversation inexplicably leaking into this, a more primitive world, where eye and hand could provide the only real contact.

"Look there," Lot said. He pointed at the island's rim. "There they are. People. See them? Nikko, they look like you."

Nikko saw them. They had emerged from some hole, or perhaps come over from the other side. He saw three people. They stood on the rim, lit from below by the upwelling light. *They look so tiny.*

Still over a mile away, he saw them in perfect detail. There were two men and one woman, clinging to the tubal network with prehensile toes. No. There was another woman below them, crouched among the tubes. Through a small scope Nikko could see her fingers where they curled twice around a grip. In the flickering light he could not be sure of the color of her scales. Bronze, perhaps. Amber lights flitted at the edge of her clinging kisheer.

"They're not exactly like you," Lot amended. "They have lights on their bodies and snakes on their heads."

Nikko choked on his kisheer. *"Snakes?"* He could see a crest of quills rising in a sunburst from the islanders' heads. The quills did not look at all snakelike to him. "Consider that they might be able to overhear the transmission from your suit radio."

"Sooth. We should speak their language. Look. I think they've seen us." Lot raised his arm and waved.

Nikko found himself abruptly conscious of the strangeness of Lot's human-original build: not so tall, but so much heavier than Nikko's own slender body.

"You're an alien to them," he said softly. Or a being out of myth.

"Their language," Lot reminded, using the islanders' tongue. "It's only polite."

On the island, the standing woman waved back, her arm moving in long, slow arcs, while the lights that danced across her kisheer shifted in a rapidly beating amber cadence.

Lot's arm dropped. "Nikko, we need to ask them if we can cross over. Urge Clemantine to do it."

Lot had switched so easily to the new language. It was harder for Nikko. The words felt awkward in his mind. His thoughts broke and stumbled as they formed. "We need to test the environment first," he said, his accent bad. "We don't want our defensive Makers at war with one another."

By contrast, Lot's voice flowed in soft syllables, the

words subtly linked, blending into one another, almost hypnotic. "Our Makers aren't hostile. They're quiescent until they're attacked, and the islanders have said their Makers are the same. We'll be safe. Nikko, we can go now."

Nikko found himself on the edge of helpless agreement. Stunned by the effect, he turned to stare at Lot. "How are you doing that?"

Lot's eyes were the only part of his countenance visible, and even those could barely be seen in the faint light cast by the radiant island. Nikko could not read his expression, but he heard the sudden caution in Lot's voice. "Doing what?" Like Nikko, he had switched back to the harsh syllables of Deception Well.

Nikko looked again across the gulf, forcing the awkward words to form in his mind. "Nothing," he said. "It's not important."

He would have to watch Lot closely.

"Nikko—"

"We're going to test for compatibility," he said sharply. "Listen. It's what Clemantine's agreeing to."

Lot left the hull, but he was restless. Nikko watched him pace the gee deck. He heard the spider mumbling in Lot's ear, repeating Clemantine's conversation as she arranged to visit Ruby as a ghost. Lot showed up in the core moments later. "Nikko! That is not right. We should meet face-to-face."

"We will," Nikko assured him, manifesting immediately.

"We don't have to go to the island. They could come here."

"They will come here. You know that. It won't be long."

Lot's hands shook as he said, "I want to go over. I want to go first."

"No."

"No?" Lot echoed, his expression mystified.

"You'll go last," Nikko said firmly.

"It's not your decision."

"It is. It's mine and Clemantine's and Urban's and Hailey's and Kiyo's."

"You've already talked about it?"

Nikko felt lousy admitting it. "We have to know if they're vulnerable to you."

Lot nodded. His skin was tinged with a hot flush. His

pulse raced. Nikko could hear it. The sense on the air was heavy and dark, hungry, frightened of itself. "You're right, of course," Lot said. His voice suddenly hoarse. "God, I feel like I can hardly breathe." He was quiet a moment. "How long do you think it will be?"

Nikko felt a stir of pity before an automatic routine engaged, siphoning away the useless emotion. "A day or two. Not long."

"I'll wait in my apartment."

"If you like."

Lot made no move to go. He stared at his hands, as if noticing their trembling for the first time. "Nikko? How long do you think we'll stay here?"

"You're not ready to push on, are you?" Nikko asked.

"No." Then he shrugged. "I don't know."

"I want you to stay off the hull," Nikko said.

Lot's head snapped up. "You think I would jump? You think I want it that badly?"

"Wait in your apartment," Nikko said. "Try to sleep."

Clemantine and Deneb went to the island. Urban ghosted in Deneb's atrium. While they were away, Lot used a patch to help him sleep. It should have lasted four hours. Nikko must have messed with it, because Lot woke exhausted, with his bladder ready to explode. Someone had stripped his skin suit off. He drifted naked among the pipeweed of his apartment. An IV line snaked into his arm. He yanked it out, spilling a trail of blood droplets onto the air.

"*Ow!* Shit."

The spider informed him that two days had passed.

He closed his eyes and tipped his head back, struggling to get some control on the awful flux of his emotions, fury and frustration and betrayal all sloshing around inside him. He felt like a baby on the verge of tears.

Someday soon Nikko would not bother to wake him at all.

The thought brought a desperate clarity. His thready heartbeat slowed, each pulse looming and falling in an unforgiving cadence. They might not even wait until he slept.

He drew in a deep breath; let it out.

He'd been behaving erratically. He would need to be far more careful.

"Lot?"

He jumped at the sound of Clemantine's voice in his ear.

"Are you feeling okay?" she asked. In her words there lay a soft concern. She loved him. They all loved him. He knew that.

"I guess so," he answered.

"Good. Get dressed. Come up to the gee deck. The islanders are here."

That didn't seem so important anymore. "Clemantine? I trust you. You know that—"

"You're on the edge, Lot."

"I know. But I don't want to be afraid to go to sleep. If you aren't going to wake me up again, tell me first. Swear that you'll tell me."

She didn't answer right away. Then, *"Damn you, Lot!"* she whispered.

"Swear it, Clemantine. Swear you'll tell me. You'll make Nikko hold off until you tell me."

"All right then! That's an easy thing to promise. We haven't ever planned a thing like that."

He believed her. Still, he knew it was only a matter of time.

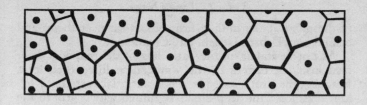

Chapter
30

Lot got a skin suit and put it on. Then he thought better of it. His skin suit mimicked the islander's vacuum-adapted hides. Wearing it, he would look at least a little like them. He wanted to look different. Ancient. Human. How much did they remember?

He didn't examine his motives too closely.

He stripped off the skin suit and replaced it with gray slacks and a black pullover. He wore no shoes. On the way he ran his fingers through his hair, which had grown out a couple of inches.

And what if the islanders *were* vulnerable to the cult?

Then Clemantine would have kept him sleeping.

His hands were sweating when he stepped out on the gee deck. His gut felt hollow.

Their presence brushed his sensory tears, faint. Alien. His pulse quickened. *Clemantine would have kept him sleeping.*

Angry with himself, he straightened his shoulders and strode deliberately toward Clemantine's house.

He found them by the koi pond. Kiyo and Hailey lay on the slope with an islander woman, all of them gazing up at an artificial sky, agleam with a midmorning light. Three other strangers lay prone on the bank, staring over the edge of the pond at the milling fish. Nikko sat near them, and behind him, Urban, Deneb, and Clemantine.

As Lot hesitated on the path, one of the islanders dribbled his long fingers in the water, then lifted them out, watching the drops fall. He was a dark, lacquered-red fellow, marbled with deep blue. He turned with a grin to the white-scaled woman beside him and spoke in a voice Lot recognized as belonging to Ruby Yan. "Listen to the sound it makes. A little like music, no?"

The woman smiled. "Planet talk."

"Yes, that's it."

The fish chomped at the drops.

Noa had been crossing the stepping-stones—Seth closing in behind him—when a look of inspiration came over his face. "Hey, listen to this!" he shouted, and he bent to scoop a great handful of water, launching it across the pond so that it fell in a spatter of rain. The white-scaled woman gasped and flinched back, while the startled fish churned their tails against the surface, sliding away to deeper water.

"Noa!" Deneb scolded in a scandalized tone.

But Ruby Yan laughed in obvious delight. He scooped up a handful of water himself and launched it into the air. Joy rushed from him as he watched it fall. "It's so amazing!" he declared. "I can't get over it. The water all runs back together, as if it were magnetic. I knew it would, of course. But to see it. To hear it." He turned back to the woman. "We should build a place like this, Charm. What fun it would be."

She frowned. "Unravel an island to make a wheel?"

"That would stir some protest," the other pond watcher said.

"Yes, it would burn the naturalists," Charm agreed.

"Could we spin an island?" Ruby asked, twisting around to look at the islander on the slope. "Sirkit?"

"Hell no." Sirkit didn't raise her head to look at him. Only then did it occur to Lot that the pseudogravity must be a burden on the islanders. No wonder they kept flush to the ground. Sirkit explained: "Put any significant rotation on an island, and the skeletal structure will tear apart. They're barely strong enough to tolerate division."

Abruptly, she rolled on her side and looked upslope at Lot. "Oh. Hello."

"Hi." He moved his head back and forth, trying to gather a better definition of this stranger.

"This is Lot," Kiyo said, scrambling to her feet. "Lot, this is Sirkit. And there by the water, that's Ruby, and Charm, and Dieter." She pointed to each in turn. Then she was beside him. She hugged him. She kissed him on the cheek. "You're hungry. I'll get you some food." Her charismata fluttered around him, tiny, nervous birds.

He pulled away, resenting her concern.

"Lot?"

"I am hungry. Thank you."

"Okay."

He walked down the slope to crouch beside Clemantine. Islander eyes watched him. Obviously, they'd been warned. He groped for something civil to say, but surely all the pleasantries and basic information had been exchanged? Well. He looked at Clemantine. "They were immune to the cult, then?"

"No."

No?

His heartbeat quickened. Dark oceans stirred and some part of himself began to drown.

"We've given them our immunity," Clemantine said.

"Oh. Good. That's good."

He looked at Ruby, and at white Charm, feeling their suspicions. Dieter was a dark blue like Nikko. Sirkit was colored like gleaming brass. Their long quills lay folded against their scalps, forming a small ridge along the midline of their skulls and down the napes of their necks. Faint lights flickered in their drooping kisheers.

"How many are you?" he asked, aiming the question generally at Ruby Yan.

Charm answered. "Only the four of us. This is all."

"Here?"

"Yes."

Lot nodded, acutely aware of their unease. But, dammit, what was he supposed to talk about? "You came from another . . . archipelago?"

"Yes."

"Recently?"

"Yes."

"You don't want to talk about it?"

"You make us uneasy," Charm said.

Us. Of course they would be having their own conversation on an atrial channel. "Well." Lot tried to keep a growing anger out of his voice. "That's good, I guess. It means the charismata don't work, because I've been trying to calm you down."

For a moment, no one spoke. Lot took bitter satisfaction in the silence. He *was* great-cult-leader. They should be afraid.

Then Urban slapped his thigh, startling everyone. "Lot! You're going to love it here. Being on the island is a real adventure. All kinds of strange fish swim in the forest."

Kiyo crouched beside him. She dropped a plate into his hands. "Eat, Lot. You'll feel better." Her charismata brushed his sensory tears. *Shut up,* she seemed to whisper. *Sit still. Don't embarrass us.* That was the sense of it. He took up the spoon and poked at a stew of fruit and curds, while Kiyo sat close to his elbow. Would she pinch him if he said the wrong thing? He grinned at the thought. Decided to test it.

Ruby was telling Deneb about a fish that appeared only when an island was ready to divide—an event of almost mythical rarity, occurring once in several millennia for any one island. The division was triggered when an island reached some critical mass. The lens shape would distort. Front and back would pull apart, splitting the island into equal slices that slid apart on natural steerage jets, doubling the surface area. It was the islands themselves that produced the mysterious and powerful radio signals Nikko had picked up ever since their passage of Alpha Cygni. They would call to each other across the void, and sometimes they would migrate in millennial journeys through the cloud.

Lot waited for a lull in the conversation, then, "Excuse me," he said. Kiyo stiffened beside him. Her hand touched his arm, while her charismata dropped kisses of warning against his face. He felt their influence for only a moment, before they vanished into the dark sea that ran beneath his skin.

He glanced at her, grimly pleased. Then he turned back to Ruby Yan, who looked as if he were reconsidering the wisdom of this visit. Lot tried on a reassuring smile. "On one of your transmissions to the city, we heard you mention a gateway."

"A gateway?" Ruby echoed. His gaze shifted to Charm, and then to Sirkit.

Lot felt a touch of satisfaction—apparently he had found a subject that had not been discussed. "We heard you mention it," he said.

"Yes." Ruby blew on the water, while his indecision leached onto the air. "The gates are an old transportation tech. You must have them." His quills lifted slightly, as he turned his head toward Lot with a questioning look. "A facility to translate electronic code into physical structure?"

"Oh." Lot couldn't stifle a rush of disappointment. This was the same technology that had allowed the resurrection of Deneb from stored code. "Yes. We do have that."

"And it won't work on Lot," Urban added cheerfully. "His body is too stacked with dynamic feedback loops. It can't be re-created."

"Well." Relief blossomed on Ruby's face. "That's too bad, isn't it?" He smiled. "You won't be able to visit the city."

Lot scowled. "Well, how far is it?"

"Far," Sirkit said. "This big, wallowing ship would take forever to get there."

Nikko laughed. "It would make for tricky navigation, anyway, threading through the islands. Still, I'm curious. Would it be possible for the rest of us to visit the city?"

"Sooth," Urban said. "I'd love to go."

Ruby was back to looking unhappy. "It would take time to construct a second. I'm not sure it would be easily approved."

"Could we ghost?" Urban asked.

"Ghost with a host?" Ruby obviously found something to admire in that suggestion. "I suppose. That's less threatening. I'll ask it."

"I'd appreciate it," Urban said.

"I'd like to go too," Deneb added.

Clemantine agreed. "I think we all would, eventually."

"Are you thinking of staying with us, then?" Dieter asked.

Lot's chin came up. His breath caught, stunned by the question. They *could* all leave through the gateway. They could.

He turned to Clemantine. She exchanged an uncertain

glance with Deneb, while Kiyo's hand tightened on Lot's arm. "It's not a thing we've discussed," Clementine said.

"And they don't know your world," Lot added. "They don't know who you really are."

Ruby laughed. "That could scare off any hearty soul! But visit us anyway . . . those of you who can." He gave Lot a suspicious, sidelong look. "Learn who we are. You must know we are fascinated by your presence. We are often a shallow people. Fads rampage through our cities faster than behavioral viruses. But something truly new is rare in the cloud. The library you carry could keep us busy for years."

"It's not clean," Nikko said. "The content is yours to copy if you choose, but be forewarned, not all of it is clean."

Charm rolled over onto her side. Her gaze swept her three companions. "That's it," she said. "We wanted to make this archipelago just another wilderness retreat, but think—what if we made it a library instead? We could contain Null Boundary's wealth here, far from the city, where any useful information could be safely extracted. Scholars could come here to study. It's the perfect site."

Lot's interest stirred at this suggestion. "So—many more people would live here?"

Sirkit sat up with a groan. "This gee deck is a cumbersome place!" Her body swayed, as if the ground moved beneath her. She looked at Lot and smiled. Not a friendly expression. "Oh yes. Many more people would come. You could probably persuade some to let you possess them. It's been done before. Happy thought, eh? Good hunting."

Lot let most of her babble slide by him, but one phrase stuck. "What do you mean it's been done before?"

It was Charm who answered, in a soft, embarrassed voice. "Some of us have reached into the past and taken things that perhaps should have been left alone."

"What things?" Lot could not keep the hunger from his voice.

"Ancient forms, taken from the cloud. Tendrils, that easily adapt to symbiotic relationships. Some have taken this ancient symbiote into themselves. The result is . . . unsettling. A communal organism that does not look human, yet it understands us perfectly."

"A seductive organism," Sirkit added. "Stealing away

the minds of good people. Sound familiar, pet? Maybe your cult *is* here, but in a different form."

And if it was? Then Lot would find a way to stay here. He swore it to himself. The cult was a cold tide within him, hardening his resolve. "Do these hybrids talk?" he asked. "Will they talk to me?"

Charm turned to Sirkit, her face pensive, worried. Lot imagined the atrial talk gushing between them. Sirkit's kisheer lit with dire red. "We don't talk to them," she said. "And this archipelago is our claim, stocked with our facilities, our links. You understand?"

"Meaning you won't let me talk to them."

Charm chased this conclusion with a quick, nervous explanation. "We don't want to be difficult. It's just that there has been . . . disagreement, about these symbiotes. There is a fear the process is not truly voluntary, and the debate has only been sharpened by the news you've brought us of the old worlds—the Hallowed Vasties. We don't think it's wise to aggravate the situation. Lot, we don't understand you, and we need to, before you get freedom among us. For our own protection. So that we don't go the way of the Hallowed Vasties."

Charismata of anger boiled out of Lot's sensory tears. Kiyo sensed it. Her arm slid around his waist; her body grew tense. *Patience,* Lot told himself.

"That is not what I want." He raised his hands, palm up, in a supplicant's gesture. "Try to understand. Things are different now. The Hallowed Vasties were taken by surprise, but there is no need to fear what we all understand—"

"*Lot,*" Clemantine cautioned him.

"What?" He turned to her, his exasperation the lace-edge of a veiled rage. "Clemantine, you've lived with me for years. Tell them! I'm no more dangerous now than an old, tamed plague."

Clemantine did not volunteer any such testimony.

"Give it time," Charm urged after a painful silence. "Let the situation settle."

Lot knew time would betray him. Maybe that was their plan. He struggled to quell a budding panic. "Will I at least be allowed to see your island?" he asked her. He turned to Sirkit. "Or is it your island? How do these things work here?"

"With unfortunate democracy," Sirkit said. "And I've been outvoted."

They had agreed to let him see the island because no one could find any prospect of harm in it. Lot told himself it was a step forward. He would find a path around their wariness. Charm had admitted to a diversity of opinion in the city. If he could make his way there, his options might widen. So he would be patient, and he would find a way around them. The cult was an ally, warm and dark beneath his skin. *Patience*. He could hold out a little longer.

Kiyo and Urban went with him when he left to get his skin suit. "Don't mind that Sirkit," Urban said when they were secure in a transit bubble. "She's got an attitude that would have gotten her popped into the monkey house in Silk."

"The news of the Hallowed Vasties has made them afraid," Kiyo said. "I don't blame them. Mostly, they're nice people. I think Hailey and Deneb really want to stay here."

Lot thought about all of them staying here, living happily ever after, but even as he visualized the scene, it was painted over in silver tints that ran together like melting worlds. Things could not go on long, not for him, not without some profound change. His fingers shook as he touched Kiyo's hand. "And you? Do you want to stay here too?" *And be part of it*.

"I—I don't know." Her kisheer brightened in a faint flush.

Urban scowled. "We haven't talked about anything like that, fury."

"Well, as long as we are here, I'd like to know more about those hybrid forms."

Urban nodded. "Sooth. It sounds familiar, doesn't it? Tendrils."

"Like the gnomes," Kiyo said. "Their tendrils had Chenzeme neural cells. It could be the same thing: tendrils that adapt easily to symbiotic relationships."

Lot imagined the gnomes' gossamer threads strung between the three of them, forever linking them as one entity. Never to be alone. It was not an ugly thought. It didn't deserve Sirkit's contempt.

The transit bubble dumped them into Lot's apartment. He pulled off his shirt. "Why are we so afraid of changing?" He held his hands out, gazing at their shape, their warm brown color. "This isn't the best we can do." His gaze went to Kiyo. "You are beautiful. You're a better person than me, or Urban."

"Lot—" she whispered.

He wanted them to understand. He wanted someone to understand. "Do you think it was easy for Nikko, being the first? Somebody had to decide to *let* him be different."

Urban fished a skin suit from one of the storage sacs behind the wall. "It's not like that for you, fury. We already know how it ends."

"We know how it ended in the Hallowed Vasties. Things are different here. This cloud is a cradle of worlds. At least thirty million years of history are here, and new things are always being made. One factor could change it all, Urban. It could make this"—he brushed his sensory tears—"into something palatable. Something with potential. You've never been touched by the cult. You don't know how *essential* it feels."

He handed the suit to Lot. "I know how you feel."

"There isn't just one answer, Urban. It isn't just yes or no."

Urban shrugged. "You know, I think you'll like it on the island. It was worth it, coming here."

The islanders had brought their sled over to Null Boundary. It sat with its feet sunk into the hull, soft amber lights merrily gleaming. Everyone clipped to short tethers in preparation for the trip back to the island. Lot hooked himself between Seth and Noa. It would be their first trip too. They all held on to the black rods of a cargo rack.

"We could make one of these sleds," Deneb was saying. "Null Boundary can spare the material."

"We've already got two more growing in a pit on the island," Dieter told her. "They'll be ready soon."

"Everybody secured?" Ruby asked. He was answered by a chorus of aye and yes and ready. "Okay then. Sirkit? Let's go."

The sled's feet slammed down with a sharp jolt, and the little vehicle popped away from Null Boundary's surface.

Noa whooped and Seth echoed his call, while Lot used one hand to rub at his strained neck. From the other side of the sled, Urban and Deneb kept watchful eyes on the boys, while Ruby and Dieter occupied the passenger slings rigged within the rack. Sirkit piloted.

Charm had elected to stay behind, while Clemantine helped her set up an access shunt to the ship's library. Hailey and Kiyo had offered to help. In his usual manner, Nikko had wordlessly vanished into the recesses of Null Boundary.

Still, with eight people on the sled Lot thought they made a comical sight, like some giant insect covered in parasites. The island plunged down upon them with frightening speed, while Null Boundary's lightless silhouette shrank behind them.

Now Seth and Noa were making excited noises about the island's hasty approach, and Lot found himself a bit anxious, wondering how long Sirkit planned to wait before slowing them. His grip on the cargo rack tightened. He started to say something; stopped himself. He looked at Urban, but he could not see his expression behind the visor of his skin suit.

Lot resolved to say something. "Sirkit—"

The sled's little jets fired at last—hard—slamming Lot against the cargo rack. "Unh—"

"Ow!" Seth growled. "That hurt."

"Sorry," Sirkit said sweetly. "Lot, did you want something?"

"Hell of an elevator."

"Thank you."

The sled rotated, so that now it fell gently, feet-first, toward a black shadowless circle on the island's back. The circle was small; Lot guessed its diameter to be only a few feet greater than the length of the sled. As they drew near, the sled's lights penetrated and defined it: a pit some twelve feet deep, its smooth walls sunk into the island's face.

They dropped between the walls, then slammed against the bottom with another hard jolt. Shadows jumped wildly. The sled jounced again as its feet shot into the floor, locking the vehicle in place.

Noa didn't wait for any go-ahead. He got himself untethered in a second. Seth had some trouble, so Lot helped him before unleashing his own tether.

"Careful," Sirkit warned. "Anyone who drifts off an island is not rescued—that's our nod to natural selection."

"Cut the bullshit," Dieter said tiredly. "You know we'll at least grab any stray kids."

Sirkit laughed, while Noa vehemently denied he would ever need a rescue. Seth moved a little closer to Deneb.

Lot felt a touch at his elbow and turned to see Ruby Yan at his side. "We excavated this pit after the island was slaughtered. It gives us fast access to our tunnels, with only a little cost to the island's natural look." He waved Lot toward an alcove in one wall of the pit. "Push past the membrane."

Lot did as he was told, and emerged into a snaking, blue-walled chamber that branched off into five other passages. His suit informed him he was in the presence of a breathable atmosphere, yet it seemed thick, almost cloudy. He swiped a hand through it, and watched a blue-tinged vapor swirl in the wake.

"Swimmers," Ruby said, coming in behind him. "The light level dropped when you came in, so they're disoriented. They'll find the walls soon, and anchor."

Even as he spoke, the air cleared. The light from the walls softened, as if a filter had been laid upon them. The swimmers formed a smooth, velvety layer.

"They clean the air?" Lot asked, as Seth and Noa burst through the membrane.

"Hey, it looks like water in here."

"It's just blue lights."

"I know that!"

"Yes, the swimmers renew the air," Ruby answered. Then he paused while his kisheer rolled free of his face, pulling away from his nose and out of his mouth. He coughed, then drew in a long breath. "Ah, home, sweet home!" Lot's skin suit picked up the external noise and piped it to his ears.

"You see," Ruby explained, "when no one's here the swimmers move freely under very bright lights. It gets their metabolism going fast. They produce oxygen for the tunnel borers as well as for us, and they also stir the air."

Seth had been looking into the different tunnels. "There's nothing in here!" he whined.

"Hush," Noa scolded. "Deneb said to say nice things."

Both of them had let their kisheers unroll, and now they breathed the air along with Ruby. Lot's stomach knotted in fear. "Hey! Did Deneb say you could breathe the air here?"

Noa gave him a comical look of suspicion. "The air's clean, Lot. Urban tested it the first day."

"Oh."

Ruby chuckled. "It's true. Your companions have spent several hours in here, without a problem. You can take your hood off too."

"Okay." Lot told his skin suit to open. His hood rolled away from his face. Cold air touched his cheeks. He moved his head slowly back and forth, finding the air amazingly clean. He caught a trace of Noa's presence on his sensory tears. Seth might have been absent. "Are there still swimmers in the air?" he asked Ruby.

"Some. To break down any pollutants."

Like the charismata. Sooth. He glanced up the tunnels. "Where is the gateway?"

Ruby's scaled hide brightened a bit. "The gate chamber? Well, it's in the central tunnel, behind a tissue plug. We haven't used it yet. We arrived so recently, after a journey in cold sleep."

Urban and Deneb pushed through the membrane. Deneb's kisheer pulled away from her face. Urban popped his hood. "What do you think, fury? Not much to look at, is it?"

"Not yet," Ruby conceded. "We have extensive plans."

Lot was already bored. "Can we look outside?"

Ruby shrugged. "If you like." He pointed to one of the branching tunnels. "Let's go this way. It will bring us out on the surface."

They emerged into a scintillating landscape. Some eight meters overhead, colors raced one another through a canopy made of an organic mesh of narrow tubes. The weirdly inconstant light lit a rough surface of mounds and pincushion outgrowths. Some of the lumps sprouted black stalks that thrust past the mesh before dividing into crowns of branches hung with tiny points of white light.

On one of the stalks, Noa spotted a tiny silver shell no bigger than his knuckle. Ruby snapped it off for him, and the boys shrieked as the shell shot off on a tiny jet of vapor. "A puff," Ruby said. "Quite common on all the islands."

He gestured to Lot and the boys. "Come, let's get above the canopy for a minute." He launched himself toward the mesh and Noa followed. Lot went next.

"What's a fish?" Lot asked, as he wriggled through the same gap in the mesh Ruby had used. He forgot the question as he emerged into the open.

All around him, lights shot past in a weirdly joyous night display, a pulsing celebration of existence, as if to cry in defiance of the dark, *I am here, I am here.*

Against the blaze, black branches stood in silhouette, like river deltas eroded into the flashing colors. Silvery specks drifted between the tenebrous trees in slow, noble clouds.

Seth recognized them. "Gnomes!" he shouted. "Look, Lot! They're gnomes."

"Sooth." Lot watched a colony as it drifted past, a meter or so away.

Ruby, his long toes hooked around a tube, crouched close to Lot. "*Those* are fish," he said, nodding toward the passing gnome colony. "So are puffs and serpents and dust. Anything that lives here, but is not permanently anchored."

"We saw gnomes far out in the cloud."

"Gnomes? We call them webs. They're tendril symbiotes."

"Like the people Charm described?"

"People . . . ? Oh. Well, I guess it is the same general idea. Look over here now. Look at this."

They skated about the island for over two hours. Noa kicked himself into the void once, but Lot caught him just before he slipped out of reach. Deneb caught Lot.

Compared to the others, he and Urban had a hard time of it. Their booted feet were useless appendages among the tubes, and their fingers were too short for an easy grip. Lot's wrists ached, and he felt unspeakably primitive. Fatigue ran thick through his veins while the boys were still darting around like native creatures.

No, he corrected himself. Anything native had adapted to conserve energy. More than once Lot had gripped a tube, only to be startled by a flash of motion as a frightened inhabitant darted away. Ruby told them that fish could lie still for years, moving only when forced to do so. Noa and Seth were adapted to a far hotter, faster pace of life.

Lot was down under the tubes with the boys, watching them chase each other around the stalks, when he chanced upon a new, yet chillingly familiar sight. "Urban," he called softly.

"Yeah?"

"Come look at this."

Growing over the anchoring lump of one of the stalks was a glassy white apron, three meters across. Its granular surface gleamed with its own steady light.

"Philosopher cells," Urban whispered. For that was exactly what the crusty colony looked like.

Lot felt strangely justified. This was the first unambiguous sign of the Chenzeme they had found since passing through the swarm, and yet . . . what did it prove?

He dove down close to the cells to get a better look. "There's dust on them, just like on the ship."

"Don't touch it," Urban cautioned.

"Sooth. I want to get a sample, though. I want to know if there's information in the dust."

"We'll ask Ruby if he has any equipment."

Now Seth and Noa were crowding close. Urban held them back. "It's a colony of philosopher cells," he warned. "And they're active. Don't touch them, or they'll try to metabolize you."

"Eat us?"

"Slowly. So be careful. You've never been around active cells before."

Ruby and Deneb converged on them from above. "Oh," Deneb said in a voice of soft trepidation. "Where did that come from?"

"It's a dust field," Ruby said. "They're fairly common."

"Are they?"

"Uh-huh. They seem to be an artificial parasite, not optimized for their own reproduction. We really don't know what they're for. They make a lot of dust, though. They'll probably try to colonize your hull. They show up everywhere, but always in low numbers."

Lot asked if they could get a sample of the dust. Ruby shrugged and swiped at the cells' surface. Lot choked in shock, while Deneb shouted an incoherent warning. But Ruby's palm slid easily over the cells, coming away gloved in a white powder. "How much do you need?"

"The cells didn't try to bond to you?" Urban blurted.

"No. They're harmless."

"They look exactly like our philosopher cells," Urban said. He shook his head. "But our cells are definitely *not* harmless."

Noa pulled a clear pouch out of his waist bag. He held it open while Ruby rubbed the dust into it. They gathered a little more, and then Lot was ready to hurry back to the ship.

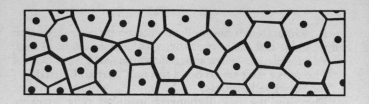

Chapter
31

This island is not alive.

This was Deneb's first thought as her visiting ghost manifested in the islander's city. She was the first of them to make the trip. Now her startled gaze looked across a gulf of space to an island she had never seen before. She faced its convex back, and the first thing she noticed was the surface tubes: though they held light, they didn't flash, and they didn't branch in the complex patterns she had seen in the wild archipelago. Instead they were formed into laddered paths and scattered arches. The stillness and the order combined to create a cultivated, static, artificial feel—as if this were a handmade copy of an island, not the real thing.

Still, the landscape was imposing. It spread out before her, filling her field of view, seeming so close at first that she might be able to take a short jump and reach it. She perceived it then as a wide plain opening out beneath her. But with no gravity to enforce a sense of up and down, her perceptions shifted. The plain became a wall, then a terrifying, looming roof—then finally the island settled into an abstract surface, and her heartbeat slowed—the simulation of her heartbeat. She was a ghost now.

She could see people moving on the laddered paths,

some toe-stepping, some aglide, winding between groves of smooth, dark trees trimmed in lines of tiny red lights. In the wild archipelago, such treelike structures had been beaded with points of white light.

The people on the trails looked unnaturally small. As she realized this, the island changed again, at once growing larger and farther away. She found the effect unsettling, and instinctively she reached out with her long toes to grasp some solid structure—then started in surprise when her foot encountered a loose web of soft gel that pulsed and vibrated with a rhythmic beat.

Easy, a deep-throated voice urged her with some amusement. *We're secure here.*

Where are we?

She looked past her feet, to find herself adrift just above a long bridge woven of glowing white strands, like the spinnings of some gigantic spider. The bridge stretched away toward a vanishing point on the island's rim. Looking through the weave, she could see other islands far below, coin circles and fingernail crescents, glowing with the same steady light as the near island.

She turned. Her host (he must be her host; he was the only other person on the bridge) waited just a few feet away. The expression in his shadowed eyes was vague as he gazed at her over the rim of his kisheer. He could see her only because her ghost existed within his atrium; all that she saw and heard and felt was filtered through his senses.

Her gaze slid past him, to follow the bridge in its unbending run to a distant island. Her host wasn't looking in that direction, but so long as he had looked there once, the atrium would remember.

Deneb finished her survey by looking overhead, confirming more islands on that side, and now she could make out the gossamer lines of other bridges stretching between them. Beneath her toes, she felt the fibers quiver.

Welcome to the Choir, her companion said. *We're drifting now at its heart.*

Deneb wasn't sure she had heard him right. *The Choir?*

It's what we call this archipelago. It was the first one settled, and we were taken by the way these islands sang to one another.

She knew all the words he spoke, yet still she felt confused. *Sang?

In radio frequencies. It's the signal you followed here. Perhaps it's not song, but it can be translated that way. It has a lovely sound sometimes. Of course, many of these islands we slaughtered. He gestured vaguely, at the near island, and at the crescents of neighboring islands all around. *A living island won't do for a home.

Deneb nodded, wondering how they had managed to skip any introductions. *Thank you for hosting me.

*It's my pleasure. Truly.

They backtracked then, and she found out that his name was Velt and he was an ecologist and an essayist and the administrator who oversaw Ruby's expedition to the wild archipelago. He was also one of the few remaining members of the original expedition still living in the city, having been born on the passage from Earth. He seemed a touch embarrassed as he explained it to her, the emotive lights on his kisheer flushing a faint pink. *You see, I convinced the council I would have a better intuitive understanding of your ancient ways, so they would let me host you.* He chuckled softly, a pleasant sound.

Deneb would have smiled, but the kisheer concealed her face. That was a cosmetic detail in the illusion of her existence. She was a ghost and she had no need of the kisheer, because she didn't really breathe. Zero pressure could not harm her. Yet the simulation of life was comforting to both of them. She gazed again down the web path to the slaughtered island, and to other islands beyond it, their distant lights unhazed by dust. *How many archipelagoes are there?

Millions, Velt said. *Perhaps billions.* There was a quickening excitement in his emotive lights. *Far more anyway than we have ever explored, and we're only familiar with a tiny portion of the cloud.* Amusement flickered in bronzy glints around his eyes. *Some of us originals thought the name 'Choir' too romantic. We wanted to call this archipelago 'Mote' instead. It seemed equally descriptive.

The abundance of territory had let them convert this entire face of the island into a park. Deneb glided with Velt along the laddered paths, pausing now and then to admire a black glossy tree in full fruit, its reproductive pods like glowing red marbles all along its skeletal form, or the puffs that crawled on the trunks, or flitted between the trees. The root zone was filled with scales of rainbow iridescence, broken now and then by clumps of crystal grasses, their whip-thin blades a blur of frantic vibration. A topaz snake lay wrapped around the black trunk of a tree, its fangs sunk into the bark as it sucked the inner liquid. Deneb touched its back. The DI within Velt's atrium concocted an estimate of how the snake would feel: smooth and slick, with a slight suction against her fingers. Then Velt touched the snake, and the sensory detail jumped. She could feel tiny ridges on its back and a terrible, sucking pressure. She snatched her hand away.

A gnome colony drifted overhead, each node in the web gleaming with a faint white light. It was a Chenzeme remnant, but the islanders hadn't known that until Null Boundary came. How must it have felt to come here, unscarred by the Chenzeme or the cult? Light was limited, but the territory so vast. What freedom they must have felt! A million potential cities . . . though the islands had been slaughtered. Ruby and Charm had shed guilt over that fact. There had been regret in Velt's voice too. So there was compromise, even here.

They left the park through a sequence of three gel locks. Velt explained they would see no vast, cavernous spaces inside the island. Instead, its hollow heart was long and sinuous: a broad, winding, pressurized tunnel that looped back on itself again and again. Velt waited until his kisheer pulled away from his face before he named it: the "Anaconda."

Slipping through the last gel lock, they emerged close to a laddered path where a family had just passed—three adults and two children touching the rungs lightly as they moved away.

Deneb grabbed a receiving rail to steady herself. The Anaconda was a rounded tunnel perhaps a hundred meters wide. They had emerged at the apex of an oxbow curve, just on the edge of a mall—Deneb could think of it as nothing else—an emporium of shops and restaurants that had been built into the tunnel walls. Light crowds flitted across the storefronts, gliding at an easy pace, their voices rolling indistinctly on the air. The mall twined around the tunnel surface in a slow spiral, the storefronts linked one to another with no space between. Their signs beckoned in color and in scent. Some stores protruded into the tunnel; others receded.

This was a fully three-dimensional world; there seemed no consensus about which way was up. Light gleamed from most surfaces, but the brightest light arose in a strip on the opposite side of the Anaconda. Deneb wondered if that was supposed to suggest a sky. Velt shrugged. "The light rotates around the walls over a period of twenty-five hours."

"There is no night?"

"There is enough night outside."

Beyond the lane occupied by the spiraling mall, there were apartments with architecturally quiet faces, their windows rounded, their doors encircled by railings. Well-disciplined vines entwined their walls. In the distance, three smaller tunnels opened on the Anaconda, all of them flattened ovals.

Deneb turned to look in the other direction of the oxbow curve. Here, more homes sprouted out of increasingly thick vegetation, their railed faces emerging overhead, underfoot, on every side. After several hundred yards, the trees took over, as a leafy thicket crowded all the way across the tunnel, forming a blockade.

Anaconda. Out of habit Deneb made to query the library about the name, but this was not Null Boundary. She was not recognized here, and no response came back to her. So she turned to Velt. "Anaconda is a familiar word. I should know it."

His scaled skin was blue, marbled in purple, but she could see a sudden flush of darker shades as he grinned. "It's a kind of immense snake, from Earth. Some wit offered it as the name for the main tunnel. So we all live in the gullet of the world snake."

Velt had a lovely smile. Gazing at him, Deneb said aloud what had been on her mind since Null Boundary reached the wild archipelago. "It amazes me that you and your people look so familiar, even after centuries of isolation."

Velt's expression sombered. "I wish it were so. Here at the heart, we tend to be conservative. We remember who we are. It's different in the outlying archipelagoes. You may see some of it. Travel by Second is common, and strange forms visit here."

Like Charm and Ruby, Velt appeared uncomfortable with this subject, but Deneb could not, in good conscience, avoid it, if there was any chance the tendril symbiotes might offer some clue to the enigma of the Chenzeme. "Charm mentioned alliances with ancient life-forms."

"Did she?" Velt's emotive lights dimmed. "Such things happen, of course. We are a free people."

"You don't approve, then?"

He let out a slow breath. "I am disturbed. People I have known for centuries have vanished into these alliances, abandoning family, friends, career. Why? The reasons given are never adequate. We are a free people, but there are unresolved questions of how freely their choice was made."

"That's what Charm said." Deneb's heart fluttered as she remembered her own anger and confusion when the cult invaded her world. The Chenzeme threat was subtle and insidious, and it would not surprise her that it could take many forms. "You're wise to be vigilant," she said. "The cult festered in Sol System for years before it bloomed."

Velt nodded. "That lesson has hit home with us. There are many here who will not stand quietly by, if coercion is ever proved."

After that, Velt guided the conversation to lighter subjects, while they wandered down the tunnel, following a trail laid out in grab bars. The mall and then the residences were left behind, and now the blockading thicket loomed before them. Deneb slowed as they approached it. It grew across the tunnel, and she could not see a way to get through. The smooth, glistening brown branches formed a tangled fence. The glossy leaves—as large as her hand—prevented her from seeing through to the other side, where children's voices could be heard shouting gross challenges and shrieking with triumphant laughter.

Velt smiled at her hesitation. "It'll let us through," he said. "Come."

He kicked off from a grab rail, launching himself toward the thicket. Deneb heard a sharp rustle of vegetation as a cluster of branches pulled open a moment before Velt would have whacked into them. He shot into the oval gap and disappeared.

Deneb's reality stuttered. Abruptly she found herself at his side, shunting through a leafy tunnel that opened as they advanced. She laughed in pleasure at their giddy pace. "Oh, I like this." Then she twisted around, looking back over her shoulder, but her view was blurred. "Velt? Look back, please."

He caught a branch and stopped, turning around, letting his gaze sweep the path they had taken. Deneb rode his senses. Now her vision snapped into satisfying clarity. The tunnel through the thicket was closing behind them, but much more slowly than it had opened. "It's a security fence," Velt explained. "To keep the pets confined to the park. Of course, wild birds like to nest here too."

Deneb looked for eyes in the branches and under the leaves. She couldn't find them.

Soon the thicket opened on a curve of the Anaconda where tall grasses covered the walls, some as high as canes. Branches bearing leaves of green and yellow and russet snaked across the tunnel's width. Kids climbed on them, and flitted through the open spaces, their kisheers clenched tight around their necks. Dogs went with them—that's what Velt called them. Deneb thought they looked like bats. Bats with pretty, perky dog faces and vari-colored hair. They barked like dogs and panted. When they'd been flying hard, mist lifted off their wing surfaces. Kids would strand themselves on a slow trajectory in the middle of the Anaconda, then call to their dogs, laughing hysterically as the creatures bumped and nuzzled them back toward a hedge or a branch or a wall. Watching them, Deneb thought about Seth and Noa. It wasn't hard to imagine them happily at play here.

She studied each child, and also the handful of adults taking their ease in the grass or clinging to the tree branches. Some were strikingly large. Others had unusual colors. A few had crests like Ruby and his companions. Most, like Velt, did not. They seemed very human. And though she looked closely at everyone who passed, she saw no one with sensory tears.

They continued to wander the Anaconda while Velt talked. His knowledge of Sol System was from a time before Deneb was born. He told her the stories his parents had told him about the Celestial Cities and the breakup of the Commonwealth and the flowering of culture that had followed.

"My parents didn't actually leave the Celestial Cities," he explained, as they entered yet another mall. "They sent their Seconds on the great ship. I told you before that I was born on the voyage here, but that's not quite true. I was born in Sol System first. My parents forwarded my pattern to the great ship. It was still close enough to do that. So I was there when my parents' Seconds awakened from cold storage. So really, I am a Second too. Even after all this time, I am uneasy with this status. I am a copy of someone I never knew and can't remember." He shook his head.

Deneb said, "I imagine you've diverged a bit by now."

That brought a hearty laugh. "A reasonable assumption, no doubt." But his humor quickly gave way to melancholy. "Over the years, I have tried to imagine their lives. I know now I got it all wrong. The news you brought confirmed a dark suspicion already growing among us. When no one followed us from Earth, we feared something had gone terribly wrong."

Deneb turned away, her gaze wandering across the blurred baskets of a restaurant that Velt had not quite looked at. "It's true. Null Boundary's records show there was little or nothing left at Sol after the cordon eroded. But hundreds of thousands of people, and probably billions of ghosts, left Sol System before the cordon was made. There were years and years of heavy emigration before anyone suspected anything was wrong."

"And this cult plague followed those emigrants outward."

"Some of them," she admitted. "But the frontier was relatively untouched, at least at the time Null Boundary left. It wasn't the cult that slowed the out-migration. It was the Chenzeme warships."

"The Chenzeme," Velt mused. "The ancient regime. We always knew we were not the first sentients to live in the cloud. We have recognized the biotechnology left behind by an earlier people—and some of us have abused it. But we have never seen anything like the warships you describe."

"We thought they came from the cloud," Deneb said. "Now I think they were made especially to harry us—or other civilizations—out there in the light. I wish I knew why your ship passed through the Chenzeme Intersection unmolested. Was it because you left so very early in our history? Or was it because you never stopped until you reached the cloud?"

"That I don't know." His gaze had fixed on her, and it was the only thing with weight in the Anaconda. "We've only known of the tragedy at Earth for a few centhours, but it's already changed us. It's made us more aware of who we are, and that we might be the last viable civilization."

Deneb did not want to agree with this. "We don't know that they're all gone. The frontier was under pressure, but it was still vitally alive when Null Boundary left. And we have no idea what happened in the other direction, outward along the galactic arm."

"Still, your own shipmates have speculated on it."

She shrugged uncomfortably. Velt could say what he liked, but there was no way to know what had become of those left behind. She let her gaze slide away, to meet a frozen tableau of the mall, the image of each passerby fixed in the aspect Velt had last seen. She smiled. Velt was a fine host, quite judicious in looking around, but just at the moment he was distracted.

"Velt . . . ?"

"Oh, pardon me." He glanced up to renew her view, and abruptly the prospect changed. A creature popped into existence on a ladder, perhaps twenty yards away. Deneb caught her breath in an audible gasp. The thing was worm-like, white, and quite long. It was still emerging from an emporium that dealt in video clips. Now the tail finally appeared and she guessed it to be perhaps three meters from end to end, and no thicker than her arm. It was covered in a long fringe of delicate tentacles that swirled like a skirt when it turned. It used some of the tentacles as tiny hands and feet to propel itself along the storefront, gliding easily and naturally in the zero gravity.

A second worm emerged from another shop. Moving on the whisper of its tentacles, it joined the first, side by side, their tentacles tapping gently as if probing for a familiar scent. Then their tails touched, and the two worms *fused*. Deneb leaned forward. Her jaw dropped in surprise. The two worms were joined. It was not like mating. They were close enough that she could see a swollen node at the point they came together, but there was no seam, no overlap, no hint they had ever been apart.

Three other worms converged on the first two. Deneb did not see where they came from, but now they repeated the behavior of the initial pair: a gentle touching of tentacles, and then abrupt fusion, all melding at the same node, which swelled in size at each addition until it became a disk. Now the conglomerate creature looked like a giant, white version of that aquarium pet called a brittle star, with five long, supple limbs, each fringed in delicate tentacles. There were eyes in the disk, and at the ends of some of the tentacles. Very human eyes, and they watched Deneb watching.

She drew back, her hand rising toward her mouth. *No.* It could not see her. She was a ghost, existing only within Velt's atrium.

He stared at the brittle star. His eyes were hard, and the turn of his mouth was bitter. "Those are a family," he told her. "No doubt they have come to show themselves to you."

"I don't understand."

"It's what you were asking about. The alliance with the symbiotic tendrils. Chenzeme tendrils, by your own speculations."

"Love and nature," she whispered. Her heart fluttered as she looked at the thing. She had imagined nothing like this. She had expected something analogous to the gnomes, humanlike nodes, linked by tendrils. She could see nothing human here, save a scattering of eyes.

"Each worm is competent on its own," Velt explained,

"but when they join they become something different. I don't know if the aggregate is smarter, but it is different from us."

Now the eerie eyes on the brittle star's central disk eased their inspection of Velt. Its limbs folded behind it in a streamlined package, like a squid. It used its fine tentacles to propel itself along the twisting path, until it passed out of sight down a side tunnel.

When it was gone, Velt turned to Deneb. "Have you ever seen that kind before?"

She shook her head, frightened as much by Velt's obvious anger as by the bizarre sight she had just witnessed. "No. I've never heard of such a thing. I don't think it's in the library."

"More and more of us feel that this is *our* Chenzeme threat."

"They have attacked you?"

His answer was the one she dreaded most. "Never. Their conquest is always a seduction. Their recruitment is always voluntary—or so they say." His kisheer shivered close to his neck. "I say it is still possible to go too far."

Deneb's thoughts turned to Lot. How far was too far? Lot was mostly human, but he was alien too. Deneb had taken some of that alien nature into herself. She had put it within the children. Their feelings spilled out around them, clearer than any words.

Velt sighed, and the tension ran out of him. He offered an apologetic smile. "My intolerance is unforgivable."

She responded cautiously. "I know this is a personal matter for you."

"Yes. Exactly. I knew so many of them, before."

Her heart raced in a thready beat, afraid to reveal herself to Velt, afraid not to. She liked what she had seen of the Choir. She liked it very much.

"You should know," she said softly, "they are not completely unlike us. We too have made a synthesis with an alien pattern."

His sharp gaze softened as she explained the charismata. "This sense has let us learn the chemical language of the Chenzeme warships," she finished. "Without it, we would not have survived."

Velt nodded. "You use this pattern," he said. "It does not use you. That, I think, is a critical difference."

It was the difference that separated her from Lot. "You are right to be cautious," she murmured.

"More so now than ever," Velt agreed. "If we are the last viable civilization, then we have a responsibility to defend what is human against any Chenzeme threat."

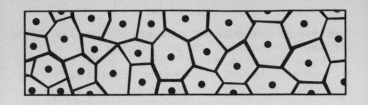

Chapter
32

The transit bubble flattened, squeezing Lot against the dormant cell tissue. The wound no longer felt soft, or yielding. The inactive cells were fearfully cold; he could not touch them, except through his skin suit. When the light from the transit bubble faded, Lot was left in absolute darkness. He moved his head slowly back and forth, but he could detect no emissions from the philosopher cells; the air in this tiny pocket was clean of everything but his own presence. Doubt fluttered on the floor of his mind like a half-seen insect with broken wings.

We will die in the cloud.

The hull cells had dismissed that warning, but Lot had to wonder again what it meant.

Just before coming here, he had walked the hull, pacing the edge of the dormant field. A smooth layer of dust still adhered to the cell faces. That would be metabolized when they awoke, giving them a burst of energy.

In his fingers, Lot rolled the sealed capsule that contained the dust gathered from the colony of wild cells. In the islanders' blue-tinted burrow, he had let a little of it brush his sensory tears, and immediately he had been plunged into a trance, a sleet storm, static wash of jumbled input, too much, or too unresolved for him to interpret. But surely the philosopher cells, working in concert, could sort meaning?

He would know soon.

"Nikko? I'm going to try to wake the field now."

The spider spoke with Nikko's voice: "I'm watching."

Lot closed his eyes. Then cautiously, he opened the gate of his fixed memory. Codes and images, sounds, scents—experiences that were not even his resided there. He left them undisturbed, seeking a simple pattern—

That slipped free, sliding into his sensory tears.

(Awaken.)

The charismata diffused outward. Swirled in the currents of his breath. Brushed the cells surrounding him.

"Ignition," Nikko said. "Measurable thermal response at your locus."

Opening his eyes, Lot felt the pressure of cell light against his retinas. It was faint at first, but it brightened, rising within seconds to a painful glare. At the same time, a torrent of activity crashed down around him—competing waves of sensation and desire. He waited for the flood of output to stabilize, but instead it continued to build, fearfully energetic, until, like an ocean swell that has grown too steep, it collapsed into a meaningless froth, losing all identity.

"Nikko—?" Lot's voice cracked in nascent panic as the cell glare threatened to blind him.

"I don't know!" Nikko snapped. "Love and nature, the cells are burning themselves up. They're pulling nothing from the ship, no energy at all."

"There must be another code to stabilize them." Lot searched his memory. There had been thousands of instructions encoded in the dust dropped by the swarm. Which ones were important? He couldn't replicate it all.

"Shut the cells down," Nikko said. "Push them back into dormancy."

"Yeah, okay." Lot felt heat at his back. *They're burning themselves up.* He closed his eyes, seeking a node of calmness, an island from which he could weave his spell of darkness.

That was when the cell field collapsed.

Lot's only warning was a crisp, glassy *crack*! Immediately, a giant palm slammed into his chest, driving out his breath while punching him through a wall that crumbled to dust as he passed. Searing pain lanced his ears. He wanted to scream, but the survival instincts that had been embedded in his ancestors would not allow it. His eyes, nose, mouth, and ears squeezed shut, buying him the necessary seconds while the hood of his skin suit slithered over his head and sealed. Lights popped, and hammers pounded in every tiny cavity in his skull, before precious air washed against his lips. He gasped it all in and there wasn't nearly enough, but more, more was coming, filling his lungs and his ears. He could hear the pounding of his heart and the heaving of his lungs. He opened his eyes.

Distant islands swung slowly through his field of view. In the foreground, he thought he could make out Null Boundary's shape, where reflected light played faintly on its surface. If that *was* Null Boundary, the hull cells had all gone dark again. Burned themselves out? That's what Nikko had said. They had cracked open beneath him.

He twisted around, straining his neck to see what lay ahead. The island, of course. It looked huge, and he was moving toward it pretty fast. "Nikko?"

"Here." An odd buzz marred Nikko's voice. "Are you stable?"

"Sooth. What happened to the cell field?"

"It collapsed. The cells consumed themselves. There's nothing left but powder."

Now Lot's rotation had brought the island into easy view. It was growing rapidly closer. "Can you grab me?"

"Sirkit's coming after you."

"Sirkit?" If this news was meant to reassure, it didn't work. "She planning to give me some extra momentum before I hit?"

Sirkit's voice buzzed painfully loud in his suit. "Now there's an idea." She dropped past him on the sled. He had only a glimpse of her, before a cargo net exploded in his face.

"Unh!" The blow knocked the air out of his lungs again. Then she hit the brakes, and he was slammed in the opposite direction. Before he was quite aware of it, the sled settled into the pit. To his mild surprise, he had survived another of her unlovely landings. He grabbed the net and

started untangling himself. "I want to go back to Null Boundary."

"What? No 'thank-you'?"

"Thank you. And please take me back to Null Boundary."

"Sorry, pet." Sirkit turned to look at him from the pilot's chair. "We have to refuel. Shouldn't take more than an hour. Or two." She climbed off the sled, disappearing into the shadows.

Lot sighed. Well, at least she had overlooked her rule about abandoning all strays to the void. He went back to untangling himself, and it was then he remembered the unopened capsule of dust still clenched in his cramped fingers. He'd never even had a chance to try it.

Ruby waved him inside the burrow. Once in atmosphere, his hood opened. Clotted blood leaked from his ears. Charm brought him food. She wouldn't look at his face. He imagined it was badly bruised. Maybe his eyes were bloodied too. Regardless, he knew he made them nervous. Damn.

Charm disappeared into one of the side tunnels. Ruby had already gone out through the membrane. The air in the burrow was clean and tasteless. "Nikko?"

"Here."

Lot fingered the capsule of dust. "Why did it happen?"

"I don't know. Apparently something stimulated a self-destructive routine."

Lot held the transparent capsule up to his eye, squinting at the cloud of white powder drifting within it. "There was dust on the cells."

"I've thought about that."

"There was dust on the wild cells too. Ruby says they produce it."

"The wild cells still function."

"Sooth."

Up till now, Lot had felt an icy calm, but suddenly frustration geysered through him. "Dammit, Nikko, we've lost the cell field again. *Again!* And this time by accident. I want to know why."

It had been so long since he'd been immersed in a real Chenzeme conversation, unpolluted by lockstep commands and dormancy codes. Ah god, he would forget how to follow the language, he would forget how to *be* Chenzeme, he would.

Yet the wild cells survived.

What were the wild cells? And . . . could he speak with *them*?

"Nikko? Ask Ruby if we can cut out the colony of wild cells. Maybe we can get *it* to function on the hull."

A few minutes later, Sirkit came into the burrow. She scowled at Lot. "You look like hell." A torch emerged from a hidden closet on the wall beside her. She hefted it. "I'll cut the dust field out for you, but it will die without nutrients from the island."

"Nikko can keep it alive."

She shrugged, then disappeared again through the membrane. He was left alone to wait.

It came without warning, making no sound. Lot first sensed its presence as a flash of motion in the central tunnel. He looked around, to see a flood spiraling down on him, white water sluicing through an invisible pipe, a snake made of water. It swept into the chamber; it coiled around him, an arm's length away. The coils of the snake melted together, and he was encased in a glistening shell. Charismata of exhilaration rained against his sensory tears, a strange, foreign sense of greeting. Tendrils reached out to him from the shell's shimmering white surface, a thousand slender white tendrils brushing him. Faint touches. Where they contacted his skin suit they retracted, but where they touched his bruised face they stayed. Familiarity flooded him, a warm sense of union that eased the black pressure of the cult forever burning under his skin. A voice whispered in his ear, produced by a trembling membrane on the end of a tendril. *"You know us?"*

He stared at the alien filament. "No. I don't know you."

"You asked for us." Its voice so soft he could barely make it out.

Tendrils pressed at his sensory tears, injecting into them a new flood of charismata. The creature's presence exploded in his sensorium, familiar, arousing. He realized: *This one is vulnerable*. Whatever it was. The cult surged under his skin. His own charismata flushed from his sensory tears, carrying the cult into the thing, linking it to him on silver currents. "Sooth, you're right. I remember now. I did ask for you."

"And so we came to you, through the gate." The creature was huge, filling the chamber, dwarfing Lot with its enclosing mass. Yet fear seeped from it. It feared him. Not as much as it desired this contact. It wanted something from him.

Lot's confidence grew. "What are you?"

"A symbiote." A dozen eyes gazed at him, human eyes, embedded in the ends of tendrils. *"We are one part of Hafaz colony. We were human once, separate creatures of singular minds, but we have re-created ourself from the life of the cloud. Something happened here long ago. We have tried to remake the past, so that we might understand it."*

Its tendrils held tight to his sensory tears. The cult parasite had been seeded in it. It would be forming now in the creature's neural center—its brain—wherever that might be. Satisfaction flowed from it, almost as if it understood and was pleased. *"You are the answer to so many questions."*

"While you are so many questions, to me."

"They have lied to you about us."

Lot smiled. He knew it was so. The islanders feared what they did not understand. It had always been that way. He closed his eyes, savoring the flavor of human desire, heightened with a wild tang of Chenzeme emotion. Never had he felt such a thing before. "Tell me your truth."

<All I remember>

Lot listened. Part of the tale flowed to him through the tendrils, in Chenzeme packets of memory. Part of it was whispered in his ear by the tiny, trembling membrane.

He saw Hafaz colony as it used to be: curious people, wondering at the symbiotic tendrils that had made biological alliances with so many life-forms, so many different clades. Curious people, yearning to know if the tendrils could make a bridge to their species too.

They could not resist trying, and they did not regret it. Success revealed to them a library of memories in the tendril's ancient neural cells. Memories that were passed from generation to generation like the memories of the hull cells, or like Lot's own fixed memory. Those who entered a union with the tendrils awakened to a past of overwhelming depth. As tendrils were added to Hafaz colony, details grew.

In swift, whispered words the symbiote related what it knew: "Once, we were drifting webs, thousands of kilometers across. Spun from dust over slow millennia, we would think as one, and at the same time, each node of us lived as a separate entity, our alliances constantly shifting as we earned respect or sex or adulation. To be cut off from all bonds was death. It did happen. By accident. Now and then out of need. To meet another colony—"

Lot gasped. He could see again what he had glimpsed in the passage of Alpha Cygni: creatures like translucent cloth blown on wind, or like fog, far away. He saw them again, but this time he understood them. "They are like us."

He hungered after them, a need like the cult hunger, a desire for union, but it was polluted by fear, hatred, anger, violence. A foreknowledge of death.

"When one net touches another, they join, and die."

"We cannot turn away."

"We cannot turn away. It's a need, like food or sex, but we don't survive it. We join and die. Something new replaces us. It remembers both us and the other, but it is not us. It is something new."

Lot found himself falling through a four-dimensional pile of history, memory. "I can look back on a thousand deaths. I remember them all, though I am not them. And it will happen to me. It will happen. Again, and again."

"Millions of deaths," the symbiote whispered. *"Millions of generations all aware of their desire, and their fate. We could not escape it. Many tried, but that was death too. The fear of loss was always with us. You understand? Even when we were singular human minds we understood it: that the worst fate is to know too much."*

"But to join without dying—"

"We have never learned how."

"Never?"

"They knew."

"Sooth." The cult was made to knit the disparate together.

"We don't know. Hafaz colony died every time a new entity was accepted into our union. What was reborn was

more sublime than what had been before, but our sense of self was lost. We are a new colony, remembering ancestors. We don't add new entities anymore."

"It doesn't have to be that way," Lot said.

Acknowledgment and hope whispered from the tendrils. Lot closed his eyes. It was so sweet to meet this relief of his solitary existence. This willing play between himself and these others—

(They *were* plural—if he slowed his breathing and listened closely to his Chenzeme senses, he could separate them, like loops of dialogue, like ghosts of individual volition, blended along some new and unfamiliar vector.)

—they desired the union he could give them. They understood what they did not possess, and they desired *him.*

"Be part of Hafaz colony," the symbiote whispered. *"The rest of ourself will welcome you. Come now. Please. Through the gate. Before it's too late."*

Lot opened his eyes to despair, like cold, cold fire in his marrow. "Not through the gate. I can't. I won't survive it. I'll come to you, though, however I can. Tell me where you are."

"In the city."

"I will—"

It ended. A flare of blue heat lanced out of the body of Hafaz colony, shooting past Lot's shoulder. He ducked, hiding his face against his thighs as the charismata vanished from the air and the scion of Hafaz colony snapped apart in a searing fog of burning flesh and twisting tendrils, some of them still clinging to Lot's sensory tears.

Something slammed him against a wall. He stuck. Like a bug in syrup. He couldn't move. The hood of his skin suit writhed beneath his head, struggling to close, to cut him off from the smoky air, but it was stuck too, a bug's wings.

Sirkit landed on his chest, a torch clutched in her hands. He arched, struggling to throw her off, but the effort only drove his head and shoulders deeper into the muck. The colony tendrils embedded in his sensory tears writhed and snapped. He felt their heads burrowing deeper. "Get off me!" he screamed. "What the fuck have you done?"

"Saved your life, pet." Sirkit's lip twitched as her kisheer rolled up her throat, toward her mouth. Her contempt cut the smoky air. She flicked the torch on.

She had killed the symbiote. And she would kill him next. Her hatred pounded at him. He thrashed in the sludge of the softened wall, but it would not let him go.

Urban landed behind him, kneeling in the sticky goo. His hands framed Lot's head, squeezing hard, forcing him to be still. "Easy, fury."

Now, Lot thought. *They will do it now.*

"Fuck you," he growled.

The torch slashed, but not at him. He flinched, his eyes all but closed against the heat and the fumes as Sirkit touched the flame against the free end of each tendril embedded in his sensory tears. Each one collapsed, a dying worm curling into ash. Lot could not breathe, he could not think. He was choking. Maybe he was sobbing.

Then it was over. She was off his chest. The wall released him and the hood of his suit slipped over his head, sealing out the repulsive air. He drifted, stunned, his cheeks wet, his suit stinking of his own slowly abating terror.

Sirkit glared at him from a corner of the chamber. She still clutched the torch. Her shoulders heaved. A blur of swimmers swarmed around her veiled face.

"You murdered them," he said. It had been a ruthless execution, in the manner of the courser at Alpha Cygni.

"It trespassed on my territory," Sirkit answered. Her voice trembled. "It did not have my permission to come through that gate."

"So you murdered them." The swimmers had become so thick, he could hardly see her. "What kind of people are you?"

She turned to Urban. "Get him out of here, before I kill him too."

Urban put a hand on his arm, but Lot was not ready for it. "*Why?*" he screamed at her. The cult a dark, despairing presence under his skin. "Why do you hate them?"

Behind the blur of swimmers, her shadow contracted. She asked him, "Do you know what spiders are? Hafaz colony is like a spider. It spins seductive webs. Touch the web, and you will want to be bound. Every member of the colony joined *voluntarily*, but what does that mean, when they have already been changed, and all resistance stripped from them? Of course, you work the same way. Clemantine told us how it used to be with her."

"Fuck you."

She kicked forward, emerging abruptly from the haze, the torch aimed at Lot's chest. In a panic, he grabbed Urban's shoulder, pushing away from him to widen the space between them. Sirkit touched the wall with a prehensile toe, arresting her motion. "Listen to me," she growled. "Hafaz colony is engaged in a conquest, and sometime soon, enough of us will accept that and we will begin to fight back."

Urban slid between them. He spoke to her gently. "I think that's what happened with the Chenzeme. I think the cult snuck up on them too, and the warships were their way of hitting back, or ensuring the cult didn't spread any farther out there"—he waved his hand—"beyond the cloud. Maybe they planned to live out there, when it was clear of the cult. I don't know. We've all been caught up in somebody else's mess, an ancient civil war between the shipbuilders and the cultists that is still spewing trouble and new hybrids thirty million years after the main action ended."

Sirkit lowered the torch. "So. I can only hope *we'll* make our counterstrike before things spread so far." Her toe tapped the floor, and she shot off, disappearing into one of the tunnels.

Urban sighed, and the tension ran out of his shoulders. He turned to Lot. "Come on, fury. Let's go home."

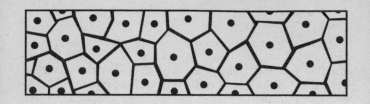

Chapter
33

A disk of tissue supporting the colony of wild cells had already been loaded on the sled, so they took it with them when they went back to Null Boundary. Lot guided it to the site Nikko had prepared for it, trying not to think too much. He watched the hull lap around it, anchoring it in position. He watched the cell light brighten as the colony extracted nutrients from Null Boundary's tissue. Then he went inside and he stripped. He slapped a patch against his neck. The cult was a cold, despairing pressure, an unbearable absence chewing at his gut. He wanted to kill Sirkit.

He descended into the darkness of sleep.

When he woke several hours later, he took a transit bubble to the site of the wild cells. They gleamed beneath his gloved hands. They looked like the old hull cells, and yet they might have been inanimate matter, for they shed no sense of any activity into the space of the transit bubble. Lot could detect no presence nor any hint of conversation.

Be Chenzeme.

Suppressing his questions, he made a charismata of greeting, but it stimulated no response. He made a charismata of threat. That too was ignored. He tried other approaches, but nothing he did produced results.

He went to see Nikko. "Do you know where the islander city is?"

Nikko hovered at the end of the core chamber. His fingers tapped at his thigh, but they made no sound. "No."

"I want to talk to Hafaz colony."

"I'll ask."

Several days passed. Lot stayed aboard Null Boundary. It was an empty ship. The others were gone most of the time, exploring the islands. Ruby had relayed his request to the city, but no reply came from Hafaz colony.

Lot tried again to communicate with the wild cells.

Nothing.

The cells continued to produce dust. He collected it, comparing it to the small quantities of dust that accumulated elsewhere on the hull.

Traces of wild cell dust could be found in every sample he collected.

He started three new clusters of philosopher cells growing, each within a separate bubble hollowed out of the ship's tissue, so that they were protected from the dust. Each new colony thrived, its cells gleaming with their signature white light. Lot could even extract rudiments of conversation from them.

He waited until the new colonies were a handspan wide. Then he exposed one to the dust gathered from the wild cells and another to the vacuum around Null Boundary. The first cell colony disintegrated immediately. The second lasted an hour. The third colony, still protected within the ship's tissue, survived.

In a sullen fury, Lot went back out on the hull. He cut out the colony of wild cells he had planted there. Nikko helped him destroy it.

"At least we know why there are no Chenzeme ships visibly active in the cloud," Nikko said. "It's inoculated against them. This dust could be anywhere. That's what the swarm tried to warn us against."

"Sooth." Lot tasted bitter frustration. "But inoculated by *who*?"

The Chenzeme themselves. There could be no other answer. Some faction of them must still be here, somewhere, and they used the wild cell dust like a fence, to keep their

cloud safe from their own warships . . . or the warships of
their shipbuilding cousins in this bloody civil war.

Charm met them on the gee deck when they went back
inside. Lot was surprised to see her; he hadn't known she
was aboard. "We've had news of an incident in the city,"
she told them, her voice strangely drained of emotion.
"Hafaz colony has ended. There was a fire in their house-
hold. No copies survived."

Lot stared at her, numb, as if a wall had been thrown up
around his passions.

"It might have been suicide," she suggested.

It was murder. Lot knew the technique. Those other
charismatics living in his memory had used it too. Crush
dissent. Eliminate any source of threat before it could grow.
He swiped at the water droplets condensing on the cold
surface of his skin suit. "Are there other colonies?"

Charm shifted, green lights gleaming in her kisheer.
"There has been . . . a small civil war. I don't think there
will be colonies left when it is done."

"Sooth." There had been peace here before Lot came. It
had been an uneasy peace, but it had taken his presence to
ignite this "small" war.

Charm drew in a long breath. The green lights in her
kisheer steadied. "I am to tell you that you will not be per-
mitted to enter the city by any means, at any time. The risk
of infection is too great."

Lot's eyebrows rose. His hand coiled into a fist, spilling
droplets of condensing moisture to the floor. "Do you think
it's that easy? The Silkens told my father the same thing,
and still, he got in."

Charm stiffened. She backed off a step. Her wariness
washed over Lot in a satisfying cloud.

Then Nikko was speaking, calm and reasonable. "Lot
will stay aboard Null Boundary—"

"The hell I will!"

"—and Null Boundary will not be moved closer to the
city. I promise you that."

Lot turned away. He walked to the end of the pavilion,
feeling trapped, furious, utterly helpless. He stared down

the path to Kiyo's house. He couldn't remember the last time they had made love. He looked back at Charm.

A pink flush had invaded her white scales. "You understand," she was telling Nikko, "these words are a formality. I didn't mean to imply you would deliberately bring him to the city—"

"He will stay here with me."

"The rest of you are welcome, that's not changed. It's just that we must be careful, not to go the way of the old worlds."

"I understand," Nikko told her. "I agree."

Darkness lay within and without: the lightless, sealed chamber of Lot's apartment cradled him, while the cult boiled in its dark ocean just beneath his skin. He floated at the interface of these two worlds, the charismata drifting outward along a hundred thousand vectors that went on forever, never touching on anything else. He remembered Hafaz colony, and he wept.

Ah god, he was so hungry for some connection! The islanders were right to be wary of him. He would do anything to ease this isolation. Anything at all. It was what he'd been made for. He was a weapon, pressed to the service of some ancient civil war. He could see it in no other light.

But whose war? Whose crusade? Where was the faction that had made him? It had to be the same faction that had made the cult.

He wanted to find them.

The cult virus had come out of the void to infect the Hallowed Vasties, carried within the flesh of a man like Lot. An ancestor: Lot could remember snatches of his life— shadowy recollections that lingered in his fixed memory— but hard as he tried, he could not uncover any memory of the moment of infection.

The islanders insisted this nameless man had not been part of their expedition. That was probably true, but hundreds of early expeditions out of Earth had never been accounted for.

History recorded the first effects of the cult in Sol System, but its influence spread swiftly outward from Earth. Behind this wave front the cordons first bloomed and then crumbled: internal collapse meeting external strife as the Chenzeme warships appeared from the direction called *swan*, to harry settlements along the frontier.

The cult and the warships: they were closely related, but they were not the same thing.

The warships attacked any life-form that might carry the cult, though they could not be touched by it themselves. Neither could they come deep into the cloud, or the wild cell dust would wreck them. The warships and the wild cell dust were like a dog and its collar—a deliberately engineered system of control. It wouldn't be hard for the ships to resist the killing dust, but apparently they did not, any more than a dog would think to remove its own collar.

So the cloud was neutral territory. The warships did not come here, and the cult was found only in impotent remnants, uniting hybrid colonies like Hafaz.

Only remnants.

What else could there be after thirty million years? Surely no culture, no war, no crusade could endure that long. Time was a ruthless sculptor, forever changing everything that would pass through it. The cult should have died out long ago, or evolved toward a truce with the Chenzeme ships.

That had not happened.

It was as if the past skipped through time to continuously reinfect the future. If so, then no truce would ever last long.

I am a weapon.

Made for this war.

Something had made him, and not so long ago. If he could retrace the path of his ancestor, rediscover that source, it might be possible to remake himself into something more potent.

Nikko watched Lot make his way to the empty core chamber. The image walls showed the view outside, the islands, and the sled moving in a slow arc as Charm and Deneb returned with the boys from a tour of an outer island.

Lot slid into the chamber. He watched the sled a moment, long enough for his restlessness to scrape the wall receptors. "Nikko?"

"Here."

"Come out, please. We need to talk."

Nikko let his ghost manifest at the chamber's bow end. He could guess the point of this conversation, and Lot did not disappoint. "Nikko, we've stayed here long enough. You know we have."

Nikko did not try to mask or edit his reluctance. Like Deneb, he had made a ghost-run to the islander city, and oh, how brightly it had reminded him of a past he had tried too hard to lock away. Nikko was in no hurry to leave the islands. Really, he wanted an excuse to stay.

An excuse?

Why could he not simply *choose* to stay?

Lot snapped at his silence. "C'mon, Nikko! You're not like Deneb. You can't really be thinking of settling down. We came this far to look for the Chenzeme—and we aren't going to find them here."

"You came because you had nowhere else to go," Nikko reminded. It was a soft shot, made to deflect the sleepy stirring of an old, familiar guilt.

Lot knew how to play on guilt. "So what? I still want to find the Chenzeme. You want that too. I know you do."

No! Nikko wanted to deny it. That was an obsession. It wasn't him. And still, he felt himself soften. "And if we were to leave? Where would we go? Where would you have us look?"

Lot's gaze was calm. Quite calm and thoughtful for someone in his position. Nikko mistrusted it. "We could go on to Nightlight," Lot suggested.

"Nightlight?" Nikko feigned confusion. "The islands were the source of the signals we heard. There's nothing at Nightlight. There can't be. That star is hardly ten thousand years old."

"You know that's the point."

Nikko wanted to end this conversation, but he couldn't bring himself to do it. Like some falling body, he felt himself caught on an inevitable track. "You're thinking of the artifact we saw at Alpha C."

"Sooth. Urban suggested it might predate the original conflict. That it might have existed in the star's primordial nebula—"

"Revealed when the star formed and the dust was blown away."

Lot nodded. "That might have happened at Nightlight too."

Nikko felt a welcome skepticism; he used it like a refuge. "Do you really think such artifacts would be that common? The islanders have never found one. They've never seen such an object in orbit at Nightlight."

"Well, how closely have they looked? The ring was dark. We would have missed it, if it hadn't been silhouetted against Alpha C. That we saw one at all could mean they're common. We should go see."

It *was* an obsession. "I'm tired, Lot."

"You can edit that."

"Yes. I can." He could edit other things too, but he never had.

"We could still find the Chenzeme," Lot coaxed.

"I doubt it. What is it you're hoping for anyway? Are you thinking they could unravel your physiology?"

A faint sense of subterfuge brushed the wall sensors. "They would have had no reason to make a key to that."

"That's right," Nikko said, pretending he had won the point.

Lot rubbed at his sensory tears. "I want to know who they were . . . or who they *are*. I want to know why they made us part of their war. You want it too."

Nikko nodded. Why try to pretend he did not? "You want to leave soon, then?"

"Sooth." Lot looked at the image wall. Nikko followed his gaze to where Hailey stood on the rim of the island, waving at the approaching sled. "Will you leave a copy of yourself here?" Lot asked. "I think you should."

"As insurance?"

"Yes. As insurance."

"I don't think so."

Lot turned to him in alarm. "But why?"

Because it was an obsession. Copied into every copy. "Oh, because then I would always wonder what happened to you."

"So? You could come back and tell yourself."

Nikko chuckled. This *is* me. "Ha. We're a frontier people. We never go back."

"Nikko, this is serious. You don't want to be alone again."

"I don't think I will be. Now come on. We need to say good-bye."

Nikko was right. They did not leave alone. Urban, Clementine, and Hailey all chose to send along the data patterns that defined them. Urban pleaded with Deneb to do so too, but she refused, telling him, "We're welcome here. Why should we go? Why should Seth and Noa have to face more danger, more unknowns? They're safe from the cult here. I won't do it."

"You'll make me go on alone, then?"

Anger flashed in her eyes. "Not you," she reminded him. "Only that still unmade copy of you—and that's what rankles. You don't want to be the version left behind. Look at yourself! So jealous—of a ghost."

Her assessment was deadly accurate. The restlessness that had driven Urban out of Deception Well was still in his nature. Then, he had run away from his old man without leaving any version of himself behind.

That was a long time ago.

"Deneb, you know I love you."

"You love many things, Urban."

And now he had to choose between them.

In the zero gravity of his apartment, he held her, his arms around her hips, his cheek pressed against her smooth belly, knowing she was right, that he did not want to stay behind in the islands, not in his heart, and still, he could not bring himself to leave her or the boys.

Such reluctance might be excised. Astute editing might banish this oppressive sense of obligation—though he didn't think he could ever untangle his more complex feelings. Love ran deep, and when he thought about it hard, he knew he would never willingly write himself out of their lives.

"*I want you forever,*" he whispered fiercely. "It's that poor bastard trapped aboard Null Boundary who will be the jealous one, because I'll have you and the boys."

"And Ruby's map of the archipelagoes," Deneb added in a wry and knowing voice. "With worlds for you to explore to fill a thousand years. Urban, I don't think you will be too bored."

Like Deneb, Kiyo didn't put her pattern aboard Null Boundary. *Threads break.* Clemantine had warned her of it, and now she saw it was true. Lot had been carried away from her on a dark tide that had snapped her delicate chain of charismata. She could not reach him anymore. He no longer seemed to see her.

So she stood with Hailey on the rim of the island while Null Boundary pulled away on a frail acceleration. Watching the gulf between them widen, Kiyo felt hollow and frightened, and strangely, relieved.

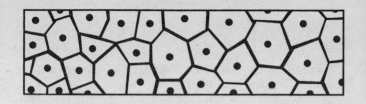

Chapter
34

During the passage to Nightlight, Nikko's ghost became reclusive, rarely visiting the cardinals, so Urban found himself commanding more and more of the ship's functions. His persona expanded into the empty spaces. The ship's senses were once again his senses: the tension of the reef, the hot sting of dust against the prow, the sighing, crackling song of radio emissions, the glow of nebular gases heated by Nightlight's intense ultraviolet radiation. He played with his time sense, so that the past and future both squeezed hard against a long, unfurling present. Deneb remained always only a moment away. If he were to look back quickly enough, he might find her beside him, while Nightlight loomed, imminent, just ahead.

All through the long approach, Urban kept a pair of telescopes trained on Nightlight. The islanders had never noticed any satellites around the supergiant star, but after a number of years Urban was able to pick out two tiny objects. One lay close to Nightlight, trotting across its face four times a year. Urban watched it suspiciously, wondering how the islanders could have failed to mark its presence. The second object was far harder to see. It had a dark, eccentric orbit, far from Nightlight's searing energies. It emitted no radiation and reflected no light. Urban saw it only as it passed briefly across Nightlight's turbulent face. How many other, similar objects might be forever hidden in the neighborhood of the giant star?

There was no way to tell.

Abruptly he was aware of Nikko, as an unseen mass at his back. Checking in at last?

"I can't discern what they are yet," Urban told him. "They're tiny, like the artifact at Alpha C, though we're still too far away to detect a ring shape."

Nikko said: "A natural object would reflect more light."

Urban had to agree. "Null Boundary will boil again if we take it past the inner object. I don't want to risk that. So I'm going to focus on the outer satellite instead."

"The outer satellite won't be easy to find," Nikko pointed out.

"We'll use radar."

"It might not reflect radar."

"Sooth," Urban agreed. "But radar might wake it up."

Lot awoke from cold sleep, with the cult hunger burning under his skin. No one waited at the chamber door to greet him. "Nikko?" he asked. "Are we at Nightlight?"

The spider answered in Urban's voice: "Yeah, fury. We are."

Lot jerked free of the last of the suspension threads. "And the artifact? Have you found one?"

"I've found two objects. One's in a close orbit around the star—too far away to say for sure what it is."

"And the other?"

"It's a ring, exactly like the artifact at Alpha C. It seems to be aware of us."

Extrapolating from his brief observation, Urban had estimated the position of the outer satellite. When he finally located it through faint radar reflections, he found his estimate had been off by only 212 miles.

Now, even without radar, the object was visible. A faint heat signature could be detected in the distinctive ring shape they had seen at Alpha Cygni, viewed at an oblique angle. The artifact was stirring, its temperature rising above the background galactic average—though what that might portend, Urban could not guess.

Urban made himself incarnate again. As Lot slipped into the core chamber, Urban turned to greet him, but Lot hardly spared him a glance. His gaze fixed on the image wall and the ring's blurred and ghostly shape. "How long before we reach it?"

No "hey Urban." No hello. There was something hollow and too hungry behind Lot's focused gaze. It made Urban's hackles rise. "A few days, fury. More or less, if we want it."

"Less."

"Huh?"

"Get us there as soon as you can."

"Okay. I'll work on it."

Lot's gaze shifted, fixing on Urban with a speculative light. "Is the ship yours now?"

Urban answered quickly, "No," wondering if it was a lie.

Lot studied him, his head moving slowly back and forth. "You're afraid of me." His expression broke into a grin, though there was little humor in it. "You almost gave me Silk, remember? Now that's a scary thought."

"You didn't want it," Urban reminded him.

"Sooth. I'm glad I left Silk. I'm glad it's far away now—or I might try to convince you to take me back." Lot clung to a grip with a white-knuckled hand, his posture hunched, as if a fire burned under his skin. Urban did not know what to say to him. He knew exactly what Lot needed, but he would not give it to him.

Goddamn the Chenzeme!

And their heartless meddling.

Some things could not be unmade.

Lot was looking at the ring again. "There must be billions of them. Trillions. You know? Scattered all through the cloud."

"Sooth. Most of them would be impossible to find."

"Whoever built them must have planned it that way."

This had occurred to Urban too. Cold, dark, inactive,

and therefore nearly undetectable, the artifacts might conceivably survive for hundreds of millions of years. Or longer?

"You think they're the source of the cult virus, don't you?" Urban asked.

Lot straightened up. "Fuck, I hope so. I want to know where it came from. I want to know who did this, *what* did this, how it was done . . . I want to know why."

They debated sending a probe ahead, but Lot was against it. He was on edge, and Urban worried he would not be rational if they waited even a few days more. So together they lobbied for an all-or-nothing shot.

The plan was simple. Hailey would remain aboard Null Boundary while the rest of them deployed in a drop pod that Urban was building on the hull, from a library design augmented with the addition of a reef. Once separated from Null Boundary, the pod would decelerate, while the great ship continued on, conserving velocity in a slow fall past Nightlight. By the time the pod made contact with the artifact, Null Boundary would be far away, and safe.

The drop pod had a gateway. If things went well, they would use it to return their ghosts to Null Boundary while Lot waited aboard the pod in cold sleep, until the ship could return and pick him up. If things went poorly . . . well, they would also leave ghosts aboard the great ship, so their existence wouldn't end. Except, of course, for Lot, but that was a chance he was willing to take.

The drop pod's passenger capsule was mounted on a gantry, between the reef and a classic engine employing reaction mass. As Lot crawled through the hatch, he could feel a faint pull from the idle reef.

Inside the capsule, four acceleration pouches were packed around a central column. Lot sank into one of them. Relief washed over him, allaying for a few minutes the dreadful craving for the cult that ate at him, ate at him all the time now. So. He would know soon if the rings were part of it, if they were the source of the cult virus. He hoped they were. He hoped that in some metaphorical sense he was retracing the path of his ancestor. That first charismatic had probably not come as far as Nightlight, but he might have stumbled over another ring, at Alpha C, or at some other star even closer to the frontier.

If Lot gained nothing else, it would be a victory to know where he came from.

He settled his shoulders against the enfolding membrane. Clemantine bent over him. "Okay?" she asked. Their suits were already sealed, so her voice reached him through the radio.

"Sure."

She drifted past, to clamber into the pouch on his other side. He was cozied between Urban and Clemantine. Nikko was on the opposite side. Their backs were to the column, so he couldn't see anyone's face.

Even if he could, their faces would be hidden behind hoods or kisheer.

Acceleration gel flowed into the chamber from a conduit in the central column. It filled the whisper-thin space between his shoulder and Clemantine's, between his shoulder and Urban's. He felt as if he were sinking backward into a quagmire of it; it flowed over his visor. "Okay, fury?" Now Urban wanted to know.

"Sooth."

The pod DI reported their progress. Lot felt a kick of motion as they were boosted free of Null Boundary's hull. The Dull Intelligence warned of pending acceleration. It would be a negative thrust. They needed to severely reduce their velocity relative to the artifact. Initial thrust would be generated by the classic engine, leaving the reef to finish the job. The DI initiated a countdown from ten. Lot steeled himself as the chant hit zero and the pod kicked at almost twelve g's.

Eight hours passed. The classic engine was cold, the fuel tank empty. They rode on the silent flux of the reef. The gel had drained away, but there was no room to move around. Hailey's voice reached them through the com, giving updates that amounted to "no change" intermixed with position information. Her voice acquired an increasing delay, as the distance between the pod and Null Boundary grew.

Urban listened to her while memories bubbled up in his consciousness, old stuff that he hadn't thought about in years.

"Hey, Lot."

"Yeah?"

"You ever think about Silk?"

"Sometimes."

"Remember that baby-sitter city authority appointed for you?"

Lot groaned, while Clemantine chuckled. "He smelled funny," Lot said. "Some perfume he always used. Made me want to puke."

Urban could almost smell it himself. His nose wrinkled in remembered contempt. In those days he had felt like the lord of the city, fifteen years old and almost immune to censure, his old man head of the city council and Lot in his pocket, this strange, helpless kid whom city authority feared. Never since had he felt quite so invulnerable. "Remember that first time you took off from that creep, and we went down to Splendid Peace?"

Clemantine objected. "He wasn't *that* bad."

"Like you know," Urban countered.

Lot laughed. "I remember it. I was ten. Just a step away from growing up, that's what I thought. I was going to run away and live under the bridge at Splendid Peace."

"That's right! You got me to swipe beer for you. You were going to drink it under the bridge at dinner."

They'd had it at lunch instead, then dared each other to walk on the bridge's arched railing as it rose over a rocky swath of white water. Had they really been that young?

"Freedom," Lot mused. "That was a wild day."

"Until Clemantine wrecked it."

"Yeah," Lot agreed. "That is what happened. Clemantine, you remember? Security sent you to bring me back. They always sent you."

"And a good thing too. You and Urban tottering on that railing. It almost made my heart stop. I thought sure you would fall."

"I was an easy drunk."

"Yes, some things never change."

Lot laughed again, while Urban asked, "Why do you think he used that awful perfume anyway?"

It went on like that for hours, talk, talk, talk—talk that messed with time, words that resurrected people and long forgotten places: favorite restaurants and the flavors of famous dishes, arcades and the raging popularity of insect sims, concert halls and the music they had and hadn't liked, Lot getting laid for the first and second time in the same night . . . they picked that one apart until Urban's belly hurt from laughing.

And all the while they talked, Urban could feel time flowing past his hand in an incessant current. So much time, and yet never enough. *Remember how it was? Remember?*

Until finally he understood: This was how they said good-bye.

They were within four hours of the ring, when Hailey's voice tore through the com, riding a wiry panic that replicated itself in Urban's chest.

"Null Boundary has sighted another vessel. It's coming up out of the glare of the star."

"Is it the other satellite?" Urban snapped, his suspicions alight. Maybe the islanders had no record of it because it hadn't been there long.

The delay that preceded her response was excruciating. "Urban, I don't know. But . . . it could be. I can't see the inner satellite anymore, and I should."

"Is it a ring?" Nikko asked.

"No. It has the profile of the courser."

The courser. Urban felt something close inside him, a connection that had waited years to trigger. He had thought the courser long gone. He had let himself believe that it had returned to the frontier.

What if it had run ahead of them instead? Anticipating their foray to Nightlight.

"What's its heading?" Clemantine demanded. "Is it targeting you?"

"No. I think it's making for the ring."

"That's impossible," Lot said. "The wild cell dust should have destroyed its hull cells. It should be blind. Or dead."

"It's running dark," Hailey said after a long delay. "The hull cells are not active. So . . . how can it know where it's going?" Her voice caught. "Oh Lot. It's happening now. The courser is breaking dormancy. The cells are waking. The light is spreading, brightening . . ." Her words trailed off on a note of dire expectation.

"Hailey?" Clemantine queried, when the silence had gone on too long.

Hailey answered her, sounding rattled. "The courser's hull cells are still . . . intact. The full field is active now. It looks stable. I don't see any erosion, no excess activity—"

"That can't be right!" Lot's protest was an explosion of fury and frustration. "The courser passed through the cloud. Its cells must have been coated with dust, just like ours."

"The cell field is stable," Hailey insisted.

Urban felt fear in his chest like a wad of tangled wire, all kinks and sharp ends. Nightlight's solar winds had blown a vast bubble in the cloud, eroding away the dust and gas of its primordial nebula—and the wild cell dust with it. "It came up from Nightlight," he said grimly. "Maybe it learned something from us. Maybe it stayed dark all the way through the cloud, then it snugged in close to Nightlight to burn off its parasites, just like we did at Alpha C."

"Without damaging the cell field?" Lot countered.

"The cell field is self-repairing. I doubt the dust is."

Hailey's forlorn voice spilled into the silence. "How could it navigate without its hull cells? How could it *be* here?"

How indeed? They hadn't seen their nemesis since the swarm. How could it have anticipated them? Of all the destinations they might have chosen, how could it know they would come here, now? Urban felt cold, and a little nauseous as he thought about it, until Lot spoke, in a deadpan voice. "The courser isn't after Null Boundary. I think it's here because it learned the same lesson we did at Alpha C— where to look for rings."

Urban swore softly. "Sooth. We were lucky to find this ring. It's easy to believe the courser missed it, that it was waiting down close to the star, watching."

"So we pointed out the ring to it," Clemantine concluded. "While also managing to put ourselves in its path."

Hailey's voice broke in again, this time icy calm, as if she'd performed a personality wash. "I'm making guns. I'll bring Null Boundary around as soon as I can."

Nikko had been almost wordless since they'd broken from Null Boundary. Now he abandoned his long silence. "No. Whatever's going to happen, it will be long over by the time you get back. Don't risk the ship. Leave, with all the speed you can. We'll send our ghosts after you if it's possible, but don't wait."

"What about Lot?" she demanded, when the lightspeed delay expired.

"If I live, I'll be in cold sleep, Hailey. You can come back and get me when you know it's safe. Fifty years, a hundred years. It won't make any difference to me."

"That's what the ghosts say," she admitted.

"Then go," Clemantine urged her. "Run silent, and go."

Urban wanted to tell her the same thing, but he could not. Prickles of fear had grown in his throat and the words wouldn't come. Not that it mattered. His ghost was aboard Null Boundary, and Hailey already had his advice. Clemantine and Nikko had left their ghosts aboard too. They would take Null Boundary out of the system, and someday, if it seemed safe, they might return here, or go back to the archipelagoes.

But that ghost aboard Null Boundary had become someone else. It was no longer *him*. This version of Urban was only too aware of how thin its chances had just become.

Lot spoke softly. "Good-bye, Hailey."

"Good-bye, Lot. I'll love you forever."

Urban grimaced. He had to say something. "Shit," he gasped at last. "Guess it's time to kick in the NoFears."

The drop pod's DI pilot brought them to within a hundred meters of the ring. Then it separated the passenger capsule from the reef, so the instruments would have a stable platform.

The ring was neither spinning nor turning end over end. They explored its surface from the passenger capsule, moving on weak reaction jets. Radar soundings taken over a range of frequencies insisted it was a solid object, with no hollow spaces lying within. It still emitted no visible light.

The capsule settled within five meters of the ring's outer wall. As Lot emerged, he could see the ring in infrared, like the supporting arch of some gigantic bridge, viewed from above. Its featureless surface curved away on both sides.

Urban crawled out beside him. He took a long look at the structure. "Didn't spare much budget for architecture."

Lot felt oddly disappointed. "Yeah. There aren't any surface cells."

Urban nodded. "So it's not like the ships."

"Sooth."

But what was it? It looked blank, like the clay at the beginning of the world, capable of being molded into anything.

Now Clemantine and Nikko had made their way out. "I'll go first," Lot said.

Urban put a hand on his arm. "No, fury. *We'll* get a chance to start over somewhere else, while this will probably be your last shot. So let us do the scouting."

Lot started to protest, but the cult was a black boil under his skin, eating at his energy, chewing on his will. He was sick of fighting it, and too tired to argue. Besides, Urban was right. It was a coldly brutal assessment, but with the courser coming up on them, Lot knew it was unlikely he would ever leave this place. "Okay." He settled back against the hull. "I'll follow."

Urban stared across the five-meter gap, thinking, *That was too easy.* Then he punched a cartridge of robotic bugs from his belt and lobbed it toward the ring. The cartridge burst open on impact. The bugs broke free, to crawl over the ring's smooth surface, sending back reports of dormant molecules.

Urban sighed. Time was pressing. Before long, Null Boundary would be too far away to be reached by the drop pod's gateway. Urban wanted to have something to send back by then. So he crouched against the capsule, and then he jumped.

Clemantine gasped. Lot hissed. Nikko continued his silence.

Urban hit the ring's surface with more velocity than he cared for. His body resounded at the impact. Still, the hot zones on his gloves successfully connected with the artifact. He twisted awkwardly, getting his feet secure. Then he stood. "The surface is harder than Null Boundary's hull," he reported. "Not at all pliant. It feels completely inactive." He took a tentative step, his right boot ripping clear, then reconnecting. "It's not fighting me at all."

He looked around, then decided to check the ring's inside circumference. "Wait," Lot said, when Urban announced his plan. "I'm going with you." Then he jumped, before anyone could stop him.

The four of them tramped the ring for hours, exploring the surface but finding nothing to indicate the ring's function. The continuing rise in its surface temperature was the only sign that it was active at all. Urban was nearly ready to attribute that to the residual effects of some failed reaction, when a proximity alarm went off in the capsule, blaring over the radio with a squawk to wake a dormant ghost. "What—?" He turned, ready to tramp back toward the capsule as quickly as the rip and stick of his boots would allow.

"It's nothing," Clemantine called. Both she and the capsule were out of sight, over the ring's short horizon. "The capsule has drifted into the ring, that's all."

Urban scowled. "Its position was supposed to be stable."

"There must have been an aberration. Five meters over three hours isn't much."

"It's measurable," Urban insisted, his breath puffing as he tramped toward the capsule and Clemantine. "The instruments would have shown a drift of that magnitude, but I didn't detect it at all. Something's changed."

He crested the ring's horizon, and now he could see her, still a hundred yards away. She stood beside the capsule, which rested against the ring's outer edge. Nikko approached from the opposite direction.

"Where's Lot?" Urban asked, fear cutting a saw-toothed path through his gut.

"I'm here." Lot's voice answered him. "Look across the ring."

Urban turned, to see him standing on the opposite side, waving his arm in wide arcs. He looked very small. "You shouldn't be so far away."

"Feel the deck," Lot said. "Is it more pliant than it was before?"

Nikko answered him. "It is. It's easier for me to grip it now."

"And the temperature's still rising," Clemantine added.

Using his atrium, Urban ordered the pod DI to retrieve the reef and reconnect it with the capsule, which was running low on fuel. Then he had it repeat the original radar soundings. Even with the distortion generated by the activities of the reef, it was easy to see that things had changed. The ring's interior no longer reflected as a solid. Now, thin honeycombs were revealed below the surface.

"Recheck the ring diameter," Nikko said.

The DI gave its report: The outer diameter had expanded by more than ten meters. So the passenger capsule had not drifted from its position; it had simply been overrun.

"We should retreat," Clemantine said. "Wait to see what it does."

Urban wanted to agree, but he knew Lot wouldn't go for it. "Why don't you and Nikko get back on the pod. I'll try to tap one of the hollows."

"The deck is still getting softer," Lot said, a taut anticipation in his voice. "Or anyway, it's shifting."

Urban looked down, startled by a sucking sensation at his feet. Lot was right. The ring's surface had become as pliant as Null Boundary's hull. He watched as it retracted beneath his feet, pulling him down into a hollow, first a half inch, then a full inch deep. Viscous tissue lapped into the depression, flowing over his boots.

He stepped aside, but where his foot came down the deck sank away. The hull flowed in around his ankle, like a syrup under light gravity. Clemantine shouted something he could not understand. Then she repeated it: "Get back to the pod!"

She was closest. Urban was still a hundred yards away, and now the goo was up to his calves. He tried to pull one leg free but only succeeded in driving himself deeper into the muck. "Don't move!" he shouted. "Don't try to move. There's nothing to use for leverage. You'll only sink deeper."

"I'm sinking deeper anyway," Clemantine said.

She was calf-deep in it too. Urban told her: "Call the pod. Let it pull you out."

The vehicle was already moving. Who was controlling it now? *Nikko*. Urban could see him beyond Clemantine. His long, prehensile toes were locked in the sucking goo, but he showed no sign of panic. His gaze was fixed on the pod as it drifted toward Clemantine. She raised her arms to meet it.

Urban felt something slip loose beneath him. The stop-jerk progress of his descent was over. Something had given way, and now he was being drawn inward with a steady pressure, at least an inch every few seconds, up to his hips now. "Nikko, *hurry*!" The shout was out before he could summon another dose of NoFears. By the Unknown God. His heart was trying to break free of his chest as Clemantine caught the edge of the open hatch in both her hands. "Back it off!" she growled, as if through gritted teeth.

The pod hovered. Ripples flowed in the deck, where exhaust feathered the semiliquid tissue. Then the pod rose, and Clemantine with it, her calves clearing the quagmire, then the silvered curve of her ankles and finally her booted feet. In the moment that her toes popped free, Urban gasped for breath, unaware that he'd been holding it. The goo was past his waist.

Now the pod glissaded above the surface of the ring, sweeping toward him while Clemantine scrambled into the hatch. Urban twisted in the quagmire, forgetting his resolve to stay quiet, to stay calm. "Where's Lot?" he screamed. "Fury? Where are you?"

The pod floated over his head. Clemantine braced herself in the hatch. She leaned down, her hands held out to him. "Grab my hands, Urban. Come on. I'll pull you free."

He raised his arms. He lunged toward her. Big mistake. He felt himself slide down to his chest, to his armpits. Shit.

She caught his hands anyway. He felt a flush of heat in his palms as her gloves bonded to his. "Hold on," she grunted. "You're coming out . . . now . . . now. . . ."

He could feel pressure on his arms, but it was an exercise, nothing more. He slipped down to his hooded chin. "Where's Lot?" he screamed at her.

"He's next." She did not relax her grip.

"Get him now! Get him *now*!" He sent a signal to his gloves that forced them to decouple.

"*Urban!*" she shouted, as he dropped away from her panicked eyes. The ring tissue lapped up around his head. His elbows were caught in it. Clemantine was making frantic efforts to reach him, but he evaded her. "It's too late for me!" he screamed at her. "Get Lot! Get him now."

She froze, her gaze locked beyond him. "*Urban.*"

"Go," he told her. "Go."

And the pod glided away over his head in austere silence. Nikko's voice still reached him over the radio: "I can't see Lot anymore."

I can't see shit, Urban thought, as the quagmire rolled over his visor. He felt like he'd been slapped into a body bag, or dropped back into the vent tube aboard the dark courser, heinous pressure squeezing his whole body. He tried digging his hands into the tissue, but it went soft beneath his fingers, allowing him no grip. Shit, shit, shit. Nothing to grip and nothing to hold on to and no telling how soon he'd die.

So at least they had found a way inside.

Shit.

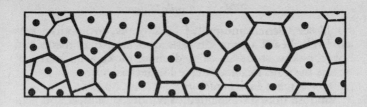

Chapter
35

Lot was not immune to terror as the deck softened beneath his boots, yet he did not resist or cry out. Here was one more chance for him. The game was not ended; not just yet. He might still deny the rot of his own congealed programming.

The cult concurred. It crouched inside him like a separate mind, a self-aware beast absolutely desperate to reproduce, weighing the odds of success in this new twist and finding them better than any other prospect.

So Lot did not resist. He did not cry out. Terror was unavoidable, but he did not wish for a rescue.

The ring tissue understood. Soft and secret, it flowed over his ankles. Gentle tug. Tug. As if asking him to conspire.

"Don't move!" Urban was screaming. *"Don't try to move. You'll only sink deeper."*

Lot resolved to hurry the process. He made his legs fold, so that he fell to his knees. The deck sank farther to receive him; the tissue flowed over his thighs like heavy strands of smooth muscle. He placed his gloved hands upon it. *As they say,* he thought with a sardonic smile, *Take me.* The deck complied and he felt himself drawn deeper.

Death or change, whatever it was to be, it was coming fast enough now to satisfy him.

Across the empty span of the ring's inner diameter, he

could see Clemantine pulled free by the pod and he was glad. He heard Urban's frantic cries and that made him sorry. Nikko stood in calm decline, looking back at Lot across the gulf. His gaze made Lot feel ashamed.

This is what I was made for.

Smooth muscles extended over Lot's shoulders and gently around his throat so that he had to strain just a little to breathe. The skin suit hardened to protect him from the pressure, while Nikko's voice cut off the panicked debate running between Urban and Clemantine: "I can't see Lot anymore."

Lot received these words with a mixture of horror and relief. Fear flashed cold across his skin, but at the same time he felt a keen sense of victory. He wanted to *know*. He wanted this chance, whatever it might mean.

The ring tissue touched his hood. He tipped his head back in an archaic reaction—as if there might be air to breathe if only he could keep his lips above the surface— and discovered Clemantine a few feet overhead, ensconced in the pod and looking down at him. Her sudden presence startled him. "Go on," he told her roughly, forcing the words past the constricting pressure on his throat. "Don't help me."

"Nikko," Clemantine said, leaning far out of the open hatch. "Take control of the pod. I'm going with him."

Lot squirmed as her meaning wormed its way into his brain. "No!" His protest came too late. Clemantine dived, her legs snapping, her arms an arrow point so that she drove herself into the consuming tissue of the ring, just as Lot slipped under.

Take a breath.

He forced air past the pressure on his throat and chest. It was dark here. Tissue flowed against his visor and he could not see, but the suit still nourished him. Clemantine's voice still spoke through the radio, audible even over the terrified pounding of his heart. "Lot," she asked, her voice calm, and so clear he knew she had to be using an atrial channel, "are you all right?"

"So far," he grunted, forcing each word. "You?"

"Yes."

He couldn't see her or feel her. He wondered how far away she was and what lay ahead of them. How long before their skin suits would collapse from the pressure, or dissolve? "Clemantine . . . you shouldn't . . . have done that."

She snorted. "Why not? All I'm risking is a ghost. We came here to investigate this thing, didn't we?"

"Sooth."

"And I'm leaving a relay line of robotic bugs. My ghost could still find its way back."

"You think the . . . bugs will survive?"

"I don't know."

Lot didn't think he could feel any more afraid. "The pressure's really hell," he whispered.

Each breath was becoming a more laborious exercise, when suddenly heat erupted all across his skin.

"That's metabolic heat," Clemantine assured him. "Our Makers are battling whatever devices inhabit this brew."

Lot could feel something thick and wet oozing across his cheek. He bit down hard on an urge to scream. "I don't . . . think our Makers . . . are winning."

Clemantine did not reply.

"Clemantine? Clemantine!"

Her sudden silence brought him to a new peak of terror—his mind's capacity for fear seemed far greater than what his body could endure. So his medical Makers kicked in, calming him. Or was it something else? "Clemantine," he called again, as a sticky lethargy invaded his senses. Hollow exhaustion seeped into all his muscles. His awareness did not collapse, and yet he sensed that more time passed than he could account for. Hours. He dreamed his life and all the while his open eyes looked out on darkness.

Sometime in that undefined age true awareness stirred in him again. *Take a breath.* Now it was easy. He could freely move his arms and legs. Darkness still surrounded him, but the terrible pressure was gone. His left foot kicked something solid. He drew that foot cautiously back.

"Clemantine?" He called her name again, tentatively, startled at the weak rasp of his voice. "Urban? Nikko . . . ?"

He got no answer. Alive or dead or somnolent: he had no way to tell. So he spoke to his suit instead, and was relieved to find it could still respond. At his request the suit's surface lit with a soft white glow.

The light fell upon the crinkled white walls of a narrow cavern, formed from the merger of several irregular clefts and passages. Tiny loops and ridges patterned the surface, so that it looked like coral, or the marrow walls of large bones. Narrow, branching channels perforated the delicate mesh, none wider than his fist.

The ring had been solid when they first surveyed it, so this cavity could be no more than several hours old.

He touched the wall with a gloved hand, half expecting the lacy surface to crumble beneath the pressure of his fingers. That didn't happen. Still, he could feel a tremor running through it, and he wondered if the ring was still expanding.

It had been a mistake to call that first ring at Alpha C an artifact. Naming it had channeled their thinking. They had come here expecting dumb structure, or at most, structure enlightened by ghosts. They had never paused to consider that the ring itself might be the organism they hunted. Lot's stomach knotted at the possibility, but there was no going back now.

His suit DI informed him the cavern was pressurized, with an atmosphere that replicated the air within his suit. He didn't think it a coincidence.

The suit also alerted him to the presence of devices in the air. Nanotech. The alien Makers were equally common inside his suit, so it took only a little argument to convince the DI that he would lose nothing by opening his hood.

The air that washed his sensory tears was warm and quite thick with an empty humidity. Lot moved his head back and forth, but he could get no trace of any human presence beside his own.

"Clemantine?" he called softly, though he was fairly sure she would not have opened her suit. His voice echoed in the darkness of the adjoining tunnels. He called her again, louder this time: "Clemantine!" And then with less confidence: "Nikko?"

He got a response, though not the one he'd looked for. Motion drew his eye to the farside of the chamber. Wriggling into sight from one of the little channels that riddled the walls was a pale white tentacle with a flattened, spatulate tip. It was the width of his finger, and it wove through the air, looking like a worm questing after dirt. Memories stirred in his mind, of Hafaz colony, and of the tendrils that bound the gnomes, and he knew these were all of the same kind, the same clade. He watched the worm's approach with dread fascination, unable to turn away, while it continued to emerge from the hole. Now it was as long as his body. The amplitude of its motion narrowed to a neat sine wave centered on his position. Every instinct in his system screamed at him to flee. Yet he held himself still. He wanted to know if the cult lived here.

His curiosity spilled onto the air, mingled with his fear. Was the tentacle a discrete organism? Or the appendage of something greater? Or both? The distinctions he'd learned in his own life might have no meaning here. If the ring was an organism, this questing tentacle might be an organ in its gut—even a temporary organ—or perhaps a sentient one.

The tentacle wormed to within a foot of Lot's face. He held himself still as it danced before him, though he breathed in short, shallow snatches. He could taste something new on the air, a foreign echo of his own curiosity. Had this thing already learned his biochemistry? Its surface glistened like a continuous skin of sensory tears.

Now the tentacle's waving motions slowed, then ceased. It locked on his position, as if cued by the density of charismata leaking from him. His emotions glinted on the air: fear and hope and his own original curiosity.

The spatulate tip quivered in tiny, tight vibrations, moving closer until it was millimeters from his face. His skin tingled with the nearness of it. Sweat gathered on his cheeks but he did not retreat, even when it touched his face.

It was only a whisper of contact. The tentacle immediately withdrew. But it must have planted a molecular trigger against the sticky surface of his sensory tears, because Lot felt the cult flare inside him: he cried out, as dark need and a sense of dreadful isolation burned through him. Of all things, the cult demanded he must not be alone, and yet he was. So alone he would drown in it. Ah god, he would die of it. They had all turned away from him. Why had he let them do it?

His charismata flooded the air, sparkling silver in his sensorium, the code of his desire, a need for Communion worse than any other hunger. He could not touch what he needed. "Ah, please," he begged, as self-hatred flared. He had been a fool. He had let the Silkens dupe him. He should never have left the city. He should never have left Deception Well. He had even let Clemantine engineer her independence. Why? To buy this isolation? It was perverted! Why had he let the Silkens convince him that his gift was wrong?

Another tentacle emerged from another hole. This one trailed tiny white filaments from its spatulate tip that drifted like sea grass in the absence of gravity. With it came a new flood of charismata: Lot felt his own desire circling back to him, but stripped of its anguish, bearing the promise of a softer, vaster awareness that stroked his sensory tears in pops and crackles of blazing Communion. He groaned, unable to endure the fleeting separations.

The new worm approached the first one and they touched. Then it turned toward Lot, startling him with the sight of its eyes, nestled in the bed of filaments. Not human eyes, like Hafaz colony. These were too large, too round; the iris was pink. The eyes blinked: two membranes moving together from either side. A bead of moisture popped off. It drifted toward him, to stick against his sensory tears.

At first Lot felt only a flush of heat, but gradually his senses heightened. He heard stirrings of sentience all around him, tiny motives, whispering unintelligible phrases that he somehow understood to be a song of ecstatic union.

"Lot!"

The tinny sound of Clemantine's voice issuing from the radio in his hood shattered the half-heard chorus. "Clemantine?" He strained to peer up the connecting clefts, hardly able to believe she still existed in his world. "Clemantine!" His shout echoed weirdly, while the walls shimmered and a sweetness filled the air.

If she was here, then it was not too late. He could have her again. All of her this time; for the first time. He could finally make it right, and she would understand.

"Lot?" Her answering cry reached him through the open air, though her voice was distant.

"I'm here!" he called to her. "In a cavern."

"This whole place is made of caverns! And cracks and

blind alleys—it's like crawling through a fault line." Her words blurred by echoes. "Try following my voice, Lot. Help me find you."

The worm contemplated him with its two round eyes. "I don't think I should move," Lot shouted. "There's . . . a thing that lives here. It's watching me. Maybe you should hurry."

This plea had its desired effect. Fear rode in the rising timbre of her voice. "You stay away from it! You hear me? Goddamn it. Why do these things find you? *I* haven't seen anything alive here. So why you?"

It was what he'd been made for.

A whisper of motion caused him to glance around. For a moment he thought the walls boiled, for at dozens of points around the cavern more worms emerged from the ubiquitous perforations, their tips wriggling obscenely, some with eyes and a dress of filaments like slender versions of Hafaz colony, but most naked and blind, glistening wet. They seemed to sample the air. Or flavor it? Suddenly the cloying harmony of the cult was everywhere, viscous as water, flowing over him, blurring his individuality.

Now two worms left their holes completely. He could not tell anymore if they were the original pair. Each trailed a rootlike anchor, and as Lot watched, the twin tangles reached for one another, melding into a knot of tissue smoothed together by some active nanomech. A third and then a fourth joined the conglomeration while the gentle fist of the cult kneaded at Lot's hybrid neural system. Round, pink eyes blinked at him. He could feel ecstatic snatches of a deep awareness, a familiar persona, flavored like the persona of his father, Jupiter, but heavier, vast in time, strong, strong, strong.

The buzz of a camera bee snapped his attention back to Clemantine. "Lot, get out of there!" she screamed from somewhere not so far away now. The panic in her voice was unaccompanied by any corresponding charismata, so it failed to move him. He remembered again how she had engineered her independence, forcing him to live alone. So. She would be here soon.

Now the worms filled the cavern with a loose vinework of enwrapping tentacles that intersected at nodes of fused tissue. Dense clusters of filaments migrated to the nodes. Some of these stretched toward Lot, extending to touch his gloved hand, his sleeve. Their moist tips lapped at his sensory tears.

His eyes widened in belated recognition. He had seen this even before Hafaz colony, in the Well, when the organ of the cult reached out to him. Then, Urban had pulled him back. Now, there was no one to interfere.

He felt a brief, stinging pain as the filaments penetrated his sensory tears, pushing deep into the mucosal layer, and then a numb pressure as they slipped into his body, sliding along the nerve pathways all the way to his brain. Other filaments slid down the front of his suit. Clemantine screamed from somewhere close by—his name, and a three-word prayer to a god she didn't believe in.

Lot couldn't see her, but he could feel her presence now, perceiving it with more sharpness, more intensity than he had ever known before. It was making him hard. "It's all right," he told her. It was what he'd been made for.

"It's not! Get out of there! Get yourself out of there!"

Out of where? Lot felt himself present here, at this discrete location. At the same time, he was spread wide in time and in position. He could see Urban and Nikko as separate animals crawling the maze of caverns. Nikko's anger steamed in puffs of helpless emotion. By contrast, Urban was dark and unreal, a monster from deep within an evil dream. Untouchable.

Lot felt the influence of the Well stir inside him. That ecology would be integrated here too, enfolded by the cult. He couldn't guess anymore what that might mean.

Clemantine appeared beyond the cage of tentacles. Her hood was off. The iris tattoos on her ears glinted gold. Her fury poured into him as she grabbed at one of the worms. It looked fragile, as if it might snap in her hand, but when she touched it, her glove slid along its moist skin, then popped free. She stared in shock at her gel-coated palm.

"Lot!" she screamed at him. "Come to me. Now."

Her desire ate at his heart, but the cult owned him now. He kicked at the encaging worms. "You come here to me."

An animalish scream of frustration ripped from her throat; at the same time she lunged toward him, wedging her elbows behind the first layer of the wormy mesh, driving herself into the tangle.

Lot watched her frantic progress with a profound detachment, feeling himself sinking into a deep, warm, luminous sea. A filament probed at the corner of his mouth, following the film of moisture inward. Others explored his ears, his nose. He felt brief discomfort as one slid along the white of his eye, into his skull. Within his suit, dozens of other filaments moved, gliding against his skin, exploring his anus and the head of his member.

"Come here to me," he whispered again to Clemantine, though his words were malformed now by the filaments trailing from his mouth.

He pondered the strange fact that he wasn't choking, and he didn't itch and he didn't feel pain, but the discrepancy failed to trouble him.

He was sinking into a warm, luminous sea, and he prayed that Clemantine would reach him while he still had the will to seize her and take her down with him.

"Lot!" Clemantine screamed, as she wriggled through the slimy maze of white eels. "You stop it! You shit. Wake up. Look at me. Don't let them get inside you. Goddamn you, Lot. Fight them!" Each sentence separated by a tearing rasp of air through her raw throat.

This had happened before. She had not seen it herself, but Urban had told her about it. In the Well, Lot had almost succumbed to the mature organ of the cult—white filaments sinking into his body, pulling his organization outward. How could the same thing exist here, so far from the Well?

She jammed her shoulders through another gap, her breasts crushed as she forced her body past it, the skin suit hardening in a valiant effort to protect her.

Grabbing the next frozen eel she risked a glance at Lot. God, was he dissolving? Thinning from the inside out. His skin suit looked too big, and it trembled with a vibrant motion. His cheeks were sunken and pale, every sensory tear a bed of filaments. The bones of his face—starkly outlined—seemed thin, too fragile. His eyes were gone, the sockets

filled with hundreds of filaments twisted together like ca-
bles. His mouth and nose were wired too. He could not
speak. How could he breathe? "*Lot!*" she roared, all her
panic, all her fear exploding in that single syllable as she
kicked her way into the center of the cage. "*Lot.*"

He could not hear her; filaments plugged his ears. And
yet, as she hovered beside him, her whole body slick with
gel, she saw his hand twitch, and rise, moving toward her,
his palm open, upturned to her in invitation. She felt his
love all around her, as she had felt it when the cult parasite
inhabited her brain, only now it was thicker, more potent
than ever before. "Ah, god, Lot."

She put a hand around the filaments that burrowed into
his eye. She pulled on them, gently at first, then with brutal
fury, wrapping her legs and an arm around the sticky cage
bars to get leverage. The cable would not budge. She
sobbed and cursed and yanked at the abomination.

His hand touched her thigh. She froze, staring down at
it. The fabric of his skin suit was still intact. His hand
moved within its glove, holding on to her, the fingers tight-
ening as if he could stop his own slide into dissolution. His
thinning leg kicked out. It struck a cage bar, and his body
flopped over.

"*Lot.*" Was it already too late? His other hand reached
toward her. She caught it. She brought it to her cheek. He
stroked her skin with tender fingers. The glove felt sticky. It
stung where he touched. Gently, she guided his hand away.
That's when the pain made itself apparent. Her cheek felt
as if sharp hooks had sunk into it at a hundred places.

She wrenched away, and drops of blood shot off into the
air. Her cheek writhed. She pinched at it, and broken bits of
wriggling filament came away in her fingers. Her breathing
was a panicked rattle, just on the edge of a scream. She
backed against the eel mesh, watching Lot's hand drift with
a drowned man's grace through the bloodied air. Filaments
wormed up through the fabric of his glove, growing toward
her like roots in a time-lapse recording.

She began to compose a ghost to send back through the
relay of robotic bugs she had left to mark her trail. Their
steady pulse still beat in her sensorium, assuring her a reli-
able link to the pod.

Nikko, she whispered. *Urban, can you hear me?

No answer. The filaments touched her cheek again in stinging contact. She thought she heard Lot whispering inside her mind *You come to me*.

She closed her eyes. Tears leached out as her ghost leaped away. "All right," she whispered. "But only for a little while. Just a little while." She went to him, and his arms opened in a sinewy embrace.

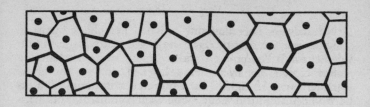

Chapter 36

Urban was first out. Five versions of his ghost uploaded to the pod, where they were relayed to distant Null Boundary. The first four experienced nothing but endless fractured spaces walled in bone. The last one had felt his body taken apart.

Whatever the artifact was, it knew everything about him now. It could rebuild him. It could change him into something like Lot. He sat cross-legged on a white data path in the library, considering this possibility while Hailey absorbed his memories.

Finally, she turned from the open window and looked at him, a haunted expression on her sculpted face. "How many times has this happened before?" she asked him. "In how many places?"

Sooth. There might be trillions, quadrillions of rings. Over a period of thirty million years. . . . "Hundreds of times, at least. Think how many species might have been drawn in."

Nikko winked into existence between them. "What version are you?" Urban asked.

"The last that will get out."

Urban had a sudden vision of perverted ghosts uploading to Null Boundary and occupying the cardinals. "We should change the access codes."

"Clemantine isn't here yet."

"Maybe she can't get out."

"Wait a little more," Nikko urged, while exchanging memories with Urban and Hailey.

Hailey was the first to lay her conclusions down. "We'll have to destroy the artifact. We have no choice."

Urban nodded, though he had no idea how that might be done. Still, he doubled himself, sending one version to develop a course that would bring them on a years-long loop back to Nightlight, pushing to its limit the power of the reef. "Clemantine's here," he announced.

He knew it a moment before she manifested behind Nikko. She stood on the data path, her shoulders heaving in a simulacrum of physical strain. Her hood was off and her cheek was bloodied. She said nothing, only flicked a hand at a hovering angel, opening a window so that her recollections could play while her ghost repaired itself.

When the scene was done, Urban had to do some fast editing just to keep a note of rationality in his voice. "I don't care what it takes. We have to go back. We have to destroy the artifact, even if it means we have to ram it." He looked at Nikko, the only one among them who had not left a copy in the islands.

For a moment Nikko's ghost seemed frozen, his kisheer perfectly still upon his shoulders. Then: "I would agree with you," he said softly, "but the ring's out of our reach now. Our velocity is too high. It would take us years to beat our way back. Nothing will be the same then. Be sure of that."

"We have to try it anyway. We have to go back."

"Maybe not," Clemantine said. Urban turned to her, ready to argue, but she held up a hand to quiet him. "If we're lucky, the courser may do the job for us."

Urban had forgotten the courser. He copied his ghost again and slipped off into the cardinals. Now he could feel the hard press of Nightlight's radiation against the bow and the tremulous pull of the reef. He dropped hours of observations into his consciousness, so that he could follow the progress of the courser on its climb up from Nightlight. A navigation submind extrapolated its heading.

He dropped back into the library, merging with his first. "It still looks like it's on an intercept course. Maybe you're right. Maybe it will treat this artifact like the one at Alpha C."

• • •

Days passed. Hailey struggled to slow Null Boundary without burning out the reef, determined to keep them within range of the pod's signal for as long as possible. The courser drew nearer to the silent ring. Urban kept two telescopes fixed on its faint and featureless point of light, while he watched the ring through the pod's cameras. That signal was already weak and intermittent, while their distance continued to grow by thousands of kilometers every second.

Still, it was a focused transmission, and if they were lucky, the courser would not detect it. Urban wanted the pod to survive at least a few seconds longer than the ring. Without the pod's observations, they might never know for sure if the ring had been destroyed.

The courser had made almost half the distance between Nightlight and the ring, when the ring began to change. Urban sat cross-legged on a data path, staring at a frustratingly low-resolution image gleaned from the pod's latest transmission. The quality was so poor it was impossible to know for sure what he was seeing, and yet he had no doubt he understood it. The white glow was unarguable: Philosopher cells were rising through the ring's malleable tissue.

"That was gleaned from Lot," Urban said. "I know it was." He twisted around, to look at Clemantine standing behind him on the library's data path. "Everything he knew is part of it now, and he understood the hull cells better than anyone."

Clemantine stared past him, her expression grim, the gold iris tattoos on her ears gleaming with a sourceless light. She bit her lip then, and turned away. It was a movement done in silence, and still it startled Urban badly. He rose. "Are you all right?"

She waved him away. "Oh sooth. Edit, edit. I am fine. Fine forever. He's just one more gone, that's all. Not the first. Not by a long way. I've had practice at this, you know."

Urban felt a strange numb sense then. He didn't know how to treat it. It felt as if a submind were operating just behind his conscious mind, neatening things up. Had he set up such a utility? He couldn't remember, and the doubt panicked him.

Clemantine caught it. "Urban?"

She was in his face, her concern snagging some vulnerable thread that pulled loose, spilling unpleasant things. "I don't want to talk about him!" Urban shouted. "Not like that. Edit it, Clemantine, because I'm not going to face it."

Her lips parted slightly. She nodded. "So fuck the Unknown God, anyway."

"Sooth." His persona was leveling out again. "He was right about it all. His ancestors were made in a place like that, weren't they?"

"I'd guess so." She folded her muscular legs, to sit two feet above the data path.

"Everything he knew is part of the ring, now."

"We have to assume it."

They heard something then, in radio frequencies. Faint. Barely detectable. Urban cocked his head. "Where is that from?" A submind brought the answer: It was from the pod. "Not voice. *Ah crap!* It's Chenzeme. The pod's been colonized? No, no. It's just forwarding some transmission from the ring."

"That *is* Chenzeme," Clemantine whispered. "Just like the warships."

"Sooth. They're all Chenzeme."

"Yes, but it's not that simple. Lot didn't think so anyway. Remember the artifact at Alpha C? The courser spent its reef to destroy it. It risked losing us. The cult and the warships, they are *not* the same thing."

"Not on the same side," Urban growled. "We are caught in an unending civil war between the shipbuilders and the cultists, but they are *all* Chenzeme."

She looked at him archly. "The ships, the ring, and Lot?"

"Hell."

"It's calling to the courser," Hailey said.

Urban looked up, to find her standing at his side. "Are you linked to the bridge?"

"Sooth. That is a greeting. It's one Lot knew."

"*Shit.*" Urban hunched over, feeling as if his ghost would split in two. "I don't want to talk about Lot anymore."

Clemantine ignored him. "Lot's seducing the courser. He likes to do it. He'll try to fuck it, the same way we spread ourselves for the dark courser."

"Shut up!" Urban shouted. His fingers dug into the data paths; a hundred files exploded open around him. "Don't talk about him like that! He's dead. He's gone. And it is not his fault!" Then he was on his feet, fists slamming into files that collapsed under his assault, while an angel hovered at his shoulder. His ghost-legs bent again. He collapsed, his forehead pressed against the gleaming white path. "Oh crap," he muttered. "Oh shit." He felt as if a worm were eating out his insides.

He stood in quiet composure, looking down on his weeping ghost. Nikko was there with him. They were discussing a new fact just reported by the pod: The courser had begun to slow.

"It's a crusade of inclusion," Hailey was saying. "The cult seeks to make all things part of an ecstatic whole. Lot knows enough about the coursers that he might be able to make it work, even on them. And he has the Well influence. That will be a new factor here. It could help him integrate the opposing systems."

Urban stared at his weeping ghost, wondering how long it would stay there. No one else seemed to see it.

His glance cut to Hailey. "Don't talk about him like that. Lot's not alive in there."

She raised her chin, and she looked away. A strange movement. "He might be," she said softly.

Oh shit, oh crap. The ghost on the floor crumbled: a strange, jerking heap of dark matter.

He might be alive.

"I want to go back," Urban said. Hailey still wouldn't look at him. The distraught ghost had vanished. Nikko stood now in the spot it had been.

Hailey said, "The pod is still there, Urban. We could ghost."

"I thought we had gone beyond range."

"Beyond the pod's range, yes. It doesn't have the power to cast a coherent signal this far, but Null Boundary does."

Huh. Urban spent a moment chewing over the possibilities. The pod still had an active reef. It had a large collection of Makers. Not much substrate. Then he frowned. "What good will it do us to ghost? The ring wiped our defensive Makers. It'll wipe any Makers in the pod's arsenal too."

Hailey's kisheer snapped in a single sharp ripple. She looked from Clemantine to Nikko, but not at Urban. The weeping ghost was gone, and Nikko wasn't standing there anymore. "We don't have to attack the ring," Hailey told them. "We could go after the courser instead."

Urban sat cross-legged, his chin propped in his hand, thinking about Hailey's suggestion, careful not to think of other things. "Why hit the courser? It's on our side now. We want it to fry the ring."

"Sooth," Hailey said, her voice soft and hesitant. "But it won't do that if it's been . . . seduced."

It's not Lot, Urban told himself. *Not really.*

Hailey crouched at his side, her hand on his shoulder. She spoke softly into his ear, obviously repeating herself, though he didn't remember hearing this before. "Urban, listen to me. I've studied records of the Makers evolved during the nanowar in Null Boundary's hull. I've adapted several of them, working in some of the Well influence. Urban, don't worry. The Chenzeme won't take us so easily again."

Hailey wanted to hijack the courser and force it to destroy the ring. Urban tried to get used to the idea, while time without meaning ran past. The pod detected a radio signal from the courser, then a burst of dust from the ring. Urban watched it all in mounting frustration. Lot had played this game before; he knew the rules.

The courser continued to slow its frantic charge.

Now the ring was changing again. Urban stared at each infrequent, low-res image, as if he could call out more detail by will alone.

The ring was closing into a spindle. This was not just an

effect of the pod's low-angle view. The ring really was taking the shape of a courser, its surface covered in philosopher cells.

Time to go.

Urban let his ghost double, then he looked back on himself. Already he'd become someone else, because *he was going*. That other version of himself would be staying here.

"Ready?" Nikko asked.

Clemantine kissed him, a ghost-touch. "The artifact is a courser now, and Lot knows his way back to the islands. Remember that."

"Sooth."

Hailey's fingers brushed his hand. She was the architect of their scheme to hijack the courser. Urban gave her a brief half-smile, feeling her cool and complex charismata through the neural bridge that she had knitted to his persona. She'd worked long and hard to improve the structure of the bridge. Now it was far more than the virtual link he had made long ago to help them understand the philosopher cells. Hailey had grown it into something more subtle and adaptive, with an intelligence of its own. If it survived the transfer to the courser, it would be translated at last into an organic entity, armed with all they knew of defensive Makers.

"Thank you for doing this," she said.

"Hey. Who better?"

Hailey smiled. Urban felt warped under her gaze, a hardassed pirate who had never learned to care quite enough. He had left his old man at Deception Well and he'd left Deneb in the islands, and now he was going to make an alliance with the hated Chenzeme, to try to slaughter the last remnants of the man who, for centuries, had been like his brother.

Who better? Clemantine couldn't do it. She hated the Chenzeme too much to ever lie down with them again. Nikko's scars were just as deep. Hailey was best with the philosopher cells, and she might have been the candidate, but the prospect of living apart from anything human worked on her with paralytic terror.

Urban glanced at his ghost standing uncomfortably on the side. He caught its jealous eye.

Who better?

Nikko's ghost went with him to the pod. They found the reef to be healthy; the power was good. The camera images that fed into their sensoriums were crystal clear. They watched the courser slide through the dust field laid down days before by the artifact. It called again in radio frequencies and the artifact responded, looking exactly like a courser itself now, though a gigantic one.

Urban had no trouble understanding the exchange. The bridge smoothly translated the greeting/challenge:

> **<synthesis>**
> self-other exchange
>
> > **(make peace)**
> > *compatible*

"He's gotten better," Nikko said. "It wasn't this easy for us that first time."

"It's not his fault."

The pod stood off, dark and quiet, while the behemoths approached one another. The artifact dwarfed the courser, which in turn would have dwarfed Null Boundary. At least Null Boundary was safely away.

Nikko and Urban began their assault while kilometers of empty space still hung between the two alien ships. From a tiny accelerator grown from the mass of the pod, wild cell dust compressed into packets was shot at the courser. It would hit in splashes no more than two or three cells wide. Those two or three cells would dissolve—just a little damage that would likely go unnoticed in the mating frenzy of the cell field.

Needles were launched behind the dust. Smooth and frictionless, they homed on the dead cells, diving deep into the courser's underlying tissue. Each one would deploy a brake at a different depth, and with any luck, at least one would find a survivable substrate where a cardinal nanosite might be constructed.

Like the cardinals within Null Boundary's tissue, each site would be a tiny processing node where Urban's ghost could lodge; a fortress in enemy territory, protected from the courser's defenses by an army of Hailey's assault Makers.

Urban waited in pensive silence, toying with his time sense while the courser slid closer, taking a position alongside the gigantic artifact.

They had no way to test the success of their invasion except to send a ghost. Enough time had passed. Either the cardinals were ready to receive him, or they would never be ready. "I'm going," Urban said.

Nikko was an unseen mass at his side. "Luck with it."

The mating process had begun. Urban watched dust fall from the courser onto the artifact. Then he launched his ghost.

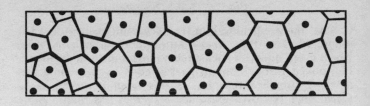

Chapter
37

Existence.

As Urban manifested within a cardinal, he was struck with a muted sense of surprise that he still continued at all. He had become a parasite within the body of the courser. Hailey's bridge surrounded him, though it was no longer virtual. It had been translated into a physical entity, busily growing outward from the cardinal, toward the courser's hull. The bridge was an extension of himself, and all along this expanding length, microscopic armies stood arrayed against him.

Panic seized him as he felt the sting of this siege, but that calmed quickly—he would not be aware of this at all if Hailey's defenses were failing. Her own armies formed a boiling defensive wall against the Chenzeme attackers, pushing them back from a thin lane of tissue where the bridge grew, in its relentless expansion toward the courser's philosopher cells. Urban's awareness slid forward into this new space, his horizon always a scorching battle line. Where was the Well influence? An armistice seemed a distant dream.

Contact.

The bridge found the philosopher cells. It linked to them, and Urban's perceptions expanded with dizzying abruptness. Machine-sharp cell-talk rolled over him in an epochal flood, opening him to a sense of vastness. He felt immersed in a deep, heavy atmosphere, Jovian in scale, where every molecule measured some moment of existence. He looked through them, gazing eons back in time; his memory stretched that far. *Is this what it means to be Chenzeme?* His own existence wavered, less than a mote against this scale.

Then he saw the artifact, and hatred narrowed his horizons.

Filtered through Chenzeme senses, the artifact was a pointillistic image of great clarity. Urban tasted its strangeness. He became a conduit for the debate raging among the courser's hull cells—**Caution/Go**, followed by an echo of eager desire—but something intruded, upsetting the unanimous waveform. A negative voice, insisting on **<wrongness>**.

With a start, Urban realized this voice was his . . . yet it had not come from him. With rising excitement he guessed at the truth: More than one copy of his ghost existed, successfully ensconced in its own cardinal fortress.

Hailey! he thought with fierce joy. *My triumphant general.*

Though he sought the other voices through the cell field, they found him first, drawing him into a powerful alliance, bridged by alien cells.

Dust from the artifact fell over the courser's hull. It brought a wave of unexpected sensation: desire without goals, loneliness, promise. Urban could identify these feelings, but to the philosopher cells they were dangerous intrusions into the fixed script of a mating. Doubt spiked within the machine-sharp debate. The dust was dissected in a search for meaningful history, but there was no history in it, only alien emotions the cells could not understand.

Urban understood it too well. This was Lot's signature: remote, and stinking of the cult, but utterly real. Horror crept over him as he realized Hailey had been right. Lot *was* alive. The knowledge destabilized his alliance with the other ghosts, bringing it to the verge of panicked collapse. *"Lot!"*

The cry sprang helplessly from the bridge, but doubt followed quickly after it. Lot could not be alive, not in the same way he had been before. Urban carried Clemantine's memory: he had seen the filaments of the cult at work. So Lot was gone, and this echo of his presence still existing in the dust was only a tool of the lying cult.

Urban steeled himself to this conclusion. He excised doubt. He dumped guilt. He forced himself to focus on his own ends, for whatever the nature or origin of this thing he faced, it was his enemy.

He immersed himself again in the cell flow, becoming a conduit for waves of confused debate. His other selves were there, each one just as stable, as determined as he. Together they made their input—*<wrongness>*—and they pumped it ruthlessly into the flow. *<Wrongness>*, over and over again.

The philosopher cells were already laden with doubt, disturbed by the strangeness of the artifact's dust, and so they offered little resistance. *<Wrongness>* rippled through them, finding fertile veins for growth. The careful truce engineered between courser and artifact collapsed. Doubt and suspicion burst forth on a cloud of hot dust.

The artifact tasted the flavor and responded in frantic, coquettish threat: Fight now. We are Chenzeme. Go: Synthesis. Or fight.

Urban steeled himself. He dumped guilt and focused on the taste of Lot as a marker for *<wrongness>*, hating himself for it, but hate blended well. The cells embraced it, drawing him deeper into the vast reaches of their internal world, where memory flowed like a bottomless ocean of heavy air. It frightened him. Yet at the same time it filled him up with awe and with a desire to be part of it. He swore he would be part of it when this was done.

So. Time to finish it.

The thought formed in his own mind at the same time it arrived on a hundred veins within the courser's cell field.

Hailey had armed the cardinals with the knowledge of wild cell dust. Cautiously, Urban constructed his suggestion. He broke the pattern of the dust into harmless components, sending each of them outward for consideration within the field of philosopher cells. *<Wrongness>* He spun false histories, to prove his weapon was good. He dared the cells to synthesize it, emphasizing *<Wrongness>*. Hailey had done so much with the bridge.

At first only a few cells acquiesced, and then a few more. Bits of dust were synthesized, then wrapped in protective skins where the components could harmlessly mix.

More.

<Wrongness>

Urban urged them on, and slowly, slowly, a frenzy of manufacture built. Mass was shunted outward to the cells, as a wave of retribution grew around the courser's hull.

<Wrongness>

Now.

The packets launched with a flash of searing heat. They slammed against the artifact's cell field in a million micro-impacts, bursting open in splotches of blazing fury, a fever that spread outward, leaving behind circles of ash that widened until ash became the color of the artifact's hull.

As the destruction finished, the courser's philosopher cells fell into an eerie silence. Weighing the possibilities?

In the stillness, Urban became aware again of the battle heat along his borders. Within the courser's tissue, Hailey's microscopic armies were still engaged in a fierce defense of his existence, operating on the simple Well protocol: Do not attack unless attacked first.

At the moment, motivation was not a problem. The courser's microscale defenses were evolving furiously in an attempt to overcome Hailey's army. One cardinal succumbed as Urban watched, its ghost vanishing from existence. An inroad pierced the defenses of another. Urban braced himself against his own fate, helpless to affect the outcome. Would he know when this cardinal failed? Would he have any warning? Probably not. His consciousness would simply—

—cease.

It was a melancholy thought, yet even as he pondered it the Chenzeme attack began to wither. The microscopic battlefront cooled. He watched as breaches in his defensive perimeter were sealed. Scout Makers tentatively probed the fray and reported sterility: the attackers had evolved so much their own policing nanomech no longer recognized them. Attacked from two fronts, the end came swiftly.

The courser did not give up on its microscopic defense. New armies were instantly made and launched against Hailey's troops, but these contained no experience of the original battle and so they were easily turned back, while Urban felt his own territory continue to expand. A neural web grew between the cardinals. His ghosts slid along these highways, blending with one another until he became one mind again, though he retained his many voices, so that his influence on the courser's cell field would not fade.

No further activity could be detected from the ash-colored body of the artifact. The courser's cells quietly debated what they had done, building scenarios of murder and playing them out. It chilled Urban to follow it, but he did not try to soothe them. Instead, he introduced another concept to them: *let us move/leave*. The scenario emerged simultaneously from every one of his multiple voices around the ship. The cells were swept up in it, and to Urban's amazement, the courser began to pull slowly away from the quiescent artifact.

Over the next hour, Urban gained new senses, pumped to him by the exploring filaments of the bridge. He could feel the courser's reef, grumbling and restless as it clutched at the zero point field. The cells disparaged it as weak, for the fast run-up from Nightlight had nearly spent it, and it would be a long time before the courser could run so hard again.

Urban found he could look back at Nightlight. So there was a telescope here somewhere, though the bridge let him feel as if he looked through human eyes. He hesitated. Was there something . . . ? His curiosity flowed into the bridge, as it continued to grow its tendrils through all the levels of the ship.

There.

He sensed it clearly now, another presence. The bridge had tapped its sensory channels. Urban could feel its commands flowing out, feedback flowing in. It was an entity separate and distinct from the philosopher cells on the hull, and also from those other copies of himself. It measured stars. Urban could feel the relentless flow of position data. It measured the hull cells, their temperature and metabolism. It measured the tremulous reef and sent suggestions to the philosopher cells, scenarios that were modified and returned.

Urban buried himself in its operations, and in time he concluded it was a mechanical mind, operating with a lesser authority than the philosopher cells and without their passion. A singular mind, without the complex plurality of the cells. An entity to run the ship when the cells were dark? Sooth.

He thought of Lot, secreted in the wound beneath Null Boundary's philosopher cells: a singular mind engaged in dialogue with the plural field. Lot had always seen himself as part of the field, but perhaps he had unknowingly taken on the role of this subservient machine-mind . . . and all his frustrating failures to dominate the cells could be laid squarely on this inferior status.

A flurry of excitement drew Urban's attention back to the philosopher cells. They had detected a stirring in the artifact. It had begun to follow the courser's retreat, and new philosopher cells were appearing on its hull.

Urban stared at them, feeling contempt for their newness, their necessary ignorance, until he realized this was an emotion spilling over from his own hull cells.

He queried the status of the main gun, and to his surprise, power flowed to it.

<Stop>

This command stirred waves of unruly objection among his philosopher cells: *Caution/Other not self*. With no command from Urban, the courser rotated, the artifact swinging slowly into its gun sights. He steeled himself, thinking *Be Chenzeme*.

A strong radio signal arose from the artifact. The bridge translated it, and Lot's voice filled the cardinals. "Urban? You are there, aren't you?"

Hearing it, Urban's mind flooded with superstitious dread. The bridge confined the emotion to the cardinals, refusing to allow it to run out into any Chenzeme system, so it echoed back, sliding in rough, repeating waves through Urban's awareness.

This is not him. He swore it to himself. He believed it. Yet he couldn't stop himself from answering. "Lot?"

"Sooth. It's me." A perfect rendition of his voice.

Quickly and carefully, Urban pruned as much emotion as he could. "No," he said. "You're not Lot."

"Urban—"

"I saw what happened to him! It was the cult. I saw it happen in Deception Well too!" Anger blossomed as he relived the memory Clemantine had shared with him. It punched past the walls set up by the bridge, slamming the cells with a Chenzeme passion *<Kill it>*. The cells fell instantly into line. The reef trembled and strained as power surged to the main gun.

"Urban!" Lot's terrified scream cut through Urban's sensorium. "I *know* what happened to me. I remember it, but it's over now. You have to believe me. You have to."

Urban didn't want to believe this voice, yet doubt assailed him. He ordered the cells to *<Hold>*. They raged at this restraint, so that he had to repeat the input *<Hold!>*.

"How can I believe you, fury?" This could not be Lot. Yet it was his voice.

"Urban, why do you want to kill me?" Lot's confusion rolled through the cardinals. "This is me. Nothing has been lost. Nothing can be lost. Not here."

"You say that? Fury, the Hallowed Vasties are lost. Heyertori is gone. Do you remember any of that?" Even as he spoke, he had to pressure the cells to *<Hold, hold, hold!>*. His sanity threatened to erode under the assault of Chenzeme fury.

"Sooth, Urban," Lot answered. "The Vasties are part of me. You're part of me too."

"The Vasties are gone!"

"Urban, listen. Nikko is calling you. Can't you hear him?"

Urban listened, but all he heard was the frantic, bubbling fury of the cell field, poised to kill. *<Hold>*

Lot said: "He tells you to kill me. Now. *Why?*"

"You know why. You have our patterns. We won't be made into weapons."

"Like me?"

"Sooth. Exactly."

"I was never a weapon."

"You thought so."

<Hold>

Lot said: "It was a gift."

"Not one we could use, fury."

"I won't harm you."

"Why can't I hear Nikko?" Urban demanded.

"Perhaps it's because you're not whole."

"And you are?"

"Now."

"And still free?"

"We are not your enemy, Urban. We have come through time to know you. We have delayed our own Communion for you, and slept here in the dark, thirty million years on the slightest chance someone would waken us. We are here, to give you all that we are and all that we know."

<Hold>

As Urban listened, he found himself wanting to believe what Lot was saying. Never had he felt this way before. The charismata had never touched him. But the man he'd been was slipping away. He wasn't human anymore. He had left that part of his life behind, to immerse himself in an alien world, where time was measured on a scale he could not truly comprehend. The vastness of this Chenzeme memory awed him. Each philosopher cell was tiny, but together they recorded an ocean of time. His own scale was not measurable against it—yet this was the world he had condemned himself to live in.

Why?

<Hold>

Memories of Silk surged in his consciousness, his old man and the theft he had done when he took himself away. And Deneb: he would never see her again, never.

Lot's voice dug at him. "You can make yourself untouchable, Urban, if that's what you want. You can fail to feel the charismata. You can edit your pain and your fear and your doubt and even your hopes if they distract you, and in the end, you will be the courser, running your probabilities, operating on an unfeeling instinct. This is you: Unconscious. Invulnerable. Untouchable. Urban? Will you do it? Or will you go back to Deneb? How much do you love her?"

<Hold>

"I don't know. I don't remember."

"How much do you love me?"

"Lot—"

"Did you edit that? So you can kill me."

"I have to do it!" The cells were frantic, boiling against his repeating restraints.

<Hold>

<Hold!>

"You are the courser now," Lot's voice told him.

"Sooth, then! It's what I am. None of us is just a man . . . anymore." He faltered, as a dreadful truth blossomed bright and hot within his heart. Lot had told him, but he had not heard. *You're part of me too.* Hadn't he lost that copy of himself in the ring? So this thing speaking with Lot's voice: It would know everything about him. It would know how to touch him, how to force him to feel what he would never choose to feel.

The cult or the courser?

This thing would have him believe there were only two choices, but it wasn't so. Firmness of purpose did not condemn him to Chenzeme brutality, and real love was not measured by the flatline of the cult. Life was a series of infinite gradations. In every moment, new decisions must be made.

"You're afraid of uncertainty, aren't you?" Urban accused. "Whatever you are. Because you're not Lot! You're afraid of choice. You're afraid of chance. You run from it. You hide from it, and you steal it away from the rest of us. You're afraid to *lose*. Lot! It's not you who's left. But I love you. You know it."

He steeled himself, giving in at last to the demands of the furious cells. *<Kill it>*

"*Urban, wait!*" It was Lot's voice screaming at him. It *was* Lot. "Urban, please listen to me."

He steeled himself. *<Kill it!>*

The reef surged. Urban felt it: as if someone had reached a hand into his guts and twisted *hard*. The main gun fired. Then searing heat and a white-hot flower of dust bloomed in his face. It stung. Eagerly, he tasted it, but it carried no sense, no purpose, blank as the beginning of the world.

Afterwards, Nikko's ghost came to visit the cardinals. He moved through them, leaving ambivalent nets strung across the paths. "They taught us how to beat them. You know that? They made Lot into our bridge."

"Sooth."

The pod had drifted several hundred kilometers away. Urban watched it with Chenzeme clarity as it slowly reformed into a broad antenna. Nikko planned to burn out the pod's reef in a one-shot attempt to get back to Null Boundary. He would have to pare his ghost to a few essential memories, and even then he might not succeed—Null Boundary was far away, and stormy Nightlight lay between them—but he would try.

Nikko's presence condensed as a faint sense of mass in Urban's sensorium. "You're going home, aren't you?" he asked.

"Sooth," Urban admitted. "I'll follow Messenger back. To Deception Well first, and then to Sol System, if it looks worthwhile. Maybe beyond. We don't have any idea what happened on that frontier."

"Do you think there'll be anyone left?"

"Oh, yes." He had to believe that someone, some *thing* had survived. "They may be hiding. I'll probably find them when they try to blow my hull open."

"Make lots of noise when you approach."

"Sooth." He remembered the fake Chenzeme encounter Deneb had found in the library, showing a communications officer turning away a trio of deadly coursers by playing a recognition code. It could happen. He believed that now.

"This age has been a bottleneck for us, but things are going to open up, I know it. The islanders aren't going to have the cloud to themselves forever."

"I'll look for the wave front," Nikko said. "Then I'll know you made it."

"You're going back to the islands then?"

"Yes."

"That's good. I'm glad."

"I don't know. We know where the cult came from, but we never found the shipbuilders."

Urban tried to imagine that faction of the Chenzeme opposed to the cult. He could appreciate the fear and anger they might have felt, watching this virus steal their world away, but he could never understand the contempt they had shown for the future. They had programmed their warships to destroy the rings that seeded the cult, but for thirty million years they had also used them to sweep away any evolving species that might become a reservoir for the cult virus—dictating an end to countless futures, perhaps even their own. "I think the shipbuilders are dead," Urban said. "Or stupid. Or lost in cold sleep or in a hidden virtual world, but I don't think they're part of *this* world anymore. They hated it too much, or they were afraid of it, or they lost control of what they did, so to hell with them—may the Well rot the balls off every one of their ships."

Nikko chuckled softly. "Urban, I have to go now."

"You won't leave a ghost?"

"No. I can't do it."

"Sooth." Nikko had too many scars to make such a close alliance with the Chenzeme. "Take care of Clementine and Hailey, then. And take care of yourself too. Be happy."

"And you," Nikko said. "Don't ever close your eyes to the world."

His ghost slipped off to the pod, then instantly it surged forth in a blaze of radio, away, away, to Null Boundary.

Urban listened to the following silence, feeling hollow, but triumphant too. He was a sculpted entity now, the soul of his own great ship, and if that ship was an alien monster, well, what was a monster but a creature new to the world?

We are a commensal organism.

Cells/reef/man/machine: the strained peace between his parts would grow stronger, as Hailey's bridge continued to knit them together, in the tradition of merciless harmony they had learned in Deception Well.

He kicked the reef. He slid away from Nightlight with his prow turned toward home. It would be a journey of centuries, and what he might find there, he couldn't begin to guess.

ABOUT THE AUTHOR

Linda Nagata is the author of *The Bohr Maker*, a nanotech thriller that won the Locus Award for Best First Novel. Her next two books, *Tech-Heaven* and *Deception Well*, firmly established her reputation as a writer of cutting-edge science fiction. *Vast* is her most recent work. Her short stories have appeared in *The Magazine of Fantasy & Science Fiction*, *Analog*, and *Amazing Stories*. In her incarnate version, she lives with her husband and children in Maui, Hawaii. In her virtual persona, she inhabits the World Wide Web address: http://www.maui.net/~nagata/

Come visit

BANTAM SPECTRA

on the INTERNET

Spectra invites you to join us
in our new on-line forum.

You'll find:

< Interviews with your favorite authors and
  excerpts from their latest books
< Bulletin boards that put you in touch with
  other science fiction fans, with Spectra
  authors, and with the Bantam editors who
  bring them to you
< A guide to the best science fiction re-
  sources on the Internet

Join us as we catch you up with all of Spectra's finest
authors, featuring monthly listings of upcoming titles
and special previews, as well as contests, interviews,
and more! We'll keep you in touch with the field, both
its past and its future—and everything in between.

Look for the Spectra Science Fiction
Forum on the World Wide Web at:

http://www.bantam/spectra.com

KAY KENYON

A renegade pilot . . .
A desperate gamble to save a dying earth.

THE SEEDS OF TIME

_____57681-X $5.99/$7.99 Canada

A small town.
A deadly game.
A galactic presence.

LEAP POINT

_____57682-8 $5.99/$7.99 Canada

Worlds of Wonder:
The Classic Fantasies of

URSULA K. LeGuin

The Novels of Earthsea

The windswept world of Earthsea is one of the greatest creations in all fantasy literature, comparable to Tolkien's Middle Earth or C. S. Lewis's Narnia. The adventures of the powerful Archmage Ged, from his willful youth through his grand destiny, continue to captivate new generations of readers.

A Wizard of Earthsea	___26250-5	$6.50/NCR
The Tombs of Atuan	___27331-0	$6.50/$8.99
The Farthest Shore	___26847-3	$6.50/$8.99
Tehanu	___28873-3	$6.50/$8.99
